A LOVE SO BRUTAL

Book Cover Design by Maria Spada @mspremades.

Editing by Maddi Leatherman, EJL Editing @ejlediting.

Proofreading and Formatting by K. Morton Editing Services LLC @kmortonedits.

1st Edition September 25th, 2025

Paperback ISBN: 9798990175334

E-Book ISBN: 9798990175327

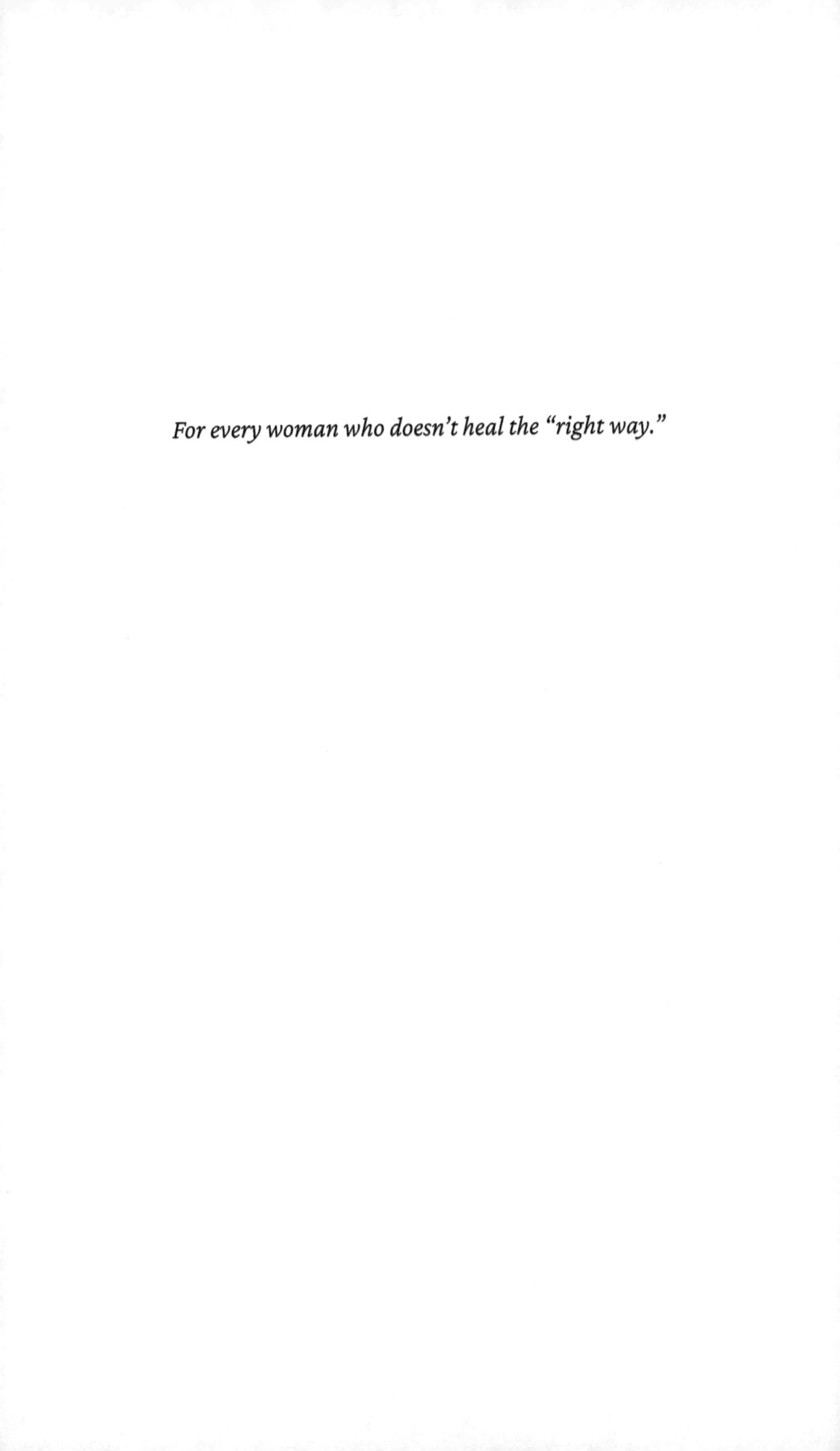

For every woman who doesn't heal the "right way."

CONTENT WARNINGS

This book is intended for audiences 18+. Please note the following content warnings before reading: sex, graphic language, graphic violence, blood, guns and shootings, murder, drug and alcohol use, PTSD, panic attacks, depression, themes and discussions of self-harm.

THE COURTS OF FAERIE

The Unseelie Court

The Seven Unseelie Houses ("The Sins")
House Pride
House Wrath
House Lust
House Sloth
House Envy
House Greed
House Gluttony
The Unseelie Magics (in order of least to most rare)
Shadow-Walkers
Empaths
Soul-Stealers

The Seelie Court

The Seven Seelie Houses ("The Virtues")
House Patience
House Benevolence
House Charity
House Chastity
House Humility
House Temperance
House Diligence
The Seelie Magics (in order of least to most rare)
Light-Walkers
Shifters
Healers

MT. BRAMBLE
CASIMIR
The SEELIE COURT
The UNSEELIE COURT
AVALON
ANWYNN
THE HUMAN REALM
FAERIE

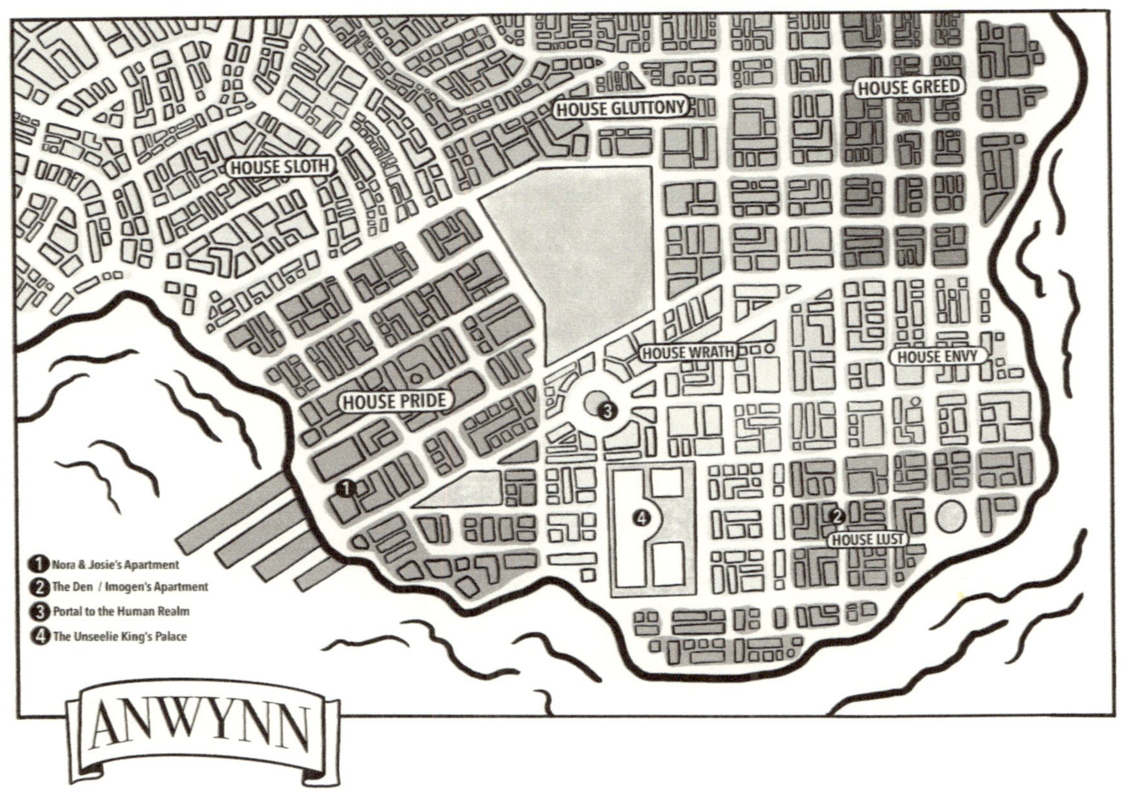
HOUSE GREED
HOUSE GLUTTONY
HOUSE SLOTH
HOUSE WRATH
HOUSE ENVY
HOUSE PRIDE
HOUSE LUST
1 Nora & Josie's Apartment
2 The Den / Imogen's Apartment
3 Portal to the Human Realm
4 The Unseelie King's Palace
ANWYNN

PROLOGUE
SILAS

FIFTY YEARS AGO

Our eyes meet in secret, the Seelie boy's an earthy brown to my midnight sky. They are stolen glances, small crimes committed over our mothers' shoulders.

Mother and I spin across the ballroom to a two-step, the hem of her bustled skirt fluttering over the floor. When the sprites pluck the last note of their tune and we stop our twirling, Mother curtsies and I bow. As I'm hinged at the waist, my gaze cuts from the black veins running through the marble to my Seelie boy.

His cheeks flush under my attention. It draws a smirk to my lips, the way he fails to fully pay attention to the fae chattering around him.

Mother *tsks*.

Maybe I'm not being as subtle as I thought.

I quickly straighten out of my bow and fidget with my cufflinks. My mother knows me better than I know myself. At times, I hate it. Occasionally, I'm thankful for it.

My back is rigid as I meet her stare. With one brow quirked and a knowing tilt to her lips, it's disarming to be under the scrutiny of her sharp features. It's the same expression I've replicated in the mirror a thousand times, all with the hope that I could strip a fae as bare as she does with only a glance.

I inherited far more from the Unseelie Queen than I did from my father: the strange colorless hair and snow-white wings, the deep-rooted magic of the Royal line, and an impish personality to match.

Mother holds out an arm, and I take it, escorting her back to the head table.

"You have eyes for someone tonight?" she asks.

"I don't know what you mean," I say, pulling out her chair for her.

The table is empty; most of the other Royals—from both sides of Faerie—are still mingling on the dance floor.

"You forget I was once young like you, Silas, even if it was centuries ago."

Her piercing eyes cut to the Seelie boy; they are a clear crystal blue, the one thing I didn't inherit from her. Instead, I have my father's near-black irises. Mother tucks a flyaway strand of hair behind her ear—the white locks are pinned into a monstrosity of ringlets piled atop her crown. It's on par with the human fashion of the time, as with her corseted dress that molds her figure into an hourglass.

"You have permission to pursue who you want, you know," Mother adds. "All I ask is that you don't get yourself killed. I don't plan on birthing a spare."

I snort and lean close to her ear, one hand braced on the chair back. "Does Father know that?"

He means well, but Father has been *overly enthusiastic* about his desire to give me a sibling. I can't tell if he loved chasing my pesky ass around the palace so much that he wants a second go… or if it's his chance to rear a better option for the Court's future leader.

Given they shipped me off to Wrath's military preparatory instead of keeping me with the Royal tutors, I'd assume the latter. I can't fault them for that—if I hadn't attended school there, then I wouldn't have met my best friend when I needed him most.

Where the hell is Robbie anyway?

I make to leave and find Wrath's grumpy son, but my mother's lithe hand snatches mine.

"Silas."

"Yes, Mother?"

"Happy Solstice," she says, a soft smile gracing her lips. She squeezes my hand, and my smirk falls, replaced by a matching soft grin. I squeeze her hand back.

"Happy Solstice, Ma," I say, then I wink. "Gonna go be a troublemaker now."

I spin on my heel, and my mother's laugh echoes behind me. It's a hearty, warm sound that fills the room. Heads snap towards her, but the courtiers quickly hide any form of scrutiny from their expressions. My mother couldn't care less either way; she's never bothered to concern herself with what others think of her. That's why she married my magicless father without a second thought.

He bounds across the room now, carrying two glasses of bubbling wine. The wings of his tailcoat billow as he bounces along. A beaming grin cuts under his brown mustache when he passes me, then somehow gets wider when his gaze falls back on my mother.

I shake my head. The man is hopelessly happy in love.

It's not a bad thing. I simply can't imagine being so taken

with someone that nothing else matters except them. I doubt there's a man or woman who could pique my interest to that degree.

I stop at the refreshments table, an elegant spread of little cakes, sandwiches, and pastries laid out for the picking. I pop a mini raspberry pie into my mouth and hum my surprise; the tart fruit compliments the buttery short-crust perfectly.

Those sprites are damn good bakers.

"Are they any good?" a smooth voice asks, the distinct presence of fluttering Seelie wings brushing my side.

Turning my head, my gaze once again clashes with the Seelie boy. Only this time, I'm close enough to note the devious sparks of gold laced into his brown irises.

"They're worth a try," I say, brows quirking up.

Rounding the boy to inspect a plate of macarons, I peek at his exposed wings—those of a monarch butterfly—and fight the urge to trace a finger over them. I pass by without making contact with the orange and black wings, but he shivers all the same.

I settle next to him, our shoulders an inch apart, and lift a delicate macaron to my lips. My teeth pierce the crisp shell, and I track the way his pupils dilate when my tongue catches a crumb at the corner of my lips.

I make sure to eat the dessert slowly.

"You recently had a birthday, right?" he asks when I'm done, and picks up his own mini fruit pie. "You're eighteen now. Officially able to claim the throne."

"Yes," I drawl. I squint at him, cautiously curious as to where this is going.

"As am I. Eighteen, that is. I'm not a Royal though." He pops the pastry into his mouth and chews. I study the flex of his jaw and the way his Adam's apple bobs when he swallows.

"But you are Royal *adjacent*," I say.

His tongue pokes at his cheek. "My father works for the Virtues."

"Ah. Happy belated birthday, then."

The boy laughs. "Same to you, Unseelie Prince."

I hum, not hiding the fact that my eyes roam south, inspecting the rest of his physique without restraint. He's in a similar suit to mine, all buttoned up with a winged collar, elegantly tied cravat, and black tailcoat tapered at the waist. He's lean, but I'd be remiss to assume his stature equates to weakness.

"I never did get your name," I say.

"Quincy," he says.

"Mind if I call you Quin?"

"Not at all. Do you mind if I call you Silas?" he shoots back.

A predatory grin cuts across my cheeks. "Only in private."

"Then maybe we should find a sitting room to continue our chat in?" he asks, facing me fully, his hip finding the edge of the refreshment table.

"You're quite forward," I say, matching his stance with crossed arms over my chest.

"I see no point in dancing around my desires."

A charged beat of silence passes between us as I make my decision. It doesn't take long; I've never been one to fuss over the carnal.

"Come," I say, launching off the edge of the table.

No one spares a second glance as I exit through the double doors next to the roaring fireplace—the ones that lead towards the old wing of the castle. It's where everyone goes for *moments alone.*

Quin's thrumming presence is constant on my back. He doesn't talk, clearly content to follow me into Casimir's depths. When we reach the end of the hall, I go to lead us up the spiral staircase but am stopped by a hand grabbing my wrist.

I focus on the point of contact, his rough fingertips pressing into the soft pulse point.

"Have you ever been downstairs?" he asks.

"No. Why?" My eyes narrow. "What good is exploring an old cellar?"

The torchlight dances in Quin's eyes.

"Because it's exhilarating," he says. *Not a lie*—to him at least—my magic notes. "You ever get off on doing something dirty and forbidden?"

I snort. "You talk as if you've taken many a stranger down there before."

He shrugs, a smug little grin playing on his plump lips. "Maybe I have."

"Fine." I roll my eyes. "I'll follow your lead, *Quin*."

He releases my wrist, though his warmth has already branded me. Not externally, but underneath; the nerves fire off, set alight by his touch.

We descend into the bowels of Casimir, and I have to give it to him—it *is* exhilarating. The cool damp clings to my skin and our footsteps ring loud between the gray stone walls. Gooseflesh crawls down my arms. Torches are few and far between at the end of the stairs, so it's dark when we finally crash together.

Teeth nibble on bottom lips. Hands rake through hair with delicious pressure. His mouth tastes of buttery short-crust and his tongue carries with it the tang of berries. Tailcoats are stripped away, cravats tossed aside. Buttons and cufflinks fly across the cellar, clinking on the stone floor.

I hardly notice the creak of the heavy door shutting until my back hits the cool metal.

Quin's hands are the perfect balance of rough and sensual running over me. And while the way his body presses into mine is divine, I still have an image to uphold in front of the Seelie.

I can't be submissive *here*.

I flip us, pressing Quincy against the door. One hand splays out next to his head, while the other grips the hair at his nape.

"Remember your place, I'm still a Prince," I rasp against his neck.

I nip at the flesh below his ear before reclaiming his lips with my raw ones. His fingers trace down my chest, pulling my shirt free and unbuttoning my trousers. I groan when he grips my length and strokes.

My hands bracket his jaw, keeping him where I want him: his mouth on mine, our tongues dancing. He's all but brought me over the edge when something sharp slides between my lower ribs.

I gasp, both from the pain and the shock, breaking our kiss.

Quin's previously warm eyes stare at me, eerily cold. My hands tighten around his neck in response, and his eyes widen a fraction at how easily I'm able to cut off his air supply. I'm stronger than my lanky frame projects.

The second stab is to the softer flesh of my abdomen.

My magic flares at the pain. Darkness fills every crevice of the room as I try to shadow-walk away, but can't.

Quincy manages to squeeze one smug word past my vice grip on his neck.

"*Iron.*"

I'd smack myself if both my hands weren't already squeezing the life out of this idiot. *Of course the fucking cellar door and walls are laced with iron.*

Quin tries to pull the dagger from my gut and stab again, but one of my hands covers his, holding the blade in place. It stings, but better to keep it in than allow both wounds to bleed freely.

His foot hooks behind my ankle and pulls, sending us both careening to the floor. The dagger is yanked from my side despite my best effort, and we grapple, each trying to overtake the other. He ends up on top, straddling me. The knife presses down on the center of my chest, and a line of red trickles over the pale expanse of skin. The pain of the iron blade slicing my flesh is dull compared to the anger burning through my chest.

"Why?" I grit out, needing to know.

We could have had fun, but he *had* to go and try to kill me. I'd love to say this is the first time I've been tempted by a honeypot tasked with my demise, but it isn't.

My mother is going to scold the living hell out of me for this.

"*Why?*" I repeat, pushing against his wrists to keep the dagger from plunging fully into my chest. A magic darker than my shadows swirls in my gut, rousing at the threat to my life. My arms shake with the effort of holding both it and the blade back, but I need information first. "*Tell me.*"

Quin grunts, and his hand holding the knife twitches.

"*Don't,*" I warn.

He twists it anyway, digging it deeper into my sternum.

Pain flares, as does my magic. It lashes out, a snake striking its prey, and Quin's arms go slack. His lifeless body crumples, and, luckily, he lands more to my side than on top of me. My head falls back with momentary relief and almost cracks at the force with which it hits the floor.

"*Fuck,*" I groan, clutching the worst of my wounds at my side.

Blood oozes between my fingers. I don't think he hit anything important, since the flow is slow and steady, rather than the rush of a hemorrhage. That and the fact that I'm not dead. *Yet.*

I suck in a single shaky breath before gathering the strength needed to stand up, kick Quin's body out of the way, and pull at the cellar door.

The door hinges creak as I yank it open, and as soon as the first step of the spiraling staircase appears, I'm consumed by shadow.

My magic drops me into madness.

Fae flee past me towards the ballroom doors—none of them stop to help me, let alone spare my bloodied appearance a second glance. Someone bumps into my shoulder, and I grunt at the impact, barely able to keep my balance. It's a blur, and I'm unable to fully focus on a single visage swirling around me until the sandy-brown hair of my best friend pops out of the crowd. His eyes widen with relief when he finds me, but a deep frown overtakes his expression as he takes in my sorry state.

"*Shit.* Silas, where have you been?" he says in that growly way of his. "I've been searching everywhere for you."

"Oh, you know, thwarting an assassination attempt," I grit out between clenched teeth.

Robbie ignores my jest, his shadows quickly unfurling from his fingertips. They thicken into something almost solid and press into my side to stave the bleeding. *Damn, I should have thought of that.*

"We need to get you out of here," he adds, one strong arm already wrapping around my shoulders. His shadows curl around us.

"Why? What else has happened?" I ask.

Robbie only shakes his head. A short, worrisome *no* that strikes dread into my already pained gut. I bat his arm away, breaking free of his shadows.

My eyes snap toward the head table, where a group of Wrath's guards stand poised in a circle, colt pistols raised in defense of someone hidden beyond a shimmering shadow-veil.

"Robs..." I keen, my already strained tone turning downright raw.

Robbie tries to shadow-walk us away, but my magic overpowers his, taking us to the center of the protective circle of his House's men.

Every emotion roiling inside of me freezes at the sight of my parents splayed on the ground. Their expressions are peaceful, strangely enough. But their chests don't rise and fall as they should. No, they're unnaturally *still*.

Twin glasses of Faerie wine are cracked and spilled around them, the golden liquid soaking into their clothes.

There are no streaks of blood, outside of the ones I stamp on them in my frantic examination of their bodies.

They are completely whole. Untouched. Except they're *dead*.

Seelie can't soul-steal. The only way they can kill like this is with poison. My focus homes in on the spilled wine, and everything else dulls. People shout around me, but it's like listening to speech underwater, garbled and slurred. I barely register them yelling to evacuate the king.

But the king is dead.

My father is right here; I'm marking his chest with a bloody handprint as I search for a heartbeat.

Arms I recognize as Robbie's pull me away from my parents. I fight him, shouting, but it's nonsense at best. My curses go ignored. The last thing I see before shadows overtake me is a set of watchful emerald eyes, staring at me from across the ballroom. They darken with fury when they realize I'm still alive.

I'll never forget those eyes.

When Robbie's arms finally release me, and we crash onto

the wet sand at the lake's edge, I scream. It's a guttural sound, one that claws up my throat with sharp talons. My magic pours out of me, a protective instinct born from pain and fear and *rage*.

Darkness descends over the Unseelie Court.

1

SILAS

When I touch the man and he dies, it's not satisfying.

There's no crunch of bone breaking under my knuckles nor the warm slick of blood between my fingers. The light simply drains from the Seelie's eyes as his heartbeat stops. The corpse crumbles to the floor with a dull *thunk* and becomes another body in the trail marking my path.

I step over the lifeless limbs, venturing deeper into the halls of Casimir.

I hate this fucking castle. Never liked it all that much to begin with. Bad memories hide here. And the first fae queen's ghost must be chronically lonely, because she seems committed to beckoning forth Death every time we visit.

I pass a portrait of her and pause. My nose scrunches as I take in the painting that's been turned askew by our chaos, the rectangular gold frame tilted on its nail. She stands poised and tall and almighty in front of her throne; white hair falls over her shoulders in soft waves, contrasting the dull blue frock that drapes over her muscular frame. Craquelure spreads across the dirtied varnish, and the tiny cracks spin a web of oil pigment rather than silk over her visage. Sprites float above her head in the picture. They are the same creatures that still live and serve us, although they've taken to their hiding spots while we march on a warpath through their home.

I right the frame, and frown when it squeaks, tilting to the side again.

A strong grip falls on my shoulder. It makes me jolt with the frame clasped in my hand—the movement pulls the portrait from its nail, and it clatters to the floor.

Oh well.

"Silas," Wrath says, a rough whisper behind me. "I thought we agreed you would use a blade. Not *that*."

"What?" I say, distracted. Then it clicks. "Oh. *That*."

He means using the rarest of my magics—soul-stealing.

Generations of Unseelie Royals have carefully bred their progeny in an attempt to pull forth this power from our blood-line. They were all met with disappointment. Until, of course, a pair of lovesick fools—half of whom didn't even have magic— managed to birth this legacy.

My parents weren't fools though, were they? More caught up in an unfortunate collision of bad luck and love-induced ignorance.

"Dead men can't gossip with anyone but spirits, Wrath," I mutter.

Candidly, I couldn't care less if everyone knows I can soul-steal. I have more important things to worry about—such as the gaggle of Patience's lackeys rushing through the doors at the end of the hall.

I sigh.

The Seelie brandish their weapons and take aim, my nose twitches at the acrid scent of spent gunpowder in the air, and the world around me instinctively swirls into shadow. My body reacts on its own. I trained for years to anticipate danger and adjust my response accordingly.

I reappear farther down the hall, Wrath at my side.

Where I reach for my foe's nape, fingertips grazing the sweat-dampened skin and my magic taking care of the rest, Wrath slices a knife across his foe's jugular. His arm jerks back, the blade meeting resistance as it saws through the layers of flesh and sinew. Hot blood sprays from the wound, splattering my white shirt.

This repeats until there's a small pile of bodies, and my clothes are sufficiently stained.

It's almost sad how pathetic they are at fighting back. Most of the Seelie we've cleared have been magicless, otherwise they wouldn't be relying so heavily on their weapons. Guns have their merits, but they are less effective against those of us who can shadow-walk, or light-walk.

I make the mistake of swiping at my sleeve and end up smearing red across the cuff. Scoffing, I roll up my sleeves, tucking them securely under the silver armbands around my biceps.

"*This* is the reason why I was soul-stealing," I pointedly say to Wrath. "Because now we've ruined a perfectly good shirt doing things your way."

"Maybe you shouldn't have worn white, like I told you not to," Wrath snarks back.

"All my dark shirts were in the wash," I pout. "It's not my fault the staff are behind on laundry, *Robbie*."

Wrath gives me a scathing glare.

I know he dislikes his given name. He prefers the title he fought for. And honest-to-gods, I've been trying. But, sometimes, it slips out... and his reaction is too funny when it does.

Still, *Wrath* is my oldest friend. When I was shipped off to military prep school at ten, he was the unlucky fellow who was assigned to be my roommate. Years later, I'd realize that set up was a strategic move on his father's part to stoke a friendship between us. To his father's dismay, that friendship led Robbie to realizing his worth. And now we're here, with Robbie serving as our Court's newest Wrath.

Wrath swipes his blade over his dark trousers, which I'm sure are soaked with blood.

Maybe I should have borrowed something of his.

"Are you good to split up after this next stretch? I'll go upstairs, and you go down to the cellar?" he asks.

I nod, and we march on.

In the weeks since Solstice, the Seelie overtook the castle. It's not something I would worry about, except the bridge connecting the island to our Court won't fall. I had willed it to crash into the murky depths of the lake a thousand times, but the magic won't listen. The ancient castle is throwing a tantrum.

Our only comfort is the shadow-veil that's still shimmering over our Court. No Seelie can breach it. For now.

The shadow-veil I created fifty years ago has been a topic of intense conversation between Wrath and me. Discussions that have led us here to address the Seelie threat head-on. Casimir —the only land bridge between our two Courts—cannot become a Seelie stronghold. On that, we agreed.

Where we differed in opinion was the whereabouts of one particular half-Seelie.

I figured Patience would have moved her by now. Wrath thinks otherwise. Either way, it is worth it to clear the building and see.

I had promised Imogen I'd bring Nora back, but I'd be searching for her even if I hadn't made that vow. The hair on my neck bristles every time I think of the raven-haired woman;

my soul has found a kindred spirit and refuses to accept her absence.

We approach the central staircase of the castle. To the left, they curl upwards, leading to the suites the original Royals occupied. To the right, the stairs swirl down into damp darkness.

I've been here before, though I was a different person back then. Forbidden kisses in the dark have much less appeal to me now.

A sick sensation squirms in my stomach.

"I don't know if she's here," I say. "Would they not have more people guarding her?"

Wrath sighs. He rubs a weary hand over his brows. We've already been over this, but my nerves need something to latch on to.

"All I know is that based on what we've been able to observe from our outposts along the river, it's unlikely that they've moved her."

"And remind me why that is?"

"Because any strategist worth their weight in silver would only move her with a sizable and secure host," he says. "*And* it'd be stupid to bring her to Avalon. They make one mistake, and she'd cause a panic, regardless of if she's cut a deal with them. Casimir is the safest location to hold her."

"It doesn't feel right," I mutter.

The nauseating twist in my gut lurches, and I'm positive that this is worry rearing its ugly head. If she isn't here, then what do we do?

Wrath's tongue runs over his teeth before poking the inside of his cheek. The expression is one of begrudging contemplation, but at least it's not a frown. One of his hands finds purchase on his hip, while the other ruffles his sandy-brown hair.

I wait. He sighs.

Those red-brown eyes meet mine, sparkling with something devious.

"Fifty dollars says she's locked in the cellar," he says.

One brow quirks up on my forehead. "You're making a bet? Right now?"

"Don't read too much into it."

"Aw," I croon. "You want to cheer me up?"

Wrath grunts, his own version of a huff of laughter. "I need you motivated enough to help clear the rest of the tower. We won't let them make it a viable outpost."

My grin is soft as I offer him my hand. He shakes it, his rough, calloused fingers gripping mine.

"I will take that bet," I say.

Wrath claps me on my shoulder. "Now, don't be stupid."

"I'll try not to be."

"And if you find her, do *not* touch her. She could be working with them, and it could be a trap."

I roll my eyes, but he can't see—he's already disappeared around the curve of the banister.

He talks a lot of smack, but Wrath trusts my ability to make competent decisions. In the same way, I trust that Nora wouldn't abandon our Court.

The woman cares too deeply for the family she's found in House Pride to betray us. And even though his Seelie blood courses through their veins, it's clear she doesn't consider Patience family.

The stairwell to the cellar is a far cry from the pristine marble steps found in the rest of the castle. The walls are dirtied, the stone turned gray and splotchy from water damage, and it reeks of mildew. The farther I go, the darker it gets. Any light filtering down from the main hall vanishes with me around the bend.

My steps slow; I descend carefully, not wanting to slip on the puddles of stagnant water that my boots squelch in. It wasn't nearly this dilapidated when we ran down the steps in a horny rush fifty years ago.

Despite my caution, my heel catches the stone the wrong way. I nearly fall on my ass—but luckily, my arm steadies me against the wall. *Unluckily*, my hand is now coated in a film of mildew.

I gag, wiping the crud onto my pants.

Fed up, I call my shadows forth. They wrap around me, my eyes barely able to tell where my magic ends and the shadows of the stairwell begin, and then I'm whisked away to the cellar. The main iron-laced door must be cracked because I find no resistance to my magic as I step through the shadows.

Wrath would smack me over the head, knowing I'm leaving the stairwell uncleared. But something tugs at my gut, urging me to hurry. Instinct, or maybe it's only my frustration lighting a fire under my ass.

I think I might have developed a complex. My need to see this woman safe can't possibly be normal.

When my magic dissipates, a thousand thoughts rush through my head at once.

Nora's thinner, her cheeks cutting sharp angles across her face. There's no sign of food or even a cup of water in the cell. *Are they not feeding her?* Her arms and legs are streaked with dirt and dried, chipped blood, and she's still wearing her Solstice dress. *They didn't let her bathe? Give her a change of clothes? How do they expect her to fight for them if they treat her as garbage?*

Her eyes snap open. Her unbroken spirit sparkles in those emerald irises.

My lips part before my brain can catch up.

"I owe Wrath fifty dollars." I pause, nose scrunching at the excessively damp smell in the air. "They really kept you down here this whole time?"

"Yeah, well, I don't think they trust me enough to keep me in Avalon." Her voice is rough from disuse, throat clearly parched.

A silence passes between us. I allow my brain to catch up to my words as I study her. In turn, she studies me. A single torch flickers in the dungeon, the warm glow dancing between the cell bars and over her pale face.

"So," she says.

"So?" I mirror.

How is this supposed to go?

My body hums with energy; I tamp it down by leaning against the wall at my back, shoving my hands in my pockets.

Nora rolls her eyes. "Are you going to kill me now? Because if you're going to do that, I'd love to get on with it."

A laugh bursts from my chest.

Come all this way to kill her? After everything? Does she think that I would do that simply because she's—

My laughter dies. It's just ridiculous.

I wipe away the stray tear gathering at the corner of my eye. But Nora doesn't look amused; her lips are pressed into a firm line.

"Nora," I say. Her name slides over my tongue, a teasing chide. "I'm not here to kill you."

"What?"

"I already knew."

Her shock is palpable between us.

"No." She shakes her head, chest heaving with deeper breaths. "No one knew."

Her body spurs into action, scrambling across the cell.

My jaw ticks at the sight of her crawling towards me. The sight is foreign, strange. Nora wasn't born to crawl.

She leans forward, holding herself up with a white-knuckled grip around the iron bars.

"*How did you know?*" she seethes.

I wasn't sure that she was part Seelie at first, but it became clear once we were at Bramble.

Her magic is too different from mine. In the beginning, I thought it was a natural variance—it's not as if I had other soul-stealers to compare with. And then I saw her magic up close. Pair that with those green eyes of hers, burning with white-hot anger after Imogen's accident, and it all clicked together. They were too similar to Patience's; I'd never forget that shade of emerald fury.

Once I realized her secret, I found that I didn't care.

Sometimes you meet someone and *know* them. You peel back their layers and find that your insides are the same tainted shade of blood-red flesh.

It's like that with Nora.

She's the closest anyone's gotten to understanding what hides deep within me. My magic might not *feel* the same as hers when we use it, but the rage we both derive from it? The push to destruct—to kill?

Our magic craves the taste of souls.

And who am I to stop it now? After everything we've done to get here?

I'm not a good man, and I'll never claim to be. There are more important things to worry about than my own morality. I'm okay with forcing my conscience on vacation while I rip my own version of peace from a dead man's hand.

The scratch of a rusted metal hinge echoes from above us, but I refuse to break eye contact, even when boots patter down the stairwell.

How did I know? It all comes down to one simple fact, dear Nora.

I quirk a single brow as the Seelie guard rushes into the dungeon and invades our space.

"Hey, you can't be down here—"

He's too young, too brash to realize what he's walked into. It's child's play, how easily I reach out and graze his skin. It could be a face, or an arm, or a shoulder—I wouldn't know and don't care. He drops dead all the same. His body crumples in a twisted heap of limbs.

"You're a soul-stealer?" Nora whispers. Is that awe in her tone? Or is it fear?

"Shadow-walker, empath, soul-stealer—a king can be many things," I say as I step around the dead man and crouch in front of the cell. I level with her, my forearms on my knees and my palms folding together. "You must have noticed in your guided research at Mt. Bramble that soul-stealers haven't emerged outside Royal bloodlines since before the split of Faerie. So, imagine my surprise when Pride revealed you to society."

"Is it wrong of me to have pretended I was special?" she says, in that same shell-shocked whisper. The soft rasp is unlike her.

"You are special. Just not in that specific way." I scratch my chin, nail scraping through day-old stubble. "Pride kept your magic well disguised and you well hidden from my spies. I always had suspicions, of course, but it wasn't until I saw your magic up close that I realized what you are."

Nora's gone entirely still. It's a wonder she's even breathing. My tongue darts out, swiping over my bottom lip.

"Something different entirely. The magic of a healer twisted in such a way that instead of life, you gift death." A huff of laughter escapes me as I grin down at her. "I wasn't lying back then, in your office, when I said I couldn't get a good picture of you."

"Is it clear now?" she asks. "The picture of me?"

"I see you clearer now than I've seen anything."

"Why doesn't anyone know about you?"

"Because I don't want them to."

"But you want me to know?"

I don't care if anyone knows anymore. But it's a comforting thought that you're the first I get to tell of my own volition.

"You and Wrath." I shrug. "It's not nearly as fun a power as yours. There's no pain with me. No finesse. No control. It's just, *poof.*"

I puff my fingers out, miming an explosion.

"So, you really aren't here to kill me?"

I barely rein in my sigh. Where is all her fight? Her spark, her bite?

"No, Nora," I say.

A moment passes where we're still and silent, then her hands release their vice grip on the cell bars and fall to her lap. Divots crinkle the dirtied fabric of her gown where her fingers dig into her thighs. She stares at her lap, jaw twitching with internal conflict.

"Are they okay?" she finally asks.

Her friends. Her lover.

"Yes. All three of them," I say. I tilt my head. "Greed and Envy lost their Seconds though. And Envy was grazed by a bullet. He's being a big baby about it, if I'm being frank."

"Are you telling me the truth right now, Silas?" Her voice cracks, but at least she looks up at me.

"Do I have a reason to lie?" I tease.

"Answer the question," she snaps.

Ah. There she is.

"I've only ever told you the truth when you've asked." I smirk, quoting the exact words she said to me only a few months ago. Too many of her words have gotten stuck in my head since then.

"So only lies by omission, then?"

"Of course," I say.

Nora nods. "What happens now?"

My smirk grows into a grin that could rival a shark's. Then I stand with a groan and lean my forearms against the iron bars above my head. Nora sits back on her heels, staring up at me.

No, kneeling doesn't suit her at all.

I *tsk*, my tongue clicking against the roof of my mouth.

"The past few weeks have been... frustrating. I've officially pardoned you, but the Sins are split on whether they want you back," I say. "Your House is also unsure if they should stand by you. Seems there's a faction growing behind a young man giving your Second a hard time. It's all unwanted chaos, given the war that's brewing. Patience has Oonagh's ear, and he's practically foaming at the mouth for bloodshed. But I'm sure you expected as much."

"I think we've established I expected to be dead by now."

"You need to have more faith in your friends, Nora." I chuckle. "We came back for you, after all."

"We?"

"Wrath is upstairs," I say.

The bastard is probably waiting with a smug frown on his face, knowing I now owe him fifty dollars.

Actually, he's more likely to be tapping his foot at how long I'm taking. My fingers twitch at the thought of being the subject of one of his lectures.

My shadows spring to life, snaking down my arms and to the padlock fixed to the cell bars. It only takes them a second to pick the lock; the clank of the metal on stone reverberates through the room.

I step back, pulling open the cell door.

"C'mon. Your lover is worried," I say. "And we still have a Virtue to kill."

I hold out my hand. It's an offering, and a statement of trust—Nora knows what I am now, just as I know what she is. Touch has always meant something more for both of us.

Something protective, borderline possessive, rips through me when she takes my hand.

2

JOSIE

I knock on the door, three small raps of my fist against the warped woodgrain.

Silence.

I shift on my feet, then knock again. My knuckles sting with the action.

Nothing.

"Mo," I call out, my breath brushing against the faded oak. "I'm coming in."

I don't get a reply, though I'm not surprised. She's been quiet these days.

The brass knob burns ice-cold as my palm wraps around it. I shiver when I step past the creaking door. The air is sharp and dry, the sensation of stinging nettles poking my skin.

Imogen sits on the bed, legs bent under a throw blanket, with a book balanced atop her knees. One hand fiddles with the corner of the page, as if she's impatient for what comes next. Her other hand fidgets at her mouth, nails tugging at the already raw and ripped skin of her bottom lip. Damp hair splays in a tangle of waves over her shoulder, and beneath the mane of golden locks, a water stain blooms on her silk pajama top.

She's going to catch a cold like that.

Her head tilts to the bottom of the page she's reading before flipping to the next. The turning paper is a whip cracking through the air; a breathy and forlorn sigh follows the lash.

I clear my throat. Imogen flinches, head snapping in my direction. She blinks hard, frozen for a second. But she comes out of the momentary trance with fluttering lashes and a ragged intake of breath.

"Hey," she whispers. Her tongue chases the word, darting out to pass over her lips as she wedges a bookmark into her book. "It's late."

I don't have to read her mind to hear the unsaid question in her tone: *what are* you *doing here so late?*

"Hattie dropped me off, but I wanted to check on you before I went to bed," I say.

I've been pulling fourteen-hour days dealing with the fallout from Casimir. Our clients aren't happy, and with Silas closing off the main portal to the Human Realm—for good reason—we're stuck with only our fae-side stock. And we only have access to part of that, given half of the House has taken up arms with Wes. It's not ideal.

"Ah." Imogen's attention falls to her lap. She toys with the blanket draped over her legs, picking at the woven fibers with her nails. I wait for her to say more, but she doesn't, and the room becomes unbearably quiet.

Silence often brings me peace. The thrum of public spaces —of people's invasive thoughts—has always been an incessant drain on my magic and sanity. I should love the fact that I can hear the way the wind brushes against the window, or how my wool trousers rustle as my footing shifts. But this brand of silence is not the peaceful kind; it's one that suffocates. It's silence born of pain, of watching flowers forced into the shade wilt, slowly, over weeks, with no clue on how to bring them the light they desperately need.

I want to crawl out of my skin, standing here. These late-night check-ins, where we dance around the darkness lurking in the corner of the room, do nothing to bring Imogen back into the light. She's stuck in the shade of Casimir's castle. Spaced out. Reclusive. Withering away.

A draft passes over me, the mountain air pulling gooseflesh to my forearms. I glance towards the empty hearth, where a dusting of gray ash sits, long gone cold. Fires rage in almost every other room in the complex, but not here. We're in the midst of winter now, and snow falls heavy and wet beyond Bramble's stone-carved walls, blanketing us in a deep chill.

"Do you want me to put on the fire?" I offer.

Imogen glances at the fireplace, a frown tugging at her lips. "If you're cold."

More of that disconcerting silence spreads between us, and displeasure at that fact tries to tug my own expression down. But I refuse to let it win as I crouch at the hearth, placing a bundle of kindling at its center and lighting a match. The pile of sticks and cotton strips easily take light, and I stack three logs on top.

Three should last long enough for her hair to dry at least.

My work takes a few minutes, and I keep my attention locked on the hearth. Red and orange embers hop from the kindling to the wood, trying their darndest to set it ablaze.

"You don't have to check on me, Josie," Imogen murmurs.

"I know." My eyes cut to her in my periphery. "But I want to."

She scoffs. "I'm fine."

Stuffing my hands in my pockets, I pace to the bed and stop

in front of her. I tilt my head and quirk a brow, though I try to keep the rest of my face neutral. Imogen glares up at me between her lashes, her unamused frown deepening.

"I'm *fine*," she repeats.

We both know she's not.

Certainly not since Solstice. But even before that, something was *off*, unsteady—even if she hid it well. Getting shot will do that to you.

I want to reach inside her head and fix it. To revive whatever piece of her died in that alley—to return whatever spark was snuffed out in the downpour in the woods outside Casimir.

I drop onto the bed with a tired grunt, my back bouncing on the mattress. My gaze finds the ceiling, the rough-hewn stone that whoever built this place forgot to polish down—or rather chose not to.

"How are you feeling about tonight?" I ask.

Imogen's inhale is soft and quick, not quite a gasp.

Did she think I'd leave her to wait this out alone?

"I'm anxious," she admits.

I turn my head, my cheek resting on the cushy pillow, to watch her nervously pick at the blanket again. My fingers that usually tap a restless beat are still, clutched together over my stomach. There's something about caring for her that has my own anxieties taking a back seat, if only for a moment.

"*And?*" I prod.

My sarcastic drawl makes Imogen roll her eyes. Her reddened lips twitch with a sad smile, though it doesn't overtake her cheeks as I hoped. Imogen places her book on the bed and lies on her side. We're face-to-face, a foot and the thin throw blanket separating us. Imogen pulls the blanket to her chin, curling her hands under it.

"*And,*" she mutters. "I want to know if she's okay. That hasn't changed, Josie. I don't know why you keep asking."

"I keep asking because it's a lot to take in."

"I've had three weeks to come to terms with it."

"Which is nothing compared to the near decade of history you share. If you don't want to see Nora when she gets back, I need to know."

"Why wouldn't I want to see my girlfriend?"

"There are at least"—I lift my hands and mime counting—"six reasons I can think of."

Imogen snorts. Her cheeks are plump, pushed high from the begrudging close-lipped smile she gives me. Something akin to pride wriggles in my gut at the sight.

"And don't lie and say you aren't mad at her," I add quietly. "You already gave me an earful for keeping this secret. Ignored me for a week."

Imogen's sigh is that of someone resigned to their fate. "I'm not mad at you anymore. I get why it wasn't your secret to tell."

"But it still hurt."

"Yeah."

"I'm sorry," I say again. And I mean it.

"It's fine." One shoulder shrugs beneath her blanket. "We all keep secrets when we think it'll save the ones we love." Imogen curls in on herself, knees pulling to her middle. "Nora and I... we'll have a lot to talk about. But I can't focus on that until I know she's okay. Every time I think about it, I get angry and then I start to feel guilty because she's..."

She doesn't finish the sentence, her throat catching on her tongue. Again, I hear her unspoken words: *because Nora's been captured, has a high chance of being tortured, and we don't know if we'll find her dead or alive.*

Imogen's dim amber irises glow the same shade as the

bronzed sconce flickering above the nightstand. They're intensely focused on the thread she's unraveled from the blanket's edge, but the raw emotion in them is palpable.

"Do you really think they'll bring her home?" she whispers, as if speaking the hopeful words too loud would jinx them.

"I do," I whisper back. "And if I've learned anything about Wrath and Silas over the past few weeks, it's that they are as stubborn as us. If not tonight, then it'll be soon."

Despite my hesitancy around the Sin and the Unseelie King, they've proven themselves trustworthy. Any time I've tried to pry into their minds to get a read on their opinion of Nora, I'm met with an open door. I can only assume I'm seeing whatever they want me to see, but the fact remains that they let me in freely.

Trust only works if it's a two-way street. I trust that when they say they'll get her back, they will. Part of me has to. I can't entertain anything else.

"It's past midnight," Imogen yawns. "Do you think they'll be back soon?"

"Depends on how many Seelie there are and how long it takes to clear them out."

Imogen hums. "Do you want to stay while we wait for them to get back?"

My lips part to say no, to say that I'll go to my own room or wait it out in the library. The gods know I won't be able to sleep. But I pause.

Is she asking because she doesn't want to be alone? Or is she asking so I don't have to wait this out alone?

Even while she's hurting, Imogen exudes a subtle kind of thoughtfulness that goes unmatched by any of our peers.

"Yeah, that would be nice," I say.

The skin around her eyes crinkles. "Do you mind if I keep reading?"

I shake my head.

Imogen shifts back into a sitting position and opens the book on her knees again. I watch as she tucks the bookmark between the end pages and starts to read, and then I close my eyes.

It's quiet again, but not the same as before.

The fireplace plays us a warm lullaby, the flames are more a gentle rustling than the sharp pops of a raging hearth. I'm thankful for that. I think Imogen is too, because I've not seen her flinch once since it flared to life—something I've noticed happens whenever the flames crack too loudly.

Eventually, her weight sinks deeper into the mattress at my side. And with the snowy mountain chill banished from the room and Imogen settled next to me, I gently fall asleep.

3
NORA

My heels crunch into freshly fallen snow. It's a stark difference to the darkness I've grown used to—the valley is bright and glowing even under only moonlight. Wrath trudges ahead of us with his men; a dozen footprints muddy the landscape, smearing red into the pristine blanket of white. My gaze bores into the familiar, cavernous hole in the mountainside, and the shimmering magic at Bramble's entrance taunts me. A beacon and a barrier, it laughs in the face of my sudden hesitance.

My steps have never stalled like this before. It's as if all the confidence I'd had grabbing Silas's hand has disappeared with his shadows.

"If you're wondering why Bramble, it's the safest place for you right now," he says.

"That was not where my thoughts were going," I mutter. I cut Silas a narrowed glance. "Why is the city not safe?"

"Envy may be calling for your head back in Anwynn." He grimaces.

"Ah," I say. That isn't a shock in the slightest.

"And I may have understated how much certain parties don't want you to come home," Silas adds.

"Well, it certainly can't be worse than the situation I was just in," I say, though my stomach twists as I mumble the words—and it isn't from hunger pains.

Everyone knows now.

Imogen *knows now.*

A fog of nervous energy settles over me as I tentatively ask, "You think they're awake?"

It's past midnight if I were to guess. Silas freed me hours ago, but it was dark then and it's still dark now, the stars and moon twinkling above us. Wrath demanded we deal with the bodies of those they had dispatched before we left, so we burned them in the courtyard. My nose scrunches, the stench of burning flesh lingering in my nostrils.

He's a better person than me; I would have left them to rot.

Silas shifts, boots mashing down the heavy, wet snow at my side. He utters his response slowly and concisely. "I think they would want to be woken up if they are asleep."

I nod. *Right.*

This twisted knot of anxiety is a foreign sensation in my chest.

"Where?" I ask.

"Fourth floor guest rooms."

I take one deep, calming breath of ice-chilled air, then force my legs to move. With the first step, a spark catches on the frayed edges of my soul. A wildfire engulfs my insides, but I trudge forward, all my emotions crumbling and scattering like ashes. Slipping through the cracks in my mental shields, they become lost to the biting wind.

I need to get a fucking grip. But fighting a wildfire with a single bucket of well-water is an impossible task. It may be best to let me burn.

Silas trails behind me, a silent but comforting presence at my back. Our movements up the stairs strike eerily similar to the night Imogen was shot and I came here to blow off steam.

It isn't until we crest the second landing that he speaks again.

"Before you go barreling in, did you want to change first?" Silas asks. "We're both a bit... gruesome."

Suddenly, my body wanes, the weakened muscles in my thighs aching to keep myself upright. I turn, bracing myself against the stone railing. Even if I wanted to wash the grime and blood from my body, I don't think I could spare the energy.

"Into what clothes?" I ask, my knuckles going white from their grip on the railing.

Silas's lip part and then mash together in a pout. "You have a good point. They have your clothes. I'd offer a spare set of mine but—you know what? Forget about it."

There's a nervous tick in his tone and a twitch to his movements, one pale hand batting at floating thoughts. I cock my head, the predator in me trained to catch such shifts in demeanor.

I almost... feel bad for him?

"That's a shame," I deadpan. "I love a good suit."

There's a beat of silence as I climb the stairs again, a gasp, and then the quick patter of his shoes as he catches up to me.

"Was that a joke?" Silas asks.

"Don't sound surprised."

"I just didn't think you'd warm back up to me so quickly," he says.

"Was I ever really warmed up to you to begin with?" I mutter under my breath, a thread of annoyance weaving through the tight hinge of my jaw.

He snorts. "Well, you did come to my room smoked as shit and looking for comfort on Solstice."

My toe catches on the next step, and I stumble up to the third landing.

"Don't say it like that," I snap over my shoulder.

"Like what?" Silas pries.

My brows furrow, my attention trained on my shoes to avoid tripping again. It's pathetic, how unsteady I am. But that's what happens when you're starved and stuck in a cell for weeks: your body starts to fall apart, even if it can heal itself faster than others.

"Like I knocked on your door for a drunk hookup," I sputter.

"I meant no such thing," he says.

"*Looking for comfort* sounds sexual. You say that to the wrong person, and they'd infer the worst about our working relationship."

Silas scoffs as if I've offended him. "I may be a shameless flirt, but I don't fuck my friends." He pauses. "Actually. Now that I'm thinking about it, I did offer to kiss Wrath when we were sixteen so he could get his first one out of the way. As a practice run, ya' know? He declined."

Gods help me.

I ignore him, but he continues, a buzzing fly in my ear. What happened to that comforting silence from a moment ago?

As we finally reach the fourth landing, my breathing is labored—why the fuck are there a million godsdamn stairs between floors in this place? Better yet, why isn't Silas offering to magic us up there?

"Also, would it be that bad to have slept with me?" Silas adds. "I'm not a leper. Many people want to fuck me. I'm the *king*."

I spin on my heel, and the action must surprise him

because he jerks back. Silas teeters on the ledge of the top step, one arm windmilling to keep his balance.

"Thank you for that reminder," I say. After three weeks of ruminating on my imminent demise, it's a suffocating thing, the familiarity with which he speaks to me. "But I think you're the one that needs it. Just because you freed me from the Seelie cage I was starving in, or because we have developed some kind of *strange camaraderie*—"

My chest heaves with my mounting frustration. I don't even know at what anymore. I'm fuming, crumbling, and latching onto what's easy. And Silas is an easy target.

"That doesn't mean that we're suddenly *best fucking buddies*. I appreciate you saving me. And I don't take it lightly that you have let me live, but do not misconstrue this as something it's not. We're not friends who joke about sex. You are the Unseelie King. I am Pride. We have shared goals. *That's it.*"

Silas's white brows rise to his hairline, an awkward beat passing between us. With it, my breathing calms, and the frantic feeling strangling my heart slips away.

"Are you done?" Silas asks.

I sigh, my shoulders slumping. "Yes."

"I'm going to ignore your outburst on the basis of you being starved, exhausted, and freshly unkidnapped," he says, pushing past me and patting me on the shoulder. He's quick to move, so I barely catch the flash of hurt in his dark eyes—or maybe I'm imagining it. "But consider your constructive criticism around my language duly noted."

We trudge down the length of the hall with a somber tension between us. A minute ago, I was raging, then I was fading into exhaustion, and now an icky sensation wriggles between my ribs. Guilt, maybe? My emotions are on a pendulum swing that I don't have the strength to slow.

Silas stops us a few feet before a wooden door. He leans against the wall, propping one foot up with a bent knee.

"Here we are," he says quietly, jerking a thumb at the door.

I lift my fist, poised to knock. Voices murmur beyond the thick wood.

My hand freezes, an inch between my knuckles and the door.

Everyone knows.

The two words haunt me. They spear me through my gut, a fatal wound with their resounding truth.

There's no more hiding.

4

JOSIE

There's a tickling sensation in the back of my brain, one I've grown begrudgingly accustomed to over the past three weeks.

My magic never shuts off, a reality that's led me to view the world with a level of fond detachment. I've always stood one step away from the group, been an observer more often than a participant. Even in my sleep, my magic catches stray thoughts, which is why I typically sleep alone; there aren't many fae disciplined enough to keep their minds to themselves in slumber. Nora is one, and now Imogen has been added to that shortlist.

But this tickling isn't an errant nightmare from someone down the hall. This is a purposeful knock on my psyche. Someone is projecting their thoughts towards me in the same way Nora and I learned to silently communicate.

My lids are heavy and slow to open, and my eyes take a lengthy second to refocus on the bedroom. Imogen is curled in a ball under the covers next to me, facing the wall. The sconce is still buzzing above us, though she must have turned down the dimmer because it barely illuminates the bed. The fire is nearly out, and the air has reembraced that winter sharpness.

I open my magic to the presence knocking in my head.

We're back. We got her. Silas keeps his message short.

I jolt up and force my magic to spread wide across the compound. I ignore the pestering thoughts of the scholars housed here, searching for Nora's presence. My heart races when I lock in on it and sense her coming closer.

They're inside, slowly inching up to our level.

I place a hand on Imogen's shoulder and shake.

"Mo, wake up," I whisper.

She rolls over, groaning. Her fingers dig into sleep-crusted eyes. "No, Joze, it can't be morning yet, I just got to bed."

I huff a tired laugh. "It's not, but you'll want to get up anyway. They're back."

That has her eyes snapping open, wide and alert; panic flashes, bright as lightning, within the golden specks.

"Shit," she says. "They got her?"

I nod. "They're headed up now."

Imogen throws the covers off her body, crawls past me, and tumbles off the end of the bed. She scurries around the room like a mouse, throwing on a robe and then attempting to tidy what few items she has strewn out on the desk and coffee table. I'm slow to follow, stretching my aching back before placing my feet on solid ground; I never even took off my boots before I passed out.

Oops.

I focus on Nora's presence again. A frantic energy leaks from her mental shields. They're cracked and terribly patched, leaking a messy mix of emotions. The closer they get, the louder she is.

It reminds me of when we were little, before she could banish her scars to the recess of her mind. Memories and sensations that would knock any empath on their ass—the kind of trauma I have no desire to filter through again.

I cut off my magic, block her out.

"Do I look okay?" Imogen asks.

"What?" I say, glancing her way. She grips the bathroom archway with white knuckles.

"Do I look okay?" she repeats.

I have to blink twice before my confusion fades. Her hair is a mess of waves and a little frizzy, but it's finally dry. With flushed cheeks and no makeup, she gives the impression that she rolled out of bed.

My neck heats.

"Of course you look okay," I mumble. "You always look okay."

"That's not what I mean," she groans and turns back into the bathroom.

I follow, watching as she attempts to cover the dark circles under her eyes with tinted powder.

"Mo, don't worry about that right now," I say, leaning against the bathroom door. "Nora thinks you're beautiful done up or not. I know that for a fact."

"It's not *that*," she says. I meet her eyes in the mirror. Imogen heaves a great sigh, a cross of melancholy and fear marring her features. "I don't want her to see me like *this*."

Broken. She doesn't want Nora to see her broken.

"Okay," I say, leaving it at that. This moment is not the time to push.

I don't think Nora's going to knock. She's been staring at the door for a full sixty seconds. You might want to run interference... Silas's concerned thoughts spear through my head.

My legs move of their own accord, quickly turning away from Imogen and stalking to the bedroom door. I rip it open and launch myself at Nora, crushing her in a hug.

My arms wrap around her ribs and squeeze; the air is pushed from her lungs in a breathy grunt at the impact. She's limp at first, but when I don't let go, burying my face in her neck, she finally lifts her arms and places them on my back. Nora's always been on the leaner side, but right now she's frail in my arms. As if I could snap her if I only squeezed a little harder.

I hold my mental defenses tight and strong, bracing them against the swell of emotion rolling off her.

"I never hear you, Nor. But you're so loud right now," I whisper into her shoulder.

"Sorry," she rasps.

Her voice lacks all the cocky confidence she normally exudes. She *also* sounds broken.

Anger swells within me, as sudden as a rogue ocean wave. How dare the first word Nora says to *me* be *sorry*?

I'm not the one she has to apologize to. I love her as a sister, but I'm not the one she pulled the rug out from under. I'm not the one that's had to rethink a whole relationship with life-altering context. I've been worried, but I'm not the one losing sleep over whether I'd see her again.

I pull back from our embrace and punch her right in the gut.

She rears back, clutching her stomach. "Fuck! What was that for?"

"For getting yourself fucking kidnapped," I growl.

"Sorry."

"Don't apologize to *me*."

A gasp sounds, and we both turn towards Imogen, who lingers behind me.

Imogen stares, lips parted as she takes in Nora's sorry state. She's still in her dress from Solstice, except it has lost all its elegance, dirtied and wrinkled and hanging looser on her body than it did three weeks ago.

I glance at Silas, who lurks down the hall. He nods his head, a silent command to leave and let them have their moment. I almost scoff at him, even though I know he's right.

I'll have plenty of time to debrief with Nora, to scold her until she rolls her eyes and then tell her how worried I was.

I step out of the doorway, then gently nudge Nora into the bedroom with a hand on her lower back.

"Be nice," I whisper, closing the door behind her.

Silas cocks his head, black eyes studying me with what I think is respect.

"You good?" he asks.

I shrug. I don't think I'll be able to say that with any certainty for a long time. There's too much up in the air. Silas bringing back Nora is only the first piece in a larger puzzle we have to solve.

"Ask me again tomorrow after we hear what she has to say." I cringe at his bloodied shirt. "You're a mess."

It's his turn to shrug. We've developed a kind of... friendly rapport as we've navigated the aftermath of Casimir.

"I blame Wrath," he says.

"You say that a lot."

"Because it's true." Silas shoots me a joking smirk, though his humor doesn't stretch past his cheeks. He stares beyond my shoulder, to the door at my back, with a level of concern that surprises me. "Do you think we should leave them alone for long?"

I scrub a hand down my face. There are too many questions I've got half-baked answers for these days. The fact that there's no yelling from the other side of the door is a good sign, though.

"They need to figure their shit out on their own," I say. "All we can do is pick up the pieces wherever they fall and pray they're whole enough to glue back together."

5
NORA

Neither of us move when the door clicks shut behind me. My lungs take no breath, my heart thumps not a single beat.

I... don't know what to do.

I don't have training for this.

Dark purple circles rim Imogen's eyes—the irises themselves are shadowed and dull, like brass in need of a polish. She's pale, lacking the sun-kissed complexion that usually lingers on her skin longer into winter than this. The smattering of freckles on the bridge of her nose have faded.

But... she's okay. I suck in a sudden, shaky breath. *She's okay.*

"Hey, Mo," I say, her name a rasped prayer in the silence.

Imogen's lips part, but she makes no move to cross the room.

I hadn't thought I'd see her again. Hadn't thought to practice this conversation in my head. Hadn't thought I'd walk back into the Unseelie Court without half a limb sliced off or a soul still attached to my body. Even when Silas shadowed us here, even as we walked up all those fucking stairs, I don't think it set in.

No, for three weeks I imagined my last stand. Me crushing my uncle's heart with my magic. Me trying to take out as many of his lackeys as I could before they inevitably gunned me down. As long as I got to see the light leave his eyes, I'd be satisfied.

It would have been worth it.

"Hi," Imogen whispers.

Whatever spell that froze her limbs breaks with the word; Imogen rushes forward and her shaking hands are on my arms, my shoulders, my neck, my face. Her thumbs stroke over my dirtied cheeks, her fingers push back my matted hair.

"You're okay?" she asks, voice still a whisper.

My hands flex at my sides but stay in place.

"Tired. Hungry. The pocket-jerky Wrath had to tide me over wasn't the most satiating," I say, the words trailing off at the end. "But I'm alive. So, there's that."

"This isn't a dream? Or a joke? Or some hallucination?"

"More akin to a nightmare, but real." I sigh, my eyes closing. "I'm here."

I sink into the careful stroke of her soft fingertips on my skin—they trace over my brows, my nose, my lips. They burrow at the nape of my neck, into my hair.

If this is the last time she touches me before she tosses me aside, I want to enjoy it.

She laughs, a single sardonic huff that catches in her throat. My lids flick open, and I catch the way the dim light dances off her glassy eyes. No tears spill over her cheeks, though. Imogen simply regards me with a deep and hollow melancholy.

I wonder how long that expression will last until it turns to disgust.

Or hatred.

Or fear.

Imogen suddenly pulls her hands from my body and wraps them around herself. Her fingers fidget with the tassel of her robe.

"Why didn't you tell me?" she whispers.

My hand goes to the back of my neck, nails raking over the skin. My mouth opens but no words come out. How do you explain hiding a part of yourself so thoroughly that you'd see that secret to your grave before revealing it?

I shrug.

"Josie knew," Imogen adds.

I steel myself for what's coming next.

Disgust. Hatred. Fear.

"Josie can read minds," I say dismissively.

"Silas knew," she says. Her hands tighten on her waist. "Why was *I* the last to know? Why did I find out that you're Seelie by watching wings burst from your back? I *felt* it, Nora, and the pain was *unbearable*—"

"Half. I'm half-Seelie," I say, my voice growing firm. As if that fact makes a difference. It doesn't. "And I didn't tell Silas. He... figured it out on his own." I step back, palms pressing into my burning eyes. "No one was ever supposed to know, Imogen."

"Did you think I wouldn't accept you?"

I huff an incredulous laugh. She asks the question like it's a simple one, as if it's ridiculous that I could ever doubt her ability to accept my lineage.

"Am I that untrustworthy that I had to be kept in the dark?"

"It doesn't matter if I trusted you or not," I snap, throwing my hands out at my side. She needs to understand it wasn't *her*. It was *everyone*. "Anyone who knew or could have connected the dots was a loose end. And I was taught to snip any dangling thread that threatened to unravel my secret. Do you get that?"

I approach Imogen slowly, giving her the chance to retreat. But she stands still, and I stop close enough to brush a strand of hair over her shoulder. My fingers graze the delicate skin where her neck meets her collarbone, the place I love to mark with my teeth.

Imogen shivers under my touch.

"Pride's grunt-men who helped rescue me? Dead not a year later. And even though that was at Pride's hand, I watched," I murmur. "Wes and Claude's father? He got suspicious. Tried to threaten Pride and take his place—and guess what? *Dead*. That time I did it. Gladly. Anyone else we thought even suspected? *Gone*. And with not a second thought given about it."

Imogen peers up at me, her expression cautious. "And Pride himself? Josie?"

"Mutually assured destruction," I say. My hand trails up her neck, and her lashes fall closed when my knuckles brush her cheekbone. I let them linger there, my thumb cresting over the plump flesh. "Pride had as much to lose as me if I was found out. And you must know the chances of me killing Josie are the same as you killing Leo. If I had told you, you'd be a loose thread, Mo. Do you understand what that would have meant?"

My hand cups her jaw, and I feel it tense before she nods. I never would have put her in that kind of danger willingly; I've only ever wanted her safe. But her knowing would have ended us. In one way or another.

"And the wings? The ones above your mantel?" she asks, eyes still shut.

"Mine," I confirm. A cruel, humorless smile cuts my cheeks. "The gods gifted me a single stroke of luck by placing me in a

House with a surefire way to hide them. They are the one thing I could not—cannot—deny or hide."

Imogen heaves a great sigh, and when her eyes open, lashes fluttering over pooling tears, all the fight drains out of her. A deep exhaustion sags her shoulders.

I'm tired too.

"I was worried sick about you, Nor," she says, voice cracking.

My throat burns. "I was worried about you too."

Imogen's head falls to my shoulder, and, cautiously, her arms wrap around my middle. I handle her with the same care, cupping the back of her head and curling myself around her. It's an unsteady truce, the air thick and heavy. Complicated emotions lurk beneath our spoken words. But we're both drained. My exhaustion is soul deep, and the only thing keeping me upright is Imogen's body pressed to mine.

I don't know how long we stand there, clinging to and soaking in each other's warmth. I should pull away, but I can't. Not yet.

At some point, Imogen detangles herself from my hold. Yawning, she glances at the clock mounted on the wall.

"It's late," she says. Then, shyly, she asks, "Do you want to lie down?"

I nod, but hesitate. My clothes and body are disgusting.

Imogen seems to understand, but instead of pushing me to the bed or the shower, she leads me to the couch with her hand tucked in mine. Palm to palm. Fingers laced. The tender touch aches, and my heart keens.

She helps me peel my dress off, but pauses when her fingers graze over the gun strapped to my thigh.

It's the one she gifted me, engraved with a terrifying promise. The question is, now that I'm back, and she *knows*, will it break?

Her hands tremble when they resume their task, dropping the soiled fabric to the rug. The holster and gun follow, falling onto the pool of fabric. Imogen kicks both under the coffee table, out of sight.

She pulls a nightshirt from a drawer and offers it to me. The cotton is soft, and I yawn as it slips over my skin.

Soon the sun will rise. And with it, all the problems prowling outside the bedroom door will come knocking. Reality will kiss our foreheads, wake us from this dream—or nightmare—and Imogen's tune will change. Of that, I'm sure. How could it not, when the disgust and the hatred and the fear finally take root? When the light shines on all of me, and the shadows desert me?

It's all I've ever known, once someone knows.

But there are a few hours yet before the sun will trickle through the blinds.

I give myself this and savor it.

We prop our feet on the coffee table, and Imogen drapes a blanket over us. She leans her head on my shoulder, and I wrap my arm around her waist, tucking her into my side.

Safe.

Imogen is protected here in my arms. If only for one more night.

I won't be a safe place for her come morning.

6

IMOGEN

Raindrops pelt us as we run, and I swipe at my face to clear the water from my eyes. It's a futile effort. Our skin is slick in the deluge, and Josie has to hold my hand in a vise grip to keep us connected. Thunder cracks, shaking the pavement under our boots, but it sounds different from the storms I'm used to. It's less a *boom* and more a *pop*, and instead of pausing for lightning, it strikes through the air in quick succession; this is no natural storm.

A mighty blast of wind hits us. I trip over my feet, and my hand breaks from Josie's grip as I tumble to the ground. Rain splatters my body, except it stings—it's not rain at all, but glass. Pain erupts in my side, and I gasp up at the sky, the storm growling its displeasure. My hands scramble, frantic to rip my dress open and expose the searing flesh beneath.

"No, no, no, no," I chant through the pain. "I don't want to die."

I search for Josie, head whipping side to side, panning over a barren street. And when I finally rip open the seam along my waist, I know tears mix with the rain on my cheeks. My fingers brush over a smooth expanse of skin, but I *feel* it. Every time the clouds *pop*, something rips open inside of me. I don't understand—I'm covered in blood, but there's no open wound.

A lithe, pale hand appears, pressing over mine on my stomach. The raspy timbre of Nora's voice cuts through the storm. "He needs to die, Imogen."

Her hand leaves mine, and my fingers chase hers. "No, don't go! Please, don't leave—"

Pop pop pop. Gunshots ring in rapid succession.

Pain sears through me, but this time, it spreads from my side to my back. This isn't my pain bursting from between my shoulder blades, but my magic pulling hers to me. I arch off the pavement, crying out—

I jolt awake from my nightmare. My cheeks are wet, and I bat at my face as I wheeze, Bramble's mountain air thin in my lungs. One hand comes to rest on my chest, pressing firmly over my pounding heart. Unsteady, it races beneath my ribcage. My lids screw shut, and I try to focus on the world around me—the *real* world.

The buttery silk of my pajamas. Chilling, damp tear tracks on my cheeks. The scratchy throw blanket sliding over my toes as I shift on the couch. The sconce above the nightstand buzzing low across the bedroom.

I manage to take a full, but stuttered, breath. It doesn't fill me, so much as it sustains me. The hollowness in my chest leaves little room for anything else but necessity.

Blinking down at the weight pressing into my lap, I suck in another stilted breath. Nora sleeps, peaceful as a babe, head cradled in my lap. One hand makes to run through her hair, but stops before it can connect with her raven locks. My fingers tremor, frozen midair. I curl them into a painfully tight fist, nails digging into my palm, before returning my hand to my side. My head tilts back and I stare at the ceiling.

I can't believe she's here.

I find the strength to look down again, and my chest tightens. Nora must have slipped her head from its perch on my shoulder in our slumber and landed in my lap. The rest of her body followed suit, abandoning the safety of the blanket and curling up on the other half of the couch. Her long legs cross together at the ankles, and the sight is perfectly innocent. I'd never think to use that word to describe Nora. But here I am, gazing down at the way her dark lashes splay over her pale cheeks, struck once again by the dichotomy of *her*.

Nora's rosy lips twitch down, and her eyebrows pinch, as if she too is fighting a nightmare she can't break free from.

I hope that's not the case. I've become unwillingly and intimately acquainted with nightmares that cage you, the ones that enjoy the chase, that relish catching you every time your lids fall shut.

Sleep isn't kind to me anymore.

There's no way I'll be shaking hands with the sandman again tonight, and given the lack of sun in the window, I couldn't have gotten much rest.

It'll have to be enough.

My soul broke apart on Solstice as Nora's pain ripped through me. It was too similar to when I was shot, the shredding of my body and the restitching of it with foreign magic. Or maybe my soul was already cracked from that night at Sal's shop, and the Seelie tonic they poured down my throat only gave me the illusion of being healed.

Maybe this is what happens when everyone around you thinks that violence is the solution to every problem.

Pain and fear and blood—repeat. Threats and plotting and more pain. Another vow of vengeance. More blood—repeat. I become collateral damage. Their rage saturates my scars, and I get lost in all the gnarled flesh.

I'm stuck in the crossfire of their war, and it isn't safe enough to stand behind my friends' shields anymore.

My thoughts drift to my family's cabin, tucked in the outskirts of the city suburbs. Maybe it would be better to simply... not be on the battlefield at all.

I sigh, banishing those fantasies. I can't think about that now, not when the woman I love sleeps in my lap. Would that not be abandoning her when she needs me most?

I gently shift Nora off my lap. Draping the blanket over her body so she doesn't grow cold, I fall fully into caretaker mode. It's an easy mask to put on, a mirror to when I step behind the bar. The tasks are clear: pull a change of clothes from the dresser; fold them along with a towel on the bathroom vanity for when she showers; go down to the kitchen to bring her back breakfast; leave her to rest. This, at least, I can do.

I linger at the kitchen table, nursing a cup of long-gone-cold tea, when Silas waltzes in. He stops short, head whipping from me to the door and back.

"Why are you down here?" he asks but doesn't wait for an answer before bopping across the small space to Cook. Silas reaches around the burly old chef to snag a pastry off a platter that will be delivered to the main dining room. He moans as his teeth dig into the flaky crust of the croissant. "Gods. Delicious as always, Cook. Imogen, did you sneak in here to try one too?"

"No, I wait until they're out at the buffet like I'm supposed to."

"Miss Gallagher has manners," Cook grumbles, pushing Silas aside. "Get out of my kitchen, boy. Can't you wait another five minutes?"

"I don't like eating in the hall with everyone else," Silas whines. "It's much nicer in here. And I get first pick of the goodies before the vultures descend. Who knew academics could get bloodthirsty over chocolate and butter?"

He reaches for a second pastry and Cook slaps his hand. Silas winces and hops back, muttering a curse. I can't help but snort at his antics.

"Oh, you think this is funny?" Silas croons.

I shrug and try to hide the amused twitch of my lips behind the curve of my mug. Silas's gaze narrows on me as he stalks over, leaning on the table with both hands.

"You need to work on keeping all of that to yourself." He waggles a pointed finger at my face, and I'm hit with the memory of my brother saying something similar to me years ago. "Even as Lust you were terrible at hiding your thoughts. You've got a terrible poker face. I assume you *are* bad at poker?"

"Or you could be exceptionally good at reading people," I offer.

Silas hums around another bite of pastry, flicking a spot of chocolate from the corner of his mouth with his knuckle.

"That is true," he says, as if he hadn't considered that option. He slides onto the bench across from me, munching on his breakfast with a pinched brow and an intense stare directed my way. "Why are you down here alone?"

I take a sip of my cold tea—throw an ice cube and some sugar in the mug and it could be a summer sweet tea.

"Nora needed to shower," I say, although it comes out more defensive than I intended.

Silas licks his thumb and forefinger; they pop between his lips as he sucks them clean of pastry crumbs. "I'm surprised, is all. I figured she'd be keeping you hostage up there for longer than a few hours."

I blink at him, and one of his white brows quirks up expectantly. My cheeks heat when I realize what he's implying.

"Why would you think that?" I say, clearing my throat awkwardly.

"Because you're lovers who have been dramatically reunited?"

"Can you honestly say you'd be jumping into bed after spending three weeks worrying yourself sick over whether your kidnapped girlfriend was still alive, while also over-thinking why she's been lying to you about who she was for nearly a decade?"

"Of course," he says.

I huff. *Unbelievable.*

"I take it the conversation beyond the bedroom door didn't go well?"

"Why do you care, Silas?" I ask.

His lips purse, and he clicks his tongue in thought. "I feel... slightly responsible for your troubles."

"What? Why?"

"I have pushed Nora down a certain path to suit my own desires," he explains slowly. "And I will be doing it again. I see... great potential in her. I want her to retake a leadership position in our Court. But I'm also aware of how that could affect you. And now a bit of guilt is wriggling in my chest."

"Nora does what she likes, Silas. It doesn't matter what you think you're pushing her towards. If she doesn't want to do it, she won't. And that includes being Pride." I frown, realizing how true that is. She's not like me, never has been in that regard. She's not easily swayed by those around her. "Plus, when have you ever felt guilty about how you've affected my life?"

Silas was the one who blackmailed me by threatening Leo's life last year. But at the same time, much has happened since then. These three weeks at Bramble have shifted my view of the Unseelie King—however slightly. I've realized that everything is more complicated than it once seemed.

Josie says she trusts Silas and Wrath. And they have kept their promise to rescue Nora, along with offering us the protection of Bramble's walls for as long as we need. Beneath all the pretty-boy charm and thinly veiled threats, Silas isn't all that different from my brother...

Is this how Conor would have turned out, had he survived that crash?

Silas runs a hand lazily through his white locks.

"Is a king not allowed to grow a conscience?" he jokes, though his smirk falters. "And I care about—"

"Here you are, Miss Gallagher," Cook says, cutting Silas off. He drops a small box of food that I requested earlier onto the table. "Thanks for your patience."

I stand, trading my mug for the food. "Thank *you*. For the tea and for wrapping this up for me."

"Anytime." Cook ambles away, carrying his tray of food out of the kitchen.

Glancing at the clock, which shows it's a quarter to nine, I decide it's been long enough. If Nora's still asleep when I get back, I'll gently rouse her so she can get something in her stomach. The kitchen door squeaks, and Silas follows me down the hall like a lost puppy.

At first, I figure he's headed to his room, up one floor from mine. But instead of continuing up the stairs when I turn down the hall, he stays one step behind me.

"What are you doing?" I ask.

"I'm coming with you to get Nora. We all need to debrief and discuss what comes next. You're welcome to attend, though I know you haven't wanted to the last few times we all talked Court politics."

"I don't know if that's a great idea…"

"Why? Because you don't want to join? Or has Nora said something about not wanting to see me?" he asks.

"No," I say, face scrunching as I stop before my bedroom door. "But she needs to rest. And why would she avoid you? Did you do something yesterday—"

"*Pshh*," Silas cuts me off, waving my concern away. "If that's all, then I'm not worried. I can deal with her tired. What does have me worried is why she isn't—"

The door opens, and our heads whip toward the raven-haired woman in question.

7

<h1 style="text-align:center">NORA</h1>

I jolt out of dreamless slumber with a gasp, frigid mountain air freezing my lungs. It's the first night in weeks that I've slept like the dead, lost so deep in my subconscious that not even my nightmares could rouse me.

My neck and shoulders crack as I stretch out from under the thin throw blanket. The room is dim, no sconces buzz and no fires roar, though the telltale trickle of morning sun leaks between the blinds.

I am also alone.

For all the mornings I've woken up to an empty room and an empty bed, it's never been this hollow before. It's only when I shuffle into the bathroom, stripping with the intent to wash the grime from my body that I realize, with clarity, that this ache is from something deeper than strained muscles.

Is this how Imogen would feel, waking up after I snuck away with the night? Did she leave this morning, overcome by the need to distance herself from me in the same way?

The creak of the faucet and the hiss of water falling into the tub are a beautiful, distracting song. While I wait for the water to heat, I plant my hands on the porcelain sink and stare at my reflection in the oval mirror.

My vibrant green eyes—my mother's eyes, *his eyes*—have darkened to match the gaping sensation in my chest. I twist my torso, putting my scars on full display.

I cannot blame her for leaving. I am not who she thought I was. I'm a nightmare.

My arm contorts to trace over the once-raised flesh. The scars are dark pink, but flat, as if my skin wanted to heal but couldn't fully rid itself of the markings I chose to brand myself with.

Magic itches beneath the scars, my new wings begging to be let out. They scratch the underside of my skin, cut me from the inside as if they are made of iron rather than chitin and sinew. The pain comes on quick and sudden between my shoulder blades, and my fingers curl around the sink's edge, nails nearly cracking against the porcelain.

I groan through the spasms, chanting in my head the mantra that's seen me through hell and back. *The pain is worth the reward, the pain is worth the reward, the pain is worth the—*

My fist strikes out and hits the mirror. It shatters, a spider-web of cracks blooming from where my knuckles bleed; relief is fleeting, but the sting helps bring me back from the edge. In the shards, my eyes are mirrored tenfold. They are a stark reminder of what I need to prioritize, and of what comes next.

I cannot afford *love*, however sweet or golden. Waking without Imogen is... a blessing.

Steam clouds over my reflection, and I know that the shower is warm.

As the water sluices down my body, washing away the remnants of Casimir, I check in on my tether to Patience. I indulge myself, sending the sensation of my clawing wings down the bond between us, willing my magic to wreak havoc on the man's own wings.

I hope he hates the way it burns.

The tips of my pointed ears twitch at the sound of voices, harsh and hushed, hissing outside the bedroom door. I pull on my trousers and slip into my shoes; the scratch of my woolen armor is a comfort, and the fabric wrapping around my hips finally rids me of Bramble's damp chill.

I don't hesitate to rip open the door once I'm decent—but find myself shocked as I home in on Imogen hunched conspiratorially next to Silas. Imogen's head whips towards me with wide doe eyes and those pretty pink lips parted.

But... didn't she leave?

Her teeth shyly bite into her bottom lip, and inconvenient desire floods me, my thumb itching to pull it free.

"This is unexpected," I say, eyes flicking critically over Silas. His hands are poised on his hips, posture casual and cocky. A smarmy smirk pokes a dimple in one cheek. "What kind of mischief are you up to?"

He tongues his cheek in turn. "I am attempting to right Imogen's negative impression of me. Despite her best efforts to avoid the inevitable, I think I'm growing on her. But I am charming and persistent, as you know."

I don't deign to give him a response—to do otherwise would only encourage him. I turn back to Imogen.

"If he's bothering you, I can punch him. Right in his stupid smirking face," I deadpan. "I have nothing else to lose."

"Hey!" Silas chirps.

Imogen snorts, her small hand reaching up to cover the sound.

"You don't have to punch him," she says.

"Are you sure? I would love the excuse," I say.

"No, Nora," she huffs. "I don't want you punching anyone."

And when a delicious pink blush rises on the apples of her cheeks, I have to glance away.

"Well, you know you only have to say the word and I'm there," I add.

Silas huffs. "You have no excuse to be this rude this morning. You can't possibly be this irritable after a good meal and a hot shower."

My stomach, as if on cue, twists painfully. It doesn't growl so much as it wails, drawing the concerned gazes of both Imogen and Silas.

"I hate to be the bearer of bad news, but no one fed me last night," I say.

"You didn't eat breakfast yet?" Silas asks. "It's nearly nine."

"This is what I was trying to tell you," Imogen groans. "I didn't want to wake her. I was going to bring her food once she was up and showered." She lifts a small cardboard box in her hand and waves it in Silas's face—this golden kitten has grown claws when it comes to the Unseelie King. "Hence the travel plate."

"No use arguing over it." I grab the box. "Food is now in hand. I can eat and talk. I assume the latter is why you're here, Silas?"

"Yes," he says.

"No rest for the wicked." I sigh, then push past the two. When I don't hear their footsteps behind me, I pivot on my heel. They both regard me with equally confused and concerned expressions. It makes my insides squirm. "Where are we doing this? In the library?"

Imogen makes to speak, but Silas cuts her off.

"Yes. We've converted one of the back storerooms into a more private meeting room," he says.

"But we have time, Nor." Imogen steels her shoulders, her posture contrasting with the soft words she speaks. "Why don't you take this morning easy? I know I needed a day before I was ready to talk about... it all."

My face pinches. "I'm not a wounded animal that needs to be coddled."

Seriously. What does she expect me to do? Hole up in my room while those who wronged me run free? While the Sins plot how to toss me out and the Court casts their judgments on me, uncontested?

"Sorry, Imogen, you've been overruled." Silas sweeps in before I have to explain any of that. "Kingly decree. Follow me, both of you."

He pats Imogen on the shoulder and strides forward.

"*You're welcome,*" he whispers as he passes me.

I hold out my hand out for Imogen to take. It's habit, reflex, and I realize too late what I've done—what I've opened myself up to.

My lungs hold my breath tight.

Her palm reaches out, as if she is also led only by instinct, but it pauses in its pursuit of mine, and the hesitation stalls my heart.

Waiting for this shoe to drop will be the end of me, I realize.

I need to stop this. I need to make a clean break before my resolve is muddied. I cannot allow my desire a chance to convince my mind that I can have both love *and* revenge. It's not a possibility anymore. Because there is a fear there, laced in the pattern of our intertwined fingers, a kind that wasn't present before.

And worse, the fear isn't wholly hers.

"What did you bring me?" I ask as we trail behind Silas. I shake the small box of food and decadent scented steam rises from the gap where it latches. "Hopefully, I won't be subjected to your scrambled eggs?"

Imogen looses a snort, her freckled nose scrunching. "You won't let that go, will you?"

The first time I stayed over for breakfast at hers—which was only two months ago, though it feels like longer—she attempted to cook for us. Imogen may be able to whip up cocktails and cookies with precision, but give her a spatula and a frying pan and somehow she burns eggs black.

"Cook is on-call all day, given everyone's hectic schedules, so you're safe!" Silas calls.

"It's rude to eavesdrop," Imogen huffs.

Silas shoots a paltry glare over his shoulder, but it quickly morphs into a dangerous mix of mirth and mischief. His steps slow until he's at Imogen's side, and we're walking three-across.

"Then I will simply insert myself back into the conversation," he says, "so I'm not being rude."

"It wasn't an invitation," Imogen mutters.

They quip back and forth, and with each barbed jab, Silas's smile only grows. A begrudging frown marks divots in Imogen's cheeks. But beneath the annoyance, if you pay close enough attention, there's a seed of respect blooming in her dimmed eyes.

Silas speaks to her the same way he speaks to Wrath. He pushes, but it's with care. It's precise, intentional. He's trying to get her out of her shell. He's trying to be her *friend*.

The realization is a sharp stabbing pain in my chest. Because I was cruel to Silas last night—when he's clearly been kind to Imogen, been there for her when I wasn't.

Everyone was there for her when I wasn't. Silas, Wrath, Josie... they're the ones who saved her on Solstice. Not me.

I'm the reason she needed to be saved in the first place.

Why is she holding my hand?

I'm about to untangle my fingers from hers when I catch Silas's eye over Imogen's head. She's ranting at him, but I don't think either of us are hearing her fully. He shakes his head; it's a swift, barely noticeable warning.

Don't you dare pull away from her, his black eyes scold.

But my skin is starting to itch; my palm grows clammy where it brushes against Imogen's. Last night, I longed for the tender coupling of our fingers to last. Now, my hand is desperate for relief.

I shouldn't be surprised. I knew this was coming.

Fear hugs us, and its damning friends lurk around the corner.

I gently remove my fingers from hers. Her scalding rant at Silas stops, and her head tilts toward me, concern knitting her brows.

"Is it okay if I eat?" I ask, hoping my excuse doesn't sound as fake as it is.

"Yeah, of course," she says. "Sorry."

"Don't apologize," I say.

I open up the container and reveal a pile of pastries and crisp bacon. No eggs. I smile around a bite of flaky, chocolatey goodness.

"Thank you," I mumble as I chew.

"You're welcome," she says shyly. Her fingers fidget, clasped in front of her as we walk the rest of the way to the library.

I decimate half the food by the time we're weaving between bookshelves. I don't take Imogen's hand again, even when I stop eating and quietly close the box to save the other half for later. Silas, the ever-watchful shit-stirrer, huffs an irritated sigh at that. I pierce him with a glare, but he meets my dagger with a shield of disappointment.

Imogen doesn't notice—or she simply ignores our change in mood—as we reach a paint-chipped door in the bowels of the library. Silas holds the door open for her but shuts it when I try to enter. He pokes a single pointed index finger into my chest.

"Sort yourself out, Nora," he whispers harshly. "Don't string her along."

My eyebrows hit my hairline. "Are you serious right now?"

"Imogen hasn't left her room in weeks. Barely spoken to anyone but Josie. And this is the first time she's joining one of our meetings with any kind of wits about her."

"Don't give me the protective older brother act, Silas. And don't pretend to care about her when you're the one who blackmailed her for the better part of a year." The words are a stretch. It's clear Silas cares. And I know better than most that shared trauma creates fast bonds—so why am I pushing back against his good intentions? I cross my arms, and more bitter barbs fly off my tongue. "It's been less than *twelve hours*. Am I not allowed some time to readjust? And my relationship with Imogen is none of your business—a fact of which I've stated many times before."

Silas sighs. "My patience for whatever has crawled up your ass will only stretch so far. You don't want to provoke me on this."

"What are you gonna do, kidnap me?" I huff. "Host an intervention on how I handle my relationships?"

"Yes."

I roll my eyes.

"I'm serious," he adds.

"Uh-huh."

"I don't think you realize how similar your Second and I are or how close we got while planning your escape. I'm sure she wouldn't turn me down on knocking some sense into your—"

"Can you two finish this later? We're all waiting," Josie interrupts. She pokes her head out from a crack in the door, her dark brown hair curling around her chin.

Silas whips around, giving her the biggest puppy-dog eyes. "Josie, Nora's being mean to me."

"Yeah?" she deadpans.

"I told her we'd have to host an intervention if she didn't stop being so rude," Silas says.

"That is not what happened—"

"Are you capable of holding in whatever you need to work through until after this debrief?" Josie's brows raise in Silas's direction, but there's mirth dancing in her deep brown irises.

Silas gawks at her, and I slap his shoulder as I pass him by. "You might be fast friends, Silas, but you've got nothing on two decades' worth of sisterhood."

Josie snorts and opens the door wider, letting me in. "You look better than last night."

"A warm shower and a night not sleeping on stone does wonders for the complexion."

"Glad to see three weeks behind iron didn't break your sense of humor," she says.

The small study room is made even more cramped by musty smelling boxes stacked high along each wall. I go to flick one open when Wrath's deep voice cuts through the air.

"Don't open those unless you want to see a youngling Silas in a diaper rag and smothered in cake."

My hand pulls back with breakneck speed. "I thought I told him to burn these if he didn't want people to see them."

I lock eyes with Wrath, who is seated at the table with Imogen, and give him a respectful nod. A dusting of blond stubble lines his jaw, and his red-brown eyes are made prominent with the purple circles lining them. It seems the only one without any markings of exhaustion is Silas.

Of course he'd be the only one getting enough sleep.

"Wrath," I greet.

"Pride," he greets back.

Interesting.

"Not Nora?" I ask.

Wrath shrugs, his almost-coy expression dropping into neutrality as his attention shifts to a series of documents on the table. It's then that I note we're missing one integral presence.

"No Leo?" I ask. Imogen and Josie share a loaded glance.

"Um... he's back home," Imogen says. Her attention falls to her lap, where her fingers twist together nervously.

"Why is he not—"

"We'll talk about it later," Josie cuts me off. "He needs some time. But we're not here to discuss the new Lust."

"I see." A rock forms in my stomach at the implication behind her words. I need to prepare myself for the worst, then. "Alright," I say, taking my seat and leveling with the few people currently in my corner. "What's first: your questions or mine?"

8

JOSIE

There's a mountain of frustration growing in the room, rising with each chapter of Nora's story. She answers every one of Wrath's questions succinctly. They span from her true history and how she came to be under Pride's protection in Anwynn, to what happened the night of Solstice. I'm thankful she doesn't rehash the gritty details for Imogen's sake; the woman's cheeks are sunken and white as a ghost as she processes the unfiltered details of Nora's childhood. I've told her bits and pieces, as I imagine Nora has too, over these last few years, but nothing compares to the full gruesome picture.

The vicious murder of Nora's parents at Patience's hand. Pride's abuse throughout our youngling years. How she systematically removed anyone who might have revealed her identity. Imogen is learning how deep Nora's hatred for Patience runs... and how profound her need for vengeance is.

I don't know if Imogen's better for it.

The conversation eventually shifts to Benevolence, and how he asked for Nora's help in killing his father, all to betray her. The bastard knocked her out before she could finish the job.

"And that brings us to last night," Nora says, clearing the rasp from her throat. "You two know how that went."

Silence cocoons us.

It allows me a moment to study the others as they digest Nora's recount. Imogen's brows are knit together with concern, her poor lip taking another beating from her teeth. Wrath's jaw feathers in deep thought, and he taps his pencil on his notepad three times before scribbling something down. Silas looks plain furious, his arms crossed and shirtsleeves straining against his chest as he leans back in his chair.

Waiting for Silas or Wrath to lead us down the next logical path of questioning proves fruitless. They are lost to their thoughts. I brace myself before cutting through the tension, my inquiry a pointed knife.

"Do you still have the tether?" I ask.

Nora's eyes cut to mine, jewel green glinting with anger, but not the kind I'd expect from her if their plan failed. It's a seething, simmering rage.

Her head shakes.

"*Damn it!*" Silas's hands slap against the table.

At my side, Imogen flinches. With a frustrated sigh, Silas stands.

"Sorry. I needed to get that out." One hand scrubs over his jaw as he paces behind his chair. "But know that I don't hold you at fault, Nora. Especially considering... you know."

"Since Patience forced a pair of wings to grow out of my back while he shot up the ballroom?" Nora says.

"Yes, that."

"It is an unfortunate development," Wrath mutters, his pencil scratching against paper. "We lose a tactical advantage, but it doesn't exactly change how we proceed."

"He needs to die. As soon as possible," Nora says.

"Of course," Silas agrees. He braces his hands on the chair back, leveling each of us with a determined stare. "However, we have other, more pressing issues to deal with first. The Seelie *will* attack, especially if Patience has the queen's ear. Last night wasn't only a rescue mission. Clearing the castle and lowering the land bridge has bought us valuable time. Between that and what's left of the shadow-veil, we have at least a few weeks before we need to be con—"

"Pardon me, Silas." My eyes narrow at the Unseelie King. "What's *left* of the shadow-veil?"

He scratches his jaw. "Yes, well, no magic lasts forever."

A dreadful beat passes between us, one that has my hackles rising.

"What is that supposed to mean?" Nora asks.

"The creation of the shadow-veil was an accident," Wrath answers, too quickly. "It wasn't made to last forever, and it's been weakening over the last decade. We have no clue when it will naturally dissipate, or how long of a sustained attack it can take from light magic before it crumbles."

"Can't you make a new one?" Imogen asks—the first time she's spoken up in the conversation. "You have many talented shadow-walkers in your Houses."

"I nearly died releasing the magic needed to create it in the first place. Half a continent is a large area to cover." Silas winces. "It's not something I plan to repeat."

"And as for strengthening what we already have"—Wrath's head bobbles back and forth—"we're researching a few things, but nothing's shown promise."

I spread my hands over the grainy texture of the table, leaning forward to stare the Unseelie King down.

"Let me say this back to you another way, so it's clear I'm understanding." My tongue swipes over my teeth, clicking when I open my mouth. "Our one security failsafe is, for lack of a better example, a bedsheet hung over a doorway. One that can be ripped away whenever the Seelie grow the balls to attack it outright. And you didn't think this was pertinent information to share until *right now*?"

Silas snaps his fingers, a finger gun pointed in my direction. "Exactly."

Nora and I have the same reaction: a string of curses tumble from our lips.

"We're not as helpless as he makes us out to be," Wrath says. "House Wrath's militia is as capable as it was a hundred years ago. We *can* fight. But we can't simply sit back and pretend we're untouchable."

"And we have some time," Silas repeats. "I personally believe that whether the shadow-veil stands or not, Patience's attempts to destabilize the Sins is a larger threat. That is the point I was leading us to before I was interrupted. If the Houses cannibalize themselves—we all lose."

"Take out key leadership. Sow descent. Splinter the Court so when they attack, we're easier to take down," Wrath adds. "It's a textbook play."

"Crack the foundation and the building will crumble," I mutter.

Nora barks a laugh, drawing all our attention.

"That fucking bastard," she says, voice dripping with disdain. "He called me his *unknowing* Trojan horse. My intentions never mattered. All he needed was to reveal who I was to the Sins in a way that brokered no argument." Her fists clench together on the table. "I played right into his hands like an idiot."

"We all did, Nora. But we knew there were risks in our attempt to mitigate a larger conflict," Silas says.

Nora slams one fist on the table, and Imogen flinches at the loud bang.

"Not like *this*," she snaps. "What kind of fool were you to commit to our plan, knowing the shadow-veil could fall? As set as I was in killing Patience, I always operated under the assumption that our people would be safe fae-side—House business human-side and my own safety be damned."

Silas sinks back into his seat with a blank expression. "We make the best choices we can in dire moments."

"You're the king. You should know better," she says. "You don't put your people in danger. It's rule number fucking one."

The veins in Silas's neck stick out from the tension skyrocketing between them. Nora's getting too worked up over this, and I know that's my cue to cut in and play peacemaker.

"There's no use throwing blame around," I say. "We should focus on what we can do right now. Outside of searching for solutions to our shadow-veil problem, what do you think is the next priority?"

"Your boy, Wes," Silas grinds out. "Patience's spy."

"We cut off all portal access to the Human Realm the day after we got back. While that doesn't stop him from shadow-walking himself, we do have eyes on him. He seems content to sit pretty as temporary head of House Pride for now," Wrath says.

"Why isn't he already dead?" Nora asks.

"Wrath and I agreed to table any discussion of his fate until you made your return," Silas says. "You're welcome."

"He's created a new faction, Nor," I cut in. "He's challenged both you and I for our positions. Claude is with him. Hattie is with us. The rest of the family is split."

As Second, I've dipped my hands in everything related to House Pride's operations, but managing this alone is another beast. I begin to tick off the list of things going wrong, counting with my fingers.

"The supply chain is a mess. Vendors and clients on both sides are pissed. Wes has control over key warehouses fae-side. The only thing working in our favor is the lockdown on the portal, which means we've got to manage with what we've got stored here. Doesn't really help us since no one is working, but it also doesn't help Wes."

Nora's tongue pokes her cheek as she processes the news. I know she's contemplating the best way to get rid of him, but there's already a plan brewing. We can take out Wes and his coup-happy comrades. Nora just has to bite.

"What do you think, Joze?" she asks.

"Think of what?"

"Do you still want to be my Second?" she asks hesitantly, and I'm surprised she even has to ask. Nothing has changed between us or in my desire to see our people thrive. It's what we dreamed of as children. We pinky promised at midnight sleepovers to make our House a better place when we came of age. "You willing to fight a civil war for that empire we wanted to build?"

"Yes," I say without hesitation.

"Then we'll take care of him. I'm not rolling over and letting anyone steal our legacy. He's no different from Patience in my eyes," Nora says.

"Agreed," I say.

The threat of his impending death hangs in the air.

"Are you guys talking about killing him?" Imogen asks quietly.

No one says a word.

Mo, our soft, sweet girl, is the only one in this room who hasn't killed; she's got an innocence that I hope is never ripped away. But the unfortunate reality is that these conflicts only end in two ways: exile or death.

I've never craved death as Nora has. But I also have no issue with Wes dying to serve the greater good of our House and Court. He's issued us a challenge. And the sitting Sin needs to retaliate with appropriate force.

"So much talk of death," Imogen says, her voice a shaking rasp. "Why can't Silas exile him?"

"He's a shadow-walker. That's not an option," Nora says. "I know you're naïve, Imogen, but don't be ridiculous. He's got to die."

"I'm only expressing my opinion. Is this not the place to do that?" Imogen says, her voice growing more powerful. "I'm sick of watching you all put yourselves in dangerous situations. It's a never-ending cycle of violence. Do none of you see it?"

Nora's fist hits the table again, and for a third time, Imogen flinches. This time, her face pales, and her chest heaves with quick breaths. "We're talking about war, Imogen. Death is a part of war. *And* he tried to kill you. I could never let that go unpunished. What did you expect?"

"I certainly didn't expect you to snap at me when all I'm doing is expressing my concern for your safety. I just got you back." Imogen's chair makes an awful scrape on the stone floor as she shoves it back. With shaking hands and head hunched low, she rushes to the door.

"Imogen—" Nora calls out, standing, ready to follow.

"Sorry, I need to go." Imogen's rasp rings out before the door slams shut behind her.

An awkward air descends upon the room.

"That's not what I meant by sorting your shit out, Nora," Silas chides.

Nora tenses, and my shoulders rise to my ears, bracing for the impact of her rage. But she falls into her chair and rubs her face with her hands. A groan slips through her fingers; it's a keening, guttural sound that rips through the room. It's a moan of mourning—and it slaps me in the face.

She's not crying, but she might as well be. And Nora never cries.

This... this shouldn't be happening.

Wrath's got this nauseated expression on his face, bug eyes staring at Nora like she's some kind of strange creature. Silas's are just as wide with surprise. Maybe he wanted to stoke her wrath, provoke her anger. Rage is an easy thing to navigate—but this? The way her nails dig into her forehead? The melancholic hunch of her shoulders?

Nora is cracking.

Panic speeds my heart. I need her strong; I need her whole. We're meant to fix our House together. It doesn't work if it's only me.

Nora cannot break. Nora cannot shatter.

I slide out of my chair and into Imogen's, the leather cushion still warm. I put my hand on Nora's back, and her breath hitches at the contact. I don't say anything at first, only rubbing small circles with my hand. Then I lean in, my forehead resting against her raven waves.

"Compartmentalize," I whisper in her ear. "Get through the rest of this meeting. Then apologize. Then take the rest day by day, hour by hour, minute by minute." The muscles in Nora's back twitch under my hand. Her body shakes, a volatile vibration. "Remember who you are. You are the girl who withstood ten hours of lashings while I sifted through your memories. You survived a shearing. You are the one who slayed the man who abused you and took his empire. *Alright?* I need you, Nora. Otherwise, none of this works. And they get away with it. And you lose it all again. *You lose it all if you break right now. Do you hear me?*"

Her head rubs against mine as she nods.

My jaw is tight as I swallow the lump lodged in my throat. "Good."

I pat her back, one firm smack between her shoulder blades, and sit up. I raise a single finger, asking Wrath and Silas to wait one more moment, and we watch as Nora regains her composure.

Nora takes her time, but piece by piece, she comes together. Her back straightens. Her hands steeple on the table, and she rests her chin upon them as if in deep thought. Her face slackens and her lips fall into a neutral line. Then, finally, her eyes flick open, revealing a cold sheen that has the hair on my neck standing on end.

"Sorry," Nora says, clearing her throat. "Let's continue."

Silas shifts in his seat, a dark expression swirling in his gaze; it's a strange mix of awe and concern.

"Right." He coughs, one fist pulled to his mouth. "Where were we?"

"They're going to kill Wes," Wrath says. "Which is fine because he's slotted for execution regardless. Might as well play it to her advantage."

"Exactly," Silas says, jumping in again, full speed. "I've already pardoned her, but that won't change public sentiment. I know that simply decreeing her as Pride won't stand with her people. They'd see it as a hand out. She needs to earn it back."

"Thanks for talking about me as if I'm not here," Nora grumbles.

"But am I wrong?" Silas says.

"No," Nora grits out.

He's not wrong at all.

I only hope we can convince our people of what they need.

9
JOSIE

I find Imogen staring at a shelf deep in the maze of bookcases. It's the only section with fiction, filled with tomes of myth and legend rather than historical records, biographies, and academic journals. Some are human fairytales, and some are tales from Faerie, though all of them burst with some combination of magic, heroes, and peculiar creatures. I only know because I've peeked at the titles that I've gently plucked from her lap as she sleeps; Imogen's developed a habit of passing out between chapters.

I lean my shoulder against the shelf and watch her. Imogen's arms are wrapped around her middle, her fingers gripping the fabric of her sweater tight as she presses her forehead against the books. Her ribs expand with steady breaths, but there's tension bunching her shoulders.

Tell me what's wrong, Mo, and I'll fix it.

"You can stop staring and help me pick out a book," Imogen says, unmoving.

"I don't know that I'd be any good at that," I say.

"Why not?"

"I'm partial to the darker stories."

Imogen's head tilts, and one red-rimmed eye cracks open. "Who says I'm not?"

"Are you?" I ask, mashing my lips together to hide my smile.

She huffs, pushing back from and staring up at the shelves. "No."

I amble over to her side and stare at the books with her. "Then I won't be any help."

"I'm indecisive today," she says. "If you're planning on sticking around, I'd sit and get comfortable."

I slide down the shelf with my back to the books and wait as Imogen reads titles with her head tilted to the side. Blond hair hangs over her shoulder, a glittering curtain of soft waves. She takes her time, pulling books out and putting them back after flicking through a few pages.

Finally, she reaches up on her tippy-toes to pluck one and then bends at her waist to pull another. One is faded red with gold lettering. The other is pale yellow with green lettering and a swirling border of gilded leaves and flowers.

"Which one?" Imogen asks, holding both up.

I purse my lips and point to the red one.

A ghost of a smile touches her lips. "I had a feeling you'd pick this one."

"Why is that?" I ask.

Imogen sits next to me. Her knees knock into mine as she pulls them up and rests the book between us. She flicks it open —the first page showcasing an illustration of a cabin in a forest. At first glance, it's a cute drawing, but Imogen's finger glides over the page, pointing out the shadows between the trees and little white eyes glowing beneath the branches.

"It's about a witch that lives in a haunted forest," she whispers.

"But you don't like the darker stories," I say, eyes narrowed.

"This one has a happy ending. I read the last page."

I quirk a brow. "Doesn't that defeat the purpose of reading the book?"

She shrugs. "I always do it. Even when I was younger. Gives me less anxiety as I'm reading when I know how it ends."

"I don't remember you reading much in college," I say.

"I didn't back then. I meant when I was in grade school."

"Ah."

"I figured I'd pick it back up as a hobby. Not like there's much else to do here," she explains.

Imogen hasn't joined the boys in any of their pastimes of choice, namely the drinking competitions Silas has instigated. Nor has she hopped into the sparring ring to learn self-defense when offered by Wrath. And she certainly hasn't asked to visit the gun-range on the roof. I don't imagine she ever will. The only thing left for her to do here is visit the library and read. Or think. And in my experience, using thinking as a form of entertainment leaves you worse off than before you started.

Imogen snaps the book shut, hugs it to her chest, and strokes her thumb over the clothbound cover. A divot forms between her brows.

"I didn't mean to storm out before," she says.

"It's okay," I say.

"I've been having these—" Imogen shakes her head. "When I—" A frustrated growl rips through her throat. "I... I am having a hard time coming to terms with everything that you all say *needs* to happen. I know it's unrealistic, but I can't help but wonder if there's another option. Or if someone would at least consider trying a different way."

I sigh. "Mo..."

"I know. *It's the way of things*," Imogen mocks. "Doesn't mean I like it."

"I didn't claim to like it either," I say, a twinge of exasperation in my tone. "I don't *want* to hurt people. My childhood being Pride's lie-detector exposed me to enough violence for a lifetime."

"Then why do you do it?" Imogen turns her body to face me, kneeling, and pressing the book to her thighs with her palms. "Why do you kill people? Why do you throw yourselves into conflict over and over again?"

I pause, licking my lips. *Is it not obvious why I do the things I do?* "Sometimes, it's what needs to be done to protect the people I care about."

"We keep going in circles," Imogen groans. "This is insanity."

"This life will make any normal person feel crazy."

"So are you immune or..."

"Oh, gods, no," I laugh. "I am as mental as the rest of them. I only hide it better."

"But you don't *like* killing," she clarifies.

I let the question hang in the air. Of all the times I've taken a life, not once did it make me *happy*. Pride conditioned us to not have much of a reaction at all to death. But I can remember a time when I experienced a sense of discomfort as I pulled the trigger.

"No. It doesn't bring me joy, if that's what you're asking," I say. *I did, however, find a sick sort of satisfaction when I filled the gut of the Seelie that hurt you with bullets.*

Imogen flops back against the shelf, body deflated.

"Lately, I've been thinking about running away." She huffs a laugh. "I wonder if giving up the title of Lust is enough, you know? Before Solstice, I would have said yes. But now?" Her freckled nose scrunches. "I'm realizing it's more complicated than that. I... don't know how to move forward balancing what I want with what I think I need. Does that make sense?"

"I think so?"

Blond lashes narrow over golden irises. "You liar."

I smile softly. "Explain it to me another way, please."

A somber expression falls over her face.

"I've been having panic attacks, Josie. I looked it up after our first week here. Anytime I hear a loud noise—the firewood popping, someone dropping a glass in the dining hall, Silas's and Nora's fists on the table before—it sends me right back to the day I got... shot."

Imogen swallows the last word, as if it's the first time she's said it out loud. And I think it may be—she's never opened up about that day since it happened. At least, not to me.

"How am I supposed to go back to the city like this?" Imogen whispers. "How am I supposed to be around you guys when you all have guns strapped to your sides? I understand the need for protection, but at the same time, I don't want to be protected if it means being exposed to that again. I know it's hypocritical. But none of my thoughts are very logical right now."

Imogen's eyes turn glassy, and she blinks hard, trying to bar any tears from falling. I shift closer and our shoulders meet. Let my body act as a grounding force for her.

"I want to support Nora. I want to support you. And Leo. And Hattie and even Wrath and Silas—which is crazy to say after everything—but you guys are ingrained in this life. You chose it. You continue to pursue it. And I... didn't. All I wanted was love and friendship and to not feel so alone. I didn't ask for any of *this*." She throws one hand out; it slaps unceremoniously on her thigh. "There's a part of me that wonders if—that hopes Nora would choose *me*. Over this vendetta she has. Over being Pride. This could be her chance to make a clean break... Is it wrong to hope for that?" Imogen huffs. "Please don't answer that."

"That's a lot to digest, Mo," I say. I hold my tongue when it comes to Nora—because we both know the sad truth there. "But I'm glad you're comfortable talking to me about this. And if you really want to move to a village out west, take on a new name, and open up a small pub and live a different life, then that's what you should do."

Imogen side-eyes me suspiciously. "You wouldn't try and convince me to stay in Anwynn?"

I chew on the inside of my cheek. I wouldn't love it. But if Imogen needs to distance herself from the city—and from us—I won't stop her. I'm not selfish enough to do that.

I shake my head. "I'd miss you like hell."

"I'd miss you too, Josie." Her lips curve, soft and sad. "And *that's* why it's a fantasy. I'm fucked up, but I would be more so if I lost all of you too." Imogen sighs again. "Hence the desire for you all to *not* engage in a civil war."

"And now we're right back to where you began. I see what you mean by going in circles. I'm already twitching." I snicker in an attempt to make light of the heavy topics. I force one of my eyes to twitch, pointing to it. "See?"

Imogen's nose crinkles as she barks a laugh.

"Shut up." She bats my shoulder, but there's no real force behind it. "In all seriousness, I don't think I can go back to the city full time yet. I could go to my family's cabin in the suburbs, but I also don't want to sit there doing nothing. Or to be alone. At least at my apartment, you'd all be around the corner if I needed you."

I hum thoughtfully. "Does this cabin have a guest room?"

"Yeah..."

"Then we could set up a rotation," I say, shrugging. "Someone could stay with you and switch out every couple of nights. Nora will demand one of us be with you anyway, knowing what's coming, and I'd have to agree. The list of people I trust to protect you is about this long." I mime an inch of space between two fingers.

"You guys would do that?" she asks.

"Mo," I chide, grabbing her hand. My palm squeezes hers. "Look at me."

She does, her amber irises burning with the smallest flame of hope.

"Every single one of us, even Silas and Wrath, would do *anything* for you," I say.

And I would—do anything for her—because even though Nora is my sister, Imogen is my closest friend.

But my words do the opposite of their intention; that spark in her eyes snuffs out, and the smoke of sadness clouds her expression.

"Except that's not really true, is it?" she whispers, and I know without question that she's talking about Nora. Imogen squeezes my hand back, and my heart aches. "But that's okay, Josie. I'm finally learning that's just the way of things."

10

NORA

"Do you want some water?"

Imogen's sweet voice, soft as a spring breeze, floats across the room, completely at odds with the vicious smack of my fist against the punching bag. Sweat drips down my back, sliding between my throbbing scars. I tug at my cotton tank top in an attempt to stop the sensation, but all it does is make the fabric suction to my damp, flushed skin.

"I'm fine," I say.

It's been three days of Imogen lingering in my periphery, hovering there like a ghost. Three mornings of her attempting small talk with me over breakfasts that I choke down. And three afternoons of her running away when my words come out too sharp. Three nights of lying awake at night, staring at the ceiling of the empty room I hide away in.

My body might have shed its soreness and sated its hunger, but I'm far from relaxed. I'm squirming under the confines of these stone walls.

"Or some lunch? You've been at it all morning," Imogen tries again.

"I said I'm fine." My leg kicks out and connects with the weighted bag. It rocks, and the chain it hangs from clinks.

The room is quiet enough that I hear the tired hitch of her sigh behind me.

"What about you, Joze?" Imogen asks, tone filled with fake chipper. "You need to eat too."

"I'm almost done. Why don't you save me a seat, and I'll be right behind you?"

"Okay. Are you sure you're not hungry, Nora?" Imogen asks again.

I finally cut her a look over my shoulder. The sight of her leaves me longing and confused.

I shake my head.

"Alright." Imogen forces a smile before disappearing down the hall.

I drop my forehead to the punching bag and lean my weight into it.

"Really, Nor?" Josie's disappointed tone smacks me right across the face.

"Don't start with me right now," I mutter into the leather.

Josie scoffs, and I glare at her as she sheds the boxing wrappings from her hands. The white gauze and tape land in a tangled pile on the floor. We stare each other down until she's done, gracefully crouching to scoop up her mess and toss it in the trash can.

"You're hopeless sometimes," Josie says as she leaves the room. "Get your ass to lunch, pronto."

I groan, bashing my head against the bag three times. I don't know what Josie wants from me—and I don't know what *Imogen* wants from me.

Actually, I do know what Josie wants from me. She wants me to apologize to Imogen for the other day, but every time I think of doing so, I get pissed off all over again.

Is love supposed to be this hard?

Yes, I regret snapping at her, but I don't regret stating the obvious. Wes will die a painful death for what he's done. I will never apologize for trying to keep her safe. But somehow, this fact has made me some kind of villain in everyone's eyes.

Must I be the one to say aloud what everyone else is too scared to admit?

It seems that this is my fate, my role to play. And stuck here, locked away in a different sort of cage than the iron bars at Casimir, I have nowhere sufficient to channel my restless energy on the matter.

I'm a walking smoking gun, with the trigger half-pulled for the next shot.

It's only when I'm holding one up at the range, the tip of my nose frozen, that the sickening sensation eases. Or when I'm working my muscles until they ache—an attempt to rebuild the strength I'd lost during my capture. Or, in secret spare moments like this, when I allow myself to connect with my magic.

The tether between Patience and me thrums as I twirl the golden thread between my fingers—at least, that's how I see it. My magic giggles as it zaps the bond, and I picture Patience's chest tightening, his breath hitching as oxygen is blocked from entering his lungs. There's resistance, though, as if our magics clash along the bridge connecting us.

I don't know with any certainty that what magic I send down the wire has its intended effect. But even if it translates to a millisecond of pain for my uncle, I'll take it.

"You seem deep in thought."

The manifestation of my magic dissipates as I whip around. The Unseelie King leans against the doorway.

"And you're as nosy as ever," I snark back.

"Nosy or concerned?" Silas chuckles, running his ringed

fingers through his white hair. A strand escapes, falling over his forehead. His eyes nearly cross as he huffs at the offending piece of hair. "I need a haircut. Thank the gods we're finally headed back to Anwynn tomorrow."

He shouldn't complain—the blizzard that's raged outside can't stop him from shadow-walking home. It was his own choice to wait until I recovered before we set off for Anwynn as a group.

It's a good thing my body bounces back quicker than most —a fact I've never openly acknowledged lest someone connect the dots of my heritage. But I don't have to hide those parts of myself anymore. And tomorrow, when I face the other Sins, they will gaze upon me in a new light. Hopefully, they will see things my way, but I have my doubts. It's likely I'll have to convince them by means other than talking.

"Did you come here to chit-chat or did you actually need something?" I ask, turning back to my drills.

I throw two head punches and a right hook to the body of the bag before hopping back on the balls of my feet. Repeating the same combination, I switch arms and land a left hook instead.

"Actually, I wanted to see if you'd spar with me?" Silas asks.

I pause, throwing a palm out to steady the swinging bag. Silas is in similar clothes to me: a ribbed cotton shirt tucked into matching athletic shorts. I've seen the man shirtless before, so all the tattoos peeking out from under the tank top are not a surprise. What does make me do a double take are his pale muscular legs, and how another tattoo—this one of a dagger—runs down the center of his right thigh. It strikes me as odd that he only has one, and not two, since all his other tattoos are symmetrical. Is he going to mark that slate of fresh skin with something else? Or is it meant to be left untouched?

There's something about a pristine expanse of flesh that makes me want to ruin it.

When my attention rises back to his face, Silas's cheeky, knowing smirk is blinding.

He's such a preening peacock.

"You can't spar with rings on," I chuff. If he truly wants to fight me, I won't say no. I only hope he realizes what he's asking. "Take them off and wrap your hands. I don't need Wrath scolding me if you cut up your knuckles."

Silas groans when his back hits the mat. But he doesn't appear miffed by the fact he's lost every round, given the way it transitions into a throaty chuckle. It's the opposite, actually. He seems downright *delighted*.

"That was a good one," he says between deep huffs of breath, wagging a finger at me in the air. "I wasn't expecting the takedown to come right after that nasty hit to my ribs." He pushes himself upright, shakes out his arms, and hops up and down. "Once more. Let's go."

"I don't think that will bode well for your ego," I say, one hand on my hip.

"I can tell you're holding back. You haven't once tried to bruise my beautiful face. I'm not fragile. Come on, Nora. Rough me up a bit," Silas teases, stalking around me on the mat. "I'm offering to help you work out all those nasty thoughts I see roiling in your head. Take advantage."

I roll my neck. He's annoyingly perceptive.

I'm teetering on the edge of madness. Pushing my body to its limits helps, but I know that there's only one thing that'll drain me of this tension. And that's drawing blood.

"Alternative is we can talk about the way you and Imogen are tiptoeing around each other like two teenagers who don't know how to communicate." Silas shrugs. "But I didn't think that would be your pref—"

Silas grunts when my shoulder connects with his gut, and I take us both down to the mat.

"Everyone has shit to say about me and Imogen," I growl, grappling with his long limbs. My nerves fire off with every scrape of Silas's skin against mine. "I'm getting tired of it. How many times do I have to say it's none of your fucking business?"

"It is my business if it affects my Court," he grits out, managing to hook his leg around mine and flip us. My back hits the ground, and I quickly raise my arms to block his next blow. "And it is my business when I see my friends suffering."

"I don't want your pity."

My hits are sloppy, my annoyance quickly bubbling into rage. I land another punch to his ribs and Silas winces, but he manages to catch my wrists and pins them under his weight.

"I wasn't talking about *you*." His snarky smile is a taunt beaming down at me. "Sorry, did you want to finally admit that you're also struggling with everything that's happened? You know I'm always available for a late-night venting session over shitty alcohol and a cigarette. All you have to do is come knocking on my door."

Energy surges within me; I brace my feet firmly on the floor and buck my hips with all my strength. It catches Silas off balance, and I flip us once again.

"Fuck *off*," I growl into his face. I press into his forearms with all my weight, wondering if my thumbprints will be visible along the fragile underside of his wrists tomorrow. "If I want to talk about something, I will be the one to decide when and with whom I speak about it."

Our chests heave, grazing as we come down from the physical effort of our fight. From an observer's perspective, grappling never looks as intense as it truly is. But every muscle is wrought with tension when you're locked together like this.

Silas's eyes darken beneath frost-colored lashes, and his nostrils flare. His lips part to say something else, but I lift and slam his wrists into the ground with a resounding *smack*.

"*No*," I say, ending the conversation. "I'm done here. Back off."

I shove off him and quickly grab my socks and shoes from where they sit along the edge of the mat. I don't bother putting them on, my feet slapping loudly against the cold floor as I leave the room. I'm late to lunch, but that's what I wanted, isn't it? To slip in right at the end?

That way, I won't feel Josie's silent judgment. No one will have time to dissect the way my hand twitches to scratch at my scars every few minutes. They won't notice how I can't meet their gazes for longer than ten seconds for risk of being crushed by the weight of their concern. And I'll get to pretend, for a few more delusional moments, that I don't need to do what I have to.

"We don't have time for you to pull this martyr bullshit, Nora!" Silas yells.

I slam the gym door behind me. While his words make me grimace, he is right about one thing. We don't have time for my fear anymore.

11

IMOGEN

I sneak into my room when it's past dark, only cracking the door wide enough to slip my body through. The chilled air hits my back as the lock *clicks* under my fingers, and I let out a sigh. Bramble is buried under feet of snow, and I've officially stretched my luck too thin—I will have to light a fire tonight or I'll freeze. Though, there's a part of me that would rather my body shake from the frozen mountain air than from my memories.

My forehead hits the door, my skin pressing into the woodgrain. Today... was hard. Actually, every minute of the past few days has been hard.

"You're like a little mouse, scurrying all around Bramble."

My breath hitches, and I spin around. I drop my book, the clothbound tome hitting the stone with a dull *thunk*.

"I'm the cat in this analogy, I suppose, catching you unaware."

Nora lounges on the couch, arms spread wide across the back. And even though the lights aren't on in the bedroom, the moonlight filtering in from the open window is enough to set her aglow. Her cool white skin is luminescent, and her black waves are cast in a blueish sheen. She stares at me over her shoulder, those green eyes glinting—tracking me like a predator.

"You're here," I say.

"I'm here."

The wind whistles outside, a high-pitched squeal blowing through the room.

"Come sit with me," she says.

Her tone begets obedience, but my legs don't move. Stubbornness roots my shoes to the ground—she's been brushing me off since the morning after she got home, and now she shows up in my room unannounced?

"Imogen." My name is soft on her tongue—it sounds like a memory of home—and it loosens the painful tightness in my chest.

My shoulders pull back, and I hope I appear unbothered as I approach, placing my book on the coffee table and standing before her.

"What is it you want?" I ask.

Nora leans forward, elbows on her knees. She looks up at me, face unnervingly devoid of emotion. My magic rouses, prickling under my skin—hoping to pick up any trace of what Nora's thinking. There is, of course, nothing. The absence was once a marvel that piqued my curiosity, but now, it only makes my heart yearn. She's still closed off, after everything.

"I wanted to talk to you before bed. Though I didn't think you'd wait until this late to come back to your room," she says.

"Okay," I say, and my teeth bite into my bottom lip. They tug at the rough edges of skin I've already ripped apart.

"Stop that," she says.

"Why?" I ask.

"I don't like it when you hurt yourself," she says.

"I'm not hurting myself."

My tongue swipes across my raw lip, suckling at the metallic blood blooming there. Nora's expression darkens into something fierce.

"Then stop before *I'm* the one to bite it raw," she says.

My body stiffens, and I shiver at the implication. Since Casimir, I've been oscillating between frozen terror and cold numbness. And if I can't stand a fire, then maybe Nora's unique brand of heat is the kind of warmth I need. The rough scrape of her teeth on my neck, her bruising grip on my thighs, her tongue running circles over my core... her touch isn't a balmy spring day—it's a scorching desert summer.

Would it melt all the shit that's freezing me from the inside out?

As if she can sense my sudden arousal, Nora groans, her face falling into her hands. "I'm supposed to be apologizing to you, not flirting."

"You're terrible at apologizing," I say. "I think it's the thing you're the worst at."

"Yeah," Nora agrees, all the delicious bite in her tone disappearing. She reverts back to her business voice, a detached tenor that gives me whiplash. "Anyway, I'm sorry for snapping at you lately. It's not fair, and I need to work on my tone."

Nora averts her gaze. It's a simple action, but one that strikes me with that dreadful kind of panic.

We've been here before.

"You really have been a cranky bitch the last few days," I tease, but it doesn't draw her attention back to me. "But I'll forgive you if you stay here tonight. If you stop avoiding me," I add, sweetly. "Just stay. It's an easy fix."

"I don't think that's a good idea," Nora says quietly.

"Why not?" I ask, my heart starting to race.

"Because we both need rest," Nora says. She attempts to leave, but my body moves on its own—my hands grab her face, my fingers dig into her cheeks. I tilt her head back, but her eyes stay cast to the side of the room.

She's not allowed to retreat—to waltz in here, say sorry, and leave again. Fuck that.

"Goodnight, Imogen," she says. It's a dismissal, but it only makes me want to cling to her tighter. Her fingers wrap about my wrists, tugging, but I hold fast.

"Why are you shutting me out right now?" I ask, my frustration mounting.

"I'm not shutting you out, I'm—"

"Yes, you are. You forget I have ten years of you keeping me at an arm's distance under my belt. You're pushing me away right now. You're not allowed to do that."

"I'm allowed to do whatever I want," Nora snaps.

My hands drop from her face as if it burned. All my fears rush to the center of my chest, and my ribs ache as if they're going to cave in under the pressure. It's a terrible, doom-like sensation.

"Okay." I huff. "Take your time then—the gods know we've both been fucked up by what happened. So take a few days. Take a couple of months, hell, take a few years, whatever you need. Be a raging bitch. I'll get over it. I always do." I laugh, but it's humorless. "All I've ever asked of you is that you don't pull away, and right now you're pulling away. Do not deny it." Nora's lips mash together, but she still doesn't look my way. "Why are you giving up on loving me?"

"Why do you *care*? I don't understand why you would still want me."

Tortured confusion rips through Nora's facade as our gazes finally clash. It leaves her exposed; a wounded beast paces behind her mask of detachment.

The wind's keening whistle blows through the window, and it all becomes so much clearer.

"Feelings don't disappear overnight, Nora. Even if you wanted them to."

It's an undeniable fact that we are changed women. We both left Casimir different than we entered it. But as confused, angry, or broken as I may have felt over these past three weeks apart, I never once considered giving up what we were building together.

But it sounds as if Nora has.

My love? It doesn't work like that. It's never cared what kind of wings she has, or if she had them at all.

"Do you want them to?" Nora whispers.

Her head tilts up, and I'm struck with the longing there, the barest shred of hope shining in the shadowed facets of her irises. My hands reach out again, and she lets me stroke my thumbs over her cheeks.

Her eyes close.

"Do you want them to disappear?" Nora repeats.

"No," I choke out.

"Sometimes I want them to disappear," she whispers. "It would be easier that way."

Nora's face shutters, and a single teardrop falls, cresting over her cheekbone. My thumb captures it, hides it away. Lips contorted and jaw tight, she mirrors how I feel inside.

Fragmented.

What a pair we make.

"Nora, whether you're Seelie or Unseelie—want to claim both or neither—that's not what matters to me. That will *never* matter to me," I say.

Nora sucks in a ragged, heaving breath, and then presses her head against my belly. Her arms wrap around the backs of my thighs, pulling me close.

"I'm not saying that to make you feel better. It's the truth. How many times do I have to tell you I want *all of you* before you believe it?" I ask. "But every time something bad happens, you shut me out. I can't keep pulling you out of whatever cage you lock yourself in. I don't have it in me, especially now, when I'm struggling too."

Because I am. I'm... not okay.

"I'm sorry," Nora murmurs against my belly.

I cradle her head, stroking her hair before kissing her crown. "It's okay."

We still for a moment, until her head tilts up. Nora doesn't say anything, but she must want to—her brows pinch, and her lips purse.

But I don't want to hear another excuse or another dismissal. Not right now.

Right now, I just want *my* Nora.

"Can I kiss you?" I plead.

Hesitation wars in her expression. Her jaw feathers but eventually sets with resolve—she pulls me into her lap, and then we're colliding. It's a bittersweet meeting of our bodies: a slow dance set to imaginary music, one where halfway, we trip over each other's feet. My lips search hers as if they're hunting for a memory, grasping at the past; nostalgia coats my tongue and quickly sours the kiss.

Our lips fall out of sync.

Nora pulls back, and I try to follow, but the kiss breaks anyway. Our heartbeats run wild; they clash between our pressed palms. She's got that same expression on her face, the one she had when we danced at Casimir, right before everything fell to shit. The moment that felt like a goodbye, without one utterance of the word.

I don't think she heard me. Not really. But I don't know what else to say to make her *believe*, to make her *trust*, to make her—

"Stay," I beg. "Please."

Nora cocoons me like she used to, arms circling my waist and fingers digging into my back. I burrow my face into the crook of her neck and suck in a lungful of her smoke and vanilla scent. But even wrapped in her arms, it's as if she's not here.

Nora's already locked herself behind that door she keeps between herself and the rest of the world—the one I've always wanted to break down.

"I don't believe you, Imogen," Nora murmurs into my neck.

"I wish you would run away with me," I whisper into her shoulder. All those unrealistic fantasies jump off my tongue, my desperation riding me hard. "We have the money. Why can't we go live our lives and forget about the rest of it?"

One strong hand tugs at the root of my hair, pulling my head from her neck.

"I can't do that," she says.

Our gazes crash, and instead of my heart sinking at the dim sparkle of resignation in her eyes, anger rises in its place.

"Can't or won't? Just *choose me*, Nora."

"I don't think you understand what that means," Nora says, her expression twisting into something pained. "You keep telling me you want all of me. And I think you believe that. But I don't think it's true. Even before... I don't think you want the part of me that's *Pride*."

Emotion swells in my throat.

"You won't even try?" I ask, my voice cracking. "Is my love not enough for you?"

"I didn't think I *could* love before you. I didn't realize it was a *fucking option*. Do you not think I would give anything to rewind time? To make everyone forget what they know now? But that's not reality. And we're stuck with this." Nora splays one hand wide toward the blizzard outside. "And I'm not going to pretend I don't want to murder everyone who has ever hurt you! In fact, I think you should be happy that I care so much to do that for you."

It's in this moment that things shift irrevocably between us.

It's not only about the violence. It's about how we communicate, how we show we care. How we show our love. We're speaking two different languages, our words not fully processing in each other's ears.

Quiet—a volatile kind—falls upon us.

"Clearly, my kind of love isn't enough for *you*," Nora says. "My love is a brutal thing. And there's no *choosing* for me. I will have it all, or I will have nothing." Her head tilts back to the ceiling, and she huffs a laugh through a small, sad smile. "For those few weeks in fall, I was content. I guess this is the gods' way of balancing the scales."

I trace my thumb over Nora's jaw. "The gods aren't pulling these strings, Nor. You're the one sabotaging this. And you're not even giving me a chance to prove you wrong."

Her eyes flick down to my lips. They harden, cold as ice.

"The only one who is right more than me is Josie. You can't prove me wrong, Mo," she says.

My lashes flutter, and Nora blurs in my vision. I slowly slip off her lap and onto the cushion next to her. Fissures spread across my heart at the loss of her warmth.

"Then I think you need to leave," I choke out.

I lick my lips, tasting the salty tear tracks running down my face. They meet at my chin, and thick, heavy droplets fall onto my thighs, soaking my pants.

Nora's hand falls onto my knee, and my lids screw shut, breath hitching as she gives it one last firm squeeze before she stands.

The bedroom door is quiet as it closes, and I swear I hear her mutter *I love you* before the latch clicks.

12

NORA

The railing digs into my forearms as I lean over it. The center of Bramble is beautiful in its own way—an architectural feat, with its stained glass skylight skittering rainbows where they would never naturally reach. What right does a mountain cave have to sunlight? Should it not be left to its hollow darkness?

Last night, as I chain-smoked a pack of cigarettes on the rooftop range, part of me wondered if I am the same. What right do I have to sunlight, to golden happiness, when that's not what I was made for?

Breaking up with Imogen was the right thing to do. Better to have her learn now, rather than later, that she doesn't want whatever shell of me is left for her to love.

I am the carved out mountain, and inside there's only rage and pain and death, and the briefest sparkle of *her*.

She told me to leave in the end. I knew she would. She only needed a push.

At least now I'll have the freedom to do what is needed to protect her. And in turn, she can judge me without guilt. I'll be her vengeance; I'm happy to stain my hands so she never has to.

"Wrath already took Mo to her cabin to get settled with his guards. Hattie will be taking first shift staying overnight this week," Josie says, sidling up to me on the stairwell railing. I keep my stoic gaze locked on the scholars flittering around the library below us. "I'm surprised you didn't bid her goodbye… or offer to be first shift."

The corners of my mouth twitch down at her subtle prying. "I trust you all to take care of her."

Josie leans back on the railing, eyeing me with suspicion. "What did you do?"

"What needed to be done," I say.

"You truly are a dumbass." Josie scoffs and shakes her head. "So that's it?"

"She doesn't want me, Josie."

"I have a hard time actually believing that, Nor."

"You two ready to go?" Silas says, a firm *clap* of his hands cracking behind us.

Josie pushes off the railing, and I follow suit. Silas reaches his arms out to us as if offering a dance, and Josie rolls her eyes. She snatches one of his hands without hesitation.

Silas arches a single brow at how I waver from his touch. I should be used to it by now, his palm against mine, but without my gloves, it's different. My eyes catch on his pinstripe suit jacket and the white button-down that pokes out at the cuff. The fabric hides the bruises I pressed into his wrists when we sparred. They'd be gone by now on my skin, but I'm sure he doesn't heal that fast.

"Don't want to be late to the party," Silas drawls in his haughty sing-song voice. His fingers wriggle, waiting for me to take them.

I steel my shoulders.

I'm ready to take back my House. I'm ready to take back what vestiges I can of my life. Tooth and nail, I'll scrape and fight for it.

When I was a child, Pride beat into me the idea that any pain endured is worth an equivalent reward. If I look at it that way, there's one hell of a reward at the end of all this.

With a blaring reminder of what I am searing down my back, I take Silas's hand.

We step from the shadows right into the Sins' meeting room, the first to arrive. The table is set for nine rather than its usual eight, with one extra chair across from mine.

I take my seat, the one I'd claimed for myself over a year ago.

Silas cocks a brow. "You sure you want to sit there?"

"This is my seat," I state plainly.

"It might be advantageous for you to sit between Wrath and me," he says.

"No, thank you."

"He's got a point," Josie titters from where she leans against the wall. I grip the back of the carved wooden chair as I twist my body to shoot her a withering glare.

"Whose side are you on, anyway?" I ask.

"Yours, of course. Which is why I wouldn't be doing my job if I didn't agree with him." Josie nods at Silas, who sits in the head seat with a smug-as-shit grin. "It's smart to flank your-self with allies. Visually, it's a strong statement. Plus, they can magic you away if someone gets the funny idea to take you out here."

My frown deepens.

"Fine," I grunt.

My chair scrapes noisily against the floor as I shove it back. Then I yank Wrath's usual seat out—the one directly to the right of Silas—and huff as I drop my ass onto the velvet cushion.

"Happy?" I ask them both.

Josie's got this tiny smirk tilting her lips. "Yep."

Silas hums. "You look good to my right."

"Do not start with me right now, Silas." My lips curl into an annoyed sneer. It's too early for his antics.

He raises his hands defensively. "I'm only suggesting that if House Pride doesn't work out, I'd be happy to bring you on as an adviser to the Royals."

"It'll work out," I assure him, and scoot my seat closer to the table's edge.

"I don't know," Silas draws out melodically. "Two soul-stealers running the Unseelie Court with death-bound fists could be interesting."

My attention snaps back to Josie.

"He told you?" I ask.

She nods.

"I let her play around in my head a little. It was no big deal," Silas says, waving a ringed hand in the air.

I shoot him a glare. "Also, I'm not a soul-stealer. Not really."

"You're close enough," Silas chirps.

"*And* I already said it'll work out." Some of the ever-burning hatred in my gut flares to the surface. "I didn't pander to a manipulative, narcissistic sorry-excuse-for-a-father-figure for twenty years for me to *not* keep the legacy I ripped from his clammy, dead hands."

Silas blinks at me. "I'm simply giving you options—"

"Stop trying to recruit me," I snap.

Josie snorts, clearly entertained. Of course, that's when Wrath enters the room, wisps of darkness curling around his feet. He stalls mid-stride.

"You're in my seat," Wrath says, sandy-brown brows knitted across his forehead.

I throw my hands up, gesturing to the grinning shit-stirrer and my just-as-culpable Second, who is doing a terrible job at hiding her laughter behind a raised hand.

"Blame them," I say. "I'm not moving again."

"Oh-*kay*." Wrath approaches slowly. He pulls back the empty seat next to mine with caution and gracefully lowers himself onto the cushion. "Imogen's all set, by the way."

I swallow the lump that's suddenly formed in my throat. "Good."

And then we wait in contemplative silence for the rest of the Sins to stroll in.

"Ah, you're back," Sloth says between *fwacks* of his cane on the tile, the first to enter. "Surprised they let you keep your hands."

"Ever the sweet talker, Sloth," I deadpan.

The ancient man winks and falls into his seat with a grunt.

"It's good to see you again, Nora," Gluttony says, following after Sloth. Her manicured, fingers trace over the chair backs as she rounds the table. She sends a soft smile and subtle nod towards Josie, who nods her acknowledgment back.

Both of their Seconds trail behind them and take their spots at the perimeter of the room. We will be at full capacity today, though Wrath's Second won't be joining. He's permanently stationed with the Court's troops at their base outside the city.

Greed sneers at me as he strolls in, *not* late this time, which is a miracle in and of itself. His Second follows behind him with one arm set in a sling and a slight limp to his gait.

Envy has a similar expression of disdain contorting his face when he walks through the double doors. He takes his seat alone—I guess he didn't pick a replacement yet for his Second.

Stupid, if he didn't have succession already laid out.

I grind my teeth and glance back at Josie, who studies our rivals with quiet intensity.

Then again, do succession plans matter if your people don't follow them?

Leo joins next—our new Lust—but he doesn't greet me. He doesn't even look me in the eye as he settles into his seat across the table. His new Second, a man I recognize from our time in college, stands to the side with stiff posture. Leo's fingers tap nervously on the table as he ignores me, dark skin sharp against the light cream tablecloth used for today's place setting.

Silas must have some kind of misplaced faith in us keeping this meeting cordial. Bleaching out bloodstains only works on bright whites, not creams.

Leo continues to avoid my glare, and I tongue my cheek.

That's how it's going to be, huh?

And then, finally, as if they planned the most dramatic entrance, Wes walks in with Claude in tow.

The sight of the lying little fuckwit has my jaw clenching so hard I swear my molars crack.

Wes's chest puffs out as he runs his hand through his reddish-brown hair. He's dressed more formally than I've ever seen him before. I sneer; he's a boy playing dress up in his father's clothes. Truly, what does he think is going to happen here?

Claude, on the other hand, is worse for wear. The blue-tinted crescents under my former ally's eyes make him appear grief stricken. He shoots me a pleading look.

I scoff, turning away.

Claude knows what will happen to them if things don't go their way; he doesn't deserve an ounce of sympathy from me. The man has always been smart enough to hold his own, but the reason I added him to my inner circle was due to his loyal-to-a-fault nature.

It's unfortunate that unwavering loyalty is directed at someone else now. It's a waste, really, that he'll have to die.

My scowl deepens when Wes sits in my old seat.

Silas claps his hands and the room hushes. "I know we're all quite *busy*, given we're only a few weeks into the New Year, but I called this meeting to discuss—"

"That the bitch is back," Envy interrupts. His words slur together with disgust. "News travels fast, Your Majesty. We didn't need a meeting for this. Or to see her face-to-face."

I slowly let loose a sigh from my nose. *Here we go.*

Silas's chipper smile doesn't waver, but I catch the slight twitch of his right eye. I don't think he expected any flack this early on in the conversation.

"We unfortunately *do* need a meeting for this," Silas says, hands steepling under his chin. "Because there is the matter of Pride's succession at hand."

"Is that not House business?" Greed says, tone bored.

"It is," Silas relents. "Normally, I'd keep my fingers out of it, for all our sakes. However, this is an unusual case. With no blood successor and two admittedly controversial options to fill the role, my recommendation *as king* is that you all decide how to move forward. Together."

"Decide together?" Gluttony asks with narrowed eyes.

"You want to put it to a vote," Sloth snickers. The wrinkles in his walnut skin deepen with his impish grin. "Isn't that right, boy?"

Silas lifts a brow at Sloth's use of the moniker *boy*. "Yes."

Sloth chuckles. "Never a dull day with you younglings."

"For the millionth time, Sloth, we're not younglings, you're just really fucking old," Envy says.

"You want us to pick between that boy and Nora?" Gluttony asks, pointing to Wes. "Why?"

"It seems the easiest path to an amicable solution." Silas shrugs. "And the most logical. It makes no difference to me who is Pride, as long as that person adheres to the Court's rules. But this decision could have consequences for the rest of your business operations. So, I'm letting you all make that choice."

"I think where your logic falls short is assuming we *want* there to be a choice," Envy grinds out between clenched teeth. "None of us want a traitor. Approve the boy and banish that *Seelie bitch*"—he can't even say my name—"and we can be done with it and go back to our lives."

Wes might be as quiet as me, but his poker face isn't as ironclad. His lips curve up, a devilish little smile climbing his cheeks in time with Envy's vitriol. He thinks he's gotten away with his misdeeds, since none of the other Sins know his crimes.

"Let me be clear," Silas says, standing. His hands splay out on the table as he leans forward, foreboding. He points to me. "She is not a traitor. I've known about her identity for quite some time and couldn't care less. In my eyes, she's proven herself to the Court. Whether you believe the same is up to you. But if you're harboring resentment towards her for the events of Solstice? *Stop.*"

Silas's voice booms with power.

Envy blanches. At the end of the day, the man is a coward. He might be angry or sad or grief stricken and blame me for his Second dying, but those emotions hold flimsy shields up to the spear of fear.

Sometimes I forget that Silas is to be feared.

I can't deny watching Envy pale makes me smug as a demon in hell. I've always loved watching a person's confidence crumble, especially a man's. It's just so... satisfying.

Silas continues, "I had hoped we could reembrace tradition with open arms. But the reality is that Oonagh and the Virtues want us dead. I need the Sins to stand together in the face of this threat. Understood?"

"Plus, he already pardoned her, dipshit," Gluttony mutters.

"Why are you defending her?" Envy snaps at Gluttony. "Aren't your restaurants suffering after weeks of delays in the supply chain? I know my clubs are already running dry of human liquor."

Gluttony's expression darkens. "I'm only pointing out the facts, Envy. My business is my business alone. Keep your nose out of it."

"I can also defend myself perfectly fine," I say, cutting in for the first time in the exchange. I opt for an evil smile and full bravado in the face of my least-favorite Sin. "I may be half-Seelie, and my wings may be different from yours, Envy, but I sure as shit can kill you faster than you can say 'Sin.'"

Envy huffs and crosses his arms over his chest protectively, slouching back in his seat. The pallor of his beige skin contradicts his aloof demeanor.

I decide to capitalize off this moment and make my case to the rest of the Sins. I stand, staring down my nose at each one of them before speaking. Some may find it a condescending action, but I need to portray strength in spades—embrace the hardest, coldest parts of myself to convince them I'm the better choice.

Wes will pretend to be a victim. He'll make himself small, and play on their need to be on top. But I'm okay with being a threat in their eyes. I always have been. So long as I promise to line their pockets, they won't mind.

My gaze lands on Leo, and he still won't meet my eye. His dark lashes brush his cheeks, attention set firmly on the dram of whiskey he's got gripped in one hand. The single cube of ice clinks against the crystal glass as he twirls the cup.

Contempt tightens my jaw until it aches.

"You all saw one version of the truth on Solstice, but I would like to fill you in on the rest," I begin. "My mother was Seelie and my father Unseelie. An unlikely match, but it happened across the Veil, all because the Pride before me enlisted my father's help in procuring Seelie tonics." I leave out the parts about how Pride's health was failing and how my mother was originally a Seelie spy. "My mother was a healer. I'm sure you can put two and two together now."

I pause, sweeping my gaze across the Sins. Sloth seems amused, deep crow's feet etched at the edge of his eyes.

"My mother was also an exile. That might not mean much for those of you who haven't been across the Veil, but it should. Exiles are disowned and cut out of Seelie society, left to fend for themselves with no resources in the Human Realm. They only hold loyalty to themselves." My throat tightens as I recall my parents' story. "She earned the trust of my father, who was part of Pride's inner circle before he died. Sure, he wasn't Pride's Second, but he was high enough in the family. Pride trusted my father, and together, they brought her into the fold. My mother was his best kept secret human-side. Until I came along."

My eyes slide to Wes, a sharp-toothed smile cutting my cheeks.

"And of course, when my uncle killed my parents—because my mother's brother is Patience—Pride took me in as his own. He protected me. He raised me. I was *always* family to him," I say, watching as Wes's cheeks flush with ruddy splotches. It's not a complete lie, though I am painting my ugly childhood with a rose-tinted varnish; the words daughter and weapon were interchangeable for the man who raised me. "This is all to say, I have never known loyalty to anyone other than House Pride. That has not changed. I might not have shared Pride's blood, but I was his daughter in every other sense of the word. This House is my family."

"And this sob story is supposed to make us trust you? Welcome you back with open arms when you've been nothing but standoffish to us for the past year?" Greed asks lazily.

I know it's unlikely I'll convince him, but all I need is a majority. All I need is *four*. Wrath. Gluttony. Sloth. Lust.

"I think the line of succession should be honored." I make it a point to say the next part to Sloth, catering to the old man. "*Tradition* should be honored." I twist, gesturing to Josie behind me. "My Second, Josie, who was in House Pride's inner circle for years before I took the position, is next in line. If you won't have me, she should be the next Pride." I lean forward, placing my hands against the table. "Not a youngling who's barely scratched the surface of what it means to be a House Head. A boy who has two, maybe three, months of actual operations experience across the Veil. I would truly hate to see my House crash and burn under his leadership. And all of yours struggle in turn."

"Maybe we should let him speak and make his own case," Leo says, his gaze finally clashing with mine, eyes bright and sharp.

My fingers curl, forming two fists on the satin-textured tablecloth as I sit down.

"Of course," I say with a smile, dousing the sudden flames roaring in my chest.

Needs time, my ass, I think aloud, hoping Josie is listening in. *When were you going to tell me about this, Josie?*

My chances at walking out of here as Pride are a whole lot slimmer if Leo isn't on our side, and it has me spiraling into dread. But a tickle on my wrist pulls me from my thoughts. A wisp of shadow wriggles along the soft patch of skin, and I quickly unclench my hands, waving the shadow away.

I shoot Silas a side-eyed glare; his attention is set on Wes, the perfect picture of an active listener, but there's mischief swimming in those dark eyes.

"—Nora murdered my father in cold blood, the Second before her, to further herself in the family. Then she murdered Pride to take his place. I don't see how you could want to be colleagues with someone who thought the only way up in the world was to cull those above her. I mean, who's next? The king?"

I catch the end of Wes's speech and roll my eyes. Taking the monarchy would be a headache, and I already have enough of those to deal with.

"Half the Sins here deposed their parents and predecessors. We'll all be hypocrites the day we denounce someone for doing the same to their adoptive daddy," Gluttony says. She taps her nails on the table. "I think I've heard enough. Silas?"

"If that's all, then I think it's time for us to take a vote," Silas says, steepling his fingers under his chin. "I will be abstaining; however, you all know my position on the matter. Nora is, and will be, a part of this Court. This is only a matter of what role she will fill."

His low voice, tone firm and strong, blankets the room.

"Those in favor of Nora?"

Two hands raise: Gluttony and Wrath.

My eyes flick to Leo. His head is once again tilted towards his drink. He doesn't raise his hand, and my teeth grind.

"Those in favor of Wes," Silas continues.

Envy and Greed's hands shoot up, unsurprisingly.

"Lust and Sloth?" Silas asks when neither of their hands raise.

"My advisers are scared of what it means for her to take charge again, but I'm partial to her style of leadership," Sloth says. "I'm not comfortable voting either way. I abstain."

"Lust?" Silas asks.

Leo shakes his head. Disappointment isn't a strong enough word to use in this situation. *At least be man enough to pick a fucking side.*

Silas sighs, a contemplative expression crossing his face. I had planned for wins and losses, but not ties. A miscalculation on my part. *Fuck.* I've been too distracted; I need to be better than this.

"I don't wish to be the deciding vote," Silas says. "It would defeat the purpose *of* the vote."

"Why don't we let their House decide?" Greed says. He shares a look with Envy, a cunning smile claiming his full lips. His sickeningly cooperative tone immediately sets my nerves on edge. "Give them until the next meeting to sort it out themselves. As I mentioned before, House business should stay House business."

Silas studies Greed, likely noting the same suspicious undertones. We're not stupid. We all understand the violent implications of Greed's words.

It's a sanctioned civil war now.

I'm ready for a bloodbath, but are they? How much preparation has Wes done in these three weeks of roaming free?

Does he already have such strong allies in Greed and Envy? And does he realize they will undoubtedly fuck him over for their own benefit at the end of it all? They will eat him alive.

"Fine," Silas relents, shifting back in his chair. His wrists drape lazily over his chair's armrests. "But you only have until the end of the first quarter to sort it out yourselves. I won't allow this to go on for longer than that. Otherwise, I pick." Silas flicks his fingers and the double doors at the end of the room burst open with a blast of his shadows. "None of you are allowed to complain I don't give you agency. You all are dismissed."

Envy and Greed stand to leave first.

"Wes, you want to grab drinks?" Envy asks casually. "Greed?"

Clear lines are being drawn in the sand. *Everyone go pick a side now.*

Wes shoves back his chair, casting me a conniving smile. I have to hold back my hundredth eye roll.

Greed tilts his head toward Leo. "You want to join, Lust? It's important to get to know your colleagues, especially in the early days."

Leo hesitates, twirling his crystal glass once, before he nods. I seethe as I follow his trek across the room with the others.

"I have to check on something first but can meet up with you after. Where are you—" Their conversation is cut off by the doors shutting behind them.

"Idiots," Gluttony murmurs before standing. She turns to me. "If you need something, say the word. I much prefer you"—she looks to Josie pointedly—"and you, as business partners to the other one."

Gluttony leaves, and Sloth heaves a great sigh. He groans as he stands, joints cracking sharply in the dead space.

"That was fun." He chuckles. "But I'd start calling in your favors before they're offered a quick buck."

"Duly noted, Sloth," I mutter. As soon as the door shuts behind him, I twist and glare at Josie. "Did someone not think to warn me about Leo? I thought you said he needed time, not that he *hated* me."

"He does need *time*," Josie says, shaking her head and plopping down into one of the now empty seats.

I'm about to open my mouth and argue when a loud knock cracks through the room. All our heads whip to the door as it creaks open, and the man himself peeks his head in.

"Oh, good, you're all still here," Leo says, tone light and relieved as he squeezes back into the room without his Second. He sighs, back against the shut door. "That was terrible."

All I can do is stare, mouth agape with confusion, as Leo chatters on with a wide, white-toothed smile.

"I can't talk long before I have to go entertain those pricks." Leo makes a gagging noise. "But I wanted to touch base before I left." He winks at me, eyes bright. "I did pretty good, didn't I? I used to do theater as a kid. Maybe I should pick it up again."

I lick my lips, slowly, before grinding out, "I'm sorry?"

Leo's smile drops under my furious gaze. He shifts nervously from foot to foot, head canting towards Josie, then Wrath, then Silas.

"You guys didn't tell her?" Leo whines. He faces me, hands raised pleadingly. "Don't be mad at me. It was their idea."

"Their idea for *what*?" My tongue and teeth form the words sharply; hopefully they'll cut through all the bullshit clouding the air.

"For me to not vote?" Leo says the statement like a question.

Wrath appears unfazed. His frown hasn't budged the entire meeting.

Silas's eyes dart to the ceiling, suddenly interested in the crown molding.

Josie, at least, has sense enough to look a little guilty.

"We needed your reaction to be real," Josie says. "Otherwise, they wouldn't believe Leo had turned against you."

"I don't understand."

"Nor..." Josie sighs. "Your thoughts and emotions are erratic at best. Your shields flicker more than they should. Are you telling me you haven't noticed?"

I can only huff a breath from my nose in disbelief.

"After you got back, Leo offered to help in whatever way he could. The three of us took him up on the offer, but decided not to tell you," Josie explains. "We knew you'd fight Wes regardless, so we took the risk of removing Leo as a sure vote. Now this gives him an in to be *swayed* to their side. It works in our favor in the long run. Makes Wes think he's safe when he's not."

I bite the inside of my cheek hard enough to draw blood. The metallic tang washes over my taste buds.

"Why haven't you mentioned the cracks in my shield to me yet?" I ask.

"Because every time either one of us tried to talk to you about it at Bramble, you either bitched at us or ran away," Josie says. She's got that tough love tone in her voice, the one that's like nails on a chalkboard in my ear.

"I didn't run away. You're not my fucking shrinks. And I don't appreciate being kept out of the loop."

"Maybe this should be a private conversation..." Silas tries to interject.

"Then grow the fuck up and talk to us," Josie snaps right back. "You went through something traumatic, and you refuse to take advantage of the support your friends want to lend you.

Be better—if not for yourself, then for Imogen. She's going through enough as it is."

"Do you not think I *know* that already?" I growl. "That's why we are no longer together."

Awkward air suffocates the room.

"That... is new information that definitely needs to be discussed. However, I do have to go. Otherwise, they'll be suspicious," Leo says. "Keep me posted on phase two."

He shoots us a thumbs up before slipping from the room.

I clear my throat and stand. Josie, Wrath, and Silas stare at me, all waiting, I imagine, on bated breath for me to explain further. Or to argue with them more. Or to deflect.

I do none of those. Maybe this is growth. Or maybe it's a cowardly retreat.

My scars itch and ache, and I grit my teeth through the sensation.

"I'm going to go take a lap," I say. "Then I'm going to have a smoke. And on the way back to the apartment, you can tell me about this plan you've concocted with Leo. And *then* I will answer any questions you have about my *feelings*. Okay?"

Josie leans back in her chair, pursing her full lips as she studies me. "Fine."

13
SILAS

Nora stares out the window, stoic, save for a small crease between her brows. The glass is tinted, designed so outsiders can't peer in, but from the inside we can see every-thing with clarity; there's a circus in view, beyond the palace gates.

Not a real circus, of course, but the kind of media spectacle that's filled with leering newsies and the occasional flash of a camera. I'm sure that tomorrow we'll see something printed in the papers, and the radio hosts will be gabbing about Nora's return. Everyone is desperate for the next shocking headline. And some are willing to lug a bulky camera across the city and plop it onto my front yard to get a single, blurry shot of the *soul-stealer Seelie.*

They could come up with a better name for her. Or a more accurate one. *Or,* better yet, they could mind their own damned business.

"Are you sure you don't want me to shadow-walk you home?" I ask.

Nora doesn't startle, and I wonder if she's known I was there from the second I laid my eyes on her. How long ago had I slipped from the shadows to watch her scrutinize the crowd? An embarrassingly long time. But I've never been one for embarrassment.

My face scrunches, my smile leaning towards a grimace as Nora's gaze glides over me, expressionless to the point of boredom. The corners of her red-stained lips are tense, turning down, as her attention settles back on the windowpane.

I've noticed that outside of those big, rageful moments, it's quite hard to read Nora. All her tells are subtle, and I take delight in deciphering them all.

"I'm not going to hide from them," she says.

"Okay," I say. My tongue runs over my teeth. I know when to pick my battles when it comes to stubborn fae.

"Might as well let them get their fill. Once they realize I'm not going to flash my wings at them, they'll move onto the next story. Some drunken scandal with one of the Royals or socialites will do." She sighs. "Since you enjoy sticking your nose in my business, you could make yourself useful and handle that much, right?"

She mutters the last bit—a pointed barb aimed to make me recoil, but I may be a masochist, because it only draws me closer.

I lean against the window, facing her on the opposite side. The foyer is dark; the main entrance isn't one I normally use, so why would I waste gas to light sconces here? At least the large windows that spread on either side of the entrance bathe us in soft sunlight. The thin wooden separators between each glass pane cast hatch marks over us. One shadow slices through the center of Nora's face, a matching angle to the sharp slope of her nose.

"Or you could call in those favors Sloth mentioned to cause

said scandal?" I ask, fidgeting with the cufflink on my sleeve. The only indication she hears me is the slight crinkle at the edge of her eyes. "He sounded ominous. Who could you pull favors from outside of the Sins? Or do you have some Royals in your pocket?"

Nora presses the side of her head to the glass. Her eyes, bathed in direct light, glow bright green, pupils contracting to a pinpoint.

"Did you think my predecessor kept me and Josie locked up and hidden away until we were introduced to society?" she asks, words dripping in sarcasm.

I frown. When I don't answer her, she sighs through her nose and continues.

"There are darker circles in this city, Silas. The Sins are the big sharks, but there are plenty of other predators lurking in the murky waters." She pauses, catlike curiosity drawing her gaze over me. Gooseflesh spreads down my arms. "I figured you knew about it…"

"The black market?" I shrug, and the line between her brows deepens. "I leave that stuff to Wrath's team. I don't have a pressing need to crack down on under the table deals unless they have larger implications."

"Like if I had started selling those tonics rather than going to you with my proposal?" A small note of humor fills her voice as she reminisces.

"Bingo." I snap my fingers. "Where did those go, anyway? We should consolidate the stock and redistribute to key strongholds along the river. The Royal coffers will pay, of course."

"The stock was lost in the warehouse fire in the fall. Along with our supplier," Nora says. Her expression darkens. "And we used the one other sample I had to save Imogen."

I hum. I'm desperate to hear about what happened

between them; was what I said to Nora as we sparred what pushed them to breaking up? That wasn't my intention—I was encouraging the opposite. And I hate the idea that I'd have any role in pushing them apart.

Gravel cracks as one of my drivers pulls a car around for Nora and Josie, and the paparazzi foam at the mouth.

"Are you *sure* you don't want me to shadow-walk you both back?" I ask again.

There *is* a reason why I magic myself everywhere, rather than driving. It's not for shits and giggles, as much as it is fun to drop in places unannounced.

"I don't need them to like me, Silas. I never have," Nora says, pushing away from the window. She tosses a hand over her shoulder. "I'll ring you if I need anything. Stay in your lane and keep us posted on the Seelie and the shadow-veil. Let me deal with House Pride."

I watch her bank around the hallway corner, and with one last glimpse of her raven hair, my shadows curl around me, whisking me across the city.

The Queenstown Fort, which is nestled north of Anwynn, along the river that bisects Faerie, has seen better days. Squinting against the bright sun and biting wind, I turn in place, carefully avoiding loose bricks that have tumbled from the walkable wall surrounding the stronghold.

The old military base could be considered ancient, as it was built in the early days of the Court. It's switched hands and Houses too many times to count, but now it resides under Wrath's purview. He hasn't found the time to fix it up, though we might be expediting repairs if this is where we want to experiment with our ambitious 'Plan A.' Also known as *fix the shadow-veil.*

There are only so many ways to bridge the natural divide separating our Courts. The Seelie have three realistic options for a land invasion: cross the river, funnel through the Casimir bridge, or use the portal from the Human Realm.

Of course, some *could* light-walk directly into Anwynn if the shadow-veil falls. But that's a small fraction of their population with the same limitations as our shadow-walkers. They can only go places they've seen or know.

I squint out over the river.

Most shadow-veils are opaque, but this one functions like tinted glass. It's as thin as a strand of hair and nearly transparent. But my eyes are used to quickly homing in on the quivering air, and the grayish shimmering curtain materializes in front of me.

My magic has always been a smidge different from my peers, fluid and wild in its expression—resembling our ancestors' magic or that which the sprites use.

Eighteen-year-old me was elated that my magic hadn't lowered a blackout curtain over the entire Court. We could still see the river, the sun, the blue sky and all its little cloud friends —*and* we could keep the Seelie out.

It was too good to be true.

And it *was* too good to be true.

It was three years ago that I noticed it fading. It was subtle, but I started waking up with more energy. I could have chalked it up to new strength that came with age, but my instincts knew better. My shadows got darker, and the shadow-veil got thinner.

Ever since, Wrath and I have been splitting our attention between Anwynn and Bramble, researching how to reinforce our greatest advantage—to no avail.

And now we're here.

I had hoped we could nip all our problems in the bud with Nora, but... it was a long shot. One I thought was worth the risk. If the shadow-veil falls and Patience still lives, we're bound for war regardless.

My breath dances in a cloud around my nose as I search for Wrath. I rub my hands against my arms, the chill seeping through the layers of my suit—*why didn't I put on my jacket before I left?*

Oh, right. Nora.

The distraction of a lifetime, that woman.

My shivers are quickly forgotten though, as I spot the man of the hour. He's talking with fervor, hands motioning towards the shimmering shadow-veil, and his body is suspiciously close to a tiny little thing with a mess of blond curls.

I snicker as I hop over fallen bricks on my way over to them.

How very, very interesting.

Hattie's crystal blue eyes are locked on Wrath with rapt attention. Her bob of ringlets bounces as she nods along to what he's explaining—I'm sure I already know whatever it is he's talking about. What's more interesting to me is the way Hattie beams up at my friend. And the way her grin turns as evil as my own smirk when she catches me sneaking up behind Wrath.

I've only met the girl a handful of times, but each was as memorable as the last. She's a handful, definitely an acquired taste of wild, but I find her lack of a filter endearing. Plus, from the first moment she whispered sweet nothings about murder into Wrath's ear, she had him blushing.

Even now, as Wrath turns to me with a withering glare and his signature frown, his cheeks are pink. They could be flushed from the bitter wind, but I know better.

He's smitten.

It's fucking adorable.

I want to pinch those pink cheeks and tease him about his little crush on the shadow-walker. He rarely engages in relationships of any kind, so I never get to bug him about this sort of thing. But now that I know he's harboring an infatuation?

All bets are off.

Or on, if we're placing wagers. I give it a month before she eats him alive.

"You're late," Wrath says. "Which boggles me because we were *just* in the same place and you only left to grab your jacket."

I straighten to my full height, side-stepping him so the three of us make a triangle in the walkway.

"I got distracted," I say, winking at Hattie.

"Understandable," she says.

"Right," Wrath grunts. "I was explaining our current predicament to Hattie. Nora and Josie say she's their strongest shadow-walker, and I figured bringing her out here could offer a new perspective."

"I'm all for *new perspectives*," I say, waggling my brows at Wrath.

"And you're sure Your Majesty here can't zap it with some extra juice and call it a day?" Hattie asks, jabbing a thumb over her fur-coat-clad shoulder.

I click my tongue. "Unfortunately, we tried that years ago. Bounced right off."

"We've been trying to find a way to infuse it with more power, but with little success," Wrath adds.

"Maybe we could... actually, give me a second to think," she says. Hattie's lips purse as she blows out a sigh and glances at the shadow-veil. She mutters musical *do-do-doo's* as she squints into the purple and orange-streaked sky.

I sneak a peek at Wrath and catch him staring at her puffed cheeks and pink lips longingly. I hide my quivering smile behind a hand and a cough, lightly jabbing my elbow into his side.

He jolts, and the flush spreads down his neck. I tilt my head at Hattie and then give him a thumbs up.

Stop it, Wrath mouths.

Why? You like her. I approve, I mouth back.

Wrath's face contorts with fury. *Shut up*, he mouths.

Let me be your wingman, I mouth, nudging him again with my elbow.

Wrath's lips pinch together as he bats my elbow away.

I will, in fact, not shut up about this. Ever. Or, at least, not until they get together. I let loose a snicker, poking my cheek with my tongue. The action is not an explicit gesture, per se, but Wrath still takes the bait.

His hand shoots out, but I smack it away, and we devolve into a childish fight made of muted slaps and shoves.

"You two good?" Hattie drawls.

Both Wrath and I freeze; we slowly turn to the small woman, who has one blond brow cocked at us with an amused smile plastered across her face. One of her hands is planted on her hip, fingers poking through the tufts of fur, and the other holds a small knife pointed out towards the shadow-veil.

I nod. Wrath grunts. He's always grunting; she's going to think he's a caveman. Women don't find cavemen attractive.

Hattie waves the sharp point of the knife between the two of us.

"You sure?" she asks.

I cough to cover my laughter. Wrath elbows my side, and I grunt—his jab much harder than it needed to be.

"Yes, please continue," Wrath says, righting his wool jacket.

"Good," Hattie says. "As I was saying, I know you two like your science-y stuff, but my gut says this veil was a friggin' fluke. Once in a lifetime type of stuff. When we're in stressful situations, magic tends to react in kind. You know how adrenaline can give you a physical strength boost? Same thing happens with magic. We *could* recreate the scenario—"

"—not an option—" Wrath interrupts, but Hattie continues without pause.

"—but I don't think we should waste our time on long-term solutions, given the timeline. It's not worth the effort or magic to save it."

"I don't think I'm following," Wrath says.

Hattie sighs, as if we're idiots. Then she asks, "What do you do with a battery that dies?"

We're both quiet, stupefied by her chosen metaphor. Hattie rubs her temple. I imagine her brain moves too fast for her tongue, given the way we're not tracking her train of thought.

"You *throw it out*," Hattie says, trying to coax the same words from us, gesturing with her hands. "And then you get a new one."

Wrath, again, shuts that path down. "Silas nearly died the first time—that's a no."

Hattie shakes her head.

"You're misunderstanding. I'm saying we use the fading shadow-veil strategically and have replacements ready in predetermined locations to bottleneck the fuckers"—she mimes slicing her knife across her neck—"and then slice 'em down. Use it as bait. Let the Seelie waste their magic on taking it down. Most won't have much juice left to take on another blockade afterward. They'll take the few openings as a win, but we'll be ready on the other side."

That's... actually very smart.

"Why didn't you think of that?" I ask Wrath.

His sandy-brown brows are knitted as he takes in Hattie's suggestion. "I guess I only thought of it as an either-or kind of thing. But that could work."

Hattie shrugs. "You're welcome."

"I didn't say thank you," Wrath says. But Hattie is undeterred by his prickly nature. She beams up at him, then bounces on her toes as she *boops* his nose.

"But you were thinking it," she says.

Wrath puffs up like cat, flustered and pissed. My laughter shakes my shoulders and booms into the sunset sky.

"I think you're my new favorite person, Hattie," I say, wiping a tear from my cheek. The warm droplet stings against my cold skin.

Wrath elbows me again, and I shoot him a warning glare, daring him to do it again.

Jeez, sensitive much?

"But if you truly want my opinion on it all, and I hope I'm not overstepping by saying so," Hattie adds, suddenly much more serious. "I don't think we should wait for the Seelie to attack. Of course, we should have a plan of defense, but you might want to consider an offensive strategy too. I've watched a lot of human conflict in my time, from both the winning and losing sides. More often than not, it doesn't end well for the ones who sit and wait to act."

It's an interesting thought, one said with wisdom that goes beyond Hattie's apparent years. She doesn't look a day over twenty-five, but fae age slowly—and at a snail's pace when they're powerful.

"Sounds as if there's a few intriguing stories behind that wisdom, Hattie. Care to share?" I ask.

"Nope. I'm a mystery with a history." She winks. "And that's the way I like to keep it."

"Fine. Keep your secrets. I'll have Wrath pull them from you one way or another," I say.

"I will do no such thing," Wrath says, turning a darker shade of pink.

The blues of night descend as our laughter fades. Shivers run down my spine from both the cold and the prospect of the impending conflict.

I had thought we were one step ahead of the man who plotted against my parents—against me, Nora, and the Court. But Patience proved we've been working two steps behind. And, more importantly, playing right into his hand.

"Thank you for your perspective, Hattie. I'm still partial to finding a way to reinforce the current shadow-veil, but with every day that passes, the reality of us losing its protection presses closer." I place a strong hand on Wrath's shoulder, and pat Hattie's with the other, my fingers brushing against the soft tufts of her fur coat. "I want you and Wrath to work together on a few options to move forward with. Think outside the box. It's needed."

"You got it." A dangerous glint shines in Hattie's crystal eyes. Then she tongues her cheek, nodding at Wrath. He stiffens under my grip. "You know where to find me—it's a date."

Then she disappears in a plume of smokey shadow.

Wrath wastes no time once the last wisps of her magic dissipate and comes at me with a growl. "*Silas.*"

I raise my hands, ready to placate the man who has transformed into a raging bull.

"Oh! I almost forgot!"

Wrath freezes, and I spin around to find Hattie blipping back into existence. She digs around in the pockets of her coat, pulling out two small pieces of cardstock.

I take the card she extends towards me, quickly reading the handwritten scribbles that invite me to her birthday party in a few weeks.

"I expect a good present since you're a king," she says.

I snort. "Noted."

Hattie poofs into shadow, reappearing in the small space between my back and Wrath. She hands him his own card.

"You too. You're a Sin. I know how much you guys make. Don't cheap out."

I choke on my laughter, watching as she *quite literally* pokes the bear, jabbing Wrath in the chest before disappearing for good.

"Oh, you are so unbelievably fucked, my friend," I croon, bent over, my side hurting from my cackles.

There must be something in the water in House Pride to raise such uniquely bold women.

I fucking love it; it's the most entertained I've been in years.

But then Wrath's hands are on my chest, shoving me backwards. I tumble over the crumbling ledge of the fort and plummet towards the rocky shore of the river. I linger in the fall, the wind rushing around me; my amusement mixes with adrenaline, a euphoric combination, before my shadows engulf me. They hug my body, warm arms cradling me to safety. Wrath huffs as I hop out from the black tendrils, unscathed.

"Now, that wasn't very nice," I tut. "Some would call that treason."

The man simply rolls his eyes before waving the cardstock

invitation in the air. It makes that silly wriggly noise, and I smile.

"You're going to make me go to this, aren't you?" Wrath asks.

I wrap my arm around his shoulder, tugging my friend to my side. "Of course I am. You know I'll always force you to do the things you're too scared to do alone."

14

JOSIE

The car inches through a swarm of leering newsies; the driver huffs, clearly frustrated with their lack of civility as we pull up to our apartment building. This is, unfortunately, how it's been ever since the rumor mill caught wind of Nora's secret. They're mostly harmless, more annoying than anything else, with their incessant presence and intrusive barbs posed as well-meaning questions about public safety.

It made me laugh at first, their concern over Nora's true identity. They shouldn't be worried about the fact that she's got Seelie blood. She might have a shiny new pair of wings, but she's only ever had loyalty to the Unseelie Court.

It's the rest of her that they should be worried about. Nora's always been a force of nature, for better or worse. Rain can gift the earth life, but there's a risk of flooding if the deluge comes on too fast.

Nora peers out the window with ice-cold condescension; the press are ants to squish under her heel.

She taps the driver on the shoulder. He flinches but quickly recovers.

"Don't bother trying to get through all this mess. Let us out here," she says.

He puts the car in park, and she pops the door open.

The crowd is deafening. Paparazzi scream at us, some throwing questions and others hurling obscenities. The latter is new; I've only been the subject of their questions anytime they've lingered outside our residence. They don't fear me the same way they do her.

Their thoughts are loud too, battering my mental shields. Large crowds always pose such a problem, but this is a harder battle than I've had to fight in ages. At family dinner, our people know to keep their shields up and thoughts closed off. They are trained to do so from an early age. And when I'm at the Den, it's easier to tune out. While everyone's inner monologues ramble without much of a filter there, it's all happy and heady.

These are sharp, cruel thoughts.

Despite their overwhelming vocal presence, the crowd parts for Nora with ease. Her hands are ungloved, but I have an inkling that even if they weren't, the newsies would be skittish to make physical contact with her. They talk and think a lot of shit, but few have the guts to back it up with action.

It's why they are the masses, and we are the leaders. They lack the courage to act.

Nora and I stride forward with our heads held high. Cameras pop and flash. When we reach the glass doors to the lobby, the two guards posted there nod at me. One clutches their gun to their chest while the other opens the door.

Nora pushes me through the door with a firm hand on my back, but instead of following, she turns back to address the crowd.

"I'm only going to say this once. Are you all listening?" Her voice booms. "If you're desperate for my story, here it is. An orphan girl, half-seelie, half-unseelie, was taken in by a powerful man because she had powerful magic. She grew up to be the scourge of this city, stealing souls for her House. And then she became Pride. The end." She flips them off. "Now, fuck off! I own this sidewalk, and my friends here have guns they aren't afraid to use."

For one brief moment the city hushes.

Then they have one of two reactions: outrage or fear.

The smart ones choose the latter and scurry off with whatever quotes they can spin for tomorrow's headlines. The stupid ones stay.

Nora gives them her back, but as she turns, one of the overzealous newsies rushes forward. It happens fast; the second the man's hand brushes between her shoulders to grab her attention, Nora's gun is out. There's a single, devastating *pop*, and the man screams.

My mask slips, and I curse.

The man writhes, splayed on the pavement, clutching his leg. A bullet hole oozes blood, soaking his wool trousers.

"Do *not* touch me," Nora commands.

"I only wanted to ask for a picture. You fucking shot me!" the man screams.

Nora ignores him and walks away, tucking her gun in her holster.

I quickly school my expression, but confusion and outrage fight for dominance in my throat. I know better than to question her out in the open—so I nod at the guards, a silent command. They burst into action, trained to clean up these kind of messes. The crowd scatters like pigeons, fleeing the scene, and I follow suit, rushing after Nora.

I catch her at the elevator, where she violently presses the call button with a shaking knuckle. When it doesn't light, she mashes it three more times.

I clear my throat.

"Nora…" I start.

"Freddy?" she calls to the man at the front desk, ignoring me. "Damn call light is broken again."

"I'll get a maintenance request in right away, Pride," he replies, the title rolling off his tongue easily.

"Thank you," she says, staring at the elevator doors.

My jaw feathers.

She shot a *civilian*, and she's going to walk away as if it's nothing?

It doesn't matter if he was pushy, or touched her. He didn't *attack* her. Everyone in our House is used to violence… but it's always purposeful. Even her own bloodiest acts have been enacted on those who deserved it. That was part of why we took the reins from Pride in the first place. His vicious hand was indiscriminate.

My magic slithers out, prodding at Nora's mental shields, and I can immediately tell they'd break if I put too much pressure on them.

"Nora," I say again as the elevator doors open for us. We step inside and she punches the button for the penthouse floor. I tread lightly, my voice purposefully calm. "Was that necessary?"

Nora casts me a blank look. "Does it matter?"

I'm shocked still by her response, and we ride up the forty floors with stiff shoulders. The upbeat jazz that filters through the elevator speakers doesn't help the awkwardness.

The bell dings, our ascent to the top floor complete. The doors squeak open, like they also don't know how to act in this moment. Nora steps out first, and I follow—we both pause, lingering in the small foyer where three halls diverge.

"Tea?" she asks. "I owe you a conversation and would prefer to get that over with."

"Sure…"

I don't recognize this Nora; there's a darkness pressed into every slow, deliberate movement of her body, like it pains her to keep her shoulders back and head up.

A fissure runs through my heart. It's been doing that a lot lately, cracking apart as I watch my two best friends claw their way through the aftermath of Casimir. It's starting to set in that our entire family left that castle different than we entered it. And I can't help but wonder what that means for the future we all had planned.

We end up drinking something harder than tea by the end of the night.

We may or may not be developing an unhealthy habit, emptying the bottle plucked from Nora's liquor shelf at the rate we are. It was the same at Bramble though; Silas, Wrath, and I all sharing a nightcap after each day running damage control around Anwynn.

The clock ticks loudly from its mount on the wall.

I poke Nora's side with my foot; I'm curled up on the old green sofa, while she sits hunched, forearms on her knees. She stares into the void of the crackling fire, glass cradled in both hands.

My cheek presses into the velvet cushion.

"Nor," I say.

She sighs.

She knows. *I* know.

It's late, and we can't stay like this forever. Teetering on the edge of this cliff we're facing is no way to live. There's something draining her, causing the haunted gleam in her eyes. A shroud has fallen over them and dulled their shine.

But I can't help her if she won't talk to me.

Her stare shifts above the mantle, where the wings Pride sliced from her back more than a decade ago hang.

It wasn't her choice to preserve them. Pride kept them as some kind of sick hunting trophy. He relished the reminder of his *great feat* in 'obtaining them from the Human Realm'. In reality, all he did was manipulate a child into believing she needed to cut a part of herself away to survive. To cleave away and deny half of herself was posed as a service to our House.

I fell prey to Pride's cruel manipulations too, but the past is something I came to terms with long ago. I am content in knowing we're changing the culture of our House for the better.

I will be the last to bear these scars.

"Tell me what's wrong, Nor," I whisper.

A violent shiver racks her body, and one hand reaches back to scratch between her shoulder blades. I don't know if she realizes she's done it three times in the past hour.

"I'm being eaten from the inside out, Joze."

The whiskey burns as it slides down my throat. "Yeah?"

"I don't know what else you want me to say."

My expression softens. "I want you to be honest that you're struggling. All we want to do is help you."

Nora downs the rest of her drink, slamming the empty glass onto the coffee table. She stands, the couch creaking at the shift of weight, and walks to the fireplace. A cautious hand reaches up, light skin glowing against the dark green wallpaper before she caresses the preserved wings.

"Do you know why I kept them?" Nora asks. "After we

moved in? I could have thrown them out. Or had them burned."

"I imagine it had something to do with spite?"

"That's a good guess, but no."

"Then why?"

Nimble fingers trace over the wings' veins. "I told Imogen they're a reminder of what's at stake if I fail."

I shift, placing my drink on the table. "Did you lie?"

"Not exactly."

"You're killing me with the suspense here, Nor." I huff a laugh, but it falls flat.

Her head shakes as she turns around. The resulting sight is something to behold.

Standing at their center, Nora's framed by her wings. They hover over her shoulders, descending on her like an evil spirit. She's backlit by the fire, an eerie orange glow that opposes all the green and black behind her. Her face is shrouded in shadow; the darkness consumes her.

"Sure, they served as a reminder to keep my secrets close. But really, it was proof that I'd become who I truly am inside," Nora says, rubbing her chest. "I might have Seelie blood, but I'm not Seelie, Josie. Never was. I loved my mother, but I hated those wings. I *hate* these wings."

I hold my breath, my empath's gift turning into a curse as it tosses warning signals left and right. When I was younger, no one told me how understanding people's emotions is a form of pattern recognition. And when you recognize a pattern, you know what comes next.

Nora's hand whips out, pointing to the wings. "I am not that. I am not *him*."

I'm going to despise what she says next, aren't I?

"Will you..." Nora pauses, the words getting caught in her throat. "Will you clip them for me?"

Yeah, I hate everything about what she just asked.

"Please?" Nora asks.

The pain in her voice slaps me—and I have to glance away. I focus on the rug and the intricate designs woven with the fibers.

It was one thing when we were sixteen and Pride held the knife. We were set in our convictions, and the shearing of our wings was the only way to climb the ladder. But now... it's not the same.

"Nor..." I choke out. "No."

"Josie, *please.*"

I shake my head.

Her feet slap across the hardwood, then turn to muted *thumps* on the rug before she stops in front of me. She crouches on the ground, forcing herself into my line of sight.

"At least look me in the eye when you deny me this," she seethes.

I meet her gaze. Nora's ghosts squeeze my chest and force my pulse into my ears; all I can hear is the harried, whooshing beat.

"Nora, I can't do that," I rasp.

I made a promise. *We* made a promise. I would be the last. *Why would she ask this of me?*

"Why not? It's already been done before." Her fingernails dig into my knees as she pleads. "You want to help me? Gift me freedom from this distraction. It's been a month now, and it consumes my every waking moment."

"I will not mutilate you. I refuse," I say firmly. "Find another outlet for what you're feeling. Go to the boxing gym and punch someone. Drown yourself in work. Yell at the sky. Have Silas take you to Bramble to shoot at the range—I do not care." I take a deep breath and place my hands over hers, squeezing. "But do not ask me to do *that*. Never again."

Nora's throat bobs, and her expression shutters into something blank. She rips her hands from mine and stands, giving me her back. Her nose sniffles, and she runs her fingers through her hair.

A minute passes in painful silence.

"Nora—"

"I'm going to bed," she cuts me off. "Douse the fire whenever you're done."

And then she leaves.

I know that wasn't the answer she hoped for. But, this is a line I cannot cross.

I only hope she doesn't see it as a betrayal.

When I shut the vents on the fire, it takes its time to flicker out, slowly dying.

15
NORA

I sense the shadows condense at the entrance of the alley before he appears. Vinnie is an old friend—if you can consider the man who arranged your underground, underage fighting matches a friend. The unaffiliated fae of this city may deal in shady shit, but Vinnie's always been oddly protective of his charges. If someone lays a finger on his fighters outside of those four lines of rope, they best expect a knife of shadow in their gut.

"How ya' doing, Nory-baby?" Vinnie says, sliding next to me.

I roll my eyes and hold out my carton of cigarettes to him.

"Here," I say in lieu of a hello.

"Always so hospitable," he snarks, but plucks one out anyway. We both light up. Vinnie puffs his cigarette, smoke unfurling around his curly brown hair. "To what do I owe the pleasure of your company?"

I nod my head down the alley. "Let's walk and talk."

We cross the intersection leading into the city's largest park and meander down one of the winding paths.

"You still pushing people to Moretti when they graduate?" I ask once we're in a more private area.

"Yeah…"

Moretti is the leader of one of the more influential mafia families human-side. House Pride used to trade with him regularly, but we've distanced ourselves from his organization after one too many slimy deals. And because he runs the Pits.

Hattie would hate me for going back there, but what she doesn't know won't kill her. She and I share a sordid history with the supernatural fighting ring human-side. And after my argument with Josie, I figured it was the perfect way to kill two birds with one stone. A plan quickly wrote itself as I stared at the ceiling of my bedroom, and now I plan to cash in on one of the favors I'm owed.

Josie wants me to blow off steam by going to the *gym*? That shit didn't work at Bramble. And it's not going to work here.

No, what I need is to draw blood.

The Pits offers me the ability to do that *and* get something I can use against Wes in return. Moretti's family is known for their arms dealings. And since Wes has commandeered the warehouses that contain our weapons stores, I now have the opportunity to even the playing field.

"I need you to set up a match for me," I say.

"For you or for *you*?" Vinnie asks.

"The latter."

"Gotcha," he says. We meander for a while longer, until his curiosity gets the better of him. "Am I allowed to ask why?"

"Nope. You owe me, remember?" I say.

The man chuckles. "Crazy to think I got stuck owing a favor to a sixteen-year-old."

"Crazy to think you were stupid enough to get shot in your own office."

"Even crazier that you were right there to apprehend the

burglar and patch me up. Almost like it was planned," Vinnie drawls.

An evil grin dances across my lips as I relive the memory. I was a vindictive little shit and had decided he needed to be punished for pitting children against each other—and for pushing them towards more dangerous rivals across the Veil. It didn't stop Pride from forcing me to participate in Vinnie's ring or the Pits. But pocketing a favor all those years ago was paying off.

Even if it was a set up, I still saved his life.

"I guess that's the risk you take when you're in your line of business, Vinnie." I flick my dying cigarette onto the path and stamp it out. Gravel crunches under the sole of my boot. "Can you set it up or not?"

"Yeah, I can get it goin'," he relents. "But the portal's closed. You got someone with enough juice to get you across and back by themselves?"

We emerge from the park, right into the heart of Wrath's territory. His office building towers above us, a few steps across the white lines marking the crosswalk.

"Don't worry about me," I say, stepping onto the street. "I've got it covered."

Wrath stares at me with an unwavering frown; the man could be made of marble with the way the wrinkle between his brows is carved into his face.

"You want me to escort you across the Veil so you can *blow off steam?*" he asks.

"Josie said I need an outlet for all my pent-up energy." My tongue chases the half-truth across my teeth. I do have to address this *need* coursing through me, but I'm also misrepresenting her intention. Josie did *not* encourage me to go on a killing spree. I shrug. "And, it'll help our plans to have Wes scrambling into Leo's trap. We need to push him. This is how we do that."

Wrath stews on my words. His lips pucker, as if they're sour on his tongue. "Fine, but I need a favor in return."

My eyes narrow on the Sin. "Shoot."

He leans back in his office chair, one strong hand swiping over his stubble. "Hattie invited me to her birthday party. Silas is making me go."

"Okay..."

"I don't trust him to help me"—Wrath clears his throat—"to help me choose a gift."

My lips part. "And you think *I* am the best person to help with that?"

"Aren't you friends with her?"

"Sure."

"Then it shouldn't be a big problem for you to solve." Wrath's arms cross over his chest.

"Fine." I stand, buttoning my coat. "A weird fucking favor to ask when I can think of fifty better ones, but fine."

"Believe it or not, I'm not a complete ass." Wrath busies himself with shuffling papers on his desk. "You seem like you need this. And I'd rather you go beat up some schmuck human-side than one of our upstanding citizens."

"Right," I deadpan.

"When do you need me to take you?"

"Soon. I'll be in touch," I say. "Oh, and don't tell Hattie about this."

"What? Why?" Alarm rings in his voice.

Gods, he's such a sucker. But Hattie's past isn't mine to reveal.

"I don't want to make her jealous," I warn with a wink.

16

JOSIE

Awkward coexistence unfurls between me and Nora, only speaking when she wants to delegate business my way. Because I refused to clip her wings.

I've been stewing about it all week, growing increasingly pissed off at how she's dismissed me.

We've had tiffs before, arguments that devolved into screaming matches, and even some that got physical. But we always pushed our shit aside and came together to lead this House.

Right now, I'm facing it alone. She's distant, not only from me, but from everyone on our side of this rift with Wes. She won't talk to clients. She's left me to onboard a replacement for Claude. She didn't even attend family dinner on Sunday.

My sweater takes the brunt of my frustration as I shove it into my suitcase. I trade off with Hattie for my week of staying at Imogen's cabin tomorrow and the change of scenery couldn't have come at a better time.

I'm sitting on the suitcase, trying to close the latch, when a crash of glass and a loud curse cuts through the apartment. In a second I'm on my feet, running to our shared kitchen. My shoes crunch over broken crystal as I enter, and I'm thankful I left them on when I got home from the office.

Nora sits on the kitchen table with our medical kit opened next to her. The cabinet where it was stored is hanging open, and a vase from the same shelf is cracked on the counter.

"What the fuck happened to you?" I snap, taking in her disgruntled appearance.

"I'm good. You can go. I'll clean this up later," Nora grinds out. Clenched between her pearly whites is the edge of a makeshift cotton sling. She grunts, tying a knot at her shoulder. The arm it cradles is limp. "I just need to keep this still until Doc can come and reset it."

Other than her dislocated shoulder, there are a few cuts on her cheek and brow. The latter trickles blood, dripping down her chin and onto her white tank top.

"Did you get into a fight?" I ask.

"It's none of your business."

My nails dig into my palms. "Who the hell even offered to match you? Don't tell me Silas slummed it at the local ring?"

"If you need to know, Moretti added me to a few of the lineups this month."

"I don't understand," I say. Moretti is a mafia boss human-side. He doesn't host fights in Faerie. "No one's supposed to be crossing over the Veil right now. It's a security risk."

"Yeah, well, Wrath made an exception when he found out you wouldn't give me what I needed."

Nora's cruel tone slices me, and frustration bleeds from the wound.

"That's extremely irresponsible of you," I say.

My teeth grind as she casually digs through the open med kit, pulling out pads of gauze and antiseptic. Her advanced healing will see her cuts sealed over soon, but it's still important to clean them.

I continue, "I understand I upset you, and I've held my tongue since. But I thought you've been taking time to deal with what's bothering you in a *healthy* way. The Pits could kill you."

I'd watched those fights when we were younger. They were inhumane, unfiltered acts of violence for violence's sake. Why would she go *there*?

Nora ignores me, and I take a measured step forward.

"You're our leader. You can't pointlessly risk your life. And you can't keep pushing your House responsibilities onto me. Our people need to see your face. They need to know you're still with them."

Nora's nostrils flare as she presses a moist piece of gauze to the cut on her brow. "I'm doing this *for* them."

"Getting yourself hurt does nothing for our House."

"I have a plan." Nora stands, tossing the bloodied gauze onto the table. "I asked for your help, and you said no. Don't throw a hissy fit now that I've found a way to kill two birds with one stone."

Terror fills me as I blink at Nora. She packs up the med kit in a rush. "Did they clip—"

The metal box slams shut.

"No. But it's a good distraction."

"Nor—"

"Stay in your lane, Josie. You're *my* Second." Nora shoves her good shoulder into mine when she passes. "Fall in line."

17
IMOGEN

"That's the last of it."

Wrath grunts as he drops another box on top of the small mountain of cardboard forming in the cabin's living room. If you would have told me six months ago that Wrath would be here, helping me move my belongings out of the goodness of his heart, I wouldn't have believed you.

"Do you need anything else before we go? More groceries? A cat?" Hattie appears out of shadow, dropping another box, albeit a much smaller one, next to Wrath.

And if you had told me that Hattie would be plastered to said Sin's side any time they were in the same room... well, that hasn't been as surprising. Ever since the opening of Gluttony's restaurant, she's made her attraction to the man clear.

I won't pretend to understand their dynamic. I'm only thankful that he and Hattie found a moment away from business to help pack up my apartment. Living out of a suitcase has been less than glamorous.

Wrath has grown on me much like Silas has over the last

month: slowly, like moss crawling up the side of a tree. But they have stuck by me through this whole ordeal.

I just wish I knew how to be around everyone in the ways that I used to be. There's a film between us, one we can see through, but makes everything slightly *off*.

"No, I'm all stocked up. Thanks though, Hattie," I reply, forcing a smile.

"Why would you offer her a cat?" Wrath asks under his breath.

"Why *wouldn't* you?" Hattie scolds, as if he should know better than to question her. One of her delicate hands finds purchase on her hip, while the other sweeps out at me. "She just broke up with the boss, and she's clearly depressed. Every depressed person needs a cat."

I wince, and my cheeks ache from the strain of maintaining my fake grin.

I thought I'd be worse off after processing that night at Bramble. But I've gone right back to the numb, empty state that I've come to know as my new normal. I'm not quite sure that's the appropriate response, but it's where I'm at.

Wrath meets my tense gaze, and his brows furrow, as if he's examining me in a new light.

Did he not know? No, he couldn't be that oblivious. Someone must have told him by now.

"I appreciate your concern, but you both have done enough by helping me move my things," I say, and push them towards the door.

"Alright, alright, we'll leave you alone." Hattie rolls her eyes as shadows curl around her, consuming the bright ball of light that she is. "I'll see ya' later."

Wrath doesn't leave right away, shifting from one foot to the other. He clears his throat. "Silas requests that you let him know if you need anything else during this time of transition."

"Uh, thanks," I say, matching his awkwardness.

"It's no problem." He forces a smile. The expression doesn't suit him. "Josie will be over soon, but the guards will be outside as long as you need. Have a good night, Imogen."

Josie's gaze is locked on the side yard, where the garden chairs and small glass table are lightly dusted with snow, when I open the front door. One of her hands nervously grips her neck, while the other wraps around the handle of a small leather suitcase.

"Hey," she says, dropping her hand from her neck and giving me a tight smile.

"Why didn't you have them drop you right into the living room?" I step back, holding open the door for her. Josie steps in, pulling off her scarf and throwing it over the coat stand.

"Felt too much like an invasion of privacy." Her nose scrunches up as she kicks off her boots. They land crossed over each other, snow sliding off them and onto the wood floor. "Especially the first time I come over."

"I'd rather you not stand out in the cold," I say.

"Mo, it's not that much warmer in here than it is outside," Josie deadpans as she pointedly unbuttons her coat, but doesn't take it off. "You're going to get sick if you keep doing this."

"Doing what?" I say innocently, but internally I'm cursing her observant nature. I turn around and beckon her with a flick of my hand. "Let me show you the guest room." Josie sighs, but

I ignore her. "It's small, and there are two beds because it used to be my and Conor's room, but I promise they're both comfortable. Take your pick."

I cross my arms over my chest and lean against the doorway as Josie steps into the bedroom. A cute snort escapes her.

The room is a time capsule to when I was a child, with half being distinctly pink and frilly and the other being all clean-cut gray scale. Conor had personality, but it didn't extend past his demeanor. It always confused me growing up, how he never let his room reflect his humor and joy.

I think I understand it better now. He didn't want anyone who entered his space to know what he cared about. Didn't want to give them that power over him.

He would have handled all of this better than me.

Josie inspects the room with squinted eyes that sparkle with mirth. She nods, as if ending a conversation she's had with herself, and throws her bag onto Conor's bed. It bounces once, making the old springs creak. She glances at me over her shoulder, one brown brow quirked.

"I said they were comfortable, not that they weren't squeaky," I say.

"Got it. So no jumping up and down on them at midnight."

"No, thank you. The walls are thin." My lips twitch. "I'm offended you didn't pick my side. You don't like all the pink?"

Josie huffs a laugh before flopping onto my old bed. Same as her suitcase, she bounces once before sinking into the plush covers. She sighs, and her lids fall closed.

"It's not as bad with my eyes closed."

"Rude."

One soft brown eye cracks open. "Just the truth."

I tongue my cheek. "Did you eat yet?"

"Nope."

"Are you hungry?" I ask.

"I could eat," she says.

"Soup okay?"

"Canned or homemade?"

"Do you actually want the answer to that question?" I tease.

"I'll take that as an indication it's the former." Josie laughs, and the bright sound makes the tension in my shoulders ease.

I haven't talked to Josie much since what happened with Nora, and if I'm being honest with myself, I had been worried that she'd pull away. Not entirely—I know our friendship is stronger than that—but there's a part of me that was expecting her to rescind her offer to stay out here with me. So, the fact that we're bantering back and forth as if nothing has happened? It's a comfort I didn't know I needed.

"I'll leave you to get settled and will call you when it's heated up," I say and close the door to give her some privacy.

I take my time cracking open two cans of soup and heating them over the small gas range in the kitchen. When I'm done, I yell for her and place the two bowls on the table in the dining nook. Josie shuffles into the kitchen—having changed into a cozy sweater—and drops into one of the three chairs at the table.

"Thanks," she says.

"You are quite welcome."

Josie and I eat our meal in peace, the only sounds our dainty slurps and the scrape of our spoons at the bottom of our bowls. I'm blowing away steam from a spoonful when Josie sits back, dabbing at her full lips with her napkin. She drops it onto the table and crosses her arms, staring at me. I swallow, and scoop more from my bowl. A sad smile grows on her expression.

"What?" I ask.

"Are we going to ignore the whole breakup thing or..." Josie trails off, and I choke on the hot soup sliding down my throat. I cough through it, tapping at my chest until my throat is clear.

"I'm not *ignoring* it," I say.

"Uh-huh."

I huff, dropping my spoon into my bowl. "Was I supposed to open the door for you and lead with that? *Hey, Josie, welcome to my family cabin. Want to chat about how your best friend and I broke up because she refuses to open her heart?*"

"That would have been a bit aggressive. But I *am* here if you want to talk about it. You're my best friend too." Josie tongues her cheek. "Plus, Nora and I aren't exactly on the best terms right now."

"Yeah? She self-sabotage your relationship too?" I regret the bitter retort the second it leaves my mouth. I pick my spoon up, and push around the small pieces of green bean and tomato. Then I whisper, "It's just awkward."

"So, you *do* want to talk about it?" Josie asks.

"No."

"Okay."

I narrow my eyes at her. "You're not going to push?"

"Nope."

"Even though—"

"—It was the end to an almost decade-long on-and-off partnership, and I think it would be healthy for you to talk to someone about how you're coping? Yes."

My gaze rolls over Josie's expression, and I realize she's serious. If I don't want to talk about Nora with her, she won't push.

I take a long breath and push my soup forward, my appetite disappearing. My elbows drop to the table, and I put my forehead in my hands, rubbing my temples with my thumbs.

"I don't know what else to say." My fingers dig into my skin. "I said everything I thought she would want to hear. And she shut it down. She wouldn't believe me when I said I'd love her regardless of those stupid fucking wings—" I pause, and take a breath. "And when I asked her to pick me, she said no." I shake my head. "I made a choice in that moment to let go and I don't know if I regret that decision yet. Maybe I should have fought her more on it because I—" Emotion swells again, and I sigh.

"Because you love her," Josie finishes for me.

"Yeah, I fucking loved her, Joze," I whisper. "But I don't think I can do it anymore. I'm too fucked up to fight for someone who clearly doesn't want to be loved. Or for someone who clearly can't give me what I need."

Maybe that's why I'm numb instead of devastated. These realizations hit hard, but they ring true. I peer through the space between my fingers and see Josie nodding.

"It's okay. Not every relationship is meant to be. It can be that simple," she comforts. "And it changes nothing between us, Mo."

My shoulders sag. Josie always gets right to the heart of it, the meaning and worries hidden behind the words. Can she do the same with Nora? Or am I the only one who's that easy for her to read?

"Are you sure?" I ask.

Josie nods again, clear and firm. "I've been through many seasons of Nora, seen her in all kinds of messed up situations. But since Silas brought her back from Casimir... something's changed within her."

"Casimir changed all of us," I murmur.

A beat passes between us, and Josie's throat bobs. Then she whispers, as if uttering a secret, "She asked me to clip the wings Patience gave her."

My hand slides over my mouth. "No."

"Yeah," she says.

My chest burns, and regret spreads like wildfire. Was *I* the one to push her to—

Josie's hand comes to rest over mine, squeezing. "She didn't ask me because of you, Imogen."

"But I—"

"You are *not* responsible for how she's reacting to what happened," Josie says.

It's then that I notice the dark circles rimming her black lashes. Why is she not sleeping?

Josie continues, and her frustration is clear in her tone. "You're not responsible for what happened at Casimir or to your relationship. This is not me picking sides. Nora's being... erratic. And you are entitled, just as I am, to put up boundaries regarding her behavior. Please tell me you understand this."

My throat aches, but I nod.

A heavy silence falls over us; we both turn to the window and watch as snow descends over the thicket of trees surrounding the cottage. The white crystals create a sparkling blanket over the grass and evergreen branches.

We both get lost in our thoughts.

I don't know how long passes before Josie's fingers start to tap a rhythm of anxiety on the table. I eye the bowl she cast aside; its contents are only half-finished.

"Was the soup that bad?" I cringe.

"No," Josie says quickly.

"Then you weren't that hungry?"

Her fingers stop their drumming, but the nervous beat lingers in the air. Josie shrugs, and my expression softens on her.

"Your turn," I say, and her brows furrow as she glances back at me. "What's got you stressed?"

Her head shakes, and a lock of dark hair falls from behind her ear, curling against the slope of her jaw. Short hair has always suited her.

"Besides the obvious?" she asks.

"Yeah."

Josie purses her lips, as if deciding whether to tell me. Ultimately, she relents, giving into me the same way I gave into her.

I pop a bottle of wine, and we talk about our days, our troubles, and our silent hopes. She even gets me to laugh, however briefly, at something stupid. And when I lick a drop of tart red from the corner of my lips as she rants about something silly, her gaze follows the movement.

It's easy, I realize, to open up with her. Easy to be open with each other.

Moments like these may be the medicine my soul needs to learn how to smile again.

18

NORA

I'm buzzing with restless energy by the time I leave for the Pits. It's my third night at Moretti's underground ring, and my magic writhes under my skin at the thought of getting first blood tonight. It's tried to sneak down the tether between Patience and me, but I've held it back, only letting small pokes and prods pass on to my uncle.

It's addictive, playing with him. His magic pushes back against mine, an ever-present thrumming at the back of my mind. I can't sense his emotions, but I imagine he's frustrated, wondering why I haven't tried to kill him yet—why I'm leaving him to his plotting.

Because I can. Because I want to.

This tether is no longer my revenge; it's a failsafe.

I've burrowed into my cruelty, and maybe the apple doesn't fall far from the tree; I am too selfish to end his punishment early. He hasn't suffered enough.

I pass the doorman on my way out and stop short. On the side of our beautiful building are slurs splattered in black paint. I bite the inside of my cheek, sweeping my gaze across the street. A loud *pop* and *crackle* of a camera sounds, and I lock my attention on the few newsies. They've kept their distance since I shot the one who thought it was okay to touch me. However, the incident hasn't stopped them from staking out across the street, safely tucked past the two lanes of traffic.

"You think this is fucking funny?" I yell at them, pointing at the building. Their bodies jolt as my voice echoes between the skyscrapers. I take one measured step towards them, as if I'm going to cross the street, and they scatter.

Cowards, the lot of them.

"You're giving me flashbacks of when I'd play pranks on Sloth."

I whip around to find Silas, with his hands tucked in his jacket pockets and a teasing smile on his lips, staring up at the vandalized building. Centuries old architecture, desecrated. It's an extra mess to clean up, and another reminder of how foolish I was to let my secret get out.

"Was that before or after your parents sent you away to military school for being a nuisance?" I ask.

It's a pointed question meant to provoke his ire, a warm-up to the match tonight. A verbal spar could momentarily release the mounting tension in my joints.

"Before. May have been one of the proverbial straws that broke the camel's back," he says, all mirth and no bite.

I raise an unamused brow. "What are you doing here, Silas?"

"Wrath had another obligation tonight. He asked me to help with your... errand," he says.

"Did he now?" I ask.

My tongue presses against my back molar. These excursions were only supposed to be between Wrath and me. He dropped me off, picked me up, and didn't ask questions in between. It worked easily enough that way.

"You've been up to no good, haven't you, Nora? My two best friends sneaking off to make mischief in the middle of the night. I'm honestly offended I wasn't invited sooner."

His words are so utterly ridiculous to my sleep-deprived brain that a cackle bursts from me. It immediately turns into a coughing fit that has me bracing my hands on my knees. A solid hand claps on my back, and my muscles tense.

"There, there, I've got you," he teases. "Really, what would you do without me? Keel over in the street choking on your own spit? Terrible way to go."

I bat his arm away. "You say many ridiculous things, Silas, but that ranks among the highest."

"Oh, you have a list?" he asks.

And there he goes, taking things one step too far.

Yes, I laughed. Despite my best interest. Despite feeling *on fucking fire* twenty-four seven, I laughed at his joke. And he couldn't just take that for what it was: a momentary lapse in sanity.

The Unseelie King doesn't make me *laugh*.

"Not one that I can remember," I reply, taking a definitive step away from him. He's close enough for his body heat to permeate my space, and it tickles my nerve endings.

"You have to give me some credit," Silas says. "For one second, you didn't have that angry divot between your brows."

I shake my head but take his bait anyway. "Why do you care?"

He shrugs. "Wrath said you seemed down the last time he saw you."

The dry wind whips down the street, making my eyes water. I clear my throat, and shove my hands in my jacket pockets. "That's a strange thing for him to say. I am the picture of positivity."

This part of the human city has the eerie presence of midnight oozing from every gutter and sewer drain, even at dusk. There's a damp darkness that lingers in the alleyways and claws at your boots from between cracks in the pavement.

We enter the old warehouse-style building through the back, the rusted metal door squealing on its hinges.

The hall reeks of beer and blood and body odor. Electric lights flicker overhead, illuminating the grime wedged in the tile grout. You'd think the family that runs this place would have a higher standard for their buildings, but then again, it is an underground ring and speakeasy. All Moretti needs is four standing walls, a roof, and humans needy for adrenaline, booze, and danger.

"This is... not what I was expecting when Wrath said an errand," Silas says, a step behind me.

"Did he not explain what I do here?" I ask.

"I was to drop you off and to come back whenever you told me to. He didn't elaborate more than that."

I stop short, glancing over my shoulder to catch the last second of his sneering perusal of the dingy hall. "Silas."

"Hm?"

I turn to him fully. "I assume you won't leave and come back later?"

"Not a chance," he murmurs. "I'm far too intrigued."

"Fine." I expected as much. But he still needs to know what he's getting into. *Fucking Wrath.* "Some important context to keep in mind: this place is owned by the Moretti family. They are human but are not to be messed with. Do not touch anything. Do *not* smoke one of their cigarettes—they're not tobacco. Do not drink anything they give you that you don't see them open in front of you. And *do not* go to a back room with one of the girls they will inevitably try to distract you with."

Silas straightens to his full height, his brows raising to his hairline. "Did you take us to a seedy night club?"

I roll my eyes. "I'd set your expectations lower."

I motion for him to follow me, pushing open a set of wooden double doors that lead to the main hall. And at its center is the titular *pit*—the ring that I'll be stepping into in a few hours.

"That's an iron cage," Silas says.

"Ye*p*," I say, the word popping between my lips. The floor of the ring is sunken in, with circular stands of seating rising around it. And doming over the mat is an iron cage, which prevents any escape by shadow—or light—walking. "Once you're in, the only way out is to win."

What truly makes the Pits special for the humans is not the illegal fights, the booze, or the drugs, but the fact that they can catch a glimpse of the supernatural. Moretti's standard lineup consists of matches with two human opponents, but on occasion, like tonight, the main card features a supernatural pair.

How said supernatural beings end up on the card is a whole other story. There's a steady stream of Seelie exiles who try to make a quick buck in the ring. The occasional shadow-walker will get brave enough to cross the Veil, then stumble into a match by choice or by a stroke of bad luck. Some fae, like Vinnie, push talented fighters through for training. And, of course, money. Because that's what lies at the center of most hearts.

There are others, too. Fae from families who fled Faerie hundreds of years ago—as Hattie's ancestors did. She has a long, nasty history with the humans. Pride snatched her up quickly when he saw her fighting in this very ring years ago.

And as for the other creatures that find themselves in Moretti's cage... Well, I don't know how or why they end up here. All I know is that the few vampires and wolves I've seen fight never seem to step onto the mat of their own volition.

"You're fighting," Silas says, piecing it together.

"You're so smart." My tone drips with sarcasm.

"For what?" he asks.

"A little something to help deal with Wes," I say, a half-truth.

Silas opens his mouth to ask another question, but his kingly mask snaps into place, attention darting behind me.

"The woman of the hour! How long has it been?" A booming voice fills the stale air. Moretti's deep timbre and heavy Yankee accent match his visage—olive skin and curly brown hair that's slicked back. Although, there's more gray streaking from his temples than the last time I saw him in person.

Humans age horribly fast.

"Not long enough," I say with a smile that doesn't reach my eyes.

While I've been here twice in the last two weeks, the man himself hasn't made an appearance until tonight.

Moretti's laughter shakes his thick frame. He stops before me and leans in, giving me air kisses next to each of my cheeks. He's careful not to touch his lips to my skin; he has a strong sense of self-preservation.

"You always were a firecracker. That's why you bring in the big bucks." His snake-like attention slides to Silas. "And who is this?"

"Pride's bodyguard," Silas says with a sly grin, easily slipping into a character we didn't discuss. My teeth grind as he steps forward and offers his hand.

Moretti takes it to shake, oblivious to the soul-stealing magic that runs in Silas's veins.

It still irks me, how Silas always had the upper hand in secret, the ability to kill lurking *right there* under the surface. I see every instance of casual touch from him differently now.

The two have a moment of male posturing, where their knuckles both go white, before they break apart. Moretti slaps Silas's shoulder.

"Word on the street is that you might not be Pride anymore," Moretti says, attention falling back on me. "But who am I to give credit to the roaches? Doesn't do me any good." Moretti cants his head toward the windows that sit high above the bleachers. It's the only part of the building that's shiny and new, his own personal throne to watch the matches from. "Remind me what you've been cooking up with my guys in my office, yeah?"

We climb a set of precarious metal stairs to Moretti's office. Inside, there is a set of leather chairs that sit before the windows. From the outside they are tinted dark, but from here they offer a clear view of the fighting ring. Behind the row of seats is an old wooden desk and a bar cart.

Moretti leans against the desk, crossing his shiny oxford clad feet. He's dripping in human luxury. A thick gold ring circles one finger to show the world he's married, and an even thicker gold chain peeks out from under his button up.

"I'll cut the long story short," I say, clapping my hands as I perch on the arm of one of the leather chairs, matching his casual demeanor. "I have an infestation giving me trouble. Vinnie and your very helpful right hand over there"—I point to the capo who stands guard in the corner—"struck a deal that makes everyone happy."

Moretti nods, showing he's tracking—and that I should keep going.

"Three fights, me on the main card," I say. "In exchange for a few of your rat bombs."

Sharklike teeth split his lips. "You want to smoke them out?"

"Of course. Why not wipe them out in one go? Makes things easier for me." I fake sharing a conspiratorial grin with him. "It's been fun getting back in the ring anyway. I always did have fun times here."

Moretti looks to his capo.

"You did good. I knew you were the right one to leave my baby with." Moretti's *baby* being the establishment we stand in. His slimy gaze slides over me again. "I was happily surprised when I got the call. I've been occupied with my own bullshit but had to make it back into the city to see your next performance."

"You want to clue me in on what I'm up against tonight?" The last two were Seelie shifters.

Moretti *tsks*. "You know that's not how this works."

"Worth a shot asking," I say, standing. "My payment is in the locker room, I presume?"

"Yes, ma'am," the capo says.

I nod. "Always a pleasure dealing with the family."

Moretti's nose scrunches. "I'd shake your hand, but, ya' know."

I hum and give him my back, waving my hand in the air for Silas to follow. We exit and head towards the locker room.

"You were surprisingly quiet back there," I say once we're firmly out of earshot.

"I'm not an idiot," Silas says. "But I am curious as to why you take him for his word so easily."

I shove the doors to the hall open. "Men tend to keep their

word when there is enough incentive. The money they'll get from these fights is tenfold what I'm asking for in compensation. I trust in that."

"Awfully similar to fae." Silas considers this for a moment. "This is all new information to me. How much more of this realm have you kept under wraps, Nora?"

"There's a world's worth of knowledge I could offer you. I was born here, lived it until I was six. Then I came back at Pride's behest, with a decade's worth of studying the inner workings of the human power-players under my belt."

"I'm afraid I've kept myself terribly isolated to Faerie," Silas says.

"Why would you need to learn the nitty gritty of the Human Realm? You're the Unseelie King."

"A fact you are keen to remind me of often," he mutters. I push into the locker room, and Silas stops the door before it swings shut. He leans against the frame as I open up my locker. "As if I could forget who I am. And as if it will make a difference in how I act around you."

"That is to say, I don't think it's a bad thing you spend most of your time fae-side, Silas." I toss my gym clothes to the bench and slam the locker shut. "This realm offers its own dangers along with its bounties. If you're not prepared for them, they will sneak up on you."

I point to the small crate next to the locker room door. "Now, be a doll and take that back to Faerie while I change."

19
SILAS

Nora's muscles flex and twitch, but never relax, as she ties and reties her boxing boots until they form two *just-right* bows. Her frame hunches over the bench, eyes intensely focused on the laces sliding between her fingers. At the same time, they're distant. Far off. Gazing *through*, not *at*. Is it stress? A memory wreaking havoc? Or is this how she always is before a match?

No. She's been acting strange today.

We verbally spar, but there's a dark undercurrent to it that I can't decipher. She's kept her distance since we came back to Anwynn, despite my offer to assist in taking back her House. And then, she went to Wrath for a favor. Before me. A fact that irks me greatly.

Even as we traveled here, she was careful to stay one step ahead, always leading. I recognize it for what it is: a form of leaving. She's been doing the same to her other friends too.

Her retreat only strengthens the urge to inch closer and understand why.

There's a loud knock on the locker room door. "You ready?"

Nora adjusts her tank top, tucking it deeper into sport shorts that show off her deceptively strong legs. Legs that have kicked me onto my back, wrapped themselves around my neck, and had me tapping out of one too many ego-shattering sparring sessions back at Bramble.

"You're up with Moretti in the booth," the grunt-man calls out, and I realize he's waiting, holding the door open for me.

"I'd prefer to watch by the cage," I say, jogging to catch up to Nora.

"Their house, their rules," Nora says. She reaches up to the sky, stretching, shoulders cracking with the movement. "Try not to piss them off, please."

I begrudgingly follow the human back to Moretti's office, leaving Nora to fend for herself. It's not like she *can't* handle things by herself—she has been—but that's not the point. No one should have to walk through this world alone.

I have done it most of my life; as amazing as my parents were, they were still the queen and king. I needed friends. True allies. It wasn't until Wrath that I knew what I was missing. And even though Nora is surrounded by people who clearly love her, she refuses to recognize that she *isn't* alone. What a predicament to resolve.

The office turned viewing-box is filled with made-men in ill-fitting suits and gaudy gold jewelry. There are no women present, though there are some in the unruly crowd stomping on the risers below us. What were empty metal benches before, have completely filled up, bursting with leering patrons. The rumble of the crowd penetrates the glass.

I keep off to the side, standing watch near the window's edge. Here, I can see the fight unfold without obstruction. Moretti holds court to my left, lounging at the center of the leather seats.

Nora is escorted out by two of Moretti's men, though they

keep a wide berth from her exposed skin. They lead her to the outskirts of the cage, waiting for the formal announcement for the match to begin.

"She doesn't have any weapons. How the hell is she gonna win?" one of the humans asks.

"She doesn't need any," another says.

"But how is she gonna—"

"I forgot you've never seen her before." One oily-haired man groans and leans forward, his cigar dangling between his chubby fingertips. "Here's the thing. She's the type of fae where you touch her and you're dead."

He clicks his tongue and mimes a swipe across the throat. Then he draws out the suspense by taking a puff of his cigar, letting smoke curl around the group. It's oddly similar to how Nora smokes, captivating the room in such a casual fashion. I wonder if it's a habit she picked up from being around these types of men growing up.

"The real question is, how is the other guy gonna fight someone that they can't touch?" the man finishes his dramatic explanation.

"If you think some of the other matches are bloody, just wait. She always gets cut up," another man snickers, and I suddenly have the urge to rip out his tongue. "Red everywhere. God bless the unlucky guy who's gotta scrub the mats after this."

"All of you shut your pie-holes," Moretti booms, waving his hand in the air. His dark eyes meet mine across the room, and their sharp nature sends my hackles rising. "They're about to start."

A thunderous voice echoes off the crowd a second later, with a chipper accent you only ever hear on the radio.

"Alright, ladies and gents. We've got a fun night in store for you all. Snag your drinks and take your seats," the announcer buzzes. "Bets are officially closed, so you better grab hold of your rosary and mutter your prayers."

The crowd answers him with a mix of boos, laughter, and excited jeers.

"In the red corner, we have a familiar face." Nora steps into the ring, a demonic smirk spread across her red-stained lips. She raises her hands in the air, encouraging the crowd's rowdy excitement as the announcer continues on. "You might know her as the infamous Butcher of Bedford Ave. Or, for some of our older members, you may remember her as the defending champ of our biggest supernatural series ten years ago."

My teeth grind as I do the mental calculation—*she fought here as a teen? As a youngling?*

"How lucky are we to have her back after so long?" The announcer pauses, and the crowd grows feral. "Now, how about her opponent? In the blue corner, we have fresh meat." A collective *ooo* rushes through the crowd. "That's right. This is going to be a special treat. Because not only is this a new face with shit to prove, we're pitting fae against fae."

There's a flash of light, then a muscular, blond Seelie appears, twirling long dual blades in a flamboyant fashion. He's shirtless, which is a bold decision, given who he's facing; I wonder if they refused to hint who he was up against, the same as they did with Nora.

Not that she seemed to truly care who, or *what*, she faced tonight.

The Seelie's steps falter when he gets his first true glimpse of Nora: her predator's smile and eerily calm demeanor enough to unnerve the strongest will. She hops up and down, like she's pumping herself up for a run around the block.

One of Moretti's men push the Seelie through the ring's entrance, and then the cage door slams shut with a finality that quiets the crowd. The lock automatically engages, and I realize now what Nora meant when she said the only way out was to win.

There is no handle to twist, no padlock to break. They have to be *let out* by whatever mechanism Moretti has rigged up.

"Reminder, folks, any interference with our fighters—that includes shooting them through the cage—will get *you* shot. Sit back and keep your hands to yourselves. Other than that, the rules are simple: two go in, one comes out."

My gut churns as the crowd roars for the starting bell to ring.

"Fighters ready?"

Nora and the Seelie each take positions opposite each other.

The searing heat of eyes falls on me, and I break my concentration on Nora to glance at Moretti. He smiles at me like he knows something I don't. And for the second time tonight, I find myself with the urge to rip out a human's throat.

I might be posing as a lackey of House Pride, but I *am* the Unseelie King. I'm the most powerful man in our Court; I can do as I please with no repercussions here.

Except, that isn't entirely true. There could be repercussions for House Pride. Nora's reputation. Their business.

I turn back to the iron cage, reining in whatever beast has awoken in me. Wrath would be impressed with my restraint.

The bell rings.

The crowd goes wild.

There's a moment of calm between the opponents, and then the Seelie moves. He's fast, coming in and out of view in flashes of light around the cage, all while Nora stands at the center. He has an advantage in that he can move in ways she cannot—can escape her grip faster than the average person.

The Seelie utilizes his magic at blinding speed, circling Nora as if to test her defenses. The flashes of light are disorienting, but I ignore the splotchy gray spots that appear in my vision. My focus will not be drawn away from Nora, who stands eerily still as all this goes on around her.

It's hard to tell from this far away, but I think her eyes are closed.

One of the Seelie's long blades appears and slices along Nora's cheek. She doesn't flinch as it cuts a red line across her skin and a bloody river runs down her neck. I hold in my wince. Face wounds always bleed the most.

"Here we go boys!" One of Moretti's men claps, rousing amused chuckles from the rest. "I told you she's a bleeder."

My molars threaten to crack under the pressure of my jaw.

Trust, Silas. You can do that for one night. Let her do her thing.

My faith is swiftly rewarded. The next time one of the Seelie blades bursts forth from his magic, Nora dodges, and the blade misses its target. A dance ensues, where Nora artfully evades each one of his attacks. How, I have no clue. But not one more of the Seelie's advances hits their mark.

How many hours did she train to refine these reflexes? Who taught her the art of predicting a light-walker's magic? Was it in preparation for a moment just like this?

How many times was she cut because she miscalculated in practice?

The crowd loves it. They don't see anything but entertainment—not her cruel history, which is clear in the sure, graceful movements of her body.

Her eyes are closed; that, I am sure of now. The way her muscles tense before she moves, not reacting, but *anticipating* —she must be listening, feeling, homing in on the subtle ways that magic changes the air.

Magic has a certain way that it hisses to life around us. Not many can pick up on it. It's a sixth sense anyone can develop if they train hard enough for the skill.

It's genius, applied here.

She's genius.

Nora's hand strikes out, and there's a collective gasp from the crowd. Her fingers grip around the Seelie's blade and it goes flying.

The metal clatters to the ground.

There's silence, then cheers.

The Seelie is shocked, blinking at his empty hand. He's frozen in place for *one* moment too long, and it gives Nora the opening she needs.

Her leg whips out, her boot cracking against the Seelie's ribs, and he rolls across the mat with a grunt. The next movements pass in a blur. There's a savage curl to Nora's lips as she dives for the blade, and a flash of light as the Seelie tries to recover it before her.

Nora gets to it first.

As if she can see the future, Nora jabs it out the instant the Seelie blinks into existence. His magic flares around him as he looks down in horror; his own blade sticks out of his gut.

But instead of reaching her hand out and finishing the job, Nora's leg kicks out again, pushing the Seelie off the blade. He falls to the ground with a moan.

Nora flicks the blade, splattering his blood across the floor.

The Seelie uses his magic, flashing closer to the cage's edge, but he's still on the ground, clutching his hemorrhaging gut.

Nora stalks towards the man, red lips parting with words I can't hear.

Is she taunting him?

The Seelie is outraged with whatever she says, and tries to stand, using his other blade as a makeshift cane. The sharp tip cuts into the mat as he leans on it for support.

Nora continues her slow approach, swinging her blade in a wide circle.

The Seelie yells something at her, his magic flaring around him. He appears on the opposite side of the cage, but Nora simply pivots on her heel and flips the blade between her hands. Her movements are casually cruel. Purposeful. The Seelie attempts an attack, gaining a second wind of energy.

Nora parries with her blade.

They exchange a few blows, and Nora's blade slices across his cheek, arms, and chest. The Seelie pants as he retreats, playing defense as his pallor grows gray.

It's almost painful to watch, this show she's putting on.

Except she's not putting on a show for *them*. I don't think she can even hear the crowd.

She's doing this for herself.

"Oh, shit!" Someone winces when Nora's blade slides into the Seelie's gut again.

"It's cat and mouse. Man, she's brutal," another says.

Nora's all errant rage as she stabs the Seelie until he's a slippery mess of blood. If you were to ask anyone here what Sin her visage embodied in this moment, there's no world in which they would choose Pride over Wrath. My skin runs feverish at the sight; my heartbeat pounds in my neck. Nora is fury incarnate. Primal, in a way that speaks to something I hold deep in my chest.

"Moretti, tell me again why we don't hire her out for hits?" someone asks.

"Because she's too expensive," Moretti grunts.

My attention cuts to the mafia boss, who lounges with his thick fingers steepled in front of his chin. He pulls one away and glances down at his wrist, checking his watch.

"She needs to hurry up," he says.

A crease forms between my brows.

"Why?" I say, speaking for the first time since I got up here.

"Round two, dumbass," one of his men snickers.

My shadows take over before I can order them to do so—dropping me in front of Moretti, blocking his view of the ring.

"You didn't say there were going to be two rounds," I growl.

Moretti shrugs.

He won't be shrugging when I—

"Nothing you can do about it now," Moretti says. "Maybe shoot a prayer up to whatever god you creatures worship for good luck. My money's still on your boss winning, if that gives you any consolation. Now move, you're blocking my view."

20

NORA

I give in to the crowd's pleas.

My fingers release the blade, letting it clatter to the mat to join its brother, long forgotten across the ring. I straddle the Seelie, his slick, warm blood sliding along my thighs, and lean into his face.

My magic jumps and zooms around my chest, thriving off this slow descent into carnage. And when I grip his pulse-point, it quickly leaves me, rushing through the Seelie's body. He chokes, his lungs filling with blood; it's the easiest way to recreate the sensation of drowning.

At the same time, I check in on the tether connecting me to Patience. It thrums. Pulses. It's a live wire of which I send my magic down. Can he picture himself in this nameless Seelie's place? His magic balks, caught off guard by the sudden onslaught of my own, before pushing back. Does he feel death inching closer?

A chuckle slips from my throat.

The crowd hollers. Their beer bottles clang against the risers, urging me to finish this. I relent, and the man below me expires. My shoulders fall, a weight having been lifted from them. I raise both my bloody hands up in the air and relish the roar that shakes the ground under my knees.

Sweet relief embraces me.

My scars are quiet.

My magic is satisfied.

I am me again, if only for a moment.

But when the announcer doesn't jump into his post-match spiel, my eyes crack open, and I stare up at Moretti's office, high above the risers of unruly patrons.

Silas's white hair shines beyond the window, the only one visible through the tinted glass. His arms fling up in frustration, and the hair on my neck stands on end.

Something isn't right.

I glance at the cage door behind me, still locked shut. The other times I've fought, whatever mechanism keeping it sealed has clicked open once the winner is decided.

I killed the Seelie. *I'm* the winner. But the door isn't open.

Shadows gather outside the cage, and the humans gasp as Silas appears. He says something, but it's cut off by the screech of metal. I hop off the dead man and take a defensive stance as a square hatch opens in the floor.

A pair of pale, sharp-nailed hands grip the ledge of the hatch.

"Folks, I hope you weren't expecting that to be the end of our time together," the announcer booms over the microphone. "We've got a round two for you!"

There's one second where a pin could drop in the stands, and I'd hear it. Then hell breaks loose.

Those sickly hands pull a gaunt creature from the underbelly of the pits. And it is a *creature.* If it were a man before, the person behind those red-rimmed irises is gone. It snarls, and fangs descend from its upper gums.

Vampire.

I haven't faced one before, only fae and wolves. The former I've spent a lifetime training against. The latter was easier than expected, since all I had to do was avoid getting chomped on. They aren't much different from Seelie shifters.

Vampires on the other hand... my muscles tense as I slowly reach for the discarded blade on the ground. Vampires I've only seen once; it wasn't me who fought them, and they certainly didn't look like *this*.

The gods must be laughing at me. Truly, I must be their favorite toy to play with, considering all the shit they're putting me through.

"Now our new opponent is a special friend of the family, one that's been waiting quite a while to fight," the announcer drones on, hyping up the crowd.

He's also buying time for the bookies to gather more bets. There's no way Moretti isn't milking this for all it's worth.

My magic dances on my fingertips, ready for the moment I can graze over the vampire's taught skin. A vampire which, despite its growls and clear bloodlust, is twitching in place with unnatural restraint. Almost like a rabid dog trained to heel.

"Alright, alright, I hear your cries for violence. I'm going to hand it over to the boss-man himself to get this party started," the announcer says.

I inch backwards slowly; the less space I have between my back and the cage's metal crosshatching, the better. Only I don't move quickly enough, and the sound of Moretti's smug voice over the speaker has my blood running cold.

"*Go.*"

The vampire's roar hits me a second *after* it hurls me across the cage, too quick for even my speedy magic to seep into its skin. I hit the cage, and the sharp pain in my side confirms I've broken a rib or two. Before I can recover, the vampire tosses me again. And again. *And again.* I'm flung around the ring and take one of the worst beatings of my life.

I'll be a bruised plum after this. But I *will* walk out of this. I'm too stubborn to die in the Pits. Too stubborn to die without a measure of satisfaction back in my fucked up life.

The crowd boos, probably from the lack of blood. The vampire cleverly avoids my magic, only touching the clothed parts of my body. It refuses to nick my skin with its sharp fingernails or fangs, and it doesn't move to claim one of the Seelie's blades from the first match.

Why hasn't it tried to bite me?

My best guess, knowing men like Moretti, is they tried to train this creature out of its true nature so it wouldn't end fights too quickly. A five second match with a clear winner is no good for gambling.

It won't bite, won't feed. Not unless it's told to.

My lips curve into an evil smile as an idea strikes me. I dig my nails into my palm, hard enough to draw a fresh flow of blood. The cut on my cheek has already stopped leaking, and the rest of the Seelie's blood has dried tacky on my skin.

I thrust out blindly, smacking the creature with my bloodied palm. The vampire freezes, dropping me to the ground. I'm allowed a single moment to recover as it puts distance between us. One shaky step. Then another. Its nails drag through the smear of red on its cheek, and it twitches.

A sick laugh squeaks out from my windpipe, raspy and deep.

"Nora!" Silas's worried call breaks through the crowd's jeering.

The metallic glint of the Seelie's blade shines to my left, and I quickly grab it, not hesitating to slice a long cut down my forearm. I stagger to standing, letting the blood flow freely down my arm and onto the mat.

The vampire is a blur of movement, and then I'm crushed into the floor. Its fangs pierce the flesh of my arm, but I chuckle through the pain.

"Gotcha," I say, and my magic takes over.

It acts slower than I would like—hitting a similar barrier to Seelie healing. But the vampire chokes on my blood all the same. My magic always wins, in the end.

Its fangs retract from my flesh, and it screams, clawing at its throat as if my blood is poison. Which it is, in a way.

And then it dies, falling to the mat with a dull *thump*.

I collapse onto my back, breathing heavily. I tilt my head to the side, to the cage door, and see it propped open. Framed by iron, Silas waits in the opening. It wouldn't be smart for him to step inside, lest they lock it behind him.

I close my eyes and gift myself one breath before I roll over. Pushing up and holding back my wince, I raise my bleeding arm, bracing my hand on my head. The cut is deep, but the flow should stop in a minute. Holding it up will help me from bleeding out before that happens.

The announcer's voice drones on in the background, announcing me as the reigning champ.

I stride past Silas, ignoring his questions about if I'm okay, and make for Moretti's office. The humans part for me with awe and terror. My body aches, and I know I'll need a whole twenty-four hours to sleep this off. But at the same time, the bubbling rage that's been living so close to the surface of my skin has lessened. I'm no longer a pot about to boil over. For now.

My boots clang loudly against the metal stairs leading to Moretti's office, but my steps falter as a flash of long blond hair moves through the crowd.

As quick as my heart sinks into my stomach, I shake the woman from my thoughts. That's not Imogen. That's a human.

I haven't seen Mo in two weeks.

"*Grow the fuck up, Nor,*" I whisper to myself.

"What?" Silas asks behind me.

"Nothing," I say over my shoulder.

I rip open Moretti's office door and stalk over to the mafia don. The men around him back away, their hands twitching to the guns at their waists. Moretti himself leans back in his chair with a smug smile plastered on his face.

It's only when I lean down, my hands on his arm rests and my bloody face inches from his, that fear strikes through his eyes.

"Consider this my formal retirement from the Pits," I say, pausing to sneer down at his pristine suit. "Nod so I know you understand."

He nods.

I step back, and the tension visibly rushes from his body, slumping back in the chair.

"You're also going to gift me half of tonight's profits for this little *miscommunication,*" I demand. I spit a globe of bloody saliva at his feet, and one of his men gasps. "You know who to reach out to. Get it done by next week."

Then I turn my back on them and hold out my hand for Silas.

"Let's go."

Silas disappears as soon as I step into my office, without a word. I stare at the empty spot where the smoke-like shadows curl.

"Okay, goodbye, I guess," I scoff.

I shuffle to the chaise and groan as I sit, uncaring if I get blood on it. I can always buy a new one. Closing my eyes, I take a breath.

"Fuck, I could use a cigarette."

My bones ache too much to move, so here I will sit until my magic can stitch me up to functioning. Not long passes before the air shifts with magic. I crack one eye open to find Silas swiping papers aside and dropping a medical kit on my desk. The tin clanks as he unclasps the lid and lets it fall to the wood.

"Why are you always ruining my perfectly organized desk?"

"This is only the second time I've been here, Nora," he says, his tone strained. *Why does he sound worried?*

"And both times you have made a mess of my desk."

Silas glares at me. And then, with a straight face and his gaze unwavering from mine, takes the kit and turns it over, spilling its entire contents onto my desk.

"Really?" I deadpan.

His lips twitch into a smirk as he plucks a wad of gauze and a bottle of saline solution from the pile.

"I don't need you to play nurse," I say.

Silas ignores me, dabbing the gauze with saline as he approaches. He stops before the chaise and instead of sitting next to me, or better yet, on the coffee table in front of me, he kneels on the ground. Not a crouch, or one of those squats where your ass doesn't touch the floor. He kneels.

Silas reaches for my arm, and I bat it away.

He regards me with annoyance and tries to reach for me again. I double down and smack the offending hand.

"Stop being a brat," Silas growls.

"Stop presuming I need your help. Go home." When he doesn't move at my command—*because why would the Unseelie King ever listen to me?*—I let loose a sigh. "They'll be gone by tomorrow. I only need a shower and some time." I pause, pursing my lips. "And a cigarette."

"You can heal too?" Silas asks, sitting back on his heels. "Have you been keeping secrets?"

"Not exactly," I say. His dark eyes narrow on me. "My body simply recovers faster than others. It's not something I can control. Don't go thinking this is some new piece of my magic you can research."

"I see." He stares at the cut on my arm. "Can I please clean you up now?"

"Silas, *go home*." My head tilts to the ceiling as I sigh.

"I won't tell anyone you let me," he says, voice full of amusement.

"You're a persistent bastard."

He hums. "Yes, but it's only because I care for you."

My gaze whips to his, except he's still staring at my wounds, not my face.

"Humor me. Please?" His expression is one of unconcealed concern. The weight of it puts a confounding pressure on my chest. All my fight is crushed beneath it.

Would it be so bad if I let him do this? Just this once?

"Fine," I grit out between clenched teeth.

I turn my head to the window—where the lamp's glow reflects against the glass.

The saline bottle sloshes, and I flinch when gentle fingers cradle my wrist. His skin is warm—either he runs hot, or I've lost too much blood. Sterile gauze hits my forearm, and I stifle a wince. He swipes over the sensitive skin, wiping away the dried and excess blood, before reapplying a bandage with firmer pressure.

His calloused touch is methodical as he tapes over the bandage; the graze of his thumb over my pulse makes me jolt. It reminds me of how I'd brush my thumb over Imogen's cheek.

It's too intimate.

"Do I make you that uncomfortable?" Silas asks. His tone is soft, and there's a vulnerability to his question that makes me squirm.

"No, it's—" A swell of *something* catches in my throat.

Is it his touch, specifically, that I'm avoiding?

No. I've always been like this. Touch has always been complicated. Ever since my magic came in, it wasn't something freely given to me. I learned to live without it. Learned to hate it. Touch equated to pain and death. Touch meant fear.

But then, things changed.

One day, touch started to mean trust. Suddenly, it became a marker of who was getting too close, too comfortable.

I got too comfortable.

Imogen got too comfortable.

Silas is getting too comfortable.

"It's everyone?" Silas asks, though he doesn't wait for a response. "I get it. The touch thing. It's part of why I don't tell anyone about my magic. It would complicate matters. But I don't have to explain that to you."

He lets go of my arm, and I know this is the moment I should tell him to leave. But my jaw is soldered shut, and my eyes follow suit as his nimble fingers grip my chin. Silas turns my face, and the wet gauze slides over the slash on my cheek.

"I enjoy touch, though. It feels good. And I don't mean in a sexual way either." He huffs a laugh. "But to have a friend hold and hug you? Especially when you're struggling and don't want to admit it? To care for you in that way?" He clicks his tongue. "I have a feeling you never let anyone take care of you." Silas pauses, and I'm frozen too, as his warm breath spreads over my forming bruises. "Did you... did you ever let Imogen?"

My eyes snap open, and I'm caught in Silas's dark stare. Suddenly, we're back to that night at Bramble, when we lay in the snow. When he saw right through my flesh to my soul. Except now, he's not only seeing it, but ripping it out of my chest and forcing *me* to look at it.

His pupils dilate and that small action sets me off.

Too close—he is too close.

With a burst of fury, and with all the strength I can muster, I shove Silas back. He crashes into the coffee table, bloody gauze flying from his grip. The saline bottle topples over and spills onto the rug.

"Get the fuck out," I say, pointing to the door.

Silas chuckles, pushing up on his hands. "Okay, fair. Too fresh a topic. I'm almost finished though, so—"

"No, we're done here," I snap. "You're so fucking nosy, it's nauseating. I didn't ask you for a therapy session. I don't need it. And I don't want it. I can also handle cleaning my wounds by myself, like I always have." Again, the masochistic bastard doesn't move. "*Gods*, I can't tell if you're truly that stubborn or if you can't take a hint. Well, let me be clear as a fucking summer sky, Silas. *Leave. Now.*"

Silas takes his time rising to his full height, and once he's standing, he stares down at me with an expression of disappointment. His sigh is drawn out and solemn.

"If you keep sprinting down this path, you will end up alone," he says. "Everyone has their limit on how many times they can be pushed away before they stop trying to meet you in the middle. Even your closest friends. Not everyone will realize it comes from a place of hurt."

Silas bends down to pick up the dropped gauze and empty bottle. He tosses them into the trash bin before he shoots me a sad smile. It's one of commiserative melancholy.

"You're lucky I can see right through all those pretty lies you like to tell yourself."

He disappears, and I'm left with only his words for company.

He speaks as if he understands firsthand why I do the things I do. But how can he relate to *this*? How can anyone truly understand my rage, my fears, my hopes, my sins?

21

IMOGEN

Glass shatters and the acrid scent of smoke hits my nose. I jolt up in bed, turning to wake Nora, but she's already ripping off the covers and rushing from the bedroom. The world is heavy and hazy around me, and my legs are unsteady as I tumble from the bed.

Nora's heavy footsteps pound against the creaky stairs that lead to the back of the Den. Her open button-down flutters behind her as she glides forth, a black silhouette amid an eerie red glow.

The smell of smoke is stronger here; the crash of glass shattering and ruthless laughter is louder too.

Nora curses as she enters the main part of the bar. I freeze behind her, my heart sinking to my feet.

Flames lick over the counter and up the bar, drinking up spilled and splashed liquor. The windows by the front booths are smashed in, frigid winter air whistling past the jagged frames of glass. My vision shrinks to a pinpoint, the edges blurring as my breath catches in my chest. There's shouting, but the sounds garble together, slow and strange in my ears. I can't make out the specifics, but I'm certain that the exchange is filled with vitriol.

I'm frozen. Stuck. Unable to act as I watch Nora through the haze.

She points her weapon.

More shouting.

I flinch—three gunshots echo through my home.

My body shakes as I hyperventilate; I will my arm to brace against the wall to steady myself. The gritty texture of brick catches on my nails and makes the hair on my arm stand on end.

Suddenly, Nora's standing in front of me, touching my face —cradling my cheek with one hand.

"Imogen."

I blink.

"*Imogen*," she repeats my name firmly.

I stagger forward, slipping from her grip.

The bodies come into focus. No longer specters of the night, they stare blankly up at the ceiling. Black cotton darkens at their chest, sticking to their skin in wet wrinkles.

"You killed them," I say.

"... yes."

My gaze trails over Nora. Lipstick stains linger on her pale skin, on show for the world. But my claim on her is contested, and specks of blood drip over the marks from my lips. Violence has claimed her in the same way I have.

How have I never noticed it before?

My gaze drops to the gun still drawn in her hand.

The gun I bought. The gun I gave her.

How much blood is on my hands by proxy?

My heart races. The world narrows again, and the air turns thin in my lungs.

"They needed to die, Imogen," Nora says sternly. "I did this to protect you."

Nora takes a step forward, and I take a step back.

"I don't want to be protected if it means all of this." I fling my arms out at the broken glass and ash-covered bar. "This is insane!" I squeeze my eyes shut and try to breathe. My hands cover my face in a feeble attempt to stop myself from falling. But the damn has broken, and my conflicted mind spills forth. "I want to run. And then sometimes I want to stay. But really, I want to go back to September. I want to go back to normal. Why can't you all be fucking *normal*?"

"You need to accept that isn't how the world works."

Frustration rips my hands from my face. "It was easier to accept when it wasn't shoved in my fucking face!"

Quiet, a volatile kind, falls upon us.

Shit.

She rubs a hand over her cheek and chin and laughs. Except it's a painful, stabbing chuckle of disbelief.

"I'm sorry," I say, quickly.

Why does this feel so familiar?

"I thought you loved me," Nora says.

"I do," I say. The rush of regret turns my stomach. "But you're scaring me right now. You're acting different. You—you aren't like *this*—"

Nora shakes her head, then glances over her shoulder; red flashing lights curl around her visage, blurring my vision.

"I haven't changed, Mo. You're only seeing me for the first time." Nora's dark silhouette raises one arm, and the gun is pointed at me. "You said you wanted all of me. You *lied*."

"What? No. I didn't lie. Why would I—"

The gunshot rings out, and I scream awake; there are warm hands on me, and murmured whispers of comfort hitting my ears, but I can't hear them. I scramble backwards in the bed until my shoulders hit the headboard, and my head falls to my knees. My fingers dig into the silk of my pajama top, clutching to my side where pain blooms.

I know the pain isn't real. There's no wound in my side—at least, not anymore.

But I'm choking. I can't breathe. There's a wheezing sound coming out of my mouth. But no air flows in to replace it. My heart pounds in my ears. Fast. So fucking fast. It's going to explode.

"Mo, I need you to breathe. Do it with me, okay? In... Out..." Josie's murmurs and exaggerated breathing finally registers, as do her thumbs rubbing across my shoulders. I hiccup, trying to match her rhythm. "It was only a nightmare. Okay? You're safe. Breathe with me again. In... Out..."

"It was so real," I whimper between staggered breaths. There are no tears streaming down my cheeks, but the same emotional drain that comes from crying hits me. The hollow-ness. I curl in on myself tighter, and my fingers lace into my hair. "It was too real."

Her gentle hand finds my back, rubbing small circles. There's a tingle of magic, *her magic*, sending calming waves through me. It helps. But only a little.

I suck in another stuttering breath.

"Tell me about it," Josie says.

"No. I can't," I say.

There's a pause, and then the bed dips closer to me. Josie puts her arm around me, drawing me into a side hug.

"My mom used to tell me that talking about your night-mares gave them less power over you," she whispers.

"Yeah?"

"Mhm."

My head tilts, and I peek at Josie through the crack between my knee and my arm. Her hair is askew, pieces of her bob sticking out to the side. And her pajamas—a men's striped cotton set—are crinkled.

"It was about her," I manage to rasp out.

"Nora?" she asks, brows knitting together.

"Yeah," I say, swallowing the lump in my throat. "It wasn't real, but it could have been. We were at my apartment, and someone broke in. And there was a fire. And... and she killed them." Josie doesn't interrupt as my heavy tongue finds the shape of my words. "She used the gun I gave her. *Gods*, I was so fucking stupid for letting Wes convince me that was a good present." My lids screw shut, and angry splotches of color form behind them. "And I—I was scared of her? I'm never scared of her, Joze. And then she called me a liar." I sigh. "Which I am."

"Why are you a liar?" Josie asks calmly.

"Because I said I wanted her as she is. And now I am second guessing that. Maybe it was a lie. If it was, it wasn't an intentional one. I—I wouldn't lie about loving her," I whisper. "But it hurts to accept that I... can't handle that kind of love. It doesn't serve me as it once did." My breath warms the small pocket of air trapped between my curled-up body. "I know, logically, that you all have to do things you don't *want* to do. I get that. But Nora—that's how she *shows* she cares. I don't want someone to kill for me. And I don't want someone to get revenge for me. I just want them to *stay with me*."

"You speak two different love languages," Josie says softly.

I poke my head out from its makeshift cave, huffing air through my nose.

"Yeah, you could say that." It's the same realization I had that night at Bramble. "I wish it didn't bother me. I wish I could stomach it." One of my hands falls to the bed, and I mindlessly pick at the stitching on the quilt. "Violence is Nora's first love; I cannot compete with her. And I have no desire to. Not anymore."

"And that's okay," Josie says, squeezing my shoulder.

Exhaustion washes over me, but I'm terrified of falling back into another nightmare.

"Can you stay? Just for a little bit?" I ask quietly. Josie is staring off into space, deep in thought, but my question pulls her back.

"Yeah, Mo, I can stay," she says.

It isn't lost on me that at Bramble, whenever she'd accidentally fallen asleep in my bed, I never had a nightmare. Maybe she's my lucky charm, quieting my anxieties when she's near.

We curl under the covers, facing each other. We don't talk, but Josie reaches a hand out. I rest mine on hers, and the connection grounds me. She yawns, big and dramatic, and I snort.

"Shut up," she says. "I'm not usually awake at 2:00 a.m."

"Sorry," I yawn back, much to her chagrin.

"You don't need to apologize. I'll always be here if you need me."

"Same," I promise, and she smiles.

Josie's got such a sweet smile.

Eventually, my lids fall heavy, and my lashes kiss my cheeks. But before I can fall asleep, Josie whispers to me.

"Mo?"

"Yeah?" I murmur, not opening my eyes.

"You need a softer kind of love," she says. "One day you'll find it. Your happiness, and that peace you crave."

Her words hold such certainty that all I can do is believe them.

22

NORA

After expelling my rage in the Pits and allowing myself a week to wallow in a bout of self-pity, I've successfully banished all the offending emotions swirling around my brain. They now reside in tightly locked boxes, way back in the depths of my psyche, next to where my childhood memories live.

I simply do not have time to deal with any of it anymore.

I've been working tirelessly on my plan to hit Wes where it hurts and garner an advantage in the trade war that's ensued in the wake of Casimir.

Josie says the people's unease is growing. The report she dropped unceremoniously on my desk from the last family dinner was less than ideal.

I didn't go. Again. Couldn't get myself to ride the elevator down the twenty floors.

And while it seems Wes's plan is to hold out until we self-implode, I will not allow him to make such a mockery of House Pride.

Our House fights for what we want. Even if it means I have to burn it all down to save it. I'll throw myself in the fire too, if it ensures that House Pride can become a phoenix from the ashes, stronger than before.

Right now, we are not strong. And the city knows.

The air in Anwynn sits differently in my lungs. There's a charged tension between passersby, as if paranoia breathes down their necks. Sunlight casts harsher shadows. Eerie silence lurks in side alleys. Even the city's skyscrapers stand off-kilter; they loom and leer down at me from their staggering heights, inciting a deep-seated dread where they once gifted might and vivacity.

It's a strange sensation, being home but not *feeling* at home.

A sharp knock on the car window breaks my train of thought. Hattie's wide smile presses up against the glass. It fogs up, and she snickers. With a gloved finger, she paints a crude rendition of a dead stick-figure with x's over the eyes.

I roll the window down.

"You were spacing out there, Boss. You okay?" she asks.

"I'm getting real tired of people asking me that."

"Noted. I'll save my breath for more important things. Like asking you if you'll still be coming to my birthday party next week?" Hattie shoots me a pursed-lip, eyebrow-raised look of innocence as she whispers, "You know, 'cause of Mo."

"Yes, I'll be going. Just because we're not fucking anymore doesn't mean we can't be in the same room or both be there to celebrate you. We're not teenagers," I say, though it's partially a lie. I haven't seen Imogen since Bramble, and I'm unsure how she'll react to me. Nervous, even, to find out.

"Mm-kay," Hattie titters, like she doesn't believe me.

I roll my eyes. "Get in the fucking car."

Hattie skips to the back seat, revealing an awkwardly stiff Josie standing a few feet back. I've only seen her in passing at work since she left to stay at Imogen's. And while it hurts to know they all get to go to Imogen's cabin and enjoy time with her, it's better that I stay away.

I trust them to keep her safe while I ensure *they* are safe.

I've always been the one to make the hard decisions; Josie is too concerned with keeping the peace. It's part of the reason we've always worked well as a team.

"Get in the car, Joze," I huff.

Her shoulders sag as she trudges over to the passenger side. She drops onto the leather seat and proceeds to stare at me with a frown.

"Are you still being an ornery bitch?" Josie asks.

"Are you still refusing to do what I asked?" My scars ache on cue, and I try to ignore the sensation.

"Yes," she says.

"Then my answer is also yes," I say stubbornly.

Unbelieving laughter hisses from between her teeth. "Alrighty then."

"Ugh, are you guys fighting too?" Hattie says, poking her head between us from the back.

"No," Josie says.

"Yes," I say at the same time.

I shift the car into gear, and Hattie cackles. The edges of my eyes crinkle at the sound, and in my periphery I notice Josie's do too. There's something nostalgic about the three of us setting off to wreak havoc at midnight together.

"Let's go take back our shit!" Hattie whoops as we roll into the night.

Tonight, we raid our own warehouses.

Tonight, I take back what's mine.

Then tomorrow, I seize my legacy.

I grunt as I lug the unconscious man by his feet across the floor. I'm deep in the back shelves of the tenth street ware-house, up on the second level. We'd easily forget about him back here. And the last thing we need is a forgotten body somewhere, only to come back in a week to discover the resulting rot.

I'm strong, but Artie—if I remember his name correctly—is a thick bastard, so I'm breaking a sweat by the time I drag him to the stairs.

The mustard gas I'd procured from Moretti did its job splendidly. We simply threw it into the warehouse, let it smoke up, and then popped in with our masks and gloves to clean up once the thick of it cleared. What's a few broken windows when the alternative is the fall of our House?

I kick his body off the top stair, and it flops down the metal rungs, ringing out a series of wince-worthy clanks before thud-ding to a stop at the midway landing.

Anyone Wes had stationed inside the warehouse had fallen prey to the gas. They either passed out from the chemicals or the pain. I hope for the latter. They had to suffer for their choices, after all.

"You need help?" Frank shouts from below, though it's muted behind his mask. He eyes the unconscious man, who's twisted like a pretzel on the awning.

"You couldn't have showed up five minutes ago?" I huff,

hands falling to my hips. "Help me get him to the others. Then we're going to have a nice chat."

"Got it, Boss."

I hop down the rest of the stairs, pulling my watch from my back pocket. It's coming up on two hours from when we arrived, which sets us right on track for the rest of the night. This is our largest warehouse fae-side, and we expected it to have the most guards.

Clicking the watch shut and shoving it back into my pocket, I round the corner to where we've deposited all the traitors. They sit, slumped against the bare brick wall, hands tied behind their backs. Chester, Louis, and Roy dump two more in the lineup, while Hattie and Josie watch on from the sidelines with their cold business faces. Josie catches my approach and stomps over to me before I can reach the group.

"You didn't say the gas would also burn them," Josie harshly whispers into my ear. One of the guards caught the brunt of it, with patches of his exposed skin blistered and bubbling, and his eyes red and puffed shut. "I know they need to be punished, but they're still our people."

"It's mustard gas, Josie. I don't know what you expected," I whisper back, shoving past her. "They're lucky I asked for the weaker shit."

"You said it was *chloroform*," she growls. "Those are two very different things."

I brush her off and turn back to the traitors. "Who has the salts?"

Chester digs into his pack and pulls a pack of smelling salts out. He waves them under each of the guard's noses.

"Alright, gentlemen. Remember me?" Some struggle against their restraints, while others moan their pain as they wake. I clap my hands in front of their faces. "I'm going to need you to push through whatever you're feeling right now and pay attention, because I'm only going to say this once. Got it?"

I pull out my gun—it's the one Imogen gifted me, and my gloved thumb runs over the engraving. It makes my heart ache, but it's the only piece of her I can keep, so I cling to it.

"You lot are traitors. And we all know what happens to traitors, right?" I drawl, noting how a few throats bob in fear. "I don't enjoy killing folk from my House. But when you try to take something that isn't yours, there are consequences. Now, I had hoped you all would have picked the right side, but I understand that learning about my past might have scared you. So, I'm going to give you a second chance. How wonderful is that?"

"Nora..." I hear Josie mutter a cautious warning behind me.

"This needs to happen," I snap over my shoulder. She huffs, crossing her arms, knowing better than to continue to question me in front of everyone. "You all have one chance to denounce this little coup and join back up with me. Either you do that—no harm, no foul, all is forgiven—and one of these fine gentlemen will take you to the hospital to deal with those nasty burns. Or you die. Who's first?"

One of the guards sneers at me—that Artie fellow—and decides to spit his distaste at my feet. "I'd rather die than serve some Seelie scum."

I release a slow breath.

"Unfortunate choice," I mutter. I raise my gun and shoot; his brains splatter onto the wall. "Who's next?"

"What the hell! You killed Artie," one of the traitors yells. "You can't do that!"

"Yes, I can. And I'll kill you too," I say, getting up in his face. He tries to shrink back against the wall but can't. "Ball is in your court, darling. Make your choice."

"Fuck you!" he says.

My gun goes off three more times. The others make smarter choices.

"Get the rest to the hospital," I say to Frank, who nods and sets off on his task. The other men I enlisted for this plan fall in line with him. Hattie and Josie follow me out of the warehouse while they work.

I rip off my mask, shaking out my hair and sucking in the fresh night air. My back stiffens when Josie's judgment hits my back. It's a sharp knife poking between my ribs.

I turn slowly, notching my mask between my forearm and my hip. "Say what you need to. We still have two more warehouses to hit tonight."

Josie rips her own mask off. "That was cruel. I know we have to handle this with a firm hand but—"

"I offered them a choice. That's more mercy than I was ever given in my life," I say plainly. "Don't pretend to be a saint here. If you truly didn't think it was the right thing, you should have stopped me. You didn't."

Her face shutters. "You're right, I didn't." She steps closer, lowering her voice as if to level with me. "I only feel a bit blind-sided by this—you didn't say we were culling the ranks. I thought we were commandeering the buildings and throwing the guards into some storeroom until we eliminate the one whispering in their ears. You've always led with an iron fist, and you've always been bloodthirsty, but this is overkill. Once Wes is gone, they'll come back to us."

"Josie..." I sigh, tossing my mask to the ground. I grab her shoulders and give her a slight shake. "You are usually the logical one—what's gotten into you? They won't come back to me willingly. I need to force them."

Her brown eyes flash with concern, and a dreadful, torturous idea crosses my mind—one I want to ignore but can't.

I'm not throwing myself in the fire. I *am* the fire.

And if I'm the fire, who will be the phoenix?

I drop my hands, and they leave bloody prints on her periwinkle blouse. Funny how in a world of grays, she's always wearing color. Just like Mo.

"This is what they need, okay? Trust me."

23
JOSIE

Leo leads me through a maze of hazy hallways. We're headed to the very back of Envy and Greed's gambling den, where the upper echelon of Anwynn host their private games. These rooms promise no interruptions for guests and no liability for the owners, all thanks to the iron discretely hidden in the walls.

"You sure do know your way around here," I mumble. Leo's steps haven't faltered once as he's led me to our destination.

"I've spent a lot of time here lately," Leo says, tone overly cheerful, but I can hear the sarcasm hidden in each word. "It's been amazing for my wallet."

I snort, and my nerves ease by a minuscule amount. Leo's been building up a relationship with the two Sins—Envy and Greed—all in anticipation of tonight.

It's a carefully cultivated plan, one that we planted the seeds of in the days immediately after Casimir. Despite the unknowns of Nora's whereabouts and doubts surrounding her return, Wes was always going to be an issue. Having an insider's eyes in our enemy's camp was going to be important, regardless.

My fists tighten and my fingernails dig into my palms; I had thought this plan was our chance to remove Wes with minimal bloodshed within House Pride. But Nora has decided that *maximum* bloodshed is to occur anyway. As was proven last night, when she culled our ranks with ruthless precision.

I could have stopped her, but at the same time, I couldn't.

I've never considered myself an insecure person. But there are moments where I second guess what the right decision is. It freezes me, and then I'm unable to make *any* decision. It's part of why Nora and I always worked as a team—I did the research, weighed the options, sorted the details... and she pulled the trigger.

But her killing those guards wasn't necessary. It wasn't a joint effort. She steamrolled her way through and left me and Hattie to clean up her mess.

I can't help but worry about the path she's set on. It reeks of self-destruction. And she won't listen when I try to point it out.

Leo stops outside a plain green door that stands alone at the end of the hall. The golden placard tacked to its frame hosts a gleaming *one* on it.

My eyes meet Leo's and he tilts his head in question. My magic tingles.

You good? he asks in his head.

I nod firmly. He takes a second to study me, then releases a slow breath through his nose—not quite a sigh, but close enough to one. He opens the door, and we enter.

Here we go, I think, shooting a small prayer to the gods. *Please do not fuck this up.*

But Leo can't hear my thoughts or prayers. No one can. My mind is blissfully my own.

The door slams behind me, an echoing boom of hollow metal, and we are ushered into seats by staff—one of which is his spy. Leo has worked swiftly to reestablish the network of informants House Lust was once known for.

The spies were always there, but merely inactive under Imogen's reign. I don't fault her for letting them fade into the background. She had other things to focus on after her family died.

Leo hugs Envy and Greed, and I cringe as their hands smack his back. They already stink of alcohol and cigars, but their eyes are alert as they swing over Leo's shoulder to me.

Greed's, more so than Envy's, are like a hawk's, not only tracking my muscles' every twitch but considering what opportunities my presence offers. He sits back in his seat, full lips puckering around his cigar. Smoke puffs between his cheeks.

Will the observant Royal-turned-Sin see past my acting skills? And if he does, will he intervene? Only Luck knows.

"Well, well, well..." Envy drawls, all cocky as he slinks out of Leo's hold and towards me. He looks me up and down, and I rein in my disgust, keeping my face a blank slate of boredom. "Did little miss mind reader finally read the room and realize she was on the wrong side of things?"

"You could certainly *say* that," I mutter.

"Loosen up," Envy croons, throwing his arm around my shoulders and shaking me.

If he were some guy in a bar, he'd already be keeled over, clutching his gut from where I punched him. But I need Envy comfortable. And I need him to think he's in charge. So I grit my teeth.

He tucks his head to meet my gaze. A strand of his long black hair falls in his line of sight, and he blows a puff of air to dislodge it from his brow.

"Nora's not good people. Greed and I?" Envy pauses. "We saw that a long time ago. It's about time the rest of you wised up and did too." He snaps his fingers. "Hey, will you help us get Gluttony on board for—"

"Envy," Leo warns. "Give her some space."

Envy's arm detaches from my shoulders, and he raises both hands in the air placatingly. "I'm just making conversation, Lust. Don't bite my head off."

It is an entire hour before our target arrives.

My fingers tap against the poker table in quick succession as I listen to Leo, Greed, and Envy banter back and forth. Leo's in his element, embracing the guise of a charismatic and ambitious newbie seeking guidance in the world of the Sins. Envy and Greed eat it up, their egos slurping the addictive praise with gusto.

My knuckles cease their tapping the moment the door swings open and Wes walks in. He's followed by Claude.

My jaw ticks; the room falls silent.

"Fucking *finally*." Envy tilts back in his chair. "Boy-wonder, what took you so long?"

Wes's chair screeches as he pulls it back and flops into it. It's not until he pushes his disheveled red-brown hair from his eyes that he notices me—a rookie mistake. Claude's already clocked me, his body frozen halfway between the door and the table. Wes's shoulders take on a similar stiffness.

"*You*," Wes nearly growls. He glares at Envy. "What is she doing here?"

Greed waves his hand in the air, dismissing the younger man. "Settle down. She's come to grovel."

Wes's eyes narrow, skeptical, as he should be.

"I've not come to *grovel*," I correct. "However, I am here with information. And an offer to continue giving information, for the right price."

Wes puffs up, clearly comfortable in the space. But more than that, his smile is indicative of the false confidence someone inhabits when they think they have the upper hand.

"What kind of information could you possibly provide that I need?" he postures, and that smarmy grin grows. He ticks things off his finger. "I have a majority of our House on my side. I have a majority of the *city* on my side." Envy interrupts Wes with a snort, as if he thinks it's funny half the city detests Nora. "And I have half of our warehouses locked down. You'll run out of money, men, and merchandise in weeks, if not sooner. You're not sustainable."

"But didn't you hear? They aren't your warehouses anymore," I say.

His expression tightens. "Is that a threat?"

I shrug. "I'd certainly be taking it as one, considering Nora slaughtered the men guarding those commandeered warehouses last night."

Wes does his best to keep his poker face intact, but the twitch of his left eye gives him away. This is new information to him. *Good.*

It was a gamble, letting a whole day pass between Nora's assault and this meeting. Though, she did stack the odds in our favor, since she didn't leave anybody that could go blabbing to him. All the warehouse guards are either dead or in the hospital.

"Do you not check in with your men every shift change? That is standard policy." I tsk, and Wes's confidence cracks. He glances back at Claude for support, however Claude looks just as stunned.

Now? The staff's thought echoes loudly in my head.

I play with my earring, my signal for *yes.* Then I move in for the kill.

"Nora's becoming increasingly unpredictable," I say,

perching my forearms on the table and leaning forward. It's an attempt to draw Wes into believing me with my body language. Unfortunately, I don't have to lie for that last part to be convincing. "I worry that if we continue the way we are, we will cannibalize our House to the point of no—"

Glass shatters across the room, one of the staff having dropped a bottle of Envy's most expensive liquor. An accident that is not an accident.

The staff stiffen as three Sins' eyes turn their way. Envy is about to say something unsightly, but Leo's spy—one of the waiting staff—takes the lead.

"Don't stand there! Go get something to clean this up!" they command.

The other staff panic, throwing a towel over the spill to soak up the liquor and rush from the room. Our operative takes up the rear, and their hand is the last on the handle. The door creaks closed, but it doesn't shut completely. It's that crack that ultimately seals Wes's fate.

The men around me lean back in their seats. Wes and Claude are equally angry and curious, Greed takes it all in like the conniving Sin he is, and Envy is giddy at the prospect of me turning coat. Leo is the most neutral of the five, arms crossed at his chest and watchful eyes scanning our adversaries.

"You were saying, Josie?" Greed says, sipping his drink. "This is quite a development that I'm eager to hear. I knew there was ambition in you."

"Of course she's fucking ambitious—she's my Second."

The metallic click of the door's lock engaging punctuates the deafening silence that descends. The air thickens with unease, frantic anger, and a slice of fear. Greed, Envy, and Wes are frozen, eyes on Nora, who leans against the iron door as if she owns the building. Her gun dangles in her hand.

Claude, on the other hand, is flat on his back, with Hattie's blade against his throat. She whispers something to him, but I can't hear it.

Panic flares, and Wes flickers out of existence. He reappears across the room with a frustrated grunt. Then again, and again, rematerializing in different spots, only to kick the wall out of frustration.

"You can't magic yourself out of this one," Nora taunts, tapping her gun against the door. Three clangs of metal-on-metal echo in the room. "Walls are lined with iron. Handy little security measure so no one pops out before they pay up after a game. Thanks, boys."

She winks at Envy and Greed, then reaches into her pocket. She pulls out a set of iron cuffs and tosses them at Wes's feet.

"Put those on," she orders.

"Absolutely not," Wes growls.

"By all means, you're welcome to the alternative, which is to *fight me*." Nora pauses, tonguing her cheek. When Wes stays silent, she huffs. "Put them on."

Wes spits a curse at Nora, but steps forward and puts the cuffs on.

"Hattie?" Nora calls out.

Hattie, having already put a pair on Claude, appears in front of Wes and checks that they're secured; the cuffs will stop him from being able to shadow-walk. He's truly stuck now.

"Clear," Hattie chirps.

"*Bitch*," Wes seethes.

Hattie tuts. "When did you get such a foul mouth? I'm gonna rat on you to your nan."

"Greed. Envy. Out," Nora says, pulling open the door. "The free part of the show is over."

Envy, who has sat in shock this entire time, finally regains his composure. He bolts out of his seat—though he staggers due to how much liquor he's consumed. Leo did a good job of making sure his glass was always full.

He gets up in Nora's face, a pointed finger dangerously close to her nose. "This is *my* fucking building. You can't waltz in here and—"

"*Envy*," Greed cuts him off, standing. "I recommend you walk away and let this play out."

Envy glares at Greed over his shoulder, and they have a silent conversation—like two friends usually can. He acquiesces to Greed's demand, huffing and shoving past Nora. Greed follows, though much more composed.

"I don't like you, but I respect the game." Greed stops to glance down at Wes from the doorway. The smallest sliver of pity shines in his expression. "Shame she outplayed you."

Nora shuts the door again, and this time, the clang of metal sounds like the first strike of a death knell.

"I knew she was brutal, but *jeez*," Leo whispers.

There's another crack of Nora's knuckles against Wes's face, and another wince from Leo at my side.

My frown deepens. "You can leave if you can't handle it."

Nora's been torturing Wes for an hour, and we've all stood and watched. None of us were set on letting Wes go unscathed, but an hour? As a fae who can't heal like some of the Seelie we've dealt with? I hold back my wince.

I've stood on the sidelines, a detached observer for these

types of sessions before, but this one feels different. Leo is right. It *is* brutal—and eerily reminiscent of memories of Pride striking Nora that I wish to forget.

Fuck. That's why it's different.

She's acting like *him.*

"Nora," I call out in warning. "Maybe you should—"

"He almost got Imogen killed," Nora snaps. "You don't get to stop me with this, Josie."

I hold up my hands defensively and return to my place, leaning against the wall with Leo. I give him a *look* before whispering, "Are you beginning to understand what I've had to deal with for the past twenty-some-odd years?"

"I kind of get it now, yeah." Then he adds, "It's not a pretty process, is it? This torture stuff."

"I think it's beautiful," Hattie pipes up from Leo's other side. We both grimace at her, and she shakes her head as if *we're* the crazy ones. She points to Wes. "You don't think the blood-splatter is pretty?"

"You know what? Maybe it is time for Lust to head home," Leo says.

"They don't want you!" Wes screams, and all three of us in the peanut gallery freeze. It's the first time he's said anything but expletives since Nora cuffed him to the chair.

"They need me!" Nora growls.

"*No, we don't!*" Wes bites back. His face is a puffy, bloody mess, and his words are garbled between lost teeth. "It won't matter if you kill me. The trust is broken, *Elenora.*"

He spits her name, the disrespect clear. Red-tinted spittle hits her cheek. Nora's face twitches as she slowly and methodically wipes it from her face.

Something shifts within her then. My magic can sense it, is trying to figure it out, poking at her shields. Nora tilts her head to the side, piercing green eyes shooting daggers my way.

Her shield cracks, and my magic reads a cold, deadly, calm. Acceptance, too. And something darker. Anticipation isn't the right word—it's the flurry of emotion in the moment before someone jumps off a cliff.

A door slams shut between us, and I'm locked out.

Nora turns back to Wes.

"I wish I could go back and shoot my past self for thinking highly of you. For bringing you into our circle." Nora's face is a hairsbreadth away from Wes's. Her tone is deadly quiet, almost intimate. "For trusting you with *her*. It will stand as my biggest regret in life."

The room stills.

Her back straightens.

Leo jolts at my side when the shot rings out.

Wes's body slumps in the chair, with no additional fanfare. Claude cries out, though it's muffled by the makeshift gag Hattie stuffed in his mouth. Nora strides over to where he writhes against his restraints, gun aimed for his head too. I step forward to stop her—the plan wasn't to kill Claude—but I'm too late.

A second shot rings out. A second body falls limp.

"We're done here," Nora says, voice devoid of all emotion. She motions for us to come forward. "Let's go."

Leo cringes, side stepping the pool of blood forming around Claude. "Are we going to take them with us or—"

"No," Nora says. "We're leaving the bodies. They're an example."

"Oh," Leo says. His head bobbles, but it's more a tremor than a nod. "Okay."

Nora claps him on the back, leading him to the door, not giving me or Hattie a second glance. "This is your first real lesson as a Sin, Leo..."

They leave the room, and Hattie follows, but I linger in the doorway.

As I stare at the dead bodies of those we once called our brothers, I can't help but think of Imogen and how much she'd hate this.

I'm starting to think that maybe I do too.

24
IMOGEN

"Why are there a bunch of hearts everywhere?" Wrath's tentative voice echoes down the hall in Hattie's apartment.

"It's Valentine's Day, *dummy*," Hattie says. We can't see her from our position on the couch, but the apartment's acoustics carry their voices easily enough.

"But that's a human holiday."

"So? I like it. Plus, I grew up there. It's sentimental."

Wrath grunts and Silas's animated voice chimes in—which is where I tune out. Leaning my head in towards Josie, I speak out of the corner of my lips.

"On a scale of one to ten, how excited are you to watch those two flirt all night?"

"Publicly? A neutral five. I'm not getting in their business. But between you and me?" Josie's brows raise up, crinkling her forehead. Her eyes narrow to slits as she makes a face. "Probably an eight. It's like watching a cat play with a bug before they eat it, and it's surprisingly endearing. You?"

"I'm a sucker for love, Joze, what do you think?" I mutter.

Then add, "I'm gonna give it a solid ten. I need the excitement in my life. You think they'll kiss tonight?"

There's a twinge of melancholy in my question. Getting ready for this gathering gave me flashbacks of college—memories of how Nora and I skirted around each other, the longing palpable between us.

I wish for that kind of sweet yearning again.

"Honestly, I never thought we'd be speaking more than ten words at a time to the man, let alone be commenting on his love life. Yet, here we are," Josie says.

"Here we are, and you didn't answer the question," I volley back.

Josie squints again in thought. Then spares me a conspiratorial glance, brown eyes sparkling. "I think Hattie has some schemes up her sleeve that will make him blush and all of us balk."

I snort.

"You think I'm wrong?" Josie teases, bumping her shoulder into mine. The touch sends a zing up my spine.

"No, I think you are very, very right," I say, and *ope—there's that longing again, rearing its ugly head.* "Is it bad that it makes me a little sad to talk about?"

Josie's expression softens, instantly understanding why the thought of another's budding love would make me sad. "No, it's not bad. It's normal."

Silas swaggers into the room; he unceremoniously drops a present on the kitchen counter, of which the wrapping paper is crinkled and the bow set askew.

"Good to know the Unseelie King does not have domestic talents," I mutter to Josie, and she snorts, hiding her laughter behind a hand.

"Well, this isn't much of a party," Silas pouts, flicking his hand out at me and Josie. He takes a gander around the room, inspecting the few books that sit on a mostly tchotchke-filled shelf. He sighs dramatically. "It seems the responsibility, once again, falls on me to fix everything."

Silas spins, the flaps of his coat splaying wide, and claps his hands together—Josie and I share an incredulous look.

"Hattie, where are the drinks?" Silas calls out.

"Come right this way, Your Majesty," Hattie chirps, prancing her way into the living room and into the kitchen. "Mo and Leo have me fully stocked with the finest."

She runs a hand over her curls as if to subtly tame their skewed appearance. Wrath follows her, quiet and brooding, though there's a hint of pink on his cheeks.

Josie leans in close, breath splaying on my neck.

"I told you she'd have him blushing," she whispers in an indulgent rasp. My face rushes with heat.

"Should we keep count then?" I ask, ignoring the warm tingle in my cheeks.

Josie hums, leaning back with a smile. "Could be fun."

I don't know how they convinced me to play charades, but here I am, with my eyes bugging out of my head, trying to telepathically communicate with my teammates.

I hold up two fingers.

"Two words!" Leo guesses.

A shake of my head.

"Two syllables?" Leo asks.

I throw a thumbs up.

Leo leans forward on the couch, watching me with an intense expression. Meanwhile, Josie sits back, focused but not dramatic—her *MO* has been to silently calculate the whole answer rather than piece it together out loud like the others do.

I hold my hands up on top of my head and hop up and down.

"Jumping?" Aisha, Hattie's friend and colleague from House Pride, guesses.

I shake my head.

"Bunny?" Aisha says, sitting up straight. She points one brown finger my way. "No—Rabbit?"

I wriggle my hand in the air, signaling *kind of*. My word is carrot. I never thought such a stupid word would be so damn hard to guess. I pretend to hold one up to my mouth and crunch down—which I think only confuses them.

"Chewing?" I shake my head. Leo frowns. "Mo, you're shit at this."

I pretend to nibble and hop again like a bunny. My gaze darts to the little hourglass we flipped for my turn, the sand perilously close to running out.

"Oh! I got it!" Josie pops up. "Carrot!"

"Yes!" I squeal, raising my arms and jumping. "We win!"

Leo flips the card over on the table to show that Josie's guess was correct.

He laughs. "Josie, our savior!"

The four of us collide in a fit of celebration—giggles burst from my chest alongside the spark of my magic. It perks, tentatively feeding off the energy in the room. Josie hugs me around the waist, strong arms lifting me in the air and spinning. My stomach swoops at her warm body pressed against mine.

My lips twitch up, and I feel... *holy shit, I feel good.*

A swell of emotion hits me hard and fast, stuttering my

breath as Leo joins in on the crushing bear hug. I breathe through it, pushing back against the increased beating of my heart.

"You two make a good team. I call being with you next time we play," Leo says, squeezing Josie and me around the shoulders. He lets us go and turns to the others, sticking out his tongue with a mocking noise. "We win. Suck it, losers."

"It's not fair! Josie can literally read minds," Hattie says, though there's a glint of mischief in her eyes. "She was cheating."

"I was *not*," Josie balks as if Hattie's hurled the biggest insult her way. My feet touch the floor again, and she releases my waist. "I do not cheat. I have more integrity than that. Cross my heart and hope to fade."

"Is she lying?" Hattie squints at Silas.

Silas leans back in the armchair he's claimed for his own and shrugs, lips pursed and staving off a smirk. Dramatic *ooos* ring out around the room.

"Silas!" Josie huffs, offended. She stares him down, daring him to disagree with Hattie's claim. But when he stays quiet, she marches over to him and smacks his shoulder.

"*Ouch.*"

"I barely touched you," Josie says.

"So? You don't smack the *king*," Silas balks.

"Tell them I'm not lying," Josie says.

He makes a big show of miming zipping his lips and throwing an invisible key away.

What a sore loser, I think, watching the scene play out with fond wonder. I step back, becoming one of the flowers etched into the wallpaper.

Josie lets out a frustrated growl, and her warm, tan neck flushes a rosy red.

"Useless," she mutters, flopping onto the couch. "What good are his abilities if he won't use them *for good?*"

"I'm afraid good is a subjective term, considering he's not on your team," Earl points out.

"We were clearly at a disadvantage," Silas says. "You four have known each other much longer than Wrath and I have known Hattie or Earl."

"We didn't pick the teams. Hattie did," Josie says. "Complain to her."

"Those two have been buddies for fifty freaking years." Leo jabs a finger at Silas and Wrath. "There's no excuse for why they couldn't get their shit together. Wrath lost every one of his rounds." He gathers the charades cards and rights them against the table with a few taps. "And just because it's your birthday doesn't mean we're going to go easy on you, Hattie. Step it up."

"That's rude," Hattie declares, her hand pulled to her chest dramatically. Then a wide, manic smile dances onto her lips. Her crystal-blue eyes glint with evil intentions. "I think it's time for a new game. And another drink."

The friendly bickering continues as the others gather in the kitchen. A strange sensation overtakes me as I watch them, an echo of something familiar and fleeting. My body is light, my insides floating and weightless; did Hattie put something extra in my drink to make me so loose and open? So free? Or is it seeing all my friends here in one place, without the rest of the world looming over us?

I catch Josie's arm as she passes by.

"I'm going to go to the bathroom," I murmur. "Be right back."

"Okay," she says. "I'll get you a new drink before they use up all the good stuff."

The apartment blurs around me as I slip into the bathroom. The soft click of the latch closing behind me triggers a rush of emotion to the base of my jaw, where it connects to my neck. A raw, piercing sadness hit me there, pushing past the numb that has swallowed me since Casimir.

I stumble to the sink as the tears fall; my hands grip the cold, white porcelain as my head hangs over the basin. It cradles my tears as they drip down, splattering against the brass drain.

What the fuck is happening to me? I think between sobs. *I thought I'd run dry of tears.*

The door bursts open, and I yelp, jumping back as Earl freezes in the threshold.

"Oh—sorry—" He stumbles, scrambling for the knob. "I knocked twice, but no one answered—"

"Shit—I'm sorry—I'm decent. Give me a minute to freshen up," I rush, swiping at my face. My palms come away wet, and I quickly grab the hand towel from its rung on the wall.

"All good, I shouldn't have barged in," Earl says. I watch as he goes to pull the door closed, then stops. He doesn't meet my eye when he asks, quiet and hesitant, "Want me to go get Leo?"

I shake my head and repeat, "I just need a minute."

He nods awkwardly, giving me a thumbs up. Earl's been a part of our extended friend group since college, but this is definitely the first time he's seen me cry.

When the latch clicks shut, I turn to the mirror and cringe. My eyes are red-rimmed, and my makeup is smudged. Not terribly so, but enough that I pull a few squares of toilet paper and dab at my under-eyes for damage control. Ruddy splotches bloom on my cheeks, but there's nothing I can do about that except try to pass it off as an alcohol flush.

I groan, biting back a second stream of tears.

Get it together, Mo. You're verging on pathetic here.

There's a knock on the door, the slow squeak of the hinges,

and then Josie's round face appears in the mirror over my shoulder.

"Oh, Mo," she sighs.

I toss the mascara-stained toilet paper into the trash bin and blurt out, "I'm sorry. I don't know why it's all hitting me right now."

Josie's hands find my shoulders, squeezing, and then she pulls me into a hug. Her arms band around me, cradling me with warmth. One hand presses into my lower back while the other finds the base of my skull, her thumb massaging the joint there. My face finds the crook of her neck, and I hide there, safely tucked away.

"I think you may be coming out of fight-or-flight mode finally," she murmurs into my hair.

"I haven't cried since—"

"I know. You've been surprisingly composed, even when you have your *moments*," she says. My nightmares, she means. And the panic attacks.

A beat passes where we only breathe. I close my eyes and shudder. Remembering how she had me match her breath the other night. I try to match hers now. Slowly, the overwhelm drains away.

"It's strange, feeling *good* again." My throat cracks over the words, and I blink away a final tear that manages to escape. It falls onto Josie's blouse, soaking into the silk. "Then it all crashed back down as soon as I felt myself smiling. Why do I feel *guilty*?"

Josie's hands are firm as they glide to my shoulders and push me back. Her forehead drops to mine. Concern is woven in the crinkle between her brows. There's agony, too, one that's planted in her deep brown irises. It's the color of the earth mourning her fall harvest.

Her lithe fingers wipe the fresh tear tracks from my cheek.

"I like seeing you smile," she says. She leaves her hand on the flesh of my jaw, and my lips part, my neck growing hot at the firm touch. "Healing is hard. But it doesn't have to be hard *all the time*. Don't ever feel guilty about embracing the joy. In fact, I want you to seize it."

I snap my mouth shut and nod; I sniffle and swipe at my nose. I don't want to cry again, even if the tears welling up are thankful ones.

Josie's thumb swipes over my cheek again, as if it's discovering the softness there for the first time. Her gaze scans me, then falls to my lips.

The buzzing of the light above the mirror drowns out the loud sounds of the party beyond the bathroom door. And while they are why I came tonight, I find myself wanting to stay right here, in this tiny powder room, with her.

"Thanks, Josie," I whisper.

Josie's eyes flick back to meet mine and shock fills them. She steps back, quickly releasing her grip on me. She clears her throat as embarrassment tints her cheeks.

"Of course. Anytime." Josie fumbles for the door handle and yanks it open. "I still need to get your drink. I'll be right back."

A laugh bubbles in my throat, as I grab another wad of toilet paper to fix my face. But I don't smother it, nor the smile that cuts across my cheeks.

25
NORA

Hattie all but tackles me when she opens her apartment door. Her little body crashes into me, strong arms wrapping around my neck in a tight hug.

"You're here!" she squeals.

"Happy birthday." I awkwardly pat her back and ignore the immediate squirming under my skin. While Hattie's never shied away from touching me, she's never hugged me so enthusiastically before.

"I'm glad you made it! Even though you're late," Hattie says, pulling back. Her pale cheeks are pink, and her smile is wide. "Come on, we were about to start a new game." She drags me into her cramped living room. "Guys! Nora's here and needs a drink!"

There are a few *heys* and waves, but otherwise, no one gets up to greet me, all too deep in their own conversations.

"Nora needs a drink," Hattie repeats, waving her hands in the air as if she can magic people into doing her bidding.

"I'll help myself," I say, already moving to the kitchen. I've been here once before, and I generally remember where every-thing is.

"I got it, Hats," Imogen says, hopping up from the couch.

I falter as I step through the arched threshold and onto the kitchen tile. This is the first time I've seen Imogen since that night. This is the moment of truth.

Will she yell? Scream? Sneer at me under her breath? Curse me for forcing her hand—for pushing us down the path that would keep her safest?

"You don't have to," I say quickly.

"I want to," Imogen says, squeezing by me. She glances up at me, a glint of melancholic hope in the facets of her golden eyes.

I clear my throat, and she nervously tucks a strand of hair behind her ear as she moves into the kitchen. I follow, but it's tight in here too. A true city apartment, it has little-to-no counter space and appliances that can't be opened at the same time without banging into each other.

"What would you like?" Imogen takes stock of the mixers left scattered across the counter. Some are even plopped on top of the stove to make space for the cups. "Hattie only has gin left, so your options are a shot or..." She clicks her tongue. "A Rickey, a Bee's Knees, or a Southside."

Imogen peers up at me again through lowered golden lashes, her rosy cheeks deepening. Nerves and alcohol have always been a fascinating combination on her, and I have to hold back the urge to trace over the blush.

I don't get to do that anymore.

"I'll have a Rickey," I say, turning my head to look through the hole in the wall that connects to the living room.

Leo animatedly explains whatever new game they're getting ready to play while pouring the remains of people's drinks into a single cup. He places it at the center of the coffee table. There's no doubt he's attempting to convince them to have a bitch-cup for whoever he deems the loser. I bite back a gag; that won't end well for anyone.

Imogen shifts beside me, and her hip bumps into mine as she shuffles around the ingredients for my drink.

I usually enjoy taking up space, but now, I press myself against the counter's edge in an attempt to put some distance between us. She's too close, her body heat mingling with mine in this stupidly small kitchen.

"How have you been?" I ask, my voice full of nervous formality.

Her expression twists as her attention flits between me and my drink.

"I've been… fine," Imogen says.

"That's good."

I hold my breath as Imogen reaches across me to toss a used shot glass into the sink. It clanks against the other glasses before plopping into a pot soaking with water. My lungs burn by the time she pulls away.

I knew I missed her, but I didn't expect it to be so… torturous to see her again.

The air between us thickens with tension, and my hands grow restless. I cross them over my chest, locking them under my arms.

"How are *you*?" Imogen asks, stirring the contents of my drink.

"I'm… also fine."

"That's good."

"Yeah."

An awkward breath passes before she offers me my drink. I take it from her grasp, careful not to touch her.

Because I can't. It would ruin me.

Let the last time I touched her be the kiss we shared at

Bramble. It's a fine enough memory to put in a frame and keep on the shelf of *what ifs*.

I take a sip; the drink is perfectly balanced, of course, between the gin, lime juice, and seltzer.

Imogen matches my stance, leaning against the other side of the galley kitchen.

"Nora?"

"Yeah?"

"Are we okay?" Imogen asks in a worried whisper. Her amber eyes have darkened, a complicated sheen glazing over them; understandably, it's a complicated question.

Strangely, there's a second where relief washes over me at her hint of acceptance. The fact that she is asking that question confirms as much, right?

Right?

My gut disagrees. Because while I want the answer to be yes, for everything to be fine and dandy between us, I know the answer is no.

My throat bobs—but how do I say no? How do I tell her I miss her? That I wish I could change our circumstances; that I lied before, and I'm not fine; that I hate the way everyone's been looking at me lately, with a mix of trepidation and pity; that I want to claw the wings from my back, but cannot bear to let them out to do so?

I can't say any of that. It would sound too much like regret. And I'm too far down this path for regret.

I nod stiffly. "Of course, we're okay, Mo."

Imogen breathes a sigh of relief. "Okay, good."

"Good."

A beat passes between us; I let her lead where we go next.

"I've missed you," she says, fingers twisting into the silken panels of her skirt.

"Yeah?" I tease, though my chest tightens doing so.

Imogen's brows knit, and then she huffs a laugh. "Does that mean you haven't missed me?"

"No," I say defensively. "I'll always miss you," I whisper, a bit of pain leaking into my tone. "But I stand by what I said that night, Imogen."

Her mouth twists as she bites the inside of her cheek, processing. I don't think I need to remind her what I'm referring to—I imagine neither of us will ever forget the moment I broke us apart so savagely.

Imogen nods. She sucks in a deep breath, and when she meets my eyes again, she smiles.

"Do you want to get back out there?" She points to the living room. "It's been pretty lively, and I'm sure everyone also misses you."

My lips part, but I nod instead of speaking, not trusting my words.

That's it?

Unease settles in my stomach as I trail behind the sway of her shiny golden hair.

"Well, someone *did* try to kill me the other day. But I got 'em before they got me. So, it's fine," Hattie says, throwing her hands up in the air.

"*What?*" Wrath says.

"I'm slippery. They didn't even land a jab," Hattie says.

"And this was at work?" Wrath asks.

"Yeah," Hattie says. "Maybe. I'm pretty sure."

"Hattie," I mutter, rubbing my brow. Imogen slinks back to her seat next to Josie on the couch, quiet as a mouse. "You need to report if something like that happens on the clock."

"I didn't wanna bother you guys with stupid stuff. Josie's stressed as shit as it is!"

"I'm not stressed," Josie says. "I've been very levelheaded, all things considered."

"Stress and being calm under pressure are two different things," Silas pipes up from the armchair he's turned into a throne. He sips his drink, lips smacking at something sour. Then adds, "You *can* be both at the same time."

Josie shoots Silas a glare.

"Either way, it was fine. I handled it," Hattie repeats.

"Meaning...?" Leo asks in a tipsy drawl.

"I stabbed him a few times and threw his body in the river." Hattie shrugs.

"Hattie! You can't do that!" Imogen gasps.

Silas cackles; I snort. The rest of them stay quiet—smart fae.

"Not fae-side. Jeez. Do you think I'm stupid?" Hattie whacks Wrath's chest. "I saved you some paperwork. The sharks human-side will get him."

"There are no sharks in that river, Hattie," I say, knowing exactly where she dumped the body. She's a creature of habit.

"Fine. What about the seagulls? Those fuckers will eat anything. They're the rats of the sky."

The group collectively groans, but Imogen is the only one turning pale. Josie's hand wraps around her shoulder, and she leans in to whisper something in Imogen's ear. Imogen closes her eyes and takes a deep breath, and after a moment, she shakes the color back into her face.

It's not jealousy that twists my gut watching them, but longing.

Would I be able to pull Imogen back from whatever darkness was just clouding her vision? Probably not. The others are more suited to take care of her in that way. Josie's always been a better person than me; she'll have the right words on hand to comfort.

I gesture to the cards spread around the *very full* cup at the center of the coffee table. "Maybe we can play the game you set up?"

"You're welcome. This is a fun one," Leo calls out, one finger raised in the air to remind everyone he was the one who did the work.

"No one thanked you, dumbass," Earl snickers, shoulder hitting Leo's.

"They will, though," Leo says.

"Alright, rules!" Hattie claps her hands together. "The game is Kings. Every turn, you draw a card. They each mean something different, so pay attention."

I slowly walk around the circle, eyeing the one empty space. Unfortunately, it happens to be between Silas and Wrath's armchairs.

"Two is you—you pick someone to drink. Three is me—you drink if you pick this. Four you hit the floor—your hand, not your whole body. Last one to do it drinks. Five is guys, six is chicks, seven is up to heaven—again, just your hand. Eight is mates, we all have to pick a buddy. You should do that now actually. Wrath is mine. Nine is rhymes—ha! That rhymed too. I'll explain that one when we get to it. Ten is categories."

Someone boos, and the others chuckle. I slink down into the hole between Wrath and Silas, sitting cross-legged.

"Yeah, *boo*. That ends the catchy, easy to remember rules," Hattie continues. "Ace means we drink our drinks until the person before us in the circle stops drinking or until we run out. Jack is never have I ever—should be self-explanatory. Queen is questions, first person to answer a question with something *other* than a question drinks. And king is rules, you get to make one up for all of us to follow."

"But I already do that on a daily basis," Silas snarks.

"That means nothing here," Hattie says, utterly serious.

She scans the group, eyeing everyone suspiciously, one brow arched; then she points to Imogen. "Mo goes first."

"That's not fair! I won the last game," Leo says, then slaps a hand over his face. "Sorry. I need to calm down. I'm literally the next one after her."

Imogen reaches forward, teetering on the edge of the couch, and pulls a card.

King.

She smiles, dropping it face up to start a discard pile. "My rule is that whoever pulls a king doesn't have to drink during the next round."

"Very responsible of you," Hattie mutters, unamused.

"Someone has to be after the last game..." Silas chuckles over the lip of his drink.

"They go a little crazy before I got here?" I ask him tentatively. I haven't seen him since the Pits, and I'm suddenly all too aware of how he's regarding me. It's not quite a cold shoulder, but something akin to it in the grand scheme of his antics. I shift my position, awkwardly.

"Mhm," Silas hums. Mischief dances in the dimpling of his smirk. "I hadn't realized your friends play hard and dirty, Nora."

The way my name flicks off his tongue sends spiders crawling over my skin. I get the sneaking suspicion he's planning something I won't like. He's the petty type, and we didn't exactly part on pleasant terms.

Leo's turn comes and goes without pause, and next is Earl's.

"Jack!" Earl calls out. His lips purse for a moment, and then a wicked smile crosses his face. "Never have I ever killed someone."

"Oh, that's diabolical." Hattie giggles.

"House Lust has to stick together." Earl shrugs, giving

high-fives to Leo and Imogen, the only other two in the room who haven't taken a life.

The rest of us drink.

Silas pulls a five, and all the guys drink.

A gnat hovers near the center cup, and I swat at it before picking my card. I get a king and make a rule that if someone uses their finger to point at someone, they have to drink. I call the action out *five times* over the course of the game—all of us habitual hand talkers.

Wrath gets a three, and we all laugh as he grumbles at his misfortune.

Hattie attempts to do a categories round about best places to dispose of bodies but everyone vetoes that—so she goes with something boring. Leo drinks that round.

Josie's turn comes, and she pulls the second jack. She's much faster than Earl at choosing, immediately chirping a 'never' that has the rest of us groaning.

"Never have I ever fucked a man," Josie snickers.

"Really? Even you, Mo?" Hattie asks, eyeing Imogen's tiny sip.

"I had an exploratory phase in high school," Imogen says. "It was brief. So was the sex."

Silas studies me with surprised curiosity when I take a drink, and I cock a brow. "What?"

"Nothing," he says quickly, taking a sip from his own cup. Though I note the way his midnight eyes shift back to me repeatedly throughout the rest of the game.

What is his deal?

Rounds pass, and we drink, again and again, until the available cards dwindle. All the while, whatever gnat Hattie managed to hatch from her unused bananas keeps flying around, hovering over my cup.

I try to ignore it, and focus on the game, when Silas pulls a queen and turns to me.

Of course he turns to me.

"How are you?" Silas asks.

"Is that the best question you could come up with to start?" I reply.

"Do you not like it?"

"Do you know me at all?"

"Do you *want* me to know you?" Silas teases. His tone makes it clear that the question is a jab at the other night.

"With you being king, do I get a choice?" I ask.

The peanut gallery *ooos* at our volley back and forth, impressed at our ability to think clearly enough to answer each other with questions.

"Does my persistence bother you?" Silas asks.

"Does my stubbornness bother *you*?" I reply.

"Why would it bother me?" He picks at invisible lint on his rolled sleeve.

"Don't you think it's the same reason your persistence bothers me?" I ask.

Silas huffs, and his tongue pokes at his cheek like he is tempted to answer in truth. His fingers comb through his hair, asking, "How does my hair look today?"

"Do you think switching up your questions will confuse me?" I reply.

"How would I know if I didn't try?" he teases.

"Don't you think this is getting a little ridiculous?" I huff, ready to end this round and the game.

"When are you going to slip up, then?" he whispers, leaning over the armchair. His face is a hairsbreadth away from mine.

Too close.

"What if I never slip up?" I ask.

"Then I guess I'd have to drink." Silas smirks, and it takes a second for the rest of the group to register that he lost. On *purpose.*

He downs the last dreg in his cup, shaking his head at the burn as he swallows. For someone who's paid handsomely, Hattie keeps real shitty liquor here, despite what she claims. Silas slaps his glass down on the coffee table.

"That was incredibly impressive, borderline terrifying, Nora. And I'm not scared by many things," Silas says.

"*Pshhh.* You think that was terrifying? You should have been there when she took out Wes. Scariest shit I've ever—" Leo slaps a hand over his mouth, cutting himself off.

The room is so silent a pin could drop, and we'd hear it; in fact, it's so quiet that the gnat's buzzing zooms past my ear, making it twitch.

"Wait, what?" Imogen says.

Leo's panicked gaze swings my way, and I shake my head ever so slightly. He attempts to stutter a response, but Imogen cuts him off with a raised hand. She turns to me, amber eyes glowing with frustration.

"You killed him?" Imogen asks.

I don't answer, unable to lie and unable to apologize.

"She killed him? When?" Imogen repeats the question to the rest of the group. "Was anyone planning to tell me this?"

"A week ago..." Leo finds his voice, but Imogen isn't looking at him or even listening to his explanation. She's looking at *me*, her disappointment palpable in her gaze. "We wanted to know how the aftermath shook out before asking you to come back home to the city."

"What Leo is trying to say is that I asked them all not to tell you," I say. I force my voice to be cold and detached. Clinical. *This* is the role I am best suited for. "I didn't want you to think it was safe to rush back. The situation is still in flux. I didn't think it was worth worrying you about."

"I'm not a child that needs to be kept in the dark. You could have told me in the kitchen before," Imogen snaps. "Any of you could have told me, at any point tonight." She looks around the room, her chest heaving with embarrassment as she folds in on herself. Her face pales, and her hands start to shake. "I think it's time for me to go." Imogen stands and beelines for the front door. "Happy birthday, Hattie."

"Mo, wait!" Josie calls after her, standing. The door slams, and a conflicted groan rips from Josie's throat. She's rushing after Imogen in seconds, but pauses to address Aisha. "I'm going to go after her. Can you come with me so we can get back to the cabin?"

Aisha nods. The dark-skinned woman is one of our trusted shadow-walkers, though she's always been more aligned with Hattie and Josie than me.

The door slams a second time, leaving us in an awkward silence.

There are a few sets of eyes on me. The pinpricks of their heat sear me; their judgment, their pity, their irritation, their *disappointment.*

It's suffocating.

They don't get it, what needs to be done to keep everyone safe. Maybe they never will. Maybe the people of House Pride never will either, if the people whom I considered my closest friends can't.

Or maybe it's that they don't want me to keep them safe. Maybe they don't want me here at all.

If I hadn't shown up tonight, would they still be laughing, finishing this stupid drinking game? Would Imogen still be sitting here with a smile on her face? Would Josie have had to run after her, cleaning up the mess I made?

It strikes me, a deep cut through my flesh and to my bone; if this is true, then I have a very important decision to make.

Incessant, *fucking* buzzing fills the silence, the damned gnat circling the table again.

"Hattie, why do you have gnats in winter?" Earl asks, waving at it innocently as it flies past his face.

"Um, I might have let my fruit go bad the other day?" Hattie says, scratching her chin. "But I definitely threw it out over a week ago. Maybe it's one that came up from the drain?"

"That's not how fruit flies work," Leo says.

Their conversation fades to the background as I home in on the bug. It flies back to me, hovering in front of my face, almost as if it's watching me. *It's awfully similar to—*

I slowly edge my fingers toward an empty cup and a stray card on the coffee table. Once they're within my grasp, I lunge, capturing the gnat between the cup and the card. I stare at it through the distortion of the glass.

"How the hell did you get in here?" I whisper.

"Uh, Nora, why are you talking to it?" Earl asks.

The bug, that is *not a bug*, clinks around the glass, hitting the sides in an attempt to escape.

"Hattie, you got any cuffs?" I ask.

"Yeah... like sex ones or iron ones?"

"Gods—fuck—*iron*," I growl. "Why would I need sex handcuffs right now?"

"I don't know! That's why I asked!" Hattie yelps, blipping into a plume of shadow in an instant. She comes back just as quick, tossing the iron cuffs onto the coffee table in front of me.

I stare at the bug, and it stares back at me, now still inside the glass.

"You're going to change back, and we're going to put these cuffs on you. You will cooperate, otherwise you'll be put in the freezer. Got it?" I say.

The bug floats up and down, as if to nod.

I place it on the ground and as soon as I take a step back, the glass shatters. My younger cousin's body fills the space it once occupied. He winces, his hands pressing into the broken shards as he pushes himself upright.

Wrath is quick to rip Alexander's arms behind his back, locking the iron cuffs around his wrists so that he can't shift again and escape.

The front door opens and shuts down the hall, Josie trudging back inside while Wrath cuffs him.

"Mo's home, but one of you guys is going to have to take me back aft—" Josie stops short. "What the hell is Nora's cousin doing on the floor?"

"I think a better question is how did he get past the Veil?" I ask, turning to Silas, who stares at the boy with wary curiosity.

"I told you it was fading. Maybe it flickered, and they somehow got through," Silas postures. "*Or* he snuck in. Wrath, how would that be possible? Your security is airtight."

"I'm right here, you know," Alexander sneers.

"Yeah, we can see you. Shut up and let the grownups chat for a minute, 'kay?" I snap at the little shit.

"Nora," Josie scolds.

A sound between a scoff and a snarl rips from my throat. "If he's old enough to travel to a rival Court as a fucking fly-on-the-wall spy, he's old enough to take a little sass. Plus, he's technically family. I can speak to him however I damn well please. Especially given who he reports to."

"But I'm not here for my father," Alexander grates.

"*Uh-huh,*" I huff.

"I'm *not.* I stole a ride in Wes's pocket so I could—"

"No one's going to believe you right now." I cross my arms and turn to Wrath. "I suggest we store him in the dungeon until after the next Sins' meeting. Let him sweat a little before we interrogate him."

"I'm sorry, but what the fuck is happening right now?" Leo says, still sitting on the ornate rug. His bewildered expression ping-pongs around the room. "I am still very new to this level of crazy, and I need someone to explain all this to me like I'm toasted and my head is spinning. Because I am. And it is."

"We're *all* too inebriated to handle this with any tact," Wrath says, ending the discussion *and* the party. "I'll get a few of my guys to put him in a cell. We'll figure it out from there tomorrow, after some rest. I'm sorry to cut your night short, Hattie."

"It's okay," Hattie says with a shrug. "I still have presents to open." She points at Silas with dramatic flair. "You have better spent a small fortune on me, *Mr. King*."

The others bicker as they help Hattie clean up, tossing cups in the sink and wiping down the coffee table with a wet rag. They buzz around me as I stare down Alexander until Wrath's guys come to pick him up. He attempts to goad me back into conversation, but I don't bite.

No, I study his features: the straight slant to his nose, the lean, lanky frame, and, of course, those green eyes. While the coloring of his skin and hair matches his brother, and I assume their mother, his eyes are his father's. And mine.

My fist curls around the tether to Patience; it thrums, a live wire. As if Patience can sense my unease, buzzing magic shoots to my scars. Is he laughing at me from across Faerie?

I glance at Josie, who takes charge with Wrath and his soldiers. Directing them on how to handle Alexander. Wes is gone, but I have yet to fully secure my House. I need more time for that, but I also need to eliminate my uncle as soon as possible.

I'm pulled in two directions, but I only have one body. I cannot manage both by myself.

I need to pick one.

26

SILAS

There's never been such an awkward fucking silence in one of the Sins' meetings as there is now. And I have to admit... it is entertaining.

Envy and Nora are having their typical stare-off, the grudge between them strong as ever, especially since Nora's disposed of his newest toy. Because that's what Wes was: a toy to toss around the playground to satisfy Envy's own whims. It's not unlike how I view many of the people sitting at this table, except I'm partial to calling them pawns, rather than toys.

There's a difference.

I lazily tap my ringed fingers on the table, pushing all their patience to the limit. How much longer can I hold their composure in my grip before it cracks?

Nora's striking emerald eyes cut to me, slicing my playful mood to pieces. As of late, I find my resolve buckling in her presence, and acquiescing to her demands.

It's all very confusing. Has been since the day I took her to the Pits.

I sigh. "We're all busy people. Let's skip the bullshit today, please."

All seven Sins' eyes snap to me, with varying degrees of intrigue and begrudging respect. The truth is that we don't have time for formalities.

Wrath and Hattie's assignment on the shadow-veil has been fruitless. This was expected. However, I had been secretly hoping for an update that wasn't *sorry, Silas, your options are either to die trying to erect another or to accept that you're going to war.*

My thumb spins the silver ring on my pointer finger, running over the engraved design.

Both sides of Faerie have had time to recoup from Solstice and prepare for the moment that it falls. But we've been divided as House Pride's power struggle worked itself out. It was a necessary detour, but we need to close out this chapter of Sins business for good. All our most powerful players need to turn their focus on the bigger threat.

Patience.

The man whose son we conveniently have locked away in our dungeon, no less than four floors below us.

"You've all heard the news?" I say. Seven nods and grunts of affirmation show around the table. "Then you all know Nora's challenger has unfortunately bit the pavement. By the agreed upon terms, she keeps her position as Pride. If anyone has an issue with that, save it for another day."

"Actually, Your Majesty, I have something to say," Nora says.

I blink, hoping my confusion isn't so apparent on my face. We did not discuss her making a speech. Or to comment at all. It was supposed to be a succinct acknowledgment of her status and then we would move on.

"Go on," I drawl, narrowing my eyes at the unpredictable woman.

Nora stands tall, taking a moment to stare down her sharp nose at all the Sins. Her power radiates from her, a tangible thing that pulls us forward in our seats. We wait on bated breath for those red-stained lips to part.

"I'm passing on the title to my Second. I will not be taking questions on the matter," she says plainly. "But let me be clear in that I am *still* a member of House Pride. Do not mistake this decision for a woman running. This is a leader acknowledging what is best for her people."

She pauses, letting the declaration sink in. Her head tilts towards me, those green eyes burning.

"I have bigger things to deal with now," she says.

Nora then leans forward, both hands planted firmly on the table. Her words are a whispered threat—a knife pressed to our throats. "And if I learn that any of you treat her the way you have treated me, I will kill you. That is a promise."

Nora waits for someone to clap back, but when no one does, she smiles, straightens, and walks out the door.

It's not until it clicks shut that I remember Josie is in the room; my head whips towards the woman, and there's shock there, written all over her face. She catches my gaze, and I motion to the empty chair.

Josie's face shutters into the impassive, observant expression I'm used to seeing her wear before taking Nora's seat. Under the watchful gazes of the other Sins, she sits, clears her throat, and then takes command of the room. Much like her predecessor.

"Let's get started," she says.

Nora's waiting for us when the meeting ends, casually leaning against the dungeon's stone wall with one boot kicked up and her arms crossed against her chest. Her expression is slack as she stares down the hall, not having ventured past the first empty cell.

"What the *fuck* was that?" Josie pushes past me with fury.

Nora blinks, and though her features harden, they don't lose their sunken cast. She sighs, as if expecting such a reaction from her Second—*now superior?*

"You completely blindsided me," Josie says. "Again! Why did you do that?"

"You would have fought me on the decision had I told you going into it," Nora says.

"Of course, I would have! Being Pride is all you've ever wanted!" Josie's voice echoes in the hall.

Nora shrugs.

"You're *shrugging?*" Josie's face is red, redder than the drunk flush she got at Hattie's party. "You have nothing else to say right now?"

"What else is there to say?" Nora's hands fly through the air. "Despite how much I want to be Pride, I *can't*. It's become clear that I was wrong. I thought I was what they needed, but I'm not. So I'm giving them you."

"What the fuck is that supposed to mean?" Josie shouts.

"Should we go back upstairs? Let them have this conversation alone?" I whisper to Wrath. There's a small worm of unease wriggling between my ribs.

Wrath shrugs, whispering back, "I don't think it's going to

be a long discussion. Might as well get the prisoner ready while we wait."

Wrath stalks past the two women, and I follow.

"They need to *believe* in their leader. They need to *trust* them. They don't trust me, Josie."

"Yes, they do. They'll get over the Seelie thing when we remind them of everything you've done for them. We're a *family*," Josie says.

"No, they won't."

"Nor—"

"They *won't*. Not enough to make a difference." Nora's voice echoes between the cells. "We liked to pretend it was a good thing that the people were afraid of me. That, in the early days, it would be a perfect means for control. But they will *always* be afraid. Because of who I am. It's just like with Mo. And with you. I see how you look at me now, Josie, I am too much for you all."

I wince. Wrath spares me a commiserating glance as he unlocks the iron cell. How many times had he and I discussed my soul-stealer secret in a similar way? How many times had we weighed the consequences of revealing this power, knowing that it could cause the people to fear me so deeply that it prevents them from respecting me?

The dungeon goes quiet. And either Josie and Nora's conversation has stopped, or they are talking too softly to be heard.

Wrath tugs open the cell door, the iron groaning. Nora's younger cousin could be deaf and blind, given how he doesn't flinch when we enter. To be fair, he *is* blindfolded and has plugs of cotton stuck in his ears.

A little sensory deprivation never hurt anyone.

The boy's hands are bound to his chair with iron cuffs,

cutting off his ability to change into one of the many forms a Seelie shifter can take on.

"Stop fighting me and accept that this is your path now." Nora's frustrated voice echoes down the hall once more. "Do this for me. *Help me.* After everything, you owe me this—"

"Fine," Josie cuts Nora off, and sharp, angry steps on the stone floor approach us. "I'm done talking about this right now. We have business to deal with."

"I guess their conversation is over," I whisper to Wrath with a chuckle.

His expression is deadpanned, save for the roll of his eyes as he rips the blindfold off Nora's cousin. The boy yelps, jolting in his restraints. Wrath quickly removes the cotton wedges from his ears, tossing both to some dark corner of the cell.

"Time to chat," Wrath says.

"Gods-almighty!" the boy squeals with wide, panicked eyes. Then anger pinches his expression. "Is this how you always treat your guests? By tying them up, blindfolding them, and shoving shit in their ears?"

"You're not a guest, Alexander. You're a prisoner," Nora says. "The quicker you learn that, the quicker we'll be done here."

She sidles up to me with Josie in tow. The new Pride has worry-lines cutting into her forehead but otherwise seems fine.

"Are we handling this as we normally would?" Josie grits out.

"I figured," Nora says. "If that's okay with you two?"

"I'm happy to not get my hands—or suit—dirty today," Wrath says.

"Oh, were you serious about torturing him for information?" I ask. "I thought we were going to see if he had loose lips after waiting for us."

"You're all insane!" Alexander fights against his restraints. "I never should have agreed to do this. I'm going to murder my brother when I get home."

"Who says you're going home?" Nora asks. "It would be smarter for us to kill you."

Josie steps behind the boy. "If you play your cards right, maybe I can convince her not to."

"But we're family," Alexander says.

"That's not the persuasive argument you think it is," Nora says.

The boy flinches when Josie's hand grips the back of his neck.

"How did you get into Anwynn?" Wrath asks, cutting to the chase. "Did you slip through the shadow-veil fae-side?"

"What? No. No Seelie can slip through that," Alexander says. "I've heard the rumors of those who tried. And *died*. I'm not trying to die."

"Could have fooled me," Nora says. "Enlighten us on how you got here, then."

"As I was trying to tell you the other day—" Alex squirms, twisting his head to glare at Josie. "Will you let go of me?"

"No," Josie says with a tight jaw.

"Urgh—I have nothing to hide from you people! My brother sent me. Well, *technically*, my father assigned me to watch over that idiot you guys killed. But Bennie and I have an understanding. We both despise my father." Alexander takes a breath. "Wes was the one who brought me here. I can stay in my shifted form longer than most, so it was easy for him to sneak a literal *fly* through the checks your teams had at the time."

Truth, I think, directing the thought at Josie; she replies with a glare. Somehow, I imagine Josie's version of Pride will give me more trouble than Nora's did.

"He's not lying," Josie says out loud for the group.

"I could have told you that," I say, unable to *not* tease her.

"Stop interrupting—" Wrath and Nora snap at me in tandem.

I hold my hands up defensively and retreat to the cell bars. "Fine, I'll just stand over here looking pretty."

Wrath scratches the stubble growing along his jaw. "I'm going to have to talk to my men posted at the portal. There's no reason they should have missed this."

"Not everyone can be as thorough as you, Wrath." Nora rolls her eyes. "So, Patience had you playing bodyguard. Tell us everything you know about that."

"I don't know much. They had some guy who'd meet Wes in the Human Realm. He would take letters back to Avalon," Alexander explains. "My father has his plans. But he's also paranoid. Even as his Second, I'm not privy on all the details until they're pertinent. Hence why I was relegated to body-guard duty." The boy deflates, and his young age becomes apparent with his reaction to his father's distrust. He's still searching for fatherly approval. "I imagine he was going to find a way to force Wes into smuggling more Seelie shifters through the portal. After you all wasted your time and resources on infighting, of course."

"I knew I should have killed him as soon as I stepped foot back in this damn city. If you include the weeks I was locked away, Patience has had *months* of potential information leaks," Nora seethes.

"There's not much he could truly leak. Very few are privy to our defense procedures, and as much as Wes was aware of House Pride's operations, it's only a small part of the bigger picture. That's why we let you two sort out your business on your own in the first place," Wrath notes. He crouches in front of Alexander. "Tell us more about your brother."

Alexander visibly gulps. "Like I said, we both despise our father."

"Benevolence told me as much at Solstice. Didn't stop him from knocking me out cold before," Nora says.

"Yeah, we both want him dead, but it's complicated," Alexander says, his frustration raising his voice. "In that setting, he was expected to help our father. Otherwise, the other Virtues in our father's pocket would outcast him."

"Godsdamned politics," Nora huffs, throwing up her arms.

"Bennie wants to meet. He has a proposition—don't ask me what it is, he didn't tell me," Alexander says to Nora. "All he said was for you to go to the diner on Easton Street. I would have delivered this message sooner, but it was harder than I thought to navigate the city as a fly."

"All true. There's nothing else of note in his memories of searching Anwynn," Josie confirms, shaking the boy's neck. "Stop fighting my magic. It makes it more painful when you fight it."

"Easton Street is deep in another borough, beyond what we'd consider our territory human-side," Nora clarifies, eyes narrowing on her cousin. "It's mostly dominated by the human mafia. I wasn't aware that the Seelie had much presence there."

"We don't. I think he wants to though. Bennie's fascinated with humans," Alexander says. Then adds under his breath, "I have no idea why. They're boring." He shoots Wrath a pleading look, as if he determined my infallible friend is the easiest target for a pity play. "Are we done yet? I don't know anything else."

There's a beat of tense silence, but surprisingly, Wrath stands, righting his suit.

"I think we're done for now," Wrath says, nodding at Josie.

Josie lets the boy's neck go.

"You know that's an *incredibly invasive* kind of magic?" Alexander snaps.

"I know," Josie replies.

The four of us huddle at the entrance to the cell.

"What else did you find?" Nora asks Josie.

"Not much. He's doesn't know anything about the larger militia, but there's plenty on Bennie and Patience just by way of him being family. I need more time to dig deeper if we want anything truly useful."

"Then you'll get more time," Wrath promises. "It's worth the hours to gather as much information as we can. Being a Second, he'll have knowledge of their cities, building layouts..."

"But what's the plan of action after that?" Josie asks. "Do we shore up defenses and wait it out?"

I purse my lips. The idea of being sitting ducks at the mercy of the shadow-veil's waning lifespan and the whims of the Seelie isn't one that sits right with me.

I think back to Hattie's advice as we stood before the sparkling barrier my magic created. Nothing bodes well for the ones who sit and wait to act.

A grin crawls onto my cheeks.

"It's simple," I say, turning to Nora. "We play Patience's game right back at him."

Nora's expression goes slack, and it's like she's the mind reader, not Josie. "You don't mean—"

"We make you a Trojan horse," I drawl.

"You mean to have Bennie smuggle Nora into Avalon?" Wrath asks.

I point at him with a finger gun. "Bingo."

"That's insane," Josie says. "Not to mention dangerous. Soul-stealer or not."

"I'm not a soul-stealer. You can stop referring to me as such," Nora says in a hushed rasp

Wrath and Josie volley back and forth, but Nora's not listening. Her gaze drifts off. She's lost, her mind somewhere else, sinking deep into the emerald sea. Movement catches my attention; Nora's fingers twitch at her sides, curling around what she once described as invisible strings. How many times, exactly, had I watched her check in on her tethers at Bramble? Too many to count.

Our little soul-stealer is hiding a secret.

And she *is* a soul-stealer, in the ways that matter. I'm the only one qualified to gift that title. Nora has earned it, lived the life of one long enough to claim it as her own.

"Nor." Josie yanks Nora from her trance. "If you're going to go, you need back up."

Nora shakes her head. "You can't come with us. You're too important now."

"I'll go," I say.

Josie and Wrath's attention snaps to me, gazes sharp as daggers. That was clearly *not* the answer they wanted to hear.

"You're not going to Avalon, Silas," Wrath says.

"He's the king, he can do whatever he pleases," Nora says.

Aw, is she coming to my defense?

Even if it's just her being difficult for the sake of being diffi-cult, I'm flattered.

"I can't go because I'm too important, but the *Unseelie King* can?" Josie snarks.

"We need all the Sins here, working full time to prepare for when the shadow-veil falls. Because it *will* fall," Wrath says, lifting a hand and shutting Josie and Nora's argument down. "And you, *Your Majesty*, are insane to think I'd let you traipse around an enemy territory at all."

"Nora and I are the two most lethal fae on this side of Faerie," I say. "We can handle ourselves, if that's what you're worried about."

"It's not," Wrath says.

I mash my lips together but don't say anything. If I decide to follow Nora into Avalon, no one, not even my best friend, is going to stop me. In the same way our Solstice plan was a way to prevent war, this could be too. I'm perfectly fine risking my own life in pursuit of a path that saves Unseelie lives.

"If you're set on going, you'll take one of my best soldiers," Wrath offers to Nora. "They can be ready in a few days. That also allows us time to plan contingencies. You'll be without any additional resources, and if you get caught, it isn't like last time. There won't be a rescue party."

"I understand the risks. This is part of why I passed on my title—I need the freedom to hunt Patience." Nora's words are spoken with finality, a somber eulogy. "I can't do that from the safety of Anwynn."

I take up the rear as we exit the lower levels of the palace. Wrath and Josie are farther ahead, chatting about on-boarding Josie as the new Pride. When they turn down the next hall, I catch the back of Nora's blouse with my fingers, tugging her to a stop.

Her black brows knit together, and her gaze drops to where my hand grips her shirt. I'm not touching her, but I'm certainly teetering on the edge of *almost*. Nora made her thoughts on my touch clear the night of the Pits.

From now on, the only time I touch her skin will be at her provocation.

"You've been keeping a secret, *Nora*." I lilt her name like a birdsong, a soft tease in her ear. "Do you have a tether you've been hiding?"

Nora's shoulders stiffen. It's a minuscule amount, but I've spent many days watching this woman and cataloging her tells. I know what to search for now: the tightening of her posture, a tick of her jaw, the dilation of her pupils. They're all such tiny shifts that if you're not paying close enough attention, you'd blink and miss them.

"You do, don't you?" I whisper in awe. I'm too excited by this development to be angry that she lied to us. Because this *changes things*.

"Wouldn't you like to know?" Nora replies, pulling her blouse from my hold. It's not a lie, but a clever trick to *avoid* lying.

"Were you ever going to share this with the group? The fact that you've already got him dangling on your fishing line?"

"No," she says.

Nora tries to walk away, but I shadow-walk into her path. She stops short and huffs a sigh through her nose.

"Tell me why you haven't killed him yet," I demand.

"Because it would be a mercy. And I'm too selfish to accept anything but his pulse stuttering under my palm," Nora replies quickly, her tone far too calm for the brutal words.

I hum.

I can't say I would feel differently if I were in her position. Though it would save us a lot of trouble if she did just *cut it*.

Maybe I can wear her resolve down? I wonder.

Unlikely. But I could try.

"So, our plan did work. Or would have worked, had he not shot up the party and pushed us both off a ledge we can't come back from," I say, opting for the path of least resistance. I shoot her a blinding smile; cunning has always worked better for me than force.

"Correct." She eyes me warily. "Are you going to tell the others?"

I make a show of contemplating my answer, but a plan has hatched inside my brain. One that caters to all my desires.

I've never claimed to be a good man. And while I will always put my people first, I'm still the young boy who lost his parents in a ruthless fashion. The gods are offering me—*us*—one last tempting chance at retribution.

Nora cannot do this alone, and I'm the only one who can help her.

I am a shadow-walker, after all.

"No," I say. My grin turns downright evil. "So long as you do one thing for me."

27
NORA

The cigarette doesn't calm me; nothing, it seems, can anymore. My scars cry out, and I take another drag in hopes that if I simply inhale more of the tobacco, it'll quiet the incessant whining of my wings.

Smoke rushes from my nose. It curls into the sky, mixing with the stormy shades of gray and navy. Flecks of snow fall, peppering my hair and coat. In all respects, it's the perfect winter night. A year ago, I'd be smiling with relief; crisp air and serene views are the best for smoke breaks. But I'm not stepping out for ten minutes of silence tonight. I'm not in the alley next to the Den—I'm not out with friends at all, nor am I headed back inside, high on the prospect of meeting my lover.

Too much has changed, all pretense is gone, and my eyes take in these small moments differently.

Nostalgia's a bitch for ruining this.

Bootsteps thunder down the street, pulling my attention from the sky to a familiar smug face.

"That supposed to be your disguise?" I mumble.

"Yes, ma'am." Silas spins, showing me his new getup. He's

dressed down for this: a simple wool coat and slacks. There's not a fur-lined collar in sight. The major difference is his hair, which he has dyed a coppery red.

"You couldn't have chosen something more subtle?" I ask.

Silas shrugs. "I always wondered what I'd look like as a redhead."

I mutter a curse around the dying end of my cigarette. I steal its last breath, then flick it onto the icy pavement.

"Whatever. Bennie will know who you are regardless. It's more for everyone else's sake." I unceremoniously stick my hand out for Silas to take. "If we manage to *not* get ourselves killed doing this, Wrath is going to wring your neck."

"He can't complain that much if I fix all our problems by eliminating our enemy before they get a real chance to hurt our people."

"So noble," I deadpan. "Let's get going."

"Can't I be greedy and have both noble and selfish motives?"

"Silas. We don't have time for this." I shake my outstretched palm. Why is he stalling? Even with the added barrier of our gloves, I'm not looking forward to his palm sliding against mine. The quicker he grabs it and gets us across the Veil the better. "C'mon. Let's go."

Silas frowns at my hand.

Hesitance is a new, and strange, expression on him. And I have to wonder, is it me, or is it what we're about to do that makes him pause?

Corner of Easton Street and Ninth Avenue.

As if they had tugged a train car to this plot and removed its wheels, the diner Bennie's directions lead us to sits as a single story among giants. Bold green and white paint lines the exterior, and a metallic domed roof shines under the street-lamps. A large sign squeaks, rocking on its hinges in the snow-dotted wind: *EAT HERE* in bold letters beckons forth late-night patrons.

A bell dings as we enter, and movement in the diner screeches to a halt—heads snap our way, and the clang of metal spatulas on the grill pause. A curly-haired waitress stares us down until she realizes we aren't in the wrong place, and we aren't going anywhere.

She leisurely removes herself from behind the row of counter seating and pulls menus from the small hostess stand. "Two?"

"They're with me, Ruth." At the far end of the diner, in leather booth seating, my cousin waves his sun-kissed hand.

The waitress leads us to the table, unceremoniously dropping our menus on the linoleum and stalking away. It's less crowded in this section, meant for groups rather than a single patron.

"You're awfully cozy with the waitress," I say in lieu of a greeting.

Bennie barks a laugh. "Would you believe me if I said it's my first time here?"

"No." I motion for Silas to slide into the booth before me. Just because we're in a hole-in-the-wall diner doesn't mean there aren't eyes watching. The humans are sneaky little shits when they want to be.

"I've been coming every night since Alexander left, in the event you decided to grace me with your presence. Ruth has been an exceptional hostess," Bennie says, his eyes gliding over

Silas. His confident smile flickers, but he doesn't address the Unseelie King directly. "I assumed you would have come alone."

I shrug, settling into the leather booth. "You get a two for one special tonight."

Bennie hums, and we fall into a silent stand-off. It's a measuring of wills and a test of patience.

The age-old question: who will break first?

"Coffee?" the waitress appears, holding up a steaming pot.

My head jerks a curt nod, and she pours a stream of rich-smelling black gold. She raises a thin, stenciled brow at Silas.

"Why not?" he says, pushing his cup forward with a smile.

The waitress tongues her cheek, filling his cup halfway. She uses the pot to point across the table. "Sugar and cream's over there. You three know what you want?"

Bennie shoots her a flirty grin, his mustache quirking. "I'll take a pastrami on rye, please."

Her bored gaze slides to me.

"We're good," I say.

"Thank you," Silas adds, as if to combat my standoffish attitude.

The waitress doesn't bother taking a notepad out to scribble down Bennie's order; she nods and turns away. "It'll be out in a minute."

And then we're alone again.

I could slice the tension in the air with my nail, it's so thick.

Bennie breaks first, leaning across the table, whispering, "You know I always wanted to do this. Eat at a human diner with family."

Nope. Wrong fucking thing to start with.

"Cut the family crap, Benevolence. We want to hear the details of the deal you carelessly sent your brother into enemy territory to set up," I say.

Bennie raises his coffee to his lips. "How is my brother, by the way? I hope you didn't kill him. I did tell him not to piss you off."

"He's alive," Silas quips. "Safely locked up."

"Oh, excellent!" Bennie chirps.

I shoot Silas an exasperated expression. *What the hell is he doing telling Bennie that?*

"He did crash our friend's birthday party, which I thought was in poor taste at the time, but in the end was the right call. If he'd shown himself to Nora earlier, I think she would have —" Silas makes a choking noise while running his thumb across his neck. "You know?"

Bennie's snort causes him to choke on his coffee. "I see. Well, that's unsurprising given the—"

"Enough pleasantries." I slam my hands on the table, and the cutlery clanks together in their loosely wrapped napkins. "If you haven't already guessed, I've had a shit few weeks. And my patience is about this thin." I lean forward as I hold my fingers up, a millimeter of space between my pointer and thumb. "And no, that wasn't a fucking pun. I am quite literally this close to snapping your neck for knocking me out and throwing me in a dungeon. The only thing stopping me is that you are our easiest route into Avalon."

Silas hides a laugh behind a cough and a closed fist, as if he finds my outburst cute.

"You, shut up," I snap at him.

"Here's your sandwich," the waitress cuts in, holding up a plate.

I plaster on a forced, closed-lip smile as she sets it down in front of Bennie. But once the waitress's back is turned, I snatch the plate and pull it towards me, out of his reach.

"You get this back after you start talking," I say.

My cousin sighs.

"It's not all that different from the last request I made of you," Bennie says, eyeing the sandwich hungrily. "I want my father dead. But I cannot be the one to kill him."

"Why not?"

"The why doesn't matter. I'm offering you revenge on a silver platter. It's not my fault you didn't finish him off the last time you had your hands around his neck," Bennie says. "The Seelie are all about appearances. And me killing my father? Not a good look. Let alone all the other reasons I already told you the first time we did this song and dance. I don't have the power or means to get the job done. I'm man enough to admit that."

A frown cuts into my cheeks, but I shove the sandwich towards Bennie. He greedily digs in, his teeth punching crescents out of the dark brown bread stacked with deli meat.

"Details," I demand.

Bennie talks while he chews. "I can escort you to Avalon, and I have a safe house prepared for you to stay in. I need some time to get the other pieces sorted, but then I'll get you inside the palace and you can do... whatever it is you do."

"Sounds simple," Silas says.

"The best plans are," Bennie says. "Father's attention is set on you folk across the river. He won't see an attack coming from inside our Court. It's perfect timing." He dabs the corner of his mouth with a napkin. "Well, less perfect than Solstice, but I won't beat that dead dog anymore."

"Horse," I correct.

"What?"

"The human's saying is don't beat a dead *horse*." I shake my head. "When can you take us?"

"Tonight would be best." Bennie's sandwich stops halfway to his mouth. "Both of you?"

"Yes," I say.

Bennie blinks. "Okay... we'll have to use the portal then. And there is the matter of your wings to think about."

"My wings?" I grind out.

"*His* wings." Bennie nods to Silas as he takes another bite, chewing thoughtfully. His mossy green eyes roam over the two of us before his free hand waves in the air. The telltale shimmer of Seelie light magic descends, but nothing changes, at least, for *us*.

"I've made it so if someone looks our way, they will see us chatting normally. But Silas, can you stand up?" Bennie asks.

The Unseelie King's dark eyes harden. "I might be friendly, *Virtue*, but don't presume you can order me around."

"Please, *Your Majesty*?" Bennie tries again.

"Better," Silas says, then stands. "Now what?"

"Can you take out your wings?" Bennie asks.

A beat passes, but with a muttered *okay*, Silas releases them. The white feathers unfurl from his back with the grace that only magic can provide. Stunningly pure, they match the natural locks of hair Silas has dyed over. They almost brush me, and I scoot farther away in the booth.

Bennie's fingers weave a pattern in the air, light magic taking shape around Silas's wings. "Seelie rarely keep their wings hidden. I'll craft a lasting illusion over yours so you can blend in."

The illusion takes shape, and those white feathers transform into a pearly white pair of butterfly wings. Otherworldly would be a fitting word for the way they glitter, shining even under the artificial diner lights.

Silas peers over his shoulder, admiring and flexing them in what little booth space we have.

"Fascinating," he murmurs.

"It's an intricate type of magic. Just don't put them away or the illusion will break. Oh, and if someone touches them, they'll still feel like feathers," Bennie says. Mossy green eyes slide over me. "But yours, Nora, those are real. It works to your advantage."

It's as if my wings can hear his call, and shooting pain, worse than the standard ache I've come to know, stabs my back.

Inhale. Hold it. Exhale. Endure.

My throat tightens, and my hands curl into tight fists.

I do not want to let them out; I do not want to admit this weakness.

"Is this truly necessary?" Silas asks before I can form a reply.

"If you don't want to raise suspicion," Bennie says, serious as I've ever heard him. "If you want this to work."

"Let me repeat this back to you so we're all aligned," I grit out. "You take us to the Seelie portal. Then, you drop us at a safe house for an indeterminate amount of time. There, we'll be sitting ducks in a foreign land—all while you play politics to organize some kind of setup for us to get in proximity to Patience."

"I'll fill in the nitty gritty on the way, but yes, that is essentially the plan," Bennie says.

"Why can't you magic us yourself?" I ask. "Why use the portal?"

"I'm powerful, but I don't have enough juice for three right now. There are other illusions tapping my power that must be maintained. If you both want to go, we take the portal," Bennie says.

"He's telling the truth," Silas murmurs. He raises one brow at me. "And we've done more with less."

We can go rogue from Bennie's plan whenever we want, he means.

It's not safe, not by any definition of the word. But I came prepared for danger. And I've suffered too much to *not* rip this reward from Bennie's offering hand.

I take a steadying breath.

I will let my wings loose for this. Only for this, I will bear the pain.

I nod.

"Then you kill my father," Bennie says, popping the last bite of his sandwich in his mouth. He licks his fingers clean. "And then our Courts can go back to playing nice-nice and we can move on with our lives."

I cock a skeptical brow. "You can't possibly believe that last part."

"Why not? With the bad eggs removed and the right people put in power on both sides..." Bennie shrugs, but the casual action doesn't match the intensity of his eyes. They bore into Silas. "Peace isn't impossible."

Silas doesn't let more than an upwards twitch of his lips through his composed mask. His shadowed expression is calculating. It reminds me of the first time Silas truly *saw* me. Back in his office, when we first decided we'd walk the path of vengeance together.

What is it that he's seeing in the earthy depths of Bennie's eyes? Is it lies? Is it truth? What is he seeing that I'm not?

"Do we have a deal?" Bennie asks.

Silas turns to me. "Are we doing this?"

He asks the question as if I'm the one who still needs to decide—as if *I'm* the one who can stop us. But nothing can stop this now. I have no one to hold me back but myself.

Me and my burning, aching scars.

Me and my haunting wings.

Me and my last threadbare mask of pride.

Me and my revenge.

28

JOSIE

Wes royally fucked things up in the few short weeks he had the reins on our House's operations. My fingers dig into my scalp, massaging the throbbing flesh as I lose myself in the stack of paperwork. Oddly enough, our troubles are worse fae-side than human-side. There's a mountain of dead stock we have to deal with. The alcohol is fine, but the rest? It's not *unsalvageable* but—

"Pride!" Hattie jumps onto my desk, crushing the papers. I jolt, blinking up at the beaming woman.

"Off," I scold, shooing her away.

"It's weird calling you that now." Hattie hops off my desk and proceeds to lounge in one of the leather armchairs.

I ignore her comment because she's right. It *is* weird having her call me Pride.

"Where have you been?" I ask.

"Places."

"Really?" I deadpan. "Gonna need more than that. You didn't check in this morning with shift change. How many times have I told you the importance of communication—"

"I was dealing with family stuff, okay?" Hattie huffs. She pulls a small dagger from one of the sheaths hidden across her body and tosses it in the air. It flips blade over handle, and lands back in her hand with precision.

I lean back in my chair, the hinges squeaking with the action. "Is that why you keep running off without telling anyone?"

A shroud passes over her usual preppy demeanor. Hattie's past before she joined our House is a dark and gory thing, and neither Nora nor I have pressed her on specifics. I didn't even know she still engaged with her family human-side.

"Yeah," Hattie says. "But it's fine now. I promise it won't get in the way of business again."

I run my tongue over my teeth. "Keep me posted if that changes, alright?"

She nods.

"Is everything on track with the teamsters?" I busy myself with righting the papers on my desk.

"About that..." Hattie pointedly avoids meeting my eye.

"Hattie."

"I'll have it handled ASAP."

"*Hattie*," I repeat. "You are not getting out of explaining this."

"Ugh, fine. Some of the guys—you know the ones. The traditionalists who put up a big stink when Nora was promoted to Second in the first place—"

"To the point, please," I say.

"Okay, okay. Well, they're *kind-of-sort-of-on-strike*. Again." Hattie says the last bit all fast and strung together, the speech version of ripping off a bandage.

I groan, my head dropping to my hands.

"Yeah, that's how I reacted at first too," she says with an awkward laugh.

I peek out from between my fingers, and she grimaces.

"But like I said, I'll handle it quick as a jiffy," Hattie promises.

"Did they have demands?" I ask.

"None that we'd concede to," she says, waving her knife in the air. "Something about replacing you with some old guy, *blah-blah-blah*. I stopped listening halfway through."

I swipe my hands across my face, transitioning to problem-solving mode. "Got it. Let's start with standard strike protocol and set up a meeting with their organizer. We can't afford to have any more delays, otherwise—"

A knock on the door cuts me off, followed by the squeak of it cracking open. Aisha's dark hair pokes around the wood.

"Sorry to interrupt, but Wrath dropped in to see you," Aisha says.

Hattie scoffs. I shoot her a confused glance.

"Thanks, Aisha. Let him up," I say.

Hattie pouts, sinking deeper into the chair.

"You're a seesaw today, Hatts. Happy, sad, happy, sad. What's the matter?" I ask.

"Wrath and I are... in an argument," she grumbles.

"*Okay*," I drawl. "Do I want to know more?"

She was all heart eyes and flirty with him on her birthday. What could have possibly happened to flip that on its head?

Her arms cross tightly against her chest. "No, you do not."

Another knock on the door sounds, and Wrath walks in. He pauses in the entryway, one hand gripped tightly on the brass knob. His stubbled jaw feathers as he takes in the back of Hattie's curly blond bob, then he shuts the door and straightens his suit.

Then he ignores her.

My attention flicks between the two shadow-walkers and

my magic quickly latches onto the thick waves of tension filling the office.

Yeah. Best not to get involved here.

Wrath stops a few feet behind Hattie. He clears his throat, garnering my attention.

"The Unseelie King is missing," Wrath says.

I blink. "*Pardon?*"

"I have not been able to make contact with Silas in over twenty-four hours. Which leads me to believe he has gone rogue. I suspect that he's accompanied Nora across the Veil."

"No, Nora's supposed to go meet Benevolence with your assigned guard. In *three days*," I say. The words ring hollow, though, and dread presses down on my chest.

"Can you verify if she's still in the city?" Wrath asks. "She's more limited in travel than a shadow-walker. Is she home?"

My jaw grinds together. I'd like to think Nora would follow our plans. Or would at least trust me with her reckless ideas *before* she enacts them.

But the reality is I broke her trust when I wouldn't shear her wings. And she broke mine three times over with her unpredictable decisions and volatile cruelty. Fighting in the Pits, culling the ranks, throwing this title at me... and now this. I thought killing Wes would lessen some of her frantic need for retribution, but I was stupid to have assumed.

Fuck. She's been waving red flags left and right to indicate this path. I should have known. I should've seen it, should have stopped her.

"I haven't seen her since we talked with Alexander two days ago," I say. "But that hasn't been abnormal as of late. It's my rotation at the cabin with Imogen again. Hattie, can you quickly check if Nora's at home or at any of the warehouses?"

"Sure, boss-lady," Hattie says, puffing into a plume of shadow.

As the tendrils of her magic fade, Wrath's shoulders sag.

"What do we do when she comes back and confirms what we both are thinking?" I ask.

"Only what we can, I suppose. Clean up their messes," he says.

"Story of the century," I say. My elbows hit my desk, and my forehead hits my hands. Frustration bursts in my chest. "Fuck!"

"My thoughts exactly."

"So, what? We just have faith?" I ask. "Pray that it all works out, and they manage to stop a war before the Veil falls?"

Wrath clicks his tongue. "Make sure to add that they survive to that prayer. That way, we can kill them when they come back."

"You're a bundle of sunshine today, aren't you?"

He grunts. "I'm also going to need assistance running damage control while Silas is *away on official business.*"

"Very subtle," I mumble.

"If anyone asks for details, he's at Bramble," Wrath says. He leans forward, his hands bracing the back of the chair Hattie was sitting in.

"What else?" I ask. "I can tell there's more."

"The Royals have their quarterly function coming up. Silas usually attends. They'll be pissed he's skipping out, but it's not the first time he's ditched. However, with the timing, I'm concerned about everyone colluding without him present."

I hear the hidden question in his explanation. "And you need me to attend because I can help mitigate any internal bullshit that might cause us issues in the long run?"

"I need both the new Lust *and* Pride there," Wrath says. "Nora and Imogen never attended. It's part of why tensions are high between the seven of us in the first place. We need to kick away the lines that were drawn in the sand."

My fingers tap on the desk mindlessly. Nora never deigned to attend the Royal functions, even when I would suggest that adhering to tradition to *some* extent was a good idea. But Imogen—her reasons run much deeper than shirking the status quo. Her family died on the way to one of those parties.

I steel my jaw. "I can manage that. And I'll get Leo on it too."

"Thank you," Wrath says. "That's all. I'll be in touch." He makes to leave, but stops, turns, and raises a finger. "You can bring a date if you'd like. To the function,"

I quirk a brow. "Are *you*?"

Brown eyes filled with longing cut to Hattie's empty chair. "To be determined."

As soon as the door clicks shut, my head falls back into my hands. I peer through the gaps in my fingers and groan at the half-finished paperwork.

This is such a fucking mess.

Night has fallen by the time I'm finished with work. It's brisk as I walk out the front of the building, shooting a quiet thank you to the doorman. My office wasn't put in the same building as Nora's by design. As Second, I needed to be closer to the day-to-day operations of our House, a more available presence for our department heads across our sector of the city.

Now I wonder if I should bring a cardboard box and switch offices—would Nora want that? Do *I*?

I kind of enjoy being in the thick of it.

I squint hard against the harsh wind as I wait for my driver to bring the car around. Twisting in place, I catch a glimpse of the side of the building and stiffen. I bite the inside of my cheek, and the metallic tang rushes over my tongue.

Painted in big, dripping letters: *Seelie sympathizers.*

This has happened a few times since Nora came back to Anwynn, so it's not exactly surprising. But that doesn't make it any less frustrating.

"I already called a cleaning crew to deal with that, Miss Josie—I mean, Pride," the doorman chatters nervously.

"Thank you," I grit out.

I'm not the one who's quick to anger, but it roils in my stomach all the same. I'm too tired for this—this strain, this worry. I've been holding it in for much longer than the past few months, an unhealthy habit I developed early on.

Suppress. Ignore. Push through.

I'm an excellent duck. I can put on the perfect outward appearance. Meanwhile, my mind works double time under the surface. I'm constantly blocking out everyone's thoughts, running scenarios of the future and cross-checking against the past. I worry about the minuscule details of each day as if they're equally important.

"Here's your ride, Pride," the doorman chirps, walking to open the door to the sleek automobile for me.

I step towards the car, but my boots drag on the pavement. The weight of today is too heavy to carry back to Imogen's. "Actually, I think I need a moment. I'm going to take a turn around the block."

There's a small park around the corner I can sit in for five minutes and simply breathe. To try to calm the fervid organ in my skull. *To go meditate,* I scoff internally. It was a suggestion Nora often touted at me as a joke, so I can never admit that I tried it. And that it worked.

Sometimes.

Occasionally.

A pang of hurt hits my chest, and I rub it over my coat.

"Of course. I'll have him stay here until you're ready to leave."

I start walking down the street. "Thanks, I'll only be—"

An explosion lights up the night and my body careens across the sidewalk. I roll to a stop on the concrete, my side and back immediately aching from the impact.

I groan a curse, pushing up on my hands and knees. My magic flares out, latching onto anyone in the vicinity and scanning for danger. No thoughts brush up against my magic, which means my assailant has either fled or they're strong enough to shield everything from me. Usually, I can pick up some inkling of emotion even if I can't hear someone's thoughts. But I'm entirely alone as I stand, ripping my gun from its holster under my jacket, and approaching my smoldering Cadillac.

My nose crinkles, and I raise my sleeve to act as a makeshift mask to block the acrid scent of blast powder and seared flesh.

I clear the surrounding area quickly. But outside of a few members of House Pride who come running out the front doors to check on me, there's no one.

I holster my gun and stare at the smoking mess idling in the street. It's not the loss of the car that twists my gut, but the two men who got caught in the blast. Another two people to add to the list of those I've failed. My hands shake as they flex and ball. The thick leather of my winter gloves stops my nails from cutting crescents into my palms.

I push the guttural roar that claws at my throat down, down, *way down*—a fissure in my composure rips open. A deep crack forms. My legs act of their own accord, and I turn and kick the graffitied side of our building. Boot strikes brick; the impact stings my toes.

"Gods-fucking-damnit!"

I take two seconds—*two*—to breathe through the rest of my frustration. Then I swallow it back down. I stand straight, right my singed wool coat, and get to work.

"Someone get Aisha," I say to the gathered crowd. When they continue to stare, aghast at the wreckage of the car bomb that someone—likely one of Wes's loyalists—tried to kill me with, I clap my hands. "Hey!" Their wide eyes snap to me. Fire sirens sound in the distance. "Get inside. One of you get Aisha. Follow protocol. It's there for a reason."

The underlings of House Pride scatter, but one stays behind. A young secretary lingers, twiddling her fingers.

"Pride?" she asks, quiet like a mouse.

"Yes, Leila?" I say.

"Are you okay?"

I carefully consider my response. Before, I might have given her a bit of truth. A professional *I will be*. But now, I'm Pride. I have a new set of rules to live by. And I have even less room for error.

"Of course," I say. I jerk my head to the glass doors, where the reflection of the fire flashes. "Go inside. You don't want to catch a cold out here. We've got this covered."

Her shoulders relax, if only by an inch.

"Okay. Good," she says. She flashes a quick, sad smile before scurrying into the building.

Good.

Far from it.

Imogen's hair is a wavy, frizzy mess around her shoulders when she rips open the door. Worry creases her brows, and panic makes her amber eyes shine under the porch light.

"What happened?" she asks, peering around me to see if I'm alone. But she won't find anyone. Aisha came and went by shadow as quick as a lightning strike.

I suck in a shaky breath. I can't *not* tell her the truth, but I'm hesitant to taint the energy of this house with bullshit. We've done such a good job keeping it pure and free of outside worry.

Imogen steps back, holding the red door to her cottage open for me.

I step inside, immediately hit by a wall of heat. An inkling of pride shoots through me at how she's not afraid to light the hearth anymore. It wasn't that long ago that I had to make sure there were extra blankets in her room at Bramble because she refused to. Now, she can handle all the pops of the firewood without pause.

Dropping my briefcase next to the doormat and shucking off my coat, gloves, and scarf, I cut to the chase.

"Someone blew up my car."

"What?" Imogen swiftly invades my personal space, pulling my face between her hands. She turns my head back and forth, checking for cuts and bruises, then moves to inspecting my sweater covered arms. "Are you okay?"

"I'm fine," I say, pulling my hands away as she reaches them. The soft graze of her fingertips makes my spine stiffen, and I awkwardly bend to untie my boots. "But Wrath thinks that I shouldn't go back to my apartment. At least until we deal with the stri—" I cut myself off. "Until we deal with it."

I throw my first boot into the pile of shoes under the coat rack, and I sneak a quick glance at Imogen. Her lips are pursed in concentrated thought, and her arms are wrapped tightly around her middle.

I dip my head back down to untie my other boot.

"Is it alright if I continue to stay here for a bit? I know Leo is supposed to come stay next, and I don't mean to yank your plans around. I can also ask Wrath for a favor and stay in the palace," I say. Then mutter under my breath, "Not like Silas is around to say no right now."

"Josie."

My fingers pause on the laces, and I peer up through my dark lashes.

"One: You can always stay here. No questions asked. Anytime you need to, the door is open. Two: I'm so thankful you all are still humoring me with this set up. Even though I know I'd be *okay* alone, I selfishly don't want to be. I've enjoyed having roommates again," Imogen says, a twinge of teasing snark in her tone. Then seriousness clouds her features. "Three: Do you want to talk about it? My magic is twitching out right now picking up your stress. You don't usually let your shields down enough for me to get a read on your emotions."

"Oh." My neck flushes, and I dip to finish untying my boot. "I guess I'm just comfortable here. I don't feel the need to rein in it so tightly with you." I keep my gaze averted as I pull off the boot and throw it into the pile with the others. "And thanks, I appreciate the extended stay at hotel Gallagher."

I stand, and walk to the kitchen to grab a glass of water. The soft patter of socked feet follows me.

"So?" Imogen says expectantly.

The faucet hisses when I twist it; cold water rushes into the glass. When it nearly overflows, I cut the stream off with a sharp turn of my wrist, then gulp down half.

The glass hits the counter with a firm thud.

"The cabin's a no stress zone, Mo," I say, with a wry smile.

Imogen scoffs. "Don't use my shit to avoid yours. I'm not that fragile. Will venting help you?"

"I didn't say that you were fragile."

"You didn't need to. It's baked into the way you all walk, talk, and think around me."

"It's not that," I grind out, my lips mashing together. "I don't like seeing you hurting. And I don't want to be the one to cause that."

Imogen's posture softens at my grumbled admission, but at the same time, her expression hardens with determination. "I hear you, but you're in my house. *I* make the rules. And here, when we're hurting, we talk about it."

She pushes me out of the kitchen proper and to the other side of the counter. Gripping my shoulders, she forces me to sit on one of the two stools. She gives a quick squeeze, then her presence is gone, leaving warm imprints on my sweater.

I study Imogen as she gracefully flutters around her kitchen. Golden locks sway as she spins on the tile, tugging open cabinets and reaching into drawers. She pulls out a dark maroon bottle of wine, two glasses, and a bottle opener.

"Red okay?" she asks, more as a courtesy, as she masterfully pulls the cork from the bottle with a *pop*. She already knows what I prefer, and had a few bottles delivered.

"Red is great," I say, the corner of my lips twitching.

Her wrist twists the bottle at the end of each pour, stopping the flow of deep, shimmering scarlet wine without a wasted drop. She plugs the bottle with the cork and pushes it aside, then slides a glass my way. Her middle and ring fingers bracket the stem, and there's something in the movement that strikes me as sensual.

I take a sip, swallowing the lump in my throat with the wine. We've been here before—in autumn. We may be alone this time, but my free hand still taps against the countertop, and she still studies me in the way that all good bartenders do. As if they can dissect a person's psyche with a few minutes of small talk and a few sips of alcohol.

"Tell me what happened," Imogen says. "Think of it as exposure therapy for me. I need to get used to hearing it all again without freaking out."

I stay quiet for a moment, until one of those arched blond brows ticks up, betraying her impatience.

"Mo," I sigh. "I don't even know where to begin."

The strike? Nora and Silas going AWOL? The fact I could have died tonight but escaped by literal inches? That I don't know how to cope with the crushing weight of responsibility falling on my back? That I am now a Sin, something I am technically prepared for, but never once thought would come to pass?

Imogen leans forward on the counter, soft, kind eyes leveling with mine.

"Take your time," she says quietly. "I've got all night."

I do—take my time, that is. I unload it all; the worry and the stress and all the gritty details rush from my lips. And when I finally fall silent, staring down the last sip of maroon in my glass, Imogen shifts.

"Thank you for sharing all this with me," she says.

She's slightly pale; some of what I told her had leeched the color from her cheeks. But otherwise, she's retained her composure. No panic attacks seize her lungs and no flashbacks cloud her eyes.

And strangely enough, the white noise always buzzing in my head is gone. As if simply talking with Mo emptied it.

"I think you need a day off to de-stress," Imogen says, matter of fact. I follow her gaze to the window above the breakfast nook, where thick flakes of snow fall under the porch light.

"I don't have time," I say, though it's a weak objection.

"I'll find time for you," she says. "Besides, nothing can get done in the morning if it keeps snowing like that."

She turns to me with a conniving smile. She's like a child with far too many ideas on how to trick her caretakers.

"Are you suggesting we're going to have a snow day?" I ask.

"*You*," she drawls, one finger coming up to bop my nose playfully. "Will just have to trust me and find out."

I snort, my lips twisting into a smile. Imogen winks, finishing off her wine.

Is she...? No. I'm tired and seeing things that aren't there.

She drops her glass into the sink to be cleaned later, then reaches out to collect mine. I slide it halfway across the counter, and our fingers brush as she pulls it the rest of the way.

"Josie?"

"Yeah?"

Imogen leans forward on the counter until our faces are dangerously close. I can smell the sweet wine on her breath—can see the glistening maroon tint that lingers on her smirking lips.

My mouth goes dry, my tongue like cotton.

"I'm rocking a one-hundred percent success rate when it comes to de-stress solutions. Remember, I got you to let loose and go dance that one night at the Den. You enjoyed it, didn't you?" she whispers. "You had *fun*."

I tongue my cheek, which is suddenly tingly and warm. Of course I remember. She plied me with drinks, then artfully suggested I dance with a group of over-eager women. And then I fucked one of those women with my tongue.

It *was* fun. Even after, when Imogen caught me leaving said bathroom.

Begrudgingly, I nod.

"See?" Imogen says on a breathy sigh. "I got you, Joze. Trust me."

It's a beautiful sound, her voice when it's airy and light. Unburdened, like a summer breeze.

Alarm bells ring in my head, but they're muted by the wine we've drunk.

29
IMOGEN

There's something about the challenge of caring for someone that makes it easier to forget about all the other shit going on in your life. The darkness cloying at the edges of your being shies away from the guiding light and the demons retreat. The hard feelings are banished, making way for something easier. Better. A moment of peace.

I wake before Josie with the sight of a foot of snow in the yard. The storm still flurries, though it's much lighter than last night. I press my nose to the chilled glass windowpane, and it fogs. A pristine, glittering white landscape stretches out, lined with prickly evergreens.

My smile beams, and I pull away as an idea strikes me. The plan takes shape, and childlike excitement bubbles within me. My laughter tastes sweet as I grab the supplies needed—accidentally slamming the icebox door and tripping over my sock-clad feet as I dive into the closet of winter clothes. Swimming among the musty jackets and snow-wear, I pluck out my intended targets and toss everything onto the counter.

By the time I'm done, Josie emerges from her room,

rubbing the crust from her eyes. When they land on me, her suspicion is clear. A look is enough from Josie—we've gotten to that point.

"Breakfast, *then* fun," I say, before she can voice any hesitancy.

"*Okay*," she says slowly. Her blinks take on the same lethargic cadence as she yawns. "What's for breakfast?"

"Toast and jam." I toss over my shoulder as I rummage around the kitchen. Josie usually eats her meals at work, since she's gone in the early morning and comes home late in the evening. "You cannot go wrong with bread."

A weak snort sounds from the breakfast nook; I shoot her a heatless glare.

"There's a reason why I own night-life bars and not restaurants," I say, pushing the lever on the toaster. For good measure, I move the dial back one peg; knowing my luck, I'll manage to burn the centers even when I have it on a reasonable setting. "I can make a damn good cocktail. Leo's the baker. You're the cook."

"By that logic, I should be the one making breakfast right now."

"Yeah, you probably should be," I say, leaning against the counter. The toaster heats my back, and its timer ticks a steady beat.

"Do I dare ask what all that is before I've had a chance to down my morning coffee?" Josie asks, pointing a finger at the pile of snow clothes I've gathered for our adventures.

"Are you not energized by the prospect of embracing your inner child with me today?" I say, feigning aghast.

"Who are you and where are you hiding the Imogen from the last few weeks?" Josie jokes.

I snort. "You've got it backwards, Joze. We *want* that

Imogen to stay hidden. I'm partial to keeping the original, fun version around."

It's fast, how the mood flips from teasing joy to awkward seriousness. Neither of us acknowledges outright what I've admitted.

Glimmers of the old me have emerged in random, small moments. Most of them I attribute to the woman sitting in my breakfast nook. She's been such a constant in this period of flux. And I wish to be the same for her.

This morning could be a glorious break in the clouds for us both after a *long* week of rain. The sun's warmth is shining, and I'd hate to see the rays swallowed up by the nebulous gray before we can take advantage.

Because the break will patch over again. At least for a little bit. But now, I have more tools to push through that wall of clouds. And I can survive in the overcast a while longer—can subsist on the hope that this season will pass, as sure as spring blooms after winter.

The toaster *pops*.

I busy myself with plating us each two pieces of toast and preen at how there's not a burned edge in sight. And when Josie takes a bite of her jam-and-butter-slathered piece, humming her delight, my smile hurts my cheeks with how big it grows.

My brother taught me the perfect ratio of butter to jam when I was eight. It isn't newsworthy. But the fact that you didn't have to choose between creamy and salty or sweet and sticky? That blew my youngling mind. I've used both ever since.

Josie hums as she chews. "Is this fresh raspberry preserve?"

"I get it from the market in the village. There's a cute old lady who makes it from her home garden. She's been there forever, ever since I first visited with my family."

"You know preserves are different from jam, right?" Josie teases. She covers her mouth with a lithe hand, a faint blush on her cheeks. "In a technical sense, I mean."

I lean forward conspiratorially. "It's all the same to me and the common folk: sweet, sticky, yummy. I don't need the technicalities."

Josie's shoulders bounce with silent laughter between bites. A dot of jam hangs onto the corner of her mouth, and I itch to reach over and wipe it away. Her tongue beats me to it.

Giddy gooseflesh spreads over my arms; the action clearly wasn't meant to pull such a response from my body. But it happens anyway. Has happened a few times now.

Things shifted at Hattie's party.

Maybe it was the closure I got with Nora. I wasn't surprised by what she said, but I needed to hear it from her lips. She was done. *We* were done.

I know part of me will always love her. When the dust settles, a piece of her will remain in my heart. And I know that love can be channeled into rekindling a new version of friendship between us. Maybe not right away, I'm still angry and hurt. But soon.

That conversation set me free, in a way. And while I don't quite know how I should react to *this*, I do know that whatever *this* is excites me. Gives me hope.

"You're silly," Josie says, pulling me from my thoughts.

I take a crunchy chomp of my toast and swallow it down with the sudden rush of butterflies fluttering in my chest.

"Sure, but I'm also right," I say.

My cheeks burn from the cold. I know they're terribly red, along with my sniffling nose, but I like it. The sting is nice. Fresh.

"You're doing it wrong," I say, stomping over from where I've put the finishing touches on another snowman. Josie huffs, straightening from where she's filling in the gaps of the snowballs we've rolled into boulders. We're on our last one; the two others we've made are waiting for their third to complete their family. "He's too lumpy now."

"If you're so concerned about it, you can help me," Josie snarks, tossing a lump of snow my way. I dodge it, mostly, bits of white catching in the fibers of my snow pants.

"I finished the other two already. You're the slacker," I tease, kneeling down next to her. I had shown her how to make the first one and then sent her off to complete her own. She's terribly slow and surprisingly clumsy—the middle body of her snowman falling apart every time she tries to shape it.

"However, I am a merciful host and will assist." I carve around the snow she's packed in tight, turning him from a snow-tube to a true snowman.

Josie inches closer, our thighs pressed together as we kneel.

"There," I say, giving our creation a final pat.

"Thank you," Josie says, her breath clouding around us. She pulls two carrots from her deep jacket pockets. One is crooked and knotted, while the other is stick-straight. "Which one do you think?"

"I can't do it *all* for you, Josie. Picking out his style is the fun part."

Josie snorts. "Okay, then I guess I will go with the wackiest combination I can think of."

"There you go," I drawl.

Josie crawls around me, carefully fitting her snowman with

the crooked carrot, an orange scarf, and tiny sticks for arms. He fits our snowmen family perfectly.

Their misshapen forms stand guard at the edge of the pines that surround my cabin. Their heads are topped with my brother's and mother's old hats, and a conglomeration of raisins gives them wide, curved grins.

Josie pokes in her final touches, a pair of mismatched buttons from the coat closet sewing kit.

She turns to me. "What do you think?"

"He's certainly... something." I try to keep a mask of neutrality, but it's too hard to hide the twitch of my lips. "Maybe you should stick to food creations."

"What? He's much prettier than yours."

I burst into laughter. "I'm *kidding*—he's perfect. Though you shouldn't slander his family. That's rude."

She steps towards me, stopping inches from my face. The fronts of our jackets brush as she smirks down at me. "It's not an insult to *them*. I'm poking fun at their creator."

Josie pokes my side for good measure, and I squeak, jerking away. Even with all our layers, I am ticklish. Her smirk turns evil at my reaction.

"Don't you dare," I warn.

Josie inches forward. "I don't know what you're talking about. I'm cold. Can't we cuddle for warmth?"

I inch back, the snow crunching under my boots. "I don't think your intention is to *cuddle* right now."

"But I'm cold," Josie teases. Her steps forward match my retreat, our pace quickly escalating. "Why are you afraid, Mo? I'm not going to hurt you, I promise. I just want a hug."

"Uh-huh. You do understand that I will hurt you if you think tickling me in the snow is a good idea—ah!" Josie lunges for me and I squeal, running away. It turns into a full chase across the yard, with a mini snowball fight in the middle.

And when we're worn out, we break; Josie's laugh is deep and full as she falls back in the snow. I join her, flopping over and flattening the haphazard tracks we've carved into the pristine landscape. My teeth chatter, making my smile shake, but my lips spread wide as we pant in the snow.

"I needed this," she says.

"Sometimes I come up with good ideas."

Josie snorts, and my head falls to the side, catching the scrunching of her round nose. Then, there's a wistful sigh. "I don't want to go inside yet, but my bones might actually be frozen solid."

"I don't have a pickax to chip you out of the ice, but I'm sure I can make do with a kitchen knife," I say.

Josie sits up, snow dropping off her back. The ground is indented with her figure, not quite a snow-angel—more like a cookie-cutter punch. "You're ridiculous."

I shrug, the snow crunching under my shoulders. There's a happy fluttering in my tummy, and I don't want it to go away. I beam up at her with a wide, teasing smile. "*Or*, hear me out. I'm secretly funny?"

"I've always known you were funny." Josie studies me, eyes darkening. "This just... feels different. I'm thankful to see this side of you again, and for being able to discover the parts I might have missed of you before. It's exciting."

There's a brief moment where my breath stalls in my chest and my blood freezes. You could slice me open and red crystals would fall out, lazily, like the storm that's resumed above us. But then my eyes tingle, and something potent fills my throat, and I'm scrambling upright.

"You always pull out these random one-liners that punch me in the gut." I laugh nervously. I swat at the clumps of snow that stick to the fibers of my coat, trying to ignore her intense gaze.

Josie's lips part, and her expression turns awkward, as if she doesn't know how to respond.

Suddenly she sneezes, elbow coming up to cover her face. "Excuse me," she mumbles into her coat, but it breaks the tension between us.

I hold out my gloved hand. "C'mon, let's go in before you really do freeze and join the snowmen."

She glances back at our creations, a soft smile pulling at her lips. "I'd be such an excellent addition though."

I shake my head and hold back my laugh. Wriggling my fingers, I sweeten the deal. "But doesn't a fresh, steaming cup of hot cocoa sound good right now?"

Josie takes my hand. "You're very convincing, you know that?"

"Mhm. It's a talent of mine."

I lean back, using my weight as leverage to pull her up. As I do so, my foot slips on the wet snow, and we crash back down together with a laugh. We're a tangle of limbs, and I somehow end up on top, looking down at Josie. My view is partially obscured by the fur-lined hood on my jacket; I push it back to reveal our noses are almost touching.

Our breath puffs between us as heated clouds.

"We ended up cuddling out here after all," Josie says. There's pressure on my waist—her hands grabbing the space above my hips. Her thigh slides up between mine as she shifts. My breath hitches. She huffs a laugh. "And see? No tickling."

"You do always make good on your promises," I whisper. "Do you want your hug now?"

"I won't say *no*," she teases.

The wind whips around us, pushing me closer to her, closer to her warmth. I curl my arms around her and squeeze; she squeezes me back. My head is buried in her neck, and I turn, breathing in her warm and citrusy scent. The tip of my nose brushes her neck. Blackcurrant. Bergamot. Maybe I should steal her perfume.

A beat passes, pressed against her. It's a comforting embrace.

"Thanks for not tickling me," I mutter into her skin. Though that's not exactly why I'm thanking her. It's for everything she's given me lately.

"Not something you need to thank me for."

"Then thanks for humoring me," I say, shifting to get up. And before I even realize what I'm doing, my mouth pecks hers. As if it's the most natural thing in the world to do. "Let's get inside, your lips are turning blue."

I'm standing, with my hand extended for hers to take, when it hits.

Shit. Did I really do that?

We blink at each other, reeling.

"Josie, I—"

"The last time you made hot cocoa it was way too sweet," she rasps. She scurries to standing, snags my hand, and starts to pull me towards the house at breakneck speed.

"Um, okay?"

"I would like to make it this time."

"Okay." I snort, stumbling to keep up.

And even though she's clearly ignoring what just happened, she doesn't let go of my hand. She doesn't let go of *me*. We stomp up the porch steps and fling ourselves inside, and she still doesn't let go of my hand.

A wall of heat hits us, and not another word passes between us.

Josie helps to undo the buttons of my coat and pulls off my gloves with tender care. She rubs my hands between hers to warm them up and then sits me down on the couch before rushing into the kitchen. Fifteen minutes later, she hands me a mug of steaming hot cocoa, her cheeks still flushed from the cold—or is that flush from something else?

My heartstrings play a soft tune in my chest, the song of comfort.

Peace.

We curl up on the couch; our hips and shoulders touching as we quietly sip. There's tension here between us, but it's the delicious kind. The tentative, indulgent kind. It's anticipation, it's potential, it's the precipice of *more*.

It's a surprising revelation.

I let myself linger in it.

30
SILAS

The Virtue leads us down a series of alleys and deserted crosswalks, each darker and dingier than the last. The streetlamps flicker as we pass underneath them, as if Bennie's magic calls to the light. A name change may be in order for the Seelie; the term light-eater is more fitting than light-walker, especially considering the way he snuffed it from Nora's eyes.

Those emeralds have been tarnished since the Virtue forced her hand. He didn't lie, though, which almost makes it worse. If Nora wants to cross the Veil to the Seelie Court, revealing her wings is the price.

My own wings bristle at my back. They have a mind of their own and are ruffled by her discomfort. They want to fan out and cocoon us.

In my periphery, the Seelie magic glitters, clinging to my feathers. It's fascinating, the way the illusion glints in the moonlight. And as a connoisseur of unique magic, my mind is already running the calculations on how shadows could potentially do the same.

Why the thought had never crossed my mind, I do not

know. Revelations aren't made slow; they don't hit you until they're right in your face.

Nora's footsteps, which have been quiet and steady behind me for the last twenty minutes, speed up; my ears twitch, alert.

If this isn't a trap—which I don't think it is—then we will be the first Unseelie fae to step into the Seelie Court in a very long time. If the records from Bramble are to be believed, millennia have passed since our ancestors traded freely between Courts. That was long before the fae that bore my mother's Royal line had decided we were better off hating each other.

Bennie's whistle cuts the air, the man eerily calm as he turns a corner and practically skips us across another crosswalk. My head tilts as I study his back.

His wings are tucked close to his body. The shape is similar to Nora's, except instead of black and green, they are a deep blue with white dots at the edge. I wonder how that all works compared to the Unseelie. How do their wings become what they are? How much is inherited and how much is their own?

"What are you thinking about?" Nora's deep, divinely feminine voice asks. I glance at her from the corner of my eye. "What are you seeing that I'm not?" she whispers harshly. "With my cousin?"

What do *I think of the conniving cousin?* I laugh internally. *He's not a liar. But he's a secret keeper. Must run in their family.*

I don't say that out loud, though.

"I think he's more power hungry than he's making himself out to be. I just can't figure out what his end goal is," I say.

"He's already a Virtue," Nora says, her tone tentatively curious. "What more does he want?"

"And *that* is why I'm stumped."

"It could be as simple as him wanting to clear house," she mutters. The cogs creak into gear, and the raspy narration of her thoughts scratches a deep part of my brain. "Plant his own pawns in the empty roles. Stack the Virtue's votes in his favor. Like father, like son."

I hum, her explanation not sitting quite right.

"You think it's more," she says—an observation, not a question.

We turn another corner and stop short; Bennie waits for us with his hands planted firmly on his hips. Swinging in the brisk wind above him is an old, creaking sign for a bookstore. The room behind the glass panes is dark; the curtains are drawn, and no warm glow of light flickers through the fibers to indicate it's occupied.

But beyond Bennie's shoulder, the air wavers. It's like heat over pavement in summer, except there's an extra glimmer that betrays it as magic.

"Interesting front for a portal," I murmur.

Bennie pulls a metal key from his pocket and unlocks the door with a *click*. "Why? Care to share what hides yours? Seems a fair trade."

I chuckle, dismissing his not-so-subtle dig for information. My shadow-veil may fall one day, but that doesn't mean I'm going to hand him the key to our Court *before* then. Wrath would skin me alive if I did. *Operational security* and all. I imagine Nora would incite violence upon me too, considering House Pride has gone to great lengths to keep the portal's location under wraps for centuries.

Like the Seelie's, it's hidden in plain sight—though much more accessible by automobile—masked in the shadows of a bridge underpass.

"Not happening," Nora says. "Good try though."

Her cousin laughs, but the amused sound cuts off when she tries to push past him into the shop; his arm darts out, barring her path across the entryway.

"Wings," Bennie says.

Nora bristles. "Now?"

"You walk through that door, and you step onto the streets of Avalon. Yes, *now*."

Nora mumbles a cursed *fine* under her breath. Her lashes hit her cheeks, her eyes screwing shut as if she can't stand to keep them open. It takes a moment, but the strange magic that lets our wings fold out from between the fibers of our clothes fizzles.

Nora shudders.

Twin butterfly wings unfurl from between her shoulders.

My bottom lip finds its way between my teeth, and I bite down on the flesh.

They're beautiful. The dark green membrane glitters in the moonlight, veins running through them like they're stained-glass art. Lace-like edging, black as my own shadows, swoops along the curves of her wings, ending in the curled teardrops of the lower pair.

How different would the texture be from mine? Soft? Smooth? My fingers twitch in my pockets, and I curl them into fists to tamper down the urge to reach out.

They're identical to the pair that hang above her mantle, except these are brighter. But maybe that's because they're brimming with life. Those other wings are dead, relics of a Nora who doesn't exist anymore.

I'm struck with repulsion and regret: what a waste of such natural magnificence it was to rip them from her, life-ruining secret or not. I should have outlawed the practice when I came into power.

"Ready?" Bennie's pointed question has my gaze raising to meet both his and Nora's.

Looking at them now, their relation is glaringly obvious. The same long, straight nose. The same deep-set green eyes, though slightly different shades. The same high cheekbones and broad shoulders that taper to smaller waists.

But where Bennie's expression is relaxed, Nora's is tight. Her eyes are glazed over, cold as ice. I've seen the same countenance in the mirror before, many years ago. It's a severance from the present, a coping mechanism. One that allows you to walk through the world when in complete agony.

Does she hate her wings that much?

Avalon resembles a busy village from storybooks more than a modern city.

Their portal shimmers around us, the Seelie magic dropping us in a bustling square filled with small merchant booths. Nora turns around, searching for the entrance back to the portal, but there's nothing behind us except more vendors haggling their patrons.

"How strange," I whisper, stepping deeper into the night market.

"Come." Bennie beckons us into the throngs of fae. His body language brokers no argument.

We follow.

Even though I knew he wasn't lying about the Seelie always having their wings out, it's still a shock. Every person, save for small children who clasp their parents' hands, has a pair of pearlescent wings trailing behind them.

I tuck my own close to my back, avoiding contact with passersby; and as if she was trained to, Nora slides behind me, taking up the flank position. When I glance over my shoulder, I catch her stoic gaze sweeping over the crowd. I almost tease her about being my new bodyguard, but decide against it.

Bennie leads us through the cobblestoned streets, which aren't wide enough for automobiles—only small carts, horses, or pedestrians. The buildings we pass are compact, only rising a few stories to accommodate a storefront on the bottom level and housing on top. They are nowhere near the scale of the skyscrapers in Anwynn.

"It's almost... quaint," I mutter, which pulls a booming chuckle from Bennie.

A few pedestrians turn their heads our way, but quickly disperse when they see who the laughter came from.

"You could certainly call it that," Bennie says. "Though I'd like to see more development in the coming years. Not here, exactly. This sector of the city is called Old Town. The rock here is no good to build on. Other areas though..."

His speech fades, and we weave through a few more streets without pause. But the hair on my neck stands on end the longer we walk without trouble. It couldn't possibly be *this* easy to blend in. With or without red hair dye and light-shrouded wings.

We are new. And new draws attention no matter where you are.

As if reading my mind, Nora's rough whisper hits my ear.

"Had I realized it would be this easy once we stepped through the portal, I might have gone door knocking human-side years ago."

"Maybe if you had befriended me at the same time, I could have helped," I tease.

"There was no world in which I would have instigated a friendship with you of my own accord." I can hear the eye roll in her tone. "Do you also sense there's something strange going on?"

I hum my agreement. There are eyes on us.

Pinpoints of heat smatter my body, but everywhere I look, the fae mingling are decidedly *not* glancing our way.

Nora drops back, and if I had eyes on the back of my head, I imagine I'd see her subtly thumbing her gun beneath her coat. Us predators, we have a sixth sense separate from our magic.

We turn a final corner, and once again, Bennie stops us short. But instead of a bookstore hiding a portal, we stand in a short alley leading to a three-story building. The mismatched stone facing has ivy crawling between the seams, and the wooden door is warped.

Bennie unlocks this one with another metal key. He nudges the wood, and the door creaks open, the hinges in need of oil. Beyond is the stale, dark air of the safe house.

"Here you are," Bennie says.

I don't walk over the threshold, instead leaning against the doorframe. "Before you go, I assume Old Town is yours?"

Bennie smirks, his mustache quirking, but says nothing. A non-answer is answer enough.

"And does the portal always drop fae there, in that market?" I continue.

"Light magic is similar to shadow magic, but there's a reason they're different." Bennie shrugs, then nods at the open door. "Kitchen is fully stocked. I'd appreciate if you didn't leave until I'm back to get you."

"We're supposed to sit in there and *wait*?" Nora chuffs. "For how long?"

"I thought we *just* went over this at the diner," Bennie says, like an annoyed younger sibling. At least, it's what I think a younger sibling who's exasperated by their elder sounds like. It's a vision I project onto Wrath often. "I'm not locking you up.

You'll find no iron cuffs in there. Partly because I know it'd be pointless to try to keep you chained, and partly because it would defeat the purpose of developing a *partnership*. So yes, I expect you to sit in there and *wait* for my go ahead. *Please.*"

"Fine," Nora lies. "But I'm done with the wings."

She steps under the protection of the doorway, and her wings immediately curl back into her body. Part of me is disappointed when they wink out of existence; Nora disappears in kind, stalking into the dark depths of the house.

A second passes, and a door slams.

Another second passes, and Bennie sighs. It's a forlorn exhalation that solidifies my belief that he genuinely longs for a connection with his cousin.

It's something I should use to my advantage.

"I'll come back when it's time," Bennie says. "Remember, don't put your wings away. It'll break the illusion I put on them."

I give him a salute, and in a flash of light, he disappears.

I take one moment to scan the windows across the alley. The curtains are drawn, but one corner flutters, confirming my suspicions.

I turn my back on the hidden eyes watching us and shut the door, flicking the deadbolt in place. I lock myself inside with a woman hell-bent on destruction and a growing sense that I'm about to fall into *deep fucking shit* with her.

31
NORA

Hot water scalds my back, running over my scars and down the shower drain, along with what feels like the last vestiges of my sanity. The space between my shoulder blades twinges; it's a confusing mix of my wings flexing beneath the skin and phantom pains of the past.

My body shudders, and one hand clasps over my mouth, as if to physically stop the bile gagging my throat. I swallow it back down, curling into myself at the bottom of the shower tub. My palm comes away wet, and not from the scalding water spurting from the shower head.

I *knew* this would happen, this adverse reaction to letting them out.

I don't cry.

I scrub myself with a washcloth until the itching at my back stops—or is at least masked by the rubbed-raw texture of too-clean skin.

The overwhelming disgust fades to a dull ache when the last of the shampoo washes out of my hair.

I get smaller, coiling tighter as the water flows over my

closed lids. It drips from my lashes and onto my thighs as my forehead hits my knees. I sit there in the steam, with my nails digging into the back of my neck, until the shower runs cold.

The second my teeth chatter, my aches turn to anger, as if the *thought* of freezing at the bottom of this tub any longer is an insult to my pride. It rekindles my internal fire in an instant. That glowing hearth pulses, reminding me where all this disgust and hatred should be directed. It's my rallying call, my war horn at dawn.

Patience.

My fingers release their hold on my tender flesh and, trembling, they call forth the tether linking me to my uncle. I blink against the flow of water down my face, eyeing the golden thread that ties us together. It floats between my knuckles, too strong to be broken by an emotional outburst such as this.

No, this thread must be cut as intentionally as my wings once were.

Sheared.

Pruned.

Like a weed, he'll be snipped from the gardens of Faerie. I must gut the earth of his roots. Rip every last piece of his influence from the Courts. It's the only way to get what I want—what I need.

Their safety, if I'm successful.

Some peace of mind, if I'm lucky.

Numb from the emotional drain and the freezing water, I reach back and turn the faucet off.

"Oh good, you're finally out," Silas says.

My feet stop short of the dividing line between the hallway's hardwood and the kitchen's tile. Silas lounges against the counter, munching on a bag of nuts. He tosses one in the air and catches it on his tongue, a smug, closed-lipped smile forming on his face as he chews.

"Yeah." I wince at how raw my voice sounds.

I urge my body forward, my bare feet unfazed by the cold tile. I hadn't gone looking for socks after finding a pair of trousers and a shirt in the wardrobe I raided. I continue to towel my damp hair with one hand, while the other opens cabinets, checking on what Bennie has stocked.

"It's all a bunch of boring staples," Silas says between crunches of the peanuts he's throwing back. "Good and fine for a safe house, but not up to snuff for a king."

"Meaning you don't know how to cook, so you opted for a snack," I mutter.

"You know me so well."

I slam the cabinet shut. I'm not hungry; my hands just needed something to do.

I lean my hip against the counter, flicking the damp towel over my shoulder and crossing my arms. I study the dark wood cabinetry and the quiet townhouse with a frown, the air growing thicker the longer I stay quiet.

"We're not going to wait here for days, right?" I finally ask.

"I'd hope not."

"Okay. Good." I trace circles on the counter with the tip of my nail.

"Did you doubt we'd be on the same page about not wasting our time in enemy territory?" Silas asks, brows pinching together in confusion.

I shrug. My nail catches on the woodgrain, but I keep dragging my finger across it, undeterred. "There are many doubts I have about you."

Silas barks a laugh; he always does that, as if he thinks I'm *so amusing*.

"You wound me with your verbal barbs," he says. There's another crunch of a peanut between his perfectly white teeth. "I do think we should wait a day. There are too many eyes on us right now."

Even if we do wait a day, I'd bet there are spies of Bennie's crawling all around this area of the city. We'll have to be smart in evading them.

"We need to map out the city. I'm not going to rely on Bennie leading us everywhere. That will only end in one of our destinations being a trap—by his design or someone else's," I say.

"We could find a library. They'll have archives with maps." When I shake my head, Silas adds, "Or we could snag a random passerby and see what they say. Then kill them."

"Too risky."

"You're passing up a chance to kill a Seelie?"

I shake my head again. "If we need to, we will. But it'll draw too much attention, given this is Bennie's territory. We don't know how far it extends. Or which other Virtue's borders his."

Silas leans forward, tongue poking his cheek. "Then what do you propose, oh wise one?"

"If you want information without drawing attention, you go where people talk freely."

That smarmy smirk of his makes my stomach twist. "You want us to go drinking."

"I want us to go to a pub," I clarify.

"That's the same thing."

"No, it isn't. I don't plan on drinking," I say.

"Then you won't blend in."

"*Gods.* I won't have more than one drink, then."

Silas hums, then goes back to munching on his snack. The noise of his teeth mashing the nuts together has my eye twitching. I stomp over and snatch the bag from him.

"Give me those," I huff.

"Hey," he whines but makes no move to grab them back. He just licks the salt from his fingertips, popping each between his rosy lips and sucking them clean. I'm caught off guard by the act, which is made worse by his unwavering eye contact. Silas smiles around his fingers, as if he enjoys the attention. "How are we going to pay, anyway?"

I blink, my attention flicking up to his eyes, where it should stay. "Is that a real question?"

"Yes."

"I'll fleece someone." I shrug, opening a random cabinet and tossing the bag of peanuts on a shelf. The wood slams shut with finality.

Silas chuckles, palm rubbing against his chest. "Why am I surprised to hear you have fancy fingers?"

"I don't know. You should have expected as much given all my other skills," I say.

"*Ah, yes.* The torture and murder and the stint in the mafia fighting ring should have tipped me off to your delinquent ways," he says sarcastically. He steps closer and leans in conspiratorially. "In light of all that, pickpocketing is child's play."

"It is. I was, what, nine the first time?" I say, inching back. It's a big kitchen, why is he getting so close?

"You don't talk of your childhood often," Silas says thoughtfully.

"I try not to dwell on it."

My eyes squint on some invisible spot on the wall in search

of the memory. It was one of the few nice days of my child-hood, where a poisonous sip of hope made me think that Pride could be a good man. He was patient as he taught me—anony-mous in the middle of Anwynn's streets, before the rest of the Houses knew of me or my power. Thinking back, I was a natural, swiping wallets and watches; I hadn't tested his patience yet. That bit of hope was a falsehood, a red herring in the story of my life.

I don't know why I even mentioned it, but my lips moved before my brain could stop them.

Silas hums, but it's a sad sound. It lingers in the air, like he doesn't want to let this path of conversation go.

He does.

"Where did you get those clothes?" he asks, changing the subject. "You weren't wearing those before."

I peer down at the simple garb, a cotton blouse and wool trousers. They are clearly new, but the style still lends itself an old-time-y air. From this and what we saw in the market streets, Seelie fashion seems to be slower in adopting modern styles than over in the Unseelie Court.

"The closets are full. Bennie was prepared for us—or at least me, since these fit well enough. I'm assuming any men's clothes in the other closet are his. You can use those." I shift, pulling at the collar of my shirt. The cotton rubs my back wrong, and I reach my hand up to scratch. My nails scrape, soothing the writhing sensation under my skin.

Our eyes meet, a clashing of black and green that I've grown familiar with, but not used to. Under his dark gaze, my skin crawls. I hate the way those irises *see*.

A moment passes—one where the moonlight that filters through the window snuffs out, covered by a passing cloud.

Silas's stare falls to my shoulders, boring two holes

through to my back. I pull my hand from where it was scratching and let it hang at my side.

"You'll have to bring them back out. You understand that, right?" Silas says.

I suck in a breath through my nose, slow and deep.

"Yes, I am aware," I say, the itch between my shoulder blades returning. "I'm going to bed."

"Nora—"

I hold out a hand to stop him. "I can't tonight, Silas. Please, drop it."

I turn away from the Unseelie King, but it doesn't stop the way his soul keeps poking at mine, as if it's begging for a response. But I can't afford to give it one. Not right now.

32
NORA

Someone follows us, but it's unavoidable, given our circumstances. Silas doesn't know the area—*yet*—so he cannot whisk us away with his magic. We'll just have to shake them the old-fashioned way.

Which is ten times harder with two people. One of whom is a six-foot tall man with ridiculous copper-red hair and a set of spelled wings that glitter too brightly for subtlety.

"We could embrace the spies and try to twist it to our advantage," Silas says.

I shoot a glare to my right, where he walks in stride with me.

How did he—

"How did I know you were thinking of at least ten new plans to try and lose them?" Silas chirps with a smirk. "I'm glad you asked. When you're plotting, you get a tiny crease between your brows, and your head tilts ever so slightly to the left. If you tilt to the right, then you're annoyed."

My steps falter. "Can you take this seriously for one minute?"

Silas spins, walking backwards. "I'm always serious."

"Uh-huh. I don't believe you."

The mismatched cobblestone makes my strides less steady, the heights of each stone varied. It doesn't help the unsettled nausea in my stomach, which developed as soon as Silas held the front door open for me and I had to unfurl my wings.

They twitch, stiff and aching to be spread out. But I refuse, and keep them tucked tightly against my back.

Magic shifts the air in my periphery. Whoever is following us from House Benevolence is concealing themselves, and I'm almost positive they're trailing us in the air. *Flying.*

Which means it'll take them a moment to follow us into whatever building we go into.

I spot the perfect space—a grocery—and before I can second guess myself, I grab Silas's hand.

He makes a mouse-like squeak of surprise as I drag him through the shop door. A bell dings above us, and we weave through the tight aisles of produce. And then I see it—the back entrance. We hurry down another aisle, and our view of the front door is blocked. The bell dings shortly after.

"Bet you ten dollars that was our babysitter," I snicker, eyeing Silas over my shoulder.

He's got this bewildered awe marking his features, gaze locked on our joined hands. The expression surprises me, and nerves fire off in response. Suddenly, the sticky grip of our leather gloves sends panic clawing up my neck.

I quickly drop his hand and lock in on an easy target approaching. The man is bundled in a coat three sizes too big for him, and his scarf covers half his face.

Our shoulders collide. He yelps, dropping his basket of groceries; my hand slips into his pocket and pulls out his wallet.

"I'm sorry, sir!" I say, moving out of his way.

"No, I'm sorry," he says, barely paring us a glance as he chases after a rolling can.

I jerk my head at the door for Silas to follow. We rush out, but instead of sprinting down the street, I duck us into the side alley next to the store. I force Silas behind the dumpster with me, and he gags at the pungent stench.

"Shut up and cloak us with shadows," I say.

He huffs, but the darkness of the alley comes alive, clinging around the dumpster.

Seconds later, the bell of the grocery door sounds, and a panting Seelie bursts into the alley. He pauses, head swiveling around, before muttering a curse.

He doesn't spot us.

Magic ripples the air, and the Seelie disappears from view.

We wait—one minute, then two—before the pinpricks of Seelie magic disappear.

Silas must sense it too, because he releases his own magic's hold on the shadows around us. The darkness falls back, and he straightens to his full height.

"That was... unexpected," he says.

"I saw an opportunity and took it." I pull out the stolen wallet from my pocket and wave it in his face.

Silas huffs a laugh. "When did you steal that?"

"You didn't see me shoulder-check that old man?"

I tug a small stack of bills from his wallet; it's a sizable amount, if Seelie currency is anything like human or Unseelie dollars. I snicker—leave it to the old folk to always carry so much cash on them. Tossing the empty wallet into the dumpster, I tuck the loose cash into the inner pocket of my coat.

"C'mon, dinner's on me," I say, leading us out of the alley.

"Had I known this would end in a date, I would have made you steal a man's wallet sooner," Silas teases.

I glare at his shit-eating grin. "This isn't a fucking date. This is reconnaissance."

"That is a matter of perspective." His deep laugh bounces between the old buildings, and I trudge forward, shaking my head.

"*Gods help me,*" I mutter.

I continue to scan our surroundings for danger as we make our way to a small pub. It's plenty busy, but nothing triggers that sixth sense I have that warns me trouble is lurking.

We tuck into a small booth in the back, and the waitress that approaches eyes Silas like he's a fresh cold beer poured just for her. He plays right into it, of course; the shameless flirt even winks after placing his order.

I do a terrible job of holding back my eye roll.

"Don't roll your eyes. I'm simply doing my fair share of contributing. The more stuff we get for free, the less you have to steal from some sap on the street," Silas says.

I snort. "You suddenly grow a conscience?"

He runs his hand through his red-dyed hair.

The white suits him better.

"No, but if there are innocents on our side, then there are innocents here too," Silas says, a frown flattening his lips as he glances around the pub. The tables are full, and glass steins clank together. Cheers sound as the citizens of Avalon enjoy a night out after work. Silas juts his chin towards something over my shoulder. "Look at the two at the end of the bar."

I peek over the edge of the booth. Two men with armor— like they're some kind of medieval knights—sit at the bar's end-cap. They stay huddled together, though one's hands gesture wildly as he talks.

Bingo.

"Those are ridiculous outfits," I say. "Even for Royal guards."

"Oonagh is one for tradition," Silas mutters. "As is your uncle."

"Do you want to go or am I—"

"Here you go!" The Seelie waitress appears in a blip of light. She drops food in front of Silas, her wings fluttering at her back. They're a pale pink monstrosity that matches the blush on her cheeks. "Are you new in town? I've never seen you around before."

"Yeah, you could say I'm new," Silas replies with a charming smile. He plants his elbow on the table, leans his cheek on his hand, and bats his lashes at the waitress. "If you have a moment to spare, why don't you tell me more about Old Town? I'd love to hear a real local's perspective on what we should check out."

There's a brief flash of possessiveness that churns my gut —but it's overshadowed by the vomit threatening to spew from his terrible flirting. I quickly excuse myself and slip out of the booth, but the girl has heart eyes so big for Silas that I don't think she even notices.

I slide into the empty seat between one guard and an ancient, wrinkle-faced woman sitting to his right. I call the bartender with a quiet raised hand; he approaches, throwing his bar towel over his shoulder.

"I'll have whatever she's having," I say, jerking a thumb at the ancient Seelie. She chuckles; the crow's feet around her eyes deepen as she sips at golden liquid sloshing around a block of ice. Her wings sit flat against her back, a bright, iridescent blue cape.

"Good taste," she rasps.

The bartender taps the counter in acknowledgment of my order before being called to an overzealous patron at the other end.

Perfect.

My ears twitch as I lean forward on the counter, tuning into the conversation to my left.

"I don't understand why he's the one calling all the shots now. Chastity is the one who's supposed to lead the guard. Not Patience."

"Eh, it's been this way for a while. You'll get used to it, Sammy. Keep your head low, and you'll make out fine."

"Not everyone is a jaded geezer like you, Don. Some of us actually want to *serve*. Not stand around playing sentry."

"Would you rather be up in the northern reach, draining your magic day and night? In all that fucking snow?" The older guard huffs, slamming his drink onto the counter. "Every light-walker guard with enough juice is being pulled there unless they have a station at the palace. The front lines aren't all they're made out to be. Take it from a *jaded geezer* who started serving long before you were born."

The guard grunts his distaste and flops back in his seat. He reaches for his drink, but now that he doesn't have his back to me, he jolts, realizing someone is next to him.

He's *young* young, the kind of fresh face lacking the shadows of a soldier who's seen some shit. He stares openly, with his stein pressed against his lower lip, not yet tipping it to drink.

I raise a brow. "Do you need something?"

My sharp tone shocks him out of his brazen staring.

"Sorry!" he says, quickly averting his gaze.

But he doesn't go back to his conversation with the older guard; the warmth of the Seelie's attention lingers on my cheeks.

"Sorry," he says again. "But you look familiar. Did you go to Merrymount prep?"

"Nope."

"Are you sure?"

"Yep." I tap my fingers on the bar, hoping he'll disengage and go back to talking with his partner.

"Can I buy you a drink, then, and figure out where I've seen you before? I never forget a beautiful face," he says, not getting the hint.

"Nope."

"Why not?" he pouts.

The bartender chooses that moment to drop my drink in front of me.

"I already have a drink, and I'm too old for you." I toss the bartender a few bills to cover it. Then I lean forward, addressing the older guard and ignoring the younger's perturbed expression. "You should teach him some manners."

The old man cackles like I've told the funniest joke.

I cut my losses and accept that some information gained is better than nothing. I walk back to the booth where Silas digs into the food he ordered. As I weave through the patrons, a flash of blond catches my eye. My steps falter at the golden hue, and my nose fills with florals.

What are the chances of a blond who wears rose perfume crossing my path? It's comical, really, how she haunts me.

I slide into the booth, my heart pounding in my chest.

I down a finger of my drink. It burns my throat.

The glass hits the table with a sharp *clack*, and I stare into the golden liquid. Amber, like her eyes.

My lids fall closed.

I breathe through my nose in hopes that fresh air will clear it of that cloying rose scent. But it doesn't change the fact that I *miss her.*

Is this heartbreak? To yearn for something you can never have?

"What happened?" Silas asks, far too observant for his own good.

"Nothing," I sigh, keeping my eyes closed.

"Did you get anything good?" he asks.

"Yeah."

"Are you going to share?" he draws out slowly.

"Later."

He chuffs. "I also got some good intel from the waitress. Thank you for asking."

"Silas?"

"Yeah?"

"Can you shut up? For one minute?" My elbows find the table, and my forehead finds my palms. I try to suck in my own scent, but that floral perfume clings to me. "Because I need a minute."

There's a beat of blessed silence, then the persistent moth-erfucker prods again.

"How many different ways do I have to tell you I'm here for you before you finally believe it?" he asks.

In some cruel irony from the gods, the words are eerily similar to what Imogen said the night I broke our hearts. *How many times do I have to tell you I want all of you before you believe it?* It makes anger swoop in my stomach, and I let loose a growl, lifting my head.

"Fine. You want to know what's set me off?" I ask.

"Yes," he says, serious.

"I don't know if I can love."

Silas chews on my revelation. "Why is that?"

"Because if I truly loved Imogen, wouldn't I have done more to make her happy? Changed myself to be what she needed?" I ask, my frustration palpable.

"Ah, so it's her that's got you all twisted..." Silas hums, tucking a piece of lettuce that hangs out of his sandwich back between the slices of bread. "I imagine relationships are more complicated than that."

"Either way, I couldn't do it," I say.

Silas shrugs. "That's okay."

"Is it?" I ask, my lips curling into a sneer. "It doesn't feel okay."

Silas tilts his head back and forth. "It's *okay* if it wasn't meant to be." He takes a bite of his sandwich.

I rub my chest, right above where it aches. "How long do you think I'll feel like this?"

"Hm?"

"Mo said feelings don't just go away. She was right. It's been weeks. So, when do you think they'll go away?" I ask.

Silas swallows, sets his sandwich down, and taps the corners of his mouth with a napkin. "Until you move on, I suppose."

I deflate, slouching in the booth. "That's awfully inconvenient."

Silas chuffs. "Who told you love was convenient?"

A lump forms in my throat. "No one."

"Here's what I think," Silas says, leaning forward. A lock of hair falls onto his forehead, and he blows it out of the way. "You can't fix a heart that's broken. It's the one thing in life that can't be thrown out or mended to be as it was before."

"But how do you *know*?" I ask, desperate for an answer.

"I might not have loved before, but I'm confident I've had my heart broken in other ways," Silas says. "You have to care enough about yourself to find a way to move on. I can't tell you how to do that though. I don't think my method would work for you."

My eyes narrow. "What's your method?"

"Getting under someone new," Silas mutters, lifting his drink to his lips. His eyes cut across the pub and his free hand waves a circle at me. "It just doesn't seem like your style."

There's a faint blush tinting his cheeks, and for a second I stare at him confused. Then his choice of words *clicks*.

Instead of my gut reaction being annoyance, I find I want to laugh. My lips pinch together as I try to school my expression.

"You are right," I tease, tongue in cheek. "Getting *under* someone isn't exactly my style." Silas coughs, choking on his beer. "But I get what you're saying. I could try to find someone to fuck it out of my system with."

While Silas pats at his chest to stop hacking up a lung, I glance away.

It's certainly an idea. No one could replace Imogen, but a warm body could help in other ways.

My gaze lands on the old woman, sitting at the bar. Her wings are tucked so tight to her back—*does she hate them the same way I do mine? Is that how I will end up—old and alone, nursing liquor at a pub?*

"Do I even deserve to move on?" I murmur. "I don't think I care about myself as much as I care that she's okay."

Who would want to stand by me after everything that's happened, anyway? Like Silas pointed out after the Pits, I've been pushing them all away. The only one still here is... him.

"Then maybe you need a mindset shift," Silas says, voice rough. "You can care that Imogen's okay without torturing yourself and ignoring what you need."

I shake my head, turning back to Silas, more confused than ever. "I'm not sure I know what I need anymore."

Silas pushes the second half of his sandwich toward me.

"Eat."

For once in my life, I listen.

33

JOSIE

My knuckles swipe against the frosted window, wiping a clear view of our shipping warehouse parking lot. Our trucks sit idle, four inches of snow atop their beds, lined up next to the loading dock. For two weeks, the drivers have refused to work; a picket line of white signs and red paint slashes across the sidewalk and bars anyone from entering.

Hattie hasn't had any luck getting them back to work. In fact, more are pulled to the picket line with each passing day.

I'm all for collective bargaining—if they'd give us demands. But they've refused my meeting proposals. And now they're punishing the whole House. No money comes in if no goods go out.

Vendors are angry we've paused restocks. Clients are worse, with pending orders left unfulfilled. Even Gluttony, who I've cultivated an excellent partnership with, is breathing down my neck. It's all too clear that certain members of our House want me to fail. They have not flocked to our side the way I had thought they would with Wes dead.

"I'm once again offering to kill them all," Hattie says.

My sigh fogs up the glass, and my knuckles swipe over it again. I wipe the moisture on my wool trousers as I turn around.

Hattie's sitting cross-legged on the deep maroon chaise in her office. There's no formal desk here, only a set of velvet upholstered furniture arranged around a low-sitting coffee table. File cabinets line one wall and windows line another. A gallery of art hangs on the third, and the fourth is blank, save for the door to the hall that's dead-bolted shut.

She doesn't use it—doesn't need it.

"You're not *killing them all*," I say. "That's not how I want to deal with every problem we face as a House. Plus, it'd be a pain and cost us more to find and train new drivers on the routes. Most fae still can't drive, and I don't need merchandise lost to crashes. Especially because it's winter and—"

"Jeez. I get it," Hattie groans, flopping back on the lounger. "No one can take a joke anymore."

"I have a hard time believing you were joking."

"I wasn't, but it's nice to pass it off as one every once in a while."

A shout and ruckus from outside calls me back to the window. Down below, one of the picketers slips over a patch of ice. As they try to get up, they continue to slide, unable to gain enough traction to stand. Instead of helping, the others point and laugh.

I scoff. What are they, schoolhouse bullies?

I can't wait and watch this shit anymore.

If it were Nora standing where I am, she'd have already burst down their door and forced them to the negotiating table. Meanwhile, I've been running the numbers and waiting to see what everyone else does before deciding on my next course of action.

That hasn't worked. And it's setting in that if I'm going to be Pride, I need to *lead*. I need to be the one to make a choice here.

"Hattie." I reach out my hand, not removing my gaze from the young man who shuffles on his hands and knees across the icy pavement. "Take me down there."

Her magic is quick to action, and our boots crunch softly on the snow-laden ground as we step from the shadows. Hattie stands a step behind me, my right hand in the absence of Aisha —who is human-side today, trying to soothe our vendor's worry. Wrath's still keeping the portal locked down, but he's agreed to let us try to get some business done between realms.

I don't recognize the boy on the ground; he must be one of the newer workers in training. I hold my hand out for him. A peace offering.

"Here," I say.

His bright brown eyes widen, and the boy quickly takes my hand. I pull him upright, and he falters on the thick patch of ice. With my support, he's able to clear the slippery bit and find his footing again.

The picketers have fallen quiet, glares glowing in the slit between their hats and their scarves. We're in the most bitter part of winter, those first few weeks of March where it digs its claws in and refuses to wane.

"Gentlemen," I say, hard gaze sliding over each of them. I try to log each face, but it's hard with their face half covered. There haven't been any more acts of violence made against me, but we also haven't found the person who bombed my car. Our resources are spread thin, though I would wager a high chance on it being one of these men or someone related to them. "Aren't you cold out here? Don't you want to come inside, maybe share a warm drink in the warehouse kitchen? Would be a shame if we splurged on the heating system and no one took advantage of it."

"We'd rather freeze," a man spits. He beckons the boy over. "Junior, come here."

I search my memory, trying to match a name to the voice. This part of the business was under Claude's purview, and while I know the logistics of *what*, *when*, and *how*, I wasn't a part of this group's day-to-day operations.

Then it hits me—one Sunday dinner, when I decided to sit with the guys when Nora skipped. He sat three seats down from Claude, with his wife and three boys. Offensively loud. Yelled for his boy Junior to refill his plate for him.

Rupert. A terrible name.

The boy steps forward, but my fingers wrap around the back of his coat and tug, keeping him in place. If I remember correctly, and I do, these two don't have magic. A majority of the truckers don't—that's why they work fae-side. Driving is a skill that gives them value when they lack the currency of magic.

"I've been quite patient with you. Haven't crossed your picket line, despite there being plenty of folks in the city looking for work to get through winter," I say, deadly calm. I don't have the same level of dramatic flair as Nora did, but I can make a point when I need to. "I hoped you'd have the sense to come to me with terms. Instead, you continue to let your House fall on hard times."

"That started when *she* took over," one calls out.

"The numbers state a different story, and they can't lie," I snap. "Stop kidding yourselves. All your defiance will do is ruin our business relationships when we can't deliver on our contracts. It will cause your families to starve." I let go of the boy's coat and push him forward. He stumbles into his father's stony embrace. "If you wanted Wes in power, you should have fought harder to make it so. But you didn't. Nora won, and she abdicated power out of respect for our House. Now you have me."

Magic sparks in the air as I push out my influence. I try to connect with each of their emotions, drawing out their desire for safety, peace, and harmony. I urge them to *listen*.

Okay, maybe I can be as dramatic as Nora.

"I am an empath born and raised in this city. I come from two families who have served in House Pride for generations."

Ice cracks under the men's boots as they shift uncomfortably. Using my magic may be a cheat code, but no one in this world plays fair 100 percent of the time.

"Now, you can either come inside and work out terms on how we can move forward *together*. Or I can let Hattie have her way, which is to simply kill you all and be done with it."

"And you bozos know I make good on my threats!" Hattie calls out from behind me.

My left eye twitches as I force a straight face in the wake of her outburst.

"I know which I would choose," I say, ending my speech. "I'll be inside. You have ten minutes to decide."

"I still can't believe you pulled that shit," Hattie snickers as she drops me inside Imogen's cabin. "Hey, Mo. Oh, snacks! I love when you leave these out for us."

I shuck off my jacket and boots before padding after Hattie, who scrounges food off of small plates on the coffee table like a rat.

"Pulled what shit?" Imogen asks from her spot on the couch.

"Oh, ya know, she just threatened twenty men and had them quivering in their snow boots with her sneaky empath magic." Hattie erupts into a fit of cackles, falling backwards onto the couch with a handful of cheese and crackers.

Imogen cocks a golden brow at me. "That sounds like an eventful day."

"It was amazing. *And* she got them to the bargaining table." Hattie crunches on a snack. "Now we have a tentative agreement and can resume business as usual."

"It *was* eventful," I say, ignoring Hattie in favor of focusing on Imogen. "But productive." My gaze lingers on her outfit. She's wearing one of her *going out* dresses; sparkling white beads dangle off the entire dress, ending at her calves. "You're dressed awfully nice."

Imogen hums around a cracker, chewing and swallowing before speaking again. "Leo was telling me about this party happening tonight. I hate those Royal pricks, but you shouldn't have to deal with them for the first time alone. So, I decided I'm coming with you."

"*Ha.* No," I say, grabbing a few crackers off the table.

"No?"

"No, you're not coming with me to this party." My teeth crunch into salty goodness. *What the hell is she thinking?*

Imogen pouts, one hand on her hip. "Josephine Marie An, you do not get to tell me what I can and cannot do."

I cover my laugh with my hand. "Did you just full-name me? You sound like my mother."

"Your mother sounds like she was a very sensible woman."

"Mo." I try to level with her. "You're not serious, are you?"

"It's not up for debate. I already told Leo I was going to be your date."

"My *date?*"

That's... I... no. That can't happen. Especially not after what happened in the snow. She kissed me, and no matter how casual or brief or heart-stopping it was, it was a momentary lapse in sanity on her part. A whim spurred on by the magic of circumstance. Imogen definitely does not want to be my *date.*

"Well, yes," Imogen drawls out. "Unless you're adamant about me not going. In which case, I'll ask Leo to switch just to spite you, and then you can have Earl."

"But I thought you wanted out of that world completely," I say. Imogen's excitement falls out of her expression, and a flush quickly rises on my cheeks as I try to backpedal. "Simply color me confused. I'm only trying to understand, not pass judgment."

Imogen takes her time in responding, lips pursing and fingers picking at the beads on her dress. Her gaze drops to my hands, where they're creasing my trousers in a vise grip. I quickly release the fabric and smooth it out.

"I want all of you in my life," Imogen says, plainly. "And I can't have that and fully disengage from Court politics. It's true that I needed this break, but I also need to learn how to live with one foot in that a world. This is me officially dipping my toe back in the water."

I suck in a shaky breath. "The last time you went to a Court party, you were almost shot. And then you went into shock. And then you fell into a depression that I'm not even sure is over." It's a harsh retelling of the truth, but I try to land the blows as soft as I can. "What if something happens again? The Sins aren't exactly stable right now, and Silas won't be there to keep them in check."

"I trust you to save me. You have twice before," Imogen says, though those amber eyes darken with the onslaught of painful memories. "Am I supposed to be afraid for the rest of my life? I don't want to run away forever."

I sigh. She has a point.

Hattie, who I almost forgot was in the room with us, shifts on the couch, pulling Imogen into a side hug. Imogen sinks into the touch, and their blond heads knock together.

"I think it's a brave idea," Hattie says. "There are times when running is best, and there are times when facing what troubles you head-on is better. Both instincts are in our nature. But you have to follow your gut to know which is right for you. Is your gut telling you to fight?"

"It is," Imogen says, her determination clear. "I ran. But I've been picking small fights ever since. This is the next one I need to win."

A possessive, proudful beast roars in my chest. How can I say no to that logic? How could I deny her this chance to heal?

"Then you'll come."

34

JOSIE

My heels clack against the checkered tile that extends from the hall and into the ballroom. Despite it being the smaller of two gathering spaces for Royal functions, second to the throne room, it has an aura of grandeur to it. Thick black drapery hangs in rolling swaths along the ceiling and to the windows. Golden trim lines the geometric panes, which sparkle from the lamplight filtering through the winter frost.

Imogen walks stiffly beside me, and yet still holds herself with confidence in the face of entering the lion's den.

The party is in full swing—I was already running late when Hattie dropped me off at the cabin, but it's a nonissue. The sooner this is over, the better.

Leo flags us down and presses quick kisses on Imogen's cheeks in greeting. I get professional nods from both him and Earl, as here we're colleagues, not friends.

"You missed one messy broken engagement, three fights, and double as many broken glasses that the butlers were extremely prompt in cleaning up," Leo says, casually nursing his drink.

"Sounds like some exceptional people watching," Imogen jokes. She shakes out her shoulders, and any average onlooker would see a woman shaking off the cold after arrival, but I know it's a result of our proximity. The three of us ease her nerves.

"I'm glad you came," Leo whispers to Imogen. "I miss you. And between work and Josie taking up residence in your guest room, I don't get nearly enough Mo time."

"You could always sleep in the other bed or on the couch," Imogen says, giggling when Leo makes a sour face at the thought of sharing a room with me. "When the Den's renovations are done, you'll see me more, I promise."

"Soon, right?" he asks.

"Yeah, soon," she says.

After committing to her break from the city, Imogen decided to upgrade some of the Den's facilities. When she returns, it'll be sparkling new.

I snag a drink off a passing waiter's tray; taking a whiff, I scent standard white Faerie wine. I offer it to Imogen, and she takes it with a murmured *thank you*. Grabbing a second for myself, I take a sip. A sweet hint of pear bursts on my tongue.

The party is not as formal as Casimir's Solstice Ball was, but it's a step above what goes down in the bars and clubs across the city. Jewels drip off ears, necks, and wrists. Dresses hit the floor more often than knees, though a few women still cling to the human flapper aesthetic.

I tune into my magic, cracking my shield open to get a better read of the room. An onslaught of desire, frustration, and cunning ambition hit me at once. On top of the emotions swirling in the air, the loudest thinkers project their inner dialogues to me.

My shield slams shut, but it's too late. As if all the loose thoughts in the air gain sentience, they come banging on my psyche to be let in. My fingers tap against the side of the wine glass, my body's way of working through the residual energy firing through my nerves. It's a good thing I didn't wear rings tonight, otherwise I'd be calling a toast every time my magic had me twitching.

"I'm going to grab some food," I say, distractedly walking away from the group.

I feel myself falling into a detached state, and I need to ground myself in something real to quiet the noise.

The refreshments table contains a lot of beige and leaves something to be desired; you'd think the Royals would have finer tastes, but here we are. I try one hors d'oeuvre and have to force it down my throat—too dry. I forgo tasting anything else, opting to stare at the platters until my fingers stop tapping my glass.

A warm presence sidles up to me, and the hair on my neck rises. Imogen's whispered snicker hits my ear as she peers over my shoulder.

"What's looking good? Except you, of course."

A flare of heat rushes to my cheeks—*am I reading this wrong? Is she flirting with me? No, I'm imagining it.*

"Watch it, Mo, or I'm going think you're putting a move on me," I joke. "You don't want to start that game of chicken with me. You won't win."

She chokes on her drink, coughing and tapping at her chest.

I wince. *Shit.* "Too much?"

"*No.* No, you're good." Imogen clears her throat and laughs, though it's got a nervous twinge to it. "I wasn't expecting you to respond like that, that's all."

My lips twist. "Are you surprised?"

"That you can banter?"

I tilt my head back and forth. "Yes?"

"That sounded too much like a question." Imogen's smirk finds her eyes, warming them. "No, I'm not surprised. You quiet ones always have charm sharp as a knife."

"Is that a good thing?" I ask hesitantly.

Suddenly, I need to know—need the validation from her perspective.

I've never been one for relationships, as much as I seem to be a source of advice for my friends about them. Passing hookups have always worked for my physical needs and brief stints of stress relief.

I can flirt. I can do one-night flings. It's only when the touch becomes too intimate that I have issues. I don't have the same complicated relationship with physical touch as Nora, but sometimes, in those vulnerable moments shared between two people, mental shields fall, and it's chaos for my magic.

Too much sensation fills me too quickly; their thoughts and memories rush into my head, unprovoked and uncensored. It never leaves a pleasant taste in my mouth when I kiss away the aftermath of their orgasms.

Even sleeping next to someone else proves hard with my magic.

Except... I've slept next to Mo plenty of times without issue.

"I'm sure those you're with think so," Imogen answers, pulling me from my thoughts. She steps closer, eyes roaming over me. Concern is woven into the crease of her frown. "Are you okay?"

"Yeah," I lie.

"Aren't *I* supposed to be the one having issues here, according to you?" she asks.

I stiffen. "*Are* you having issues?"

Imogen's gaze wanders across the ballroom. A sardonic note fills her voice. "I don't feel much of anything, actually. No harried breath. No blurry vision. No overwhelm. Someone even broke a glass over there, and all I did was flinch. Is apathy the next stage of healing?"

"Ah, ladies, I'm glad you could make it," Greed's deep voice interrupts us. We both spin on our heels, finding the Sin with his devilish smirk, draped in a blood-red suit. He peers around the two of us dramatically. "Though I don't see Pride—sorry, I mean *Nora*. I haven't seen much of her at all since the last Sins' meeting. She didn't want to accompany you? You're usually like this—" Greed raises his crossed fingers. His dark, plotting gaze scans over Imogen, and I instinctively step closer to her, our shoulders brushing. "But then again, I did hear some rumors. It's been a while, Imogen."

"I'd prefer if it were longer," Imogen deadpans, then turns to me. "I'm going back to Leo. Holler if you need me."

She squeezes my arm and saunters away, but not out of my line of sight. Imogen stays planted firmly in my periphery, and I relax when I notice Hattie and Wrath have joined the small group in the corner.

"Walk with me?" Greed asks.

"No."

He clicks his tongue. "Fine."

"I know we're colleagues now, but you're a dick, Greed," I say.

"How so?" he asks.

"I do not feel the need to explain that to you."

"I'll cut right to the chase then." Greed smiles, all his pointed shark teeth on display. "What is she up to?"

He doesn't have to clarify *who*. I take a sip of my drink, muttering over the rim of my glass, "What do you care?"

"Call me curious about the whereabouts of a dangerous fae who doesn't hold me in the highest regard," Greed says. "You keep tabs on all your allies and enemies, don't you?"

"Worried that you're next on her crusade for vengeance?" I ask.

Greed hums his sigh, before scratching at the sharp line of dark stubble on his chin. "Nora could have killed me that night. Envy too. You were there. You also know she doesn't see me as a true threat. I'm more worried about my dear cousin, who seems to have taken a liking to her."

I'm not shocked that he's picked up on Silas's... *preoccupation* with Nora. They have a connection that runs deeper than I think any of us can comprehend. Silas has wiggled his way into our little found family, and I can't imagine we'll be getting rid of him, or Wrath, anytime soon. They're stubborn assholes, same as the rest of us.

"Then I'm surprised you don't know the answer to your question already," I say. I can't help but take a shot at his competence. "The king is contracting her services in preparation for the impending war with the Seelie."

Greed's cunning smile twitches. He's always touted during the Sins' meetings about little birds telling him secrets, but he doesn't know shit. At least, not where Nora is concerned. No one but those in our core unit do.

When Nora and Silas didn't come home after a week, Wrath and I knew we had to create a better cover for them. We knew the Sins would sniff around eventually, and that time has finally come. But that's enough sniffing around for Greed.

It's time to do my own digging.

"Do you know anything about the rat who tried to kill me?" I ask.

"Why would I know anything about that?" he asks, playing dumb.

"Materials for pipe bombs are regulated substances. *Expensive* regulated substances that are mined by companies you have stakes in," I say. "And with the portal closed for so long, it's not as if these materials have been floating around willy-nilly. Forgive me for assuming the biggest investor in Anwynn would know about the unsavory dealings of his own businesses."

"I may need something more to help jog my memory."

I roll my eyes, catching the hint. "Six months of no transport fees for goods to House Greed."

"One year," he counters.

"Nine months," I say with finality. "Three quarters is more than generous."

Greed's smile returns, crawling up his cheeks. "It's a tale as old as time, Pride. Follow the money."

"And if I go to the banks and ask for the records, I won't have an issue?" I ask.

"One year of no fees and you won't."

I frown. There are worse things he could ask for. "You'll hear from my team."

"I like you much more than her already," Greed says, downing the amber liquid in his glass. "I think we'll get along great."

"I'm less likely to kill you in a fit of rage, that's for sure," I mutter. "But don't get your hopes up. Friendship isn't in the cards for us, Greed."

"Who said anything about friendship?" he scoffs, as if the idea of being my friend is the silliest thing I could have proposed. "I don't want friends. I want power."

"Very original," I say. I place my now empty glass down on the table and turn to leave.

"Good doing business with you, Pride," Greed calls after me.

I flip him off over my shoulder.

The rest of the party isn't torturous. By the time we're done mingling with every Tom, Dick, and Harry in Silas's extended family, our group is five drinks deep and laughing on the dance floor.

The only one of us who isn't having fun is Wrath. He stands off to the side, a comical version of a pissed off bodyguard, glaring at anyone who attempts to get within three feet of Hattie. One poor fellow sidles up to her and goes so far as to grab her hand, twirling her around. She laughs, but it's the cackle of a maniac. I wouldn't be surprised if she's turned on by the idea of his imminent demise.

Wrath's glare is molten.

"You could cut that tension with a spoon, huh?" Imogen whisper-yells in my ear, her breath spreading over the flesh of my neck.

She pulls back, hair frizzed and puffing into unruly waves with the rising temperature of the room. With the fires and the dancing, it's almost steamy—the windows have fogged, and everyone shines with a thin sheen of sweat.

"Has she told you what happened after her birthday?" I ask, leaning into the crook of her neck so she can hear me over the music.

Pressed close to her pulse, my nose flares, able to pick up the sweet scent of her happiness mixed with her floral perfume. In this moment, Imogen's a glowing image of who she used to be—bright and flushed and devoid of everything that's weighed on her lately.

Imogen shakes her head. "Has Hattie told *you*?"

"Nope," I say. "You gotta wonder though. She was *angry*."

"Have my gossiping ways rubbed off on you?" Imogen giggles.

"Maybe," I tease.

"Do you want another drink?" she asks abruptly.

I shrug. I'm flushed and in that perfect in-between state; I'm aware of my surroundings but unbothered by the crowd. With Imogen at my side, and a couple drinks in me, the pressure of their presence lessens.

"Leo, do you want another drink?" Imogen asks, tugging at his arm.

"I'm good, thanks, Mo," Leo shouts back over the roaring swing band. "We're going to leave soon anyway. You two good to get back?"

"Aisha is outside the ballroom waiting to bring us home," I say.

He smacks his forehead dramatically. "She's been out there this whole time? That's cruel, Joze."

"We *all* can't be plied with alcohol," I scold. "She understands her place as my Second and sometimes that means you have to—"

"Sacrifice, protect, blah, blah, blah, responsibilities. I get it," Leo says, waving his hand in the air.

Imogen tugs at my hand, her fingers slipping between mine. My heart seizes in my chest at the overt touch.

"C'mon, I'm thirsty," she says, leading me away from the dance floor. But before we're back to the terribly beige hors d'oeuvres, she pulls me in a different direction. "Actually, I think there's a quiet area over here."

Imogen drags me through an arched doorway and into a small, empty sitting room. While empty now, it wasn't left untouched by the party; half-filled glasses, small plates, and crumpled napkins litter every available surface.

"People are disgusting," Imogen mutters, letting go of my hand and stacking all the deserted dishes onto a side table. She peeks over her shoulder as she works, a reminiscent smile on her face. "Royals are the *worst* patrons. They always spill or break something. They never tip the waiters. And at least once a night they send a drink back because it isn't *'made right.'*" Imogen stands to her full height, blowing a stray piece of hair from her face. "As if there's any way to fuck up a glass of freaking whiskey."

"Use the wrong ice cube shape? Circle over square?" I ask, eyes tightening with mirth.

Imogen huffs. "Probably. They never tell you what's wrong with it, only that there's something wrong."

She sets the final plate aside and shows off the clean couch and coffee table with splayed arms, shimmying jazz-hands, and a sing-song *ta-dah!* Imogen flops onto the couch and pats the space next to her.

"Sit," she says.

"Didn't you want a drink?" I ask.

"No." Imogen shrugs.

"Oh." I lower myself onto the cushion next to her. "Are you feeling okay?"

"That's the sixth time you've asked me that tonight."

"Things can change quickly," I say, my defensive hackles rising. "Would you rather me not ask?"

"No. I know it means you care," Imogen says.

"So..." I say, confused.

Imogen heaves a wistful sigh. "Tonight was good. And even if this is a single good day in a sea of bad ones, at least it proves I *can* have a good day. Back here, and around all this."

I hum in understanding, settling deeper into the plush velvet couch. I curve towards her, leaning my cheek against the back cushion. Imogen matches my position, facing me.

"How's your head?" she asks, changing the subject. She reaches out, brushing a strand of hair from my forehead. "I know crowds drain you."

"Fine, for now," I say. I swallow the nervous lump in my throat as her finger mindlessly traces over my ear, curling over the pointed tip and dragging down the lobe.

"We'll each have a glass of tea before bed once we're home," she says, matter of fact.

"Do you want to head out?"

"Not yet. I want to bask in this a little longer," Imogen says, pulling her hand back. Her knees touch mine as she curls into a more comfortable position, closing her eyes.

I don't go as far as to close my eyes, but I do relax into the couch. I'm quickly lulled into a calm trance as we sit together, basking in the hum of the party.

Across from us is a large portrait, one of those ancient oil paintings that line many of the halls in the palace. This one depicts a scene of the first fae queen's children locked in battle. Silas's ancestor, with his large white wings, is wrapped in shadows. A sword of night extends from his grip, clashing against the bright steel of his brother's. Her other son has a shroud of light behind him, sparkling off his smooth, glittering white wings. It's a mighty appearance, floating down with that beaming light at his back—no wonder he was mistaken for an angel by the humans. And no wonder his brother was mistaken for a demon, with those black eyes and slinking shadows.

It has always amused me, having traveled to the other realm often, to see how our history was twisted to suit humans' understanding of the world. Before they fought and founded our Courts, the brothers had traveled across the Veil with their friends—their future House leaders—and left their mark.

Angels and devils, sins and virtues; faeries, changelings, sprites, and other creatures that go bump in the night. Humans took a few glimpses at our magic and ran with it, sometimes coming close to the truth and oftentimes landing far from it.

And now I'm part of that mythos.

I am Pride.

A soft smile curls my lips; and the tranquil silence overtakes me. I tilt my head to peer at Imogen. I can't see her expression clearly, only the apples of her plump cheeks, the smattering of freckles on the bridge of her nose, and those fluttering golden lashes.

"I missed it," Imogen says suddenly, as if she can feel my attention. Her hand raises to rub at her chest. "My magic came out to play again in full force tonight. It's been a while."

"Yeah?" I ask.

"I think I can finally say I'm excited to get the bar back up and running," she says, shifting to meet my gaze.

"Were you not excited before?" I ask.

One shoulder shrugs. "Yes and no."

"We'll have to discuss security, you know," I say softly.

"Do we have to?" Imogen's face scrunches.

I hum, amused.

"Are there still that many active threats?" she asks.

"Even if they were all gone, I'd still recommend some level of precaution."

Imogen sits up, curling her feet under her ass, and leans into my space. Her wine-tainted breath brushes over my lips, and my heart races of its own accord. If I leaned forward an inch, our lips would meet.

"And if I say no?" she asks.

"Then I'd try a different argument."

"And if I say no to that too?"

"Please don't," I whisper.

Why does it feel like we're not talking about security anymore?

"You forget that I have power too. Everyone always forgets because I never use it. *Choose* not to use it," Imogen says softly, licking her lips. There's something in the air, growing thick and heavy. "I could put my foot down, finally grow that backbone everyone wants me to have. Tell you all to stay out of my business. You'd listen."

"You don't want to do that," I say.

"No, I don't," she agrees.

"Then don't say no to me."

Her pupils dilate, overtaking all the amber. "Why did that sound so sensual?"

I glance away from her, embarrassed. "Sorry."

Gentle fingers grip my chin and force me to look at her. "I didn't say it was a bad thing."

"Oh."

Her gaze falls to my lips, lingers there for a moment, then flicks back up to meet mine, full of molten heat. I blink, the gears in my brain turning at double speed.

"I like when you flirt back," she says.

"*Oh*," I repeat.

"You should do it more."

Fuck.

Her breath mingles with mine, and I find myself pulled forward by an invisible force. Her teeth nervously bite into her bottom lip, tugging at the skin. It's going to rip if she keeps doing that—I should stop her. If I just close the gap then I could...

I jump up from the couch in a panic. "This isn't a good idea."

Shock knits her golden brows together. "What's not a good idea?"

I wave my hand between us. "Whatever is happening right now."

"Why not?" Imogen sighs, sitting back on the couch. "Because of Nora? That ship has sailed, Josie, and it's not coming back to port."

"Yes—no—because of *reasons*," I stutter, and start to pace back and forth across the room. "Because I'm Pride now. Isn't that part of why you two broke up in the first place? What if I have to kill someone? Are you going to be okay with that?" I groan, my fingers digging into my hair. "What am I even saying right now? This is crazy—"

"*Stop.*" Imogen's command strikes me, and my feet freeze to the floor. She stands and approaches slowly. "I might not always make the right choices, but at least they're *my* choices. Do you understand? I chose to pursue Nora all those years ago. And I chose to fight for our relationship for far too many years after that. Then I chose to accept that it ended."

Imogen stops, peering up at me with a glowing, hot iron will in her eyes.

"Nora's violence used to intrigue me—the fear used to thrill... until it didn't. And we couldn't figure out a middle ground. She didn't even want to try." She takes a deep breath. "Maybe it makes me a hypocrite, but I don't think your Pride will be the same as hers. You've made it clear to me that you don't enjoy it. Your violence is measured, not gratuitous. I feel safe with you."

Imogen reaches out, palm caressing my cheek and jaw.

"Everyone needs to stop deciding what's good for me. *I* decide what's good for me. And if *I* choose to flirt with you, or acknowledge that there's something *here,* or, *gods above,* kiss you. Then I'm going to do that."

We breathe in each other, and my throat bobs. I'm frozen,

not from her magic; no, this stuttering of my brain and body is all me.

"But not if you don't want this..." Imogen adds tentatively, as if coming to a harrowing realization.

"I—Mo, I—" I start and stop, my tongue unable to form words.

Her soft hand suddenly pulls away from my cheek. It covers her mouth, trembling as panic fills her expression. "Oh gods, I'm sorry. I don't know what came over me."

"No, Imogen, it's fi—"

"Forget I ever said anything. I'm going to head home. I'll tell Aisha to come back to get you when the party's over."

Imogen rushes out of the room, and I follow, if only to ensure she disappears into Aisha's shadows and not someone else's. As the black tendrils curl around her, she spares me one last nervous glance.

And then she's gone, and an empty hall stands in front of me, the upbeat swing music filtering out of the ballroom a stark contrast to my worsening mood.

35
SILAS

"You left. You said you wouldn't do that."

I lean against the doorway of the safe house, my forearm braced against the molding, smiling down at the Virtue. Benevolence seems pissed, and I'm honestly surprised by how many different expressions he's able to project with that mustache getting in the way. The curled, warm brown hair shines in the light of the sconce buzzing above us.

"Let me in," he says. "We need to talk about what you've done."

"Okay, Mr. Grumpy," I say, backing away with my hands up. He passes by me and storms into the living room. "I thought you were supposed to be *nice*."

"Where's Nora?" Bennie's head swivels, he makes haste for the bedrooms. "Is she out?"

"Whoa, there." I chuckle, grabbing onto the back of his button-down. I pull him to the living room and toss him towards the couch. "Calm down. She's just in the shower."

Bennie tosses his head back against the cushion, groaning. "How long is she going to be in there?"

"Probably longer than you want to wait here with me," I say, hands braced on my hips. Bennie's slacks are creased, and his shirt has an ink stain on it, blooming over the chest pocket. My head tilts. "What's wrong with you?"

Tan hands scrub over his face. "You left the safe house when you promised you wouldn't! And my idiot guards didn't think to tell me until today. It's been more than a week!"

"You already said that," I say. "Repeating it won't magically change the past. And you had to expect we'd explore—you're not stupid. Why is it upsetting you so much?"

Bennie's head flops forward, and his mossy gaze clashes with mine. "Besides the obvious risk? Don't tell Nora, but my father's back in town."

"Interesting." I plop into the armchair across from the couch. A plume of dust rises, and I cough, waving it away. Benevolence's men took many liberties in what *clean* meant for their preparation of this safe house. "Why don't you want her to know?"

"Because she'll go and find him before my plan is ready," he says.

"And what plan is that, exactly?" I ask, crossing an ankle over my knee. I've been content in navigating our trip without details so far, but now that the man is sitting in front of me? I'm not about to let him leave without giving me *something*. "Don't hold out on me, Bennie. You've kept us in suspense long enough, and a king only has so much patience."

Bennie leans forward, his corded forearms perched on his knees. A single strand of wavy hair falls over his pinched brow. He levels me with a somber look.

"I'm going to kill Oonagh. But it has to happen the same night as my father."

A shark's grin cuts my cheeks. What a fascinating little development.

"And you need us for that, I presume."

"Plausible deniability, and all that," he says.

It makes sense. Use the half-Unseelie, half-Seelie assassin as a scapegoat. Put someone on the throne that's in your pocket. Then, make out with the winnings and none of the consequences that treason would normally land you. Solid logic for a solid plan.

However, there's one piece missing in this puzzle.

"How does this help me?" I ask. "Explain it to me simply. Because I'm not going to let you use Nora to kill the Seelie Queen without some recompense."

"May I speak plainly?" Bennie asks, and I nod. He sucks in a deep breath. "I am also Royal."

And there we are. Puzzle complete.

"Oh?" I feign shock.

"Mother's side, not Father's."

"Of course."

"You don't seem surprised," Bennie says, cautiously.

"Because it makes everything much clearer. With no direct heir, it's fair game to any Royal. That is, if you do things like us." I finger the pilling fibers on my trousers. "This is how it will go. You're not going to place someone on the throne who's in your pocket because *you're* going to take it. And then, you're going to make sure this whole mess doesn't escalate into a war. Am I wrong about your intentions?"

"You picked that up quick."

"I'm smarter than I look."

Bennie slumps back. "And you believe me? Just like that?"

"I believe you in the same way that I believe Nora. I see some of me in you, and my gut says to trust where that goes. Some might argue it's a stupid thing to go off, but sometimes logic isn't enough to make a difference in the world." I omit the fact that I can smell his lies. It truly is a convenient magic. Still, the sentiment remains. "Is that what you want, Bennie? To make a positive difference in this world?"

"My father says it's childish to dream in such a way," he replies.

It's a yes, in so many words.

"Well, I don't think it's a childish notion," I say.

A beat passes between us. One of understanding.

Yes, there's potential here; the wheels are already turning in my head at all the opportunities.

"Silas?" Nora's voice filters down the hall. "Where the fuck are you? I'm hungry, and I'm only going to offer to make dinner once, so—what are you doing here?"

Nora stops short in the entry to the living room, draped in baggy, striped men's pajamas. She refuses to wear the women's ones that Bennie left in the wardrobe. I'm partial to these as well—they don't soften her edges too much.

Bennie stands, addressing me. "Go out and explore if you must. But for gods' sake, be back in the house by ten at night, every night. *Please*."

I nod. I can adhere to that.

"Hey, Nora," Bennie says, walking past his cousin. "Stay out of trouble, 'kay?"

"What are you, my father?" Nora scoffs.

"No, but I'm the closest thing you'll get to an older brother," Bennie calls out before slamming the front door.

Nora turns to me. "What the hell was that for?"

I slap my hands on my thighs, standing. "He came to scold us and give us a curfew. Very fatherlike behavior, if you ask me."

36
JOSIE

The migraine that's been plaguing me has finally passed. After seven days.

None of my usual coping mechanisms worked. I pushed through the best I could, but no amount of herbal tea, low-lit rooms, or attempts at sleep did anything to stave the incessant pounding. Maybe it was a punishment, self-inflicted, for what happened between Imogen and me.

Or what *didn't* happen.

Things have returned to a quiet, albeit awkward, normalcy between us since. We're both busy. She had to focus on the Den's reopening, which is later tonight, and I've been dealing with... all the shit I have to deal with as Pride.

I think we've both settled on ignoring it all together.

Which is fine.

Sort of.

It *should* be fine. But nagging thoughts cling to me, pesky little what ifs.

What if you're ruining your friendship? What if you're somehow taking advantage of her in a vulnerable state, despite how adamant her confession was about the opposite? What if this thick tension is just a trick of the mind, forged from your recent proximity? What if it's not real? Worse, what if it is? What if you made a mistake pulling away that night? What if you're playing with fire here, and Nora comes back and flips her shit? What if you had kissed her?

What if I *had* kissed her?

I take a deep breath, pressing my head to the car steering wheel.

If something were to develop between Imogen and me, we're both adults. We can all talk it out. Nora would have to buck up and deal with it. I love her as a sister, but I can't pause my life for her. Not when she fucking left.

Not just me. Not just Imogen. *She left all of us.*

Where's her consideration of *our* feelings? Struggling doesn't mean you get a free pass to be a dick to the people who love you.

Fuck that.

What *if* I kissed Imogen?

The memory of her mouth slanting over mine so briefly in the snow flashes. What *would* it be like to truly claim that pouty lower lip? Would she melt into me like she does when I cradle her after a nightmare? Would she taste like the wine we sip by the hearth? Would I be able to feel her smile, soft, tender, and sweet against my lips?

A blaring honk from someone down the street whips my head up from the steering wheel. Shit. I need to get a move on if I want to make it to the Den at a reasonable time.

I push myself out of the car and slam the door shut. With my gloved hand still pressed to the metal, I pause, staring up at the towering apartment building. The sun sets beyond the skyscraper; pink and orange meld together, a strange color combination for winter, but pretty all the same. It paints the pale stone architecture with hued shadows, darkening the grime that's notched between each crevice.

With a determined smack of my hand on the car roof, I make a decision.

I have shit to take care of, but after that, I'll talk it out with Imogen. Clear up the other night, get whatever this is out in the open, and then figure out how we want to move forward.

I'm not Nora's Second anymore. I give the orders now.

I'm a fucking Sin; I need to act like one. And that means not hiding, in any part of my life.

I pull the bag I packed from the trunk, then climb fourteen flights of stairs up to my destination.

The paint on the door is chipped, and one of the little golden numbers designating the unit hangs upside down, the top screw to keep it upright missing.

My finger is poised on the trigger of my gun when I bang on the door. A second passes, then thundering footsteps sound behind the wooden barrier. My free hand presses against the peephole. That way, they can't see my face and are forced to open the door to see who it is.

My jaw ticks as I wait.

Usually, I'm unbelievably patient. But maybe that's because if I wasn't the one pumping the breaks and demanding a slower approach to business, Nora and I would have careened towards trouble at every turn.

The door cracks open, and that's my cue to kick it in.

My boot strikes the door, and the man grunts as it smacks him in his protruding gut. He falls to the floor, flat on his back, and I stand over him, gun pointed at his head.

"What's all the ruckus abo—oh gods!" Rupert's wife comes running into the small entryway, fear coursing off her in waves.

"Where's your eldest son?" I ask. My attention flicks between her and the sneering man under my gun's aim.

"In his bedroom," the wife answers.

"Go get him," I say.

"Junior! Come out here!" she shouts. Then, she begs. "Pride, I don't know what he's done, but I promise, my boy is a *good* boy—"

"He isn't the one in deep shit," I say. "But he should see this, and then he should make a decision for himself. He's sixteen, yeah?"

"Yes, ma'am."

The teen slinks around the corner, the same boy that I helped up from the picket line's icy pavement. A shocked *o* parts his lips at the sight of me pointing a gun at his father.

"Great, now that we're here, time for a family meeting," I start. I wave the gun at the man on the ground. "I'll make this short. I know what you did, and I know why you did it. If you want to keep all your fingers, I suggest you take this threat seriously. You are going to leave this city. You are no longer a part of House Pride. And if I ever see you back in Anwynn or hear you tossing around our House name, you will die. Got it?"

"Honey, what did you *do*?" the wife squeals.

I shuck the bag I'm carrying off my shoulder and toss it onto Rupert; he grunts at the impact. "Open it."

He does, and as expected, confusion pinches his features. The bag is full of cash.

"W-what is this?" he stutters. "Is this some kind of sick joke? You're not gonna kill me?"

"No," I say.

"Why?" he asks. "That bomb I planted would have killed you. I wanted it to."

"Because I don't need to. And I'd prefer not to orphan more younglings in this city." If I were Nora, this man would be dead already. Likely the wife too. The kid would be spared, taken care of, but still scarred. But I'm not her. "If you share your father's beliefs that I'm unfit to lead us, you should go with him. Staying will only be a misery if that's the case. But if you don't, and you stay, I won't hold his actions against you. You can still claim your place in this family."

The boy and the mother stand, shocked still.

I lower my gun.

"Your debt with Envy was paid by your misdeeds. This money is meant to be an act of good faith that you'll stay away on our terms." I holster the gun. "Don't make me regret this mercy."

37
IMOGEN

The night is ripe with anticipation.

Okay, maybe not the night, but I certainly am.

My teeth bite into my lower lip and tug. There's a moment of pain, but then the comforting metallic tang hits my tongue. Tonight, the Den reopens and I get back to work. For some reason, it feels like a bigger life event than the first time it opened five years ago.

A steady trickle of guests bopped in for happy hour, but now the sun has set, and we're nearing that make-or-break window. The one where we'll know if it's going to be a good night or a slow night.

The band is getting set, the dance floor empty without its rousing beat. Most of our patrons fill the tables near the entrance, including my friends. Leo, Earl, and Hattie all clamored into their usual booth as soon as I unlocked the front door. Even Wrath came an hour after opening, pushing Leo out of the way to sit next to Hattie. He had draped a protective arm over the booth at her back, and she's been snuggled at his side ever since.

I'm glad to see they've gotten over whatever fight they were having.

I made sure to be the one to serve them but otherwise, I've taken a back seat to my staff. I am taking the phrase *dipping my toe into the water* seriously.

"You guys need anything else?" I ask, dropping off a fresh bottle of water for the table.

"Stop coddling us and go do your boss-lady shit. We're not important." Hattie shoos me away with her hands.

My hip leans against the side of the booth. "When do you think you'll all head out?"

"It's funny you think our asses aren't going to be glued to this leather until closing," Leo says.

I snort, but he doesn't laugh. "Seriously? You know we close at 3:00 a.m."

"Of course, I only worked here for five years," Leo teases. He leans close, snagging my hand and squeezing. "I'm proud of you, Mo. I missed seeing you in your element."

My throat goes tight, and I chuff, lips twisting to hide the sudden rush of emotion.

I'm slowly stepping back into my skin; or perhaps I'm shedding it like a snake, becoming a fresh version of myself.

I pull my hand from his. "Well, don't be strangers. Holler if you need something. I'll be by the band."

The chime above the entrance dings, and the sound sends hopeful butterflies scattering in my gut. But when I glance over my shoulder, disappointment has them landing as a random group of fae stumbles in.

It's a learned thing, this reaction to that bell. One that I'll have to break.

Many nights I had listened for it, waiting to see a raven-haired beauty walk through the door. Now, the thought sours my stomach. It's not the idea of Nora that twists my insides, but the guilt that tonight, until this very moment, I haven't thought about her all that much.

Didn't want to. Was scared to.

Things are different now. My love for her isn't all-consuming as it once was. It doesn't dangle me out the window of the twentieth floor and make my heart jump out of my chest. Or make me want to curl up in a ball and cry. The distance between us has given me much needed perspective, and I've come to terms with what our love story was.

A friendship. A first. A bond born of grief, circumstance, and immense effort to crack open locks long since rusted shut. A thrill. A yearning.

The bell dings again, and I can't stop my gaze from shifting from the band to the door. In its archway stands Josie, whose body heaves as if she's ran here. There's a second of stilled confusion, and then she's beelining towards me with severe determination. She passes our friends with a curt wave, and their equally confused expressions follow her across the bar. Josie doesn't stop at me, though, she grabs my hand and pulls me to the back hall.

The storage closet door is ripped open. I'm shoved into the darkness and Josie drops my hand, shutting the door behind her. There's a moment of hesitation, one where she leans forward, both hands braced against the wood, and inhales slowly. Her back flexes with the intake. On the exhale, she turns around sharply, making me flinch.

And then... nothing.

I reach up and tug on the string dangling from the ceiling. The bare lightbulb above us clicks on, buzzing as it illuminates us in a warm yellow glow.

Another beat passes of us staring at each other.

"You locked us in a closet," I say.

"Yes." Her deep brown eyes dart to the shelves of cleaning supplies.

"Um." A breathy laugh escapes me. "Why?"

"Because you're acting weird," Josie says.

"*I'm* acting weird?"

"That came out wrong."

"*You're* acting weird right now."

"We've both been acting fucking weird around each other, and I hate it," she says in one rushed breath.

My tongue darts out to nervously lick at my lips.

She's not wrong. We *have* been tiptoeing around each other. But that's because I embarrassed myself; I misread the tension between us, came on way too strong, got rejected, and then ran away.

I cringe. "Sorry."

"You don't need to apologize. You did nothing wrong."

"Okay," I say nervously. *Where is this going then?*

"I, however, have to apologize," Josie says.

"What? Why?"

"Because I made things awkward the other night," Josie says.

I shake my head. "No, I'm the one who overstepped and made some big declaration that I *definitely* should not have—"

"I wanted to kiss you too," Josie blurts out, her expression pinched and nervous. "And things are awkward because I wanted to and I didn't know how to react to that realization in the moment and then my tongue got all twisted and—*ugh*. It's happening again, but in the opposite way. Now I'm rambling."

Josie sucks a shaky breath into her lungs.

"That is all to say, I'm sorry. I didn't mean to make you feel rejected. Or imply that you weren't making sound choices. I was only afraid to make a mistake, and whenever I get afraid of making a mistake, I always end up not making a choice at all.

And that's why I stuttered and stalled and pulled away. Because I was afraid."

A cute, red blush fills her cheeks.

"That's the end of my apology, by the way," she whispers.

"Apology accepted." I don't even know where to begin to process everything she said—or the fact that I didn't have to beg her to tell me her feelings. All I know is that my body is lighter because of it.

But now that it's all out in the open and we seem to be on the same page... what the fuck do we do?

I mash my lips together, holding back my laughter.

"Why does this feel kind of messy?" I ask.

Josie's growing smile twitches. "Hate to break it to you, but you're kind of messy, Mo."

"Um, excuse me?" I tease with fake offense.

"I've seen your vanity after you do your makeup. It's like an explosion went off."

I playfully poke her arm. "That's a rude thing to say to a girl you just locked in a cleaning closet with you."

"The door isn't technically locked."

A beat passes between us, and I get the urge to brush a piece of her hair behind her ear—so I do. In the process, my thumb grazes her cheek, and she shivers. The scent of bleach and dust fades away, replaced by her warm and citrusy scent as I step closer. My heartbeat pulses through my limbs at a quickening pace, and I dare to swipe my thumb over the apple of her cheek again.

Josie leans into the contact, if tentatively, while our gazes bore into each other.

"I should get back out there," I whisper.

"You should," she says.

"It'll be busy tonight," I argue, but I'm merely trying to

convince myself. "And I'm the owner. I can't disappear all of a sudden."

"Super busy. You run quite a popular establishment. Leo's showed me the numbers," Josie murmurs, and my hand slips lower, curling around the back of her neck.

"He's not supposed to do that," I say.

"He did it anyway," Josie says, her gaze homing in on my lips. She leans forward, then stops. A hairsbreadth separates us. "Is this okay?"

"I don't know," I tease. "Didn't you say you shouldn't kiss me because you're Pride now?"

Her breathy laugh fans out over me, and the distance dissipates. "I think I'm going to do it anyway."

"Thank fuck," I mutter as her lips crash into mine.

There's no soft landing with this kiss. It's rushed, fevered passion. It's the eruption from weeks of building tension. It's electricity shooting through my veins.

Josie's hands find their way into my hair, and the sweet tug she gives them at the root is exquisite. I groan, and our kiss deepens with a swipe of her tongue over my parted lips.

A sudden bang on the door and jostle of the handle shocks us apart. Josie yelps, and covers her mouth. She quickly leans all her weight against the door, shooting me a bug-eyed look. A drunken *oops* and giggling laughter sound beyond the closet door, before going quiet again.

Josie and I stare at each other, catching our breath. And then I burst into laughter.

"What's so funny?" Josie whisper-yells, pulling her hand from her face. Her cheeks and neck are bright red, and her eyes dart to the door nervously.

"Nothing." I shake my head. "You're just cute."

She chuffs, pushing off the door. Her body stops an inch from mine, her warmth teasing my skin. "I'd normally turn my nose up at being called cute, but when it comes from you, it doesn't sound infantilizing." Josie uses her fingers to gently muse my hair back into place. "It actually sounds nice." She purses her lips, then orders, "Say it again for me."

And there we go. There's definitely a blush on my cheeks now, if there wasn't one there already.

"You're pretty cute," I whisper.

Josie clears her throat, stepping back. "We should get back out there."

I suck in a calming breath. "Yeah."

Josie's hand is mid-twist on the doorknob when sudden panic has me tugging at her sleeve.

"Wait," I say.

"What?" she asks, concerned.

"Maybe we don't... tell anyone yet," I stumble out the words. "Until we figure out what this is."

Josie's head bobs up and down, and I don't see one ounce of dissent in her features, only understanding.

"Agreed," she says. Then adds with a teasing lilt, "We don't want to make it too *messy*."

A bark of laughter slips out of me, fast and loud. "Who *are* you right now?"

Josie pulls the door open and steps aside for me to pass through first. But as I slide through the archway, her hand grazes my waist, and her electrifying whisper hits my ear.

"I'm Pride now. But to you, I will always be just Josie."

38
SILAS

What's a week or two or three in the grand scheme of life? Especially for a fae who will age well past his peers.

That's what I ask myself every night we sneak out of the safe house to explore the city of Avalon. We've hit the end of that third week, and as much as it's been fun prancing around the Seelie Court practicing my acting skills, I'm becoming increasingly concerned for my partner in crime's health.

Every day we wait drains more color from her already pale skin, and every night we spend out among the Seelie darkens the circles under her eyes. Nora's withering; hate fuels her and consumes her, a self-cannibalizing snake tightening around her neck.

Quite frankly, it pisses me off.

I'm all for her getting her revenge—but if her preferred method produces *this* result? I say we cut our losses, her pride be damned, and slash that tether that dangles between them right now. I'll figure out the rest with Benevolence later. I anticipate he'd be open to negotiations, even if we bailed on this plan we've agreed to.

Why do I even care? I don't fucking know.

That's a lie. There are a few reasons. The most prominent being that I've set my sights on Nora as a person of interest in my life, just as I did as a teen with Wrath. Once you've piqued my heart's interest, there's no escaping it. That's it. You're mine.

Wrath says I can be overbearing, inserting myself in his business and hovering in the shadows behind him. But being a domineering ass is simply how I show I care.

I know it can be a lot for some people. *I* can be a lot.

I simply don't care enough to change *how* I care.

My teeth crunch on the handful of crackers I've shoved in my mouth. The salt bursts on my tongue as my teeth grind them together. I sit at the kitchen counter, stewing in wait for Nora to exit the bathroom, as I have every night after our escapades.

As soon as I shadow-walk us back to the safe house, she storms away; her pretty little wings blink out of existence, and the bathroom door slams shut. The shower runs, and no less than a half an hour later does it shut off. Occasionally, she will come out for a snack. But most nights, she'll slip out of the steam and into her bedroom, the faint click of the lock audible from my stool.

Tonight, we're fast approaching an hour, and I have a sneaking suspicion that something is not right.

My magic is restless, my shadows curling uneasily around my fingers.

I swallow and stand, dusting salt off my fingertips with a few swipes over my trousers.

The trek across the safe house feels like miles in the dead of night, and each creak of the old floor sounds like a thunderclap in comparison to the quiet surrounding us. No steam seeps out of the crack between the bathroom door and the tile floor, yet the shower still runs. I press my ear to the wood and knock.

No answer.

"Nora," I call. "You do know I also need hot water? A king shouldn't be subject to cold showers unless he has a fever, and last I checked, I do not."

Crickets would chirp if there were any.

"I'm surprised you're not yelling at me to fuck off," I say, my concern forming a deep well in my gut. "If you don't say anything in the next three seconds, I'm coming in."

One.

Two.

Three.

Fuck. I warned you. Please don't try to kill me.

My palm grasps the brass knob, and my shadows work swiftly to unlock the door. I twist, the metal smooth under my grip, and push the door open; Nora is not in sight.

No, that's wrong. There, behind the shower's curtain, is a shadow, sitting low in the tub, but tall enough to peek over the rim.

"Nora?" I say. Again, no answer.

My feet carry me to the tub, and with gentle fingers I pull the curtain back a few inches. The metal rungs screech as they scrape along the bar they hang from. My muscles freeze, and then they move all at once, throwing it completely open and rushing to shut off the water. The faucet squeaks and a few drips from the shower head fall on my hands—they're so cold I flinch.

I drop to my knees next to the tub, hands extended, but freeze again.

Nora's curled over herself, skin rubbed red and raw across her entire body. Harsh lines from where her nails have raked over her flesh slash across her back, bisecting her faded scars. She shivers, lips blue and eyes somewhere far off.

"Nora?"

Her name echoes against the bathroom tile.

Stray droplets of water clink against the drain.

I swallow around the lump in my throat and reach out, going against my rule of letting her initiate touch between us. One dry palm connects with her soaked hair, pushing the strands away from her forehead. She flinches.

Nora's head snaps my way, and she shirks away from my hand, scuttling backwards. A switch flips, and her void expression shatters into her favorite default: rage.

"What the fuck are you doing?" Her voice cracks, raw, as if she's been screaming. Or maybe she's been crying—now that she's facing me, I note the red rimming her eyes. It makes the green of her irises shine even brighter than usual.

What a curse, for something so terrible to make you more chillingly beautiful.

I hold my hands up placatingly, and avert my gaze, staring off to the blank expanse of the wall. "I knocked and called out to you multiple times."

"*Get out!*"

I shake my head firmly. "Can't do that. You weren't answering and then I found you huddled under freezing water—"

"Give me a fucking towel then," Nora growls.

I frown but quickly pull one off the towel bar and offer it to her. She yanks it from my grip with vicious strength. I finally glance back when I hear her wet feet smack against the tile.

"I'm fine. You can go now," Nora says, pushing past me to the mirror, the towel wrapped tightly around her body.

"Absolutely not," I scoff, standing. "You're not getting out of a conversation right now. As your friend, I am concerned—"

She snorts, shoving a toothbrush in her mouth. "This isn't funny. You've been in here for a fucking hour!" I come up behind her, my reflection joining hers in the mirror. "I'm only going to ask once, or I'm bringing us the fuck back to Anwynn and you can—"

"You wouldn't," Nora seethes, green eyes glowing at me in the mirror. I stand behind her, unmoving.

"*Try me.*" I let the threat hang in the air. "What was that, Nora?"

She holds my gaze for a moment and then hangs her head with a scoff. She shoves the toothbrush back in her mouth, and the angry, frantic swipe of the bristles is reflective of the tension mounting in the room. She spits, runs the water over the brush, and drops it into the little ceramic cup on the sink top. The little *plink* sounds like a gavel pounding down with finality. Nora turns, leaning back against the porcelain basin, hugging her towel closer to her chest.

"When this is done, I would like for you to cut off my wings."

It takes me a second to process her request. "I'm sorry?"

Her nostrils flare. "You heard me, Silas. I already asked Josie. She said no. And I don't think anyone else has the stomach for it. I'd do it myself, but it's not exactly an easy spot to reach."

Disbelief parts my lips. "That's what you were thinking about that whole time?"

"Yes." Her arms cross over her chest, an extra layer of armor forming around her. It's not to protect her body, but the raw emotion she's exposed.

I knew she hated her wings, but I hadn't realized it went this far.

"I can't do that," I say softly. Her face contorts into something vicious.

"Then what good are you to me?"

I flinch. "That's a mean thing to say."

"I don't care if it's mean. It's the truth. Why can no one handle the fucking truth?" she seethes, stepping forward. "Aren't you supposed to be the one who *understands*? You're the only one still bothering with me!" Her hands try to run through her hair, but they get stuck in the damp waves, and she growls her frustration. "They *hurt*, Silas. He—he *did something* to me when he healed them. They itch and burn and *ache*. All the time. They haunt me day and night. I'm supposed to be haunting him, but it's the fucking opposite!"

With every measured step she takes towards me, I'm forced back.

"I want to be rid of it—of them—of him. He has ruined my fucking life too many times," Nora begs. My back hits the wall, crushing my wings. "In so many words, you've said that we're the same. That you see me. So why can't you see that I need them *gone*?"

Her chest heaves, nearly touching mine from how close we're standing.

Something cracks inside of me at seeing her this way. Desperate. Unmoored and reeling. She's the splintering ice of a frozen lake, on the verge of breaking open and swallowing you in its icy depths.

"I do see you," I say softly. "I see someone so lost to her rage, she doesn't know anything else. I see someone who grips so tightly to her pride because she's been taught that without it, she has no value. I see a woman who refuses to let people close, who burns bridges before they can form as an act of self-preservation..." Nora shakes her head, but the fractures in her irises spread. "And I see someone who hates herself because of it."

"No," she whispers.

"Yes," I whisper back. "Don't lie to me. Do you hate yourself, Nora?"

Her lashes flutter closed, and in their wake, a single teardrop falls down her cheek. "Yes."

"And those wings, they're a wonderful scapegoat for all that pain, aren't they?"

"Yes." The damn breaks open, and a tortured sob escapes her. It's a guttural noise. One that sounds sacred in its pain. A howl of grief cast to the moon.

Nora drops, and my shadows break her fall, cradling her knees so she doesn't bruise them. I follow, drawing her shaking body to me. I'm careful not to touch her skin, resting one hand on her mid-back over the towel, and cradling her head with the other. I don't move, don't rub circles on her back or stroke her wet hair.

"Did you know I hated my wings once?" I whisper into her crown. Her head shakes against my shoulder, rubbing left and right—a silent no. "I say we're the same all the time because we have identical trauma, Nora. Same scars, different places. We were both orphaned by the hand of a cruel man. We each have a magic swirling within us that no one else can comprehend. And we've both let our rage take us down a path of self-destruction." I suck in a deep breath as the memories of the past resurface. "Would you believe me if I said I wanted my wings gone too, years ago?"

Nora stiffens in my hold, but she doesn't pull away, staying tucked and burrowed in the crook of my neck. My wings bristle, brushing over the tile floor.

"My wings matched my mom's." A sad smile forms on my lips. "So much of me matched her. My hair, my skin, my personality. I don't know what it was about the wings, though. I could never fully claim them as *mine* like I did the rest. I could cut my hair, or dye it. I could go sit in the sun and tan. I could change how I acted depending on who I was with. But the wings? Couldn't change those. And I hated it. Hated the reminder of her. And my dad. I have his eyes."

Nora sucks in a stuttered breath; my hand on her back tightens, nails scraping over the soft fibers.

"I broke many mirrors in the palace between the ages of eighteen and twenty-eight. Less in the following decade. And then none in the past three—at least on purpose. There have been a few accidents thrown in there." I let loose a small laugh. "My point being, it might take a long time. But you gotta accept them. Learn to love them. And I get it. Of all the people in the realm, I get it. It's *fucking hard*, constantly being reminded of your pain and having no way to escape it. I'm lucky I had Wrath to pull me out of some really shitty, dark places. He never gave up on me. Which is why I *promise* I will do the same for you. But you have to *try*."

Nora shifts, and I quickly release her from my hold. She lifts her head from my shoulder and sits back on her heels.

"I don't know if I can do that," she rasps.

I pause, searching for a different route to take.

"Does it help to know I think they're beautiful?" I ask.

She blinks, slow, and a bit of her normal snark fills her voice. "Don't say that."

"Why not?" I shrug. "It's a compliment. I can't compliment you?"

"I was raised to despise the sight of them. You saying you think they're pretty isn't going to change my mind. It's not something I can be rewired for so easily."

"Then you take your time," I drawl.

Nora sighs, and covers her face with her hands, pressing her fingers into her eyes. "Who would love them, Silas?" she asks, defeated, as if she didn't hear me say as much thirty seconds ago. "Who could?"

"Um, I don't know," I tease. My hand cautiously reaches between us, popping the top few buttons of my shirt and spreading it open. "Maybe the guy with a butterfly tattoo?"

Nora's fingers spread, and one shining emerald eye glares at my chest between the digits.

"Why the fuck did you get that anyway?" she asks, and I shiver at the rough, commanding rasp of her voice.

My finger traces over the center of my tattoo, where the thin raised ridge of my scar sits.

"The tattoo artist asked a similar question when I put in my request," I say. "It's to cover another scar I had to learn to accept. My parents weren't the only ones Patience tried to kill."

"But why that *design*?" she clarifies, rolling her eyes.

There. That eye roll. That's more like her.

"Because despite the pain, I still think it's beautiful."

39
NORA

I stare, lost in my thoughts, at the two undone buttons of Silas's shirt. He leans forward, scribbling in the little notebook I bought him from the night market. The peek of smooth skin is a tease, the top half of the butterfly scrawled across his sternum barely visible.

It begs to be traced over.

He's worn his button downs like this for days, as if he's purposefully peacocking the tattoo, a badge of his commitment to seeing me *accept myself* needled into his chest.

It hasn't stopped the itching or the aching. But I haven't disassociated in the shower again. I hadn't realized it was that bad, not until he rushed in and ripped me from my episode.

It's possible that Silas's noble crusade to save me from myself isn't a lost cause. That moment was the slap in the face I needed to refocus.

Maybe I can evolve, if not for someone else, but for myself.

I've been a miserable fucking person. For longer than I want to admit. And having it laid out in front of me while I was *literally* bare and raw—it shifted something inside of me. I've held others before, been the rock in their raging sea. But for once, I let someone hold *me*.

I let him see me cry.

My head was cradled by his shoulder as I exorcised my inner most demons. Silas bore his to me in turn, and now I understand why he is able to see past my mask.

I keep hurting the few people that show up for me, time and time again. And for what? The pursuit of my own stubborn nature? Three weeks ago, I was willing to burn every bridge to get a taste of relief, and now...

I still want Patience dead. But maybe there can be more beyond that.

My magic flares at my fingertips, and the golden braid tying me to my uncle shimmers as it floats between my knuckles. It's more powerful in Avalon, as if closing the physical distance between us has strengthened it. The tether thrums, pulsing with his ancient heartbeat; I squeeze, and the cadence increases, a sensation of discomfort floating through the link.

"Anything else I should add?"

My head snaps up, and the magic fades into the ether. Silas shoots me one of his *caught you* smirks as my brain catches up to my ears. I shake my head.

We've been writing down every rumor and bit of gossip about what the Seelie forces are planning. That way, we won't miss a detail when we recount everything to the Sins. Or rather, when *he* recounts everything to the Sins.

I don't know exactly where I'll fit after all this.

"That's it," I say.

"Alrighty then," Silas says, leaning back down to finish his scribbling.

A lock of his hair falls over his eyes, and he huffs, pushing it out of the way. The red dye has faded considerably, turning a pale copper. It's better than the red, but still not as pleasant as his natural white.

"If Benevolence makes us wait any longer, I'll need to find a barber." Silas frowns as he flicks the notebook shut and tucks it into his pocket. "Do you think you could do it? Believe it or not, I trust you more with a pair of sheers near my jugular than I would some random Seelie."

"I'm not cutting your hair, Silas."

He leans back, draping both arms across the back of the booth, again drawing my attention down to the tattooed plane around his clavicle.

"But it's the perfect opportunity for you to be the menace I know you are. You could give me a terrible cut, and I wouldn't be able to say anything, because I'm the dummy who trusts you. It doesn't pique your interest at all to have me at your mercy?" His teasing smirk deepens the dimple in his cheek. "It'd be quick too. One snip and my iconic white, well *orange*, locks reduced to—"

"I'm partial to it longer," I concede, dragging my drink to my lips. "Longer hair is easier to grab on to, anyway." I swallow. "You know, for all your *exploits*."

Silas leans forward, both hands on the table, a look of pure shock on his face. "I'm sorry. Did you just tease me back—"

"Do either of you want to tell me why you are *here*, in a pub three neighborhoods away from the safe house I explicitly asked you to be inside by ten every night?"

Bennie's hands smack onto the table, and he levels us both with a searing glare. For a light-walker, he sure has plenty of shadows harrowing his expression.

"It's not ten yet," Silas says, brows furrowing. He jabs a finger at the large clock on the wall. The hands stand at a quarter to ten. "It's not as if it takes us long to get home." Silas leans forward, whispering, "I am like you in that regard."

"That clock is one hour off!" Bennie shouts, drawing attention from around the bar. "I've been looking everywhere for you!"

Silas pales and reaches into his pocket, flicking open his pocket watch. "Shit," he murmurs.

"Is it time?" I ask, standing from the booth, patting my holster to triple check my gun is still there. My wings flutter of their own accord, reacting to the sudden rush of nerves coursing through me.

"Yes, it's fucking time," Bennie growls. "You two are killing me."

Bennie's hands strike my and Silas's shoulders in a flash of lightning—the contact is brief, but potent with magic as we're shrouded in bright fae-light. I close my eyes against the blinding force, and when we land on solid ground, I have to blink away the floating blobs of gray from my vision.

"What the fuck?" I say, taking in the sight before me.

We're in a grand entryway, reminiscent of Casimir's architecture, but instead of white and pink stone, this is all creams and greens.

And red.

I lift my boot and scoff at the thick string of blood that lifts with it. Bodies of Seelie guards lie stabbed, shot, and broken across the marble, their life force seeping into the pores of the stone.

"This way," Bennie calls, tone still terse. He steps over bodies with haste as he beelines to a large archway across the rotunda. Silas and I are quick to follow. My boots squish in the entrails of the dead and snap the veins in their wings.

"Are we in the Seelie palace?" Silas asks.

"Yes," Bennie replies.

"Why?" I ask.

Our voices echo to the tall ceiling and bounce back to us;

the loud volume is a contradiction to our mission—are we not supposed to be stealthily pursuing Patience?

"Because my father is having his monthly romp in the west wing with his Royal flavor of the month." Bennie's shoulders visibly shiver, then he casts another dark glare over his shoulder. "If you two had been where you were supposed to be, I could have explained everything in more detail. But *no*, I had to go on a fucking head hunt for you."

Bennie stops under the archway and turns to us, reaching into his pocket to pull out a watch. It clicks open, the gold engraving glinting.

"Now we're here and you have"—his brows raise as he does the mental calculation—"a little more than one hour." He flicks the watch shut. "I lost the fucking map I was supposed to give you, in the rush. But he should be somewhere in this wing." Bennie points to the darkened hall beyond him. "Kill him, then meet me in the throne room before midnight, otherwise you're screwed. That's when their reinforcements will arrive." He points to the arch looming above us. "The walls beyond this point are laced with iron. Only way in and out with magic is through the rotunda or the portal in the throne room. Oh, and anyone with a green bow?" He points to a ribbon pinned to his lapel. "Please leave them alive. They're mine. Anyone else is fair game. Got it? Great. I've got people to kill, as do you."

Bennie steps beyond the arch and disappears in a flash of light, but, in a way that reminds me of Hattie, pops back into existence a second later.

"I forgot to say good luck." Bennie smiles, though it doesn't reach his eyes. The color is of the darkest moss, grown in the depths of the forest. "If you don't kill my father tonight, I will haunt you from the early grave he will surely kick me into."

And then he's gone again, his flirty little wave fading in gold light.

Silas huffs a laugh. "That was abrupt."

"Are you *amused* right now?" I say.

"Are you not?" Silas turns to meet my disbelief-stricken face, sighing. "I deal with serious situations with humor. You should know this by now."

I do know this, and yet I can't help myself to question every time it happens.

He steps through the archway, and something akin to appreciation strikes me with his choice to join me in this. It's an easy decision for me—my escape lies only with Silas or a portal. Iron walls or not, my options are the same. But with Silas, these walls are a cage, and he cannot shadow himself to safety at a moment's notice.

"You ready to do this?" he asks me, unperturbed.

I glance beyond Silas, at the quiet palace hall stretching out in front of us, my path forward lit by flickering torches.

This is my chance. I will not waste it.

Thirty minutes pass of us clearing palace rooms, mostly empty, some already sticky with the blood and guts of who I assume are Seelie Royals. With each room comes an increasing sense of urgency, as if the deeper we tread into the palace, the closer we get to our doom.

Silas, true to his nature, makes a game of it.

When my boot strikes a locked door with enough force to

send its hinges rattling, he shadow-walks at the first crack between the wood, despite not knowing what lies inside. My gun is poised, my finger ready to pull the trigger, but he beats me to it. With a snicker, whoever cowered beyond the locked door falls to the ground, the soul sucked out of them. Silas rubs imaginary dust off his hands, admiring his handiwork.

It continues like this, again and again.

I roll my eyes, slightly miffed I haven't pulled my trigger once yet.

"What are you rolling your eyes for? I never get to use this power back home," Silas whines, an exasperated smack of his outstretched palms on his thighs punctuating his words. "Let me live a little, Nor."

I choose not to comment on the affectionate use of my nickname. Or the fact that I suddenly want to pull his head back by his hair and force him to apologize for the familiarity.

Soon we come to a crossroads; do we veer left or right, or do we continue forward, venturing deeper into a palace we don't know the layout of? My little fucker of a cousin could have given us *some* directions before vanishing into thin air. But beggars can't be choosers.

I understand now, why he needed to time this correctly. It's the same trick we pulled with Wes. It's a good plan, even if it limits our range of movements here by magic along with theirs.

"Should we split up?" Silas says, though his clenched jaw notes his hesitance to do so.

"No," I say. "Too risky."

"Flip a coin?"

"Don't have any." I pace, my footsteps clack on the marble with my mounting frustration. "There's got to be a better way. We're running out of time."

I close my eyes and think.

And think.

And *think*.

And then I groan—the drink I'd been nursing at the pub must have made me an idiot. I tune into my magic, drawing forth the tether. I focus on his heartbeat, hoping, *praying*, that as I turn towards each of the halls, one feels *right*.

My prayer is answered when my magic flares as I veer to the left. I've never experienced this tug before, my magic so sure. I don't bother with conversation and trudge forward, knowing Silas will trail at my heels. We follow the golden thread of magic, through intertwining halls and up two sets of stairs.

"Time check?" I ask, quickening my pace.

Silas keeps in stride, pulling out his pocket watch. "Twenty till."

My magic flares, a beacon, a guiding light. The pulse of Patience's heartbeat whooshes in my ears. "We're getting close."

And as we round the corner to what must be a private stretch of the west wing—*gods this palace is fucking huge*—I skid to a stop. Twenty guards stand between us and a set of ornate double doors.

As quick as I calculate how we can drop all twenty without getting shot, there's a hand on my shoulder and shadows engulf me. Silas drops us on the other side of the guards, their backs to us and our backs to the door. Where we once stood, bullets are embedded in the stone.

"You go do your thing. I'll take care of these guys." Silas shoves me at the door. He doesn't leave room for argument, dissipating into a swirl of shadows and reappearing next to a confused guard.

"Don't die!" I shout, before kicking open the double doors. They crash against the wall and bounce back, closing behind me. The shouts and gunshots from the hall cut off sharply, and I glide into the room.

There's a scream, girlish and high, and my gun is aimed at the woman before her flaming red hair even hits my periphery. She's half dressed, clinging to a bedsheet between the bed and the bathroom.

She isn't what I'm here for. It's *him*.

Patience sits at the edge of the bed in a fucking bathrobe. I have to hold back my gag.

His emerald glare clashes with mine, two swords of steel meeting in the first strike of battle. The knell declares the official beginning of the end.

I nod my head at the door. "Fun's over, lady. You get three seconds to leave, or you die with him. Three..."

She squeaks, shocked and sputtering at the threat—and the second she spends doing so costs her.

"Two..."

She bolts into action, gathering the sheet around her as if to keep her dignity intact, but that's her second mistake. Her feet get tangled in the extra swath of fabric and she falls to the ground. She struggles to get up, tears and snot running down her face as panic overtakes her.

"One."

"No-no-n—"

Bang.

"Did you have to do that?" my uncle sighs.

"Yes," I say. My voice is deadly cold; my pulse is a slow, steady thump in my neck.

Then without hesitation, I shoot him too.

Patience grunts at the impact, and I let loose the entirety of my cartridge. Bullet holes riddle his gut, exposed by the gaping bathrobe. With each pop, the magic tying us together zings. He keels over, falling onto his knees in front of the bed. My lips twitch at the sight of him clutching the oozing wounds, slippery hands squelching over his stomach. Patience lifts his head, but even though pain draws a wince from his throat, he smiles widely. Blood settles in the cracks between his clenched teeth.

"Look at those *wings*," he taunts, full of vehemence, the words sharpened and hurled at me like a spear. "Don't you feel like a new woman?"

The room darkens around us and my vision comes to a pinpoint around my uncle. My wings ache, as if reminded of their duty to plague every fiber of my being. I almost force them away but stop my magic from completing the task. They fan out reflexively, the light rustle pulsing the air around me. In a way, they push me forward.

I let the wind of my vengeance carry me to him, let it flow under my wings.

Patience laughs as I backhand his bloody grin with the butt of my gun. My fingers curl around the collar of his robe, and I toss him across the floor. He's heavy, but adrenaline boosts my strength, turning me feral. My gun accidentally goes flying with him, skittering towards the doorway. Patience slides and hits a dresser, leaving a streak of red in his wake. I step along it, a perfect guide to the finish line.

I need to end this, but savagery clouds my vision—*I can play with him a little, can't I? Don't I deserve that much?*

The mania of bloodlust is addictive. And I've never been good at quitting my vices.

"My handiwork is a marvel. I'm glad I get another moment to admire it before they wither away with your life," Patience spits up at me.

I shake my head, and the hazy maroon in my periphery lessens. Can he not read the room? This is the end for him.

"This is how I feel about my new fucking wings." I flip him off.

Patience lifts himself upright with a drawer handle, at the same time pulling the thing open.

"So dignified of you," he sneers. "Did your mother never teach you manners?"

Instinct flares, a warning pulse of danger.

It comes just in time for me to dodge the slew of bullets Patience slings my way. The hidden pistol *pops*, and I dive. Two bullets graze me.

Natural epinephrine is a blessing—I don't even feel the sting of the cuts, only the dulled sensation of my sleeve and pant leg growing warm and wet. When the clicks of Patience's trigger sound and no bullets fly, I charge him. Tackling him against the furniture, the mirror attached to the armoire shatters around us.

We grapple, exchanging blows. He puts up more of a fight than at Casimir, his survival instinct finally kicking in. Patience lands a powerful jab to my ribs; pain slices through my side, warning me that something has cracked. I get in twice as many punches though, my furious youth an unmatched inferno. I manage to straddle him, and press his cheek into the broken glass. My magic bubbles to the surface, giddily leaping from my fingertips.

I don't have *that* much time to play.

Patience tries to buck me off him, but I will my magic to break the bones in his legs. The cracks are audible, and he cries out.

His magic fights mine. It's a game of tug of war with the tether; who wins will be decided by the strength of our will. The glowing thread wraps around us, curling between our limbs and circling our necks. And then it tightens.

We scream. Him from pain, and me from the effort it takes

to force my fire down his gullet. My throat becomes raw, and my teeth clench. They slice into my tongue, and I swallow down the sweet bite of my blood.

Patience tries to push me off—his slick hand smears gore across my face in the futile attempt. His fingers dig into my hair and rip a chunk free, but I hold fast.

This need is agonizing.

My magic thrums, and I relish as it takes its bounty.

One hand keeps his face pressed against the glass-ridden floor; raw blisters form on his flesh underneath my magicked fingertips. My other hand slides to his throat, obstructing his breath. My fingers squeeze along his pulse-point, cutting the flow of his arteries. And when he's a wheezing, unrecognizable mess below me, I cut the tether.

I snip it with the sharpest shears.

One burst of magic, and he's gone.

The golden thread blazes, then disappears along with his soul.

My chest heaves and a tingling sensation—pins and needles—rushes over my skin. I otherwise stay frozen, unable to release the pressure I put on Patience's limp body. The shiny marble around us quickly floods with a pool of dark red.

This... this is retribution.

And it feels glorious. That is, until it doesn't.

My tongue licks my lips clean of the blood—his or mine, I couldn't say—and that iron tang? The remnant of my brutality? It's sour.

40

SILAS

Nora doesn't notice when I slip inside the room, or that I'm staring at her blood-soaked body with something akin to reverence. Her head falls back, tilting to the ceiling, lashes falling against her cheeks; her tongue darts out to trace along her lips.

Relief.

That's what the sagging of her body softly calls out.

Patience is dead. The man who's plagued both our nightmares is gone. I watched her choke the life out of him; I witnessed the moment that tether snapped. This was different from the other times I'd seen her kill. This was rare. This was rebirth.

Nora's wings flutter, a green and black shroud curling around her—does she even realize they're fanned out in all their pearlescent glory? Does she recognize she's transformed into something new?

I take one measured step deeper into the room, then halt; Nora's head snaps my way. The glowing green eyes of a hunter stare at me, rimmed in red. Immediately, my defenses rise, my muscles twitching as I teeter on the edge of reason. My body wants me to run, but *I* want to stay.

Nora has that same exposed aura as she did when I found her in the shower. However, this time, it reflects not a sad, broken woman, but the raw, fierce being she is. There are few things more powerful than the sharp edge of her gaze.

I'm already high on bloodlust, my magic is a satisfied deviant, rushing through my veins. And that look? It brushes over me, whispering promises of cruel passion.

Fuck.

"Silas?" Nora rasps my name, and I'm done.

Fuck fuck fuck fuck fuck fuck fuck fuck —

No. This is *not* happening right now. I do *not* get turned on by my friends.

I don't think my cock considers her a friend anymore.

It clicks, suddenly, that *this* is what that nagging, confusing concern I've had for her is: attraction.

Nope. *No.* No, no, no. Lies. The falsehood instantly sours my mouth. This is not attraction. Attraction is a paltry word that common folk use to describe something casual. Everything between us has been anything but casual.

I take a measured breath in through my nose, count to ten, and square my shoulders. Okay. Freak out over. No use in beating around the bush on this one.

"Can I make a confession?" I blurt out.

A puzzled frown cuts across her face. "If I say no, won't you say it anyway?"

"You're learning." A smirk toys with my lips. "I may have just come to the controversial conclusion that I am a teeny, *tiny* bit, soul-crushingly obsessed with you."

Nora blinks. Once. Twice. Then a third time, with a shake of her head for good measure, at which point she finally processes what I said.

Her face contorts into an expression of pure exasperation. "What?"

"I think you heard me, but I can say it again if you ask nicely—"

"No! Stop!"

Nora mutters a string of curses so profane that *I* wouldn't even repeat them as she pulls herself away from Patience's dead body. She rubs her face on her sleeve, but all that does is smear the blood closer to her hairline.

"Did one of those guards knock you over the head?" Nora asks.

"If I said yes, would you kiss my wound better?" The flirty quip escapes me against my better judgment.

"No!" Her flustered scowl is almost comical.

"Why not?" I ask.

"Because I don't want to."

I wince. "That stings, Nor. But I'm a patient man. I'll wait."

"No, you're not," she scoffs.

Gods, what the fuck am I doing, goading her? My tongue has a mind of its own. But is that a flush rising up her neck? Or is that a bloodstain I didn't notice before?

"You're right. Persistent is a better word—"

"*Silas.*" Nora slaps a hand over my mouth. I jolt, and my back hits the door. "*Shut the fuck up.*"

There she goes, rasping my name again. Her voice always has that dominating edge to it, like her word is law to anyone who hears it. Her nails dig into my cheek as her bare palm presses over my mouth. I would lick over her heart lines if I had the courage to part my lips.

I'm careful to breathe through my nose and stay completely still as her potent gaze trails over me. I can see the gears turning double time behind her eyes.

"This isn't the time or the place for *confessions of love,* or whatever the fuck that was," she sneers. "Are you sure you didn't hit your head?"

"Obsession," I clarify, though it's muffled by the cover of her hand. Her hand slides to grip my jaw, freeing my mouth. "Seems a better fit for us than love, don't you think?"

One of Nora's black brows ticks, and it's with that micro-expression she hangs a deadly threat in the air. It dares me to speak, to push. It's a delicious sort of tension that makes my dick throb. *Fuck*, this is uncomfortable. I shift in a subtle attempt to put space between us. Nora is awfully close, and the last thing I need is to accidentally rub my cock against—

Nora peers down at the boner straining against my trousers.

"You can ignore that," I say.

She squints up at me, searching my face for the lie.

She won't find one.

I know her boundaries; outside of pulling her back from the brink of her own darkness the other night, I will not touch her without permission.

"Does this happen a lot because of me?" Nora asks, a hint of morbid curiosity in her tone.

I shake my head. "First time."

Her fingers dig harder into my jaw.

Nora's attention falls back to my covered cock. Her tongue swipes over her lip, catching a runaway drop of blood that's gathered there, but her lips curl at whatever she tastes.

An internal war wages in those few seconds of silence.

"Fuck it out of my system," she mutters under her breath. At least, that's what I think she says. It's hard to hear over the whooshing of my pulse in my ears. Then again, I could be concussed and dreaming all of this. She huffs a humorless laugh, shaking her head. "What else do I have to lose?"

Or dead. Probably dead. Because there's no way her hand is

still gripping my face with such delicious force. And there's certainly no way her other hand is reaching down, digging into my pocket. My body shivers as she pulls out my watch. Nimbly, her fingers crack open the case. The faint *tick-tick-tick* of the hand drives me wild, stealing my breath with every notch around the watch. Five terribly long seconds go by before she clicks it shut and drops it back into my pocket.

"Fuck it."

In a move so sensual it should be outlawed, her free hand trails one nail up my front.

My muscles seize at the touch. It stops where my shirt lies unbuttoned, the sharp tip tracing over the edge of my tattoo peeking out. I hiss, but the noise only draws her closer, and the pressure of her nail into my flesh increases.

"Ninety seconds," Nora says, and my heart drops into my stomach. Her predatory gaze peeks through her dark lashes; it holds me captive, as if she's shackled my wrists and ankles with iron. "And don't say a fucking word unless it's for me to stop."

My head bobbles, my tongue too cottony to form words.

The distinct sound of my belt buckle clinks as Nora deftly unbuckles it; she doesn't slide it from its loops, instead letting the leather hang open. Her hand doesn't graze over me fondly. No, she reaches right into my boxers and—*fuck.* Her hand is ice-cold around the length of me.

I don't dare break eye contact, meeting her blow-for-blow in this strange encounter we've found ourselves in.

Her hand glides down to the base and squeezes. Up and down, methodical and slow, she repeats the motion until my hips shift, trying to meet her strokes. She ignores my body's plea for more friction, keeping her pace torturously slow. The pressure builds until my cock is twitching in her vise grip, balancing on that line between pleasure and pain.

It's somehow the fastest *and* slowest hand job of my life.

A sound akin to a whine slips from my throat. Nora huffs, amused.

The hand squeezing my jaw slides down to my throat and *tightens*.

I fall over the edge.

After the last pulse of my orgasm, Nora pulls her cum coated fingers from my pants and lifts them to her mouth. I watch, awestruck. And the noise—*gods*—the noise that comes out of my mouth when her pink tongue darts out to lick the taste of me off her?

Nora hums, one of those short judgmental thrums that says much is left to be desired.

And those dreadfully cold eyes—they stare straight into my soul and suck it right out of my body. Now I'm the one who's stripped bare before her, even though my cock is still tucked in my pants.

She didn't even take it out.

I'm so fucked.

"You don't taste half bad," Nora says, tongue darting out to caress her bottom lip. "Thanks. I needed something to wash down the taste of his blood." She steps back, removes her hand from my neck, and frowns at my cum-stained boxers. "Clean yourself up and let's go."

41
NORA

"Are we not going to talk about what just happened?" Silas calls after me.

What the fuck was I thinking? What demon possessed me to unbuckle his belt and get him off with ten strokes in his pants like a schoolboy?

Why did I not hate it?

Because I felt myself teetering on the edge of something dark, spurred on by the hollow satisfaction left in the wake of Patience's death. And Silas was right there, an easy outlet.

Because there's a part of me that craves the moment someone powerful submits.

Because I clearly have issues.

"Nora!"

"Absolutely not. We only have ten minutes to find the throne room," I say, somehow managing to keep my tone all business. My wings rustle with my hurried pace out of the room, and I force them back into my faded scars.

My foot catches on one of the bodies strewn in the hall and the Seelie groans, not yet dead. *Oh, wonderful.* I grab the man by his shirt and slap his face until his painful, glazed over expression clears.

"Give us directions to the throne room, and I'll give you a chance to live by not finishing his botched job right now," I say, tossing a thumb over my shoulder at Silas.

The Seelie's teeth chatter uncontrollably. "Up a floor, towards the north wing. It's a left at the landing with the purple curtains."

I drop him and move on. Silas sidles up next to me, matching my brisk pace.

"Do you not actually like men? Because I thought at Hattie's birthday you said you—"

"No," I say. Then add, confused, "Yes?" I let loose a frustrated groan, attempting to keep one step ahead of Silas. My body buzzes, flustered and still coming down from the power trip.

"Sorry, I don't think I follow," Silas huffs as we enter the stairs and climb them two at a time.

"I find both attractive, but there have been very few men who have ever pulled my interest." I don't know why I feel the need to clarify, but I've always hated when people put me in a box that wasn't accurate. I shake my head. "But that doesn't matter."

"So, what I'm hearing is that I'm special, and I might have a chance."

I spin at the top of the stairwell, gripping the railing with white knuckles. Silas peers up at me with a smirk and a determination that could only be drawn from delusion.

This is too much.

Any semblance of composure I was clinging to snaps; it's a ski cut in the mountainside, an avalanche of snow breaking from the icy drifts.

"A chance at *what*, exactly?"

He blinks. "To woo you, of course. For a repeat performance."

"That was a onetime, spur-of-the-moment reaction to the comedown from adrenaline. It was not an invitation for you to *court me,*" I growl.

"That's fine for you to think." Silas shrugs.

"I can't believe we're talking about this right now!" I throw my hands up and storm away, spying the purple curtains and turning left. "I'm not entertaining any of what *wooing* entails. Forget the last ten minutes ever happened, or I may kill you and blame it on the Seelie, consequences be damned." I know he's about to spear me with another retort, but I beat him to it, snapping over my shoulder, "We have more important shit to deal with. Remember where we are, *Your Majesty.*"

Reverting to the honorific has his jaw snapping shut. He's definitely perturbed by its use, based on the way his lips mash together. But his attitude does shift.

"Fine," he grumbles.

It's a blessing, the way he retreats into his kingly shell and refocuses on the task at hand. The confines of his title keeps him at a distance; this is the last wall I can force between us.

I don't have a title to hide behind anymore. No longer Pride. Not a Second. Not even a soul-stealer. I'm only Nora.

He's intimately acquainted with *Nora.* And that makes what has occurred all the more dangerous.

I stop short outside what I assume is the throne room; the dead guards in golden armor sprinkled down the hall is a clear indicator. A black sunburst of blast powder stains the wall, and my nose crinkles at the lingering scent of sulfur. Pieces of the guards' armor are shattered, and my boots crunch over the metal shrapnel. The throne room doors are hanging off their hinges, the iron reinforcements bent and melted from the heat of whatever bomb detonated.

My ears twitch; despite all the death, it's *too quiet*.

There's merely a gentle thumping of a boot heel on stone, the nervous energy of someone in wait. The *who* behind the little clacks is obvious as we enter the room, my cousin's knee bouncing as he sits on the Seelie throne. All gold and glittering, the chair is a magnificent complement to his tanned skin.

Dead Seelie, guards and Royals alike, stare up at him in blank-eyed veneration. Rigor-mortis set in as they crawled towards the light; at the top of the throne, a glowing ball of Seelie magic hovers within an ornate etching of the sun. It casts a halo around Bennie's brown hair, but his presence is anything but angelic.

The bouncing of Bennie's knee halts, the last clack of his heel on stone rings out like a death knell. Because of him, the whole palace will be haunted by daybreak.

"Did you kill him?" Bennie asks.

The hair across my body stands on end, the pinpricks of a thousand needles poking my skin as I note the sizzle of magic in the air. It's hanging all around us, like a heavy blanket of summer humidity.

No matter how hard I squint my eyes, I can't tell where it begins and ends. Which either means Bennie's cloaking the entire room, or he's extremely good at blending his illusions into their surroundings. It's a fifty-fifty guess.

I nod.

"Excellent."

Silas steps around me. "Did you kill her yet, or do you still need us to?"

The question takes me off guard.

"Not yet," Bennie says. A shark's smile, one I've seen in the mirror before, overtakes his face as he slowly descends the stairs. There's the sharp snap of his fingers, and whatever illusion masks the outer rim of the throne room breaks. Shattering into a million shards of glittering magic, twenty of his men are revealed, all of them wearing the same green ribbon as the one on his lapel. And to the left of the throne, chained in iron and struggling against the hold of two men, is Oonagh. The Seelie Queen.

Oonagh's a ruffled mess, with a matted patch of blood-stained hair on the side of her head. One strap of her opalescent dress hangs off her shoulder, broken. Her wings flutter frantically at her back, and her face is contorted in anger.

"Now," Bennie says with a clap of his hands. "Slight change of plans. I need you to shoot both of us. It's an optics thing. One well-placed shot should work."

"What are you talking about?" I ask. Bennie ignores me and motions to his guards; they bring the Seelie Queen closer, dropping her to her knees behind him.

"He's going to be the next Seelie King, Nora," Silas mutters. "Go with it."

"What?"

"Yeah, cous', I thought you were quicker than that," Bennie teases. "Didn't ever wonder about who my mother was, did you?"

The pieces click together, fast and swift. "You're Royal?"

He holds his fingers up, about an inch a part, peering at me with a one-eyed gaze through the space. "Enough for it to count."

I turn to Silas. "You knew?"

Silas's head bobbles. "We... had a chat."

"We have an agreement," Bennie clarifies. "King to future king. We would be stupid to not take this chance for change. I'm happy to prove my father and our ancestors wrong and broker peace rather than continue some endless war."

"We have collateral, Nora," Silas reassures me. He seems to grow inches as he releases his aura into room. Silas often downplays his powerful nature, letting it lurk in the undercurrent where it's always poised to strike. Now it's out in full force. Bennie tilts his head as Silas stalks forward, shadows curling around his feet. "Alexander stays in Anwynn until Benevolence lives up to his word. He's got the burden of proving they've scaled back their war efforts. And who knows? If he's speedy, maybe his brother will be home by next Solstice."

"We'd need to have regular contact to prove that," Bennie says, brown eyes narrowed. "Meetings. Information exchanges."

"Nora will be our liaison," Silas says, volunteering me with a devilish smile over his shoulder. My expression tightens, my head shaking on instinct. "She can meet you once a month at that dinky little diner."

An equally devilish smile crosses over Bennie's face. "Business and family bonding time. How considerate of you, Silas."

"I can be an excellent partner when given the opportunity," Silas says, and somehow the words don't sound aimed at my cousin. Silas stops a foot away from Bennie.

"Deal," Bennie says, his smile growing into something blinding.

He reaches his hand out, and I hold my breath when their palms touch.

Silas does not kill my cousin. His shadows coil around their joined palms, and Bennie's hand glows golden, a meeting of magic. The illusion on Silas's wings breaks, and his white feathered wings unfurl gracefully.

My breath leaves my lungs in a rush.

"Boss, we've got reinforcements incoming on the first floor!" a guard pants, rushing into the throne room.

The spell breaks, and Bennie and Silas step back from each other.

"Well, that seems to be our cue," Bennie says.

Oonagh cries out, a last-ditch effort to escape Fate, but her pleas go ignored. Silas pulls out his gun and shoots Bennie clean through the gut; the bullet lodges itself into Oonagh's chest, her body convulsing in agony.

"Oh, that hurts like a motherfucker!" Bennie groans, falling to his knees and clutching his side.

Then, for good measure, Silas leans around Bennie and shoots the Seelie Queen in the head, right between the brows.

"That's for my parents," Silas spits at her limp body. "Heartless bitch."

The guards jolt at his vehemence, and some even raise their weapons, but a single raised palm by Bennie has them pausing.

"Everyone stand down," Bennie grunts, stumbling as he rises to one knee. "Mila, take them to the safe house."

"But Benevolence..." A female guard steps forward. She must be one of his inner circle based on the concern tightening her features.

"Do it, Mila. The reinforcements will have a healer," he says. But when everyone stays frozen, he snaps, "Now! You all know what the plan is. Execute it!"

There's a flurry of action, and Silas and I are ushered up the dais.

"Help! In here! They've killed the queen!" Bennie screams, the pain in his voice real.

A flash of light blinds me, and a harsh whisper sounds next to my ear. "Don't move."

A strong grip lands on my arm, and light magic flares. I close my eyes, nausea consuming me as the combined magic of this Seelie and the portal whisks us across realms.

Shadows are never this unsteady.

Silas and I stumble out of the light and onto the dead city streets of the Human Realm. The street signs show we're at

Fifth and Sixty-Second, which is the heart of no-man's-land and nowhere near the Seelie portal we entered Avalon through.

We are alone, only the glittering remnants of Mila's magic left to prove she was once here.

Silas and I catch our breath, and then, without another word, he extends his hand. The silent offer is always the same: *do you trust me?*

When I give him my hand, his magic wraps around me like a warm blanket on a cold night, cushioning my fall into the darkness. He drops us into a version of that cold night, settled in the snowy valley before Mt. Bramble. Above us, a storm brews. Swirling gray clouds hurl chips of ice at us, and I shield my eyes with a cupped palm.

"Bramble? Not Anwynn?" I yell through the squall.

"This was the first place I thought to go!" he shouts back.

We trudge through the drifts, and by the time we reach the cave, we're both soaked and shivering.

"Sh-showers first, to clean the grime off and warm up, then we sh-should tell Wrath—"

"Nora," Silas says, cutting me off. "I already have a plan. Don't worry about it."

"Oh."

The events of today hit me like a truck, fast and hard. My body is drained, my magic is buzzing, and my mind is reeling.

The clear midnight of Silas's eyes bores into me, and I shiver. He looks upon me with far too intimate a gaze; it's almost timid in its vulnerability.

"Are you okay?" he whispers.

"Yeah." I manage to choke the word out without chattering my teeth. And even though I know he can tell I'm lying, I do it anyway. "Of course, I'm okay. Why wouldn't I be?"

42

NORA

I lie awake in a bed that feels more like my own than the one that I slept in for most of my life; when did that change? Was it the weeks I spent here with Silas and Wrath, burrowing so deep into my magic that it's now connected to this place? Or is it that the *idea* of home has soured, as if stepping back into the facade I embraced in Anwynn would ruin me?

I should go back to sleep.

Rolling over, I stare at the hearth that is burning strong. Only a few hours have passed since my lids fell shut. The storm still swirls outside my window, and the wind throws hail at the glass like a lover tossing pebbles.

There's simply too much on my mind for slumber.

Patience and the memory of his dying breath under my tight grip. Benevolence—his gripe for power unsurprising— but his secret brokering of peace with Silas a concept I'm still trying to wrap my head around. My wings, and the small blessing that is the absence of pain under my scars.

I roll out of bed, grabbing a carton of cigarettes and my lighter from the nightstand.

I won't hold my breath, hoping it's a permanent solution. I'm not that lucky.

I'm smoking in the kitchen, nursing my third whiskey, when Silas shuffles in half after ten. He yawns while rubbing the crust from his eyes, his hair deliciously sleep-rumpled.

I frown. Has he always looked like that in the mornings?

He's also barefoot and shirtless, and that stupid ornate butterfly on his chest pulls my gaze.

"You're going to give yourself a cold, walking around like that," I say.

"I remember there was a time, not too long ago, that you traipsed around this kitchen barefoot." He pours himself a cup of coffee, then leans against the counter. Silas's early morning smile is slow to rise, but when it does, it shines brightly.

"That's different. I don't get sick. You can," I say, sucking on my cigarette. The smoke unfurls from my nose on my exhale, burning my nostrils.

Silas clamors over the bench across from me, leaning forward on the table. The steam from his coffee wafts between us, fusing the air with the earthy, bitter scent.

"Oh, you care about my well-being now? That's cute."

"You're a fucking brat," I mutter, rolling my eyes.

"I could be, for you." His expression dances with mirth as he takes a careful sip.

I shake my head, mumbling a curse. The idea of putting Silas in his place is tempting, and it's frustrating that the thought even crosses my mind. That's how I know I haven't slept enough for this conversation.

I don't know where to begin with Silas. Or how to process the memory of him coming apart in my hand. I've barely processed the night I broke apart in his. I was stupid to indulge in any aspect of the carnal with him. It muddles an already complicated dynamic. And if I'm to believe him, then I'm about to become a liaison between the Courts, whether I like it or not.

I need him as an ally... and as a friend. Not a lover.

The knuckle of my thumb jabs into my forehead, massaging from the center to my temple.

"Did Wrath get back to you?" I ask, changing the subject. I watch the ash crumble off the end of my cigarette as I tap it over the ashtray.

Silas hums thoughtfully, and his mug hits the table with an audible *thunk.* "He'll be here in a couple of hours with Josie and Leo."

"Good, you all can discuss what comes next," I say. "It's important to internally align on that deal you made before you take it to the rest of the Sins."

Silas tilts his head at an odd angle, inserting himself into my line of sight.

"I'd like for you to be a part of that conversation too," he says with hope.

"What does my opinion matter?" I ask, sitting straighter in my seat. Silas mirrors my movements. "I'll do as I'm told and won't make a fuss."

"Why wouldn't it matter?" Silas asks.

"Would you rather me say that I think we should *not* do as you promised Bennie?" My jaw ticks, but a sardonic laugh bursts from my chest. "Question your judgment in front of your lessers? Suggest we launch an attack before he can think to betray you?" I take one last drag of my cigarette, breathing the toxic chemicals in deep, before flicking the butt into the ashtray. "We know where their portal is. You can shadow-walk anyone anywhere we've been in Avalon. There are ways to make it work. And we know they're vulnerable right now. We could end them if we do it right."

Silas only looks disappointed by my confession. "You'd kill the last of your family so easily?"

"Family is who you choose," I say. "I don't choose him."

"Could your opinion not change with time? With getting to know him?" Silas asks.

I shake my head, but it's a half-hearted motion. Because as angry as I am with my cousin, there's a part of me that recognizes that Bennie is a product of his circumstances. As I am. As we all are.

"And what would you do with all the Seelie innocents?" Silas continues. "Would you lead them to the slaughterhouse too? There's an entire Court to consider."

"Bennie is his father's son," I say. "I simply think searching for an ally in a snake pit is a fruitless endeavor."

"History does prove collaboration between the Courts is unlikely. I will give you that," Silas says. "But how many of my ancestors *tried*? When has anyone tried, really? This is the first time in modern history that we have someone uniquely fit to bridge the gap. *You*, Nora. You can be the one to help us build lasting peace with the new Seelie King. A man who didn't lie to me once."

I am at a loss for words—at a loss for further anger. "You truly trust him?"

Silas levels with me, a knowing smirk. "Aren't you the one who told me that men tend to keep their word when there is enough incentive? I'm only taking a page out of your book."

I sigh. I'm arguing with a wall. The Unseelie King made his

final decision last night, when he shook the Seelie King's hand and didn't steal his soul. There's no going back.

"You'll come to the meeting, right?" Silas asks. "We need you."

A sudden lump forms in my throat.

That damned word. *Need.* I thought I was what House Pride needed, what my friends needed. What Imogen needed. And now that I've done all the things I convinced myself they *needed me* to do, the fire in my chest snuffs out. Because I was wrong.

It was I who *needed*—to fall, to burn.

And now, of all the people in the world, the Unseelie King is saying *he* needs *me*? It's almost comical.

"Fine," I rasp.

"You're not going to argue more?"

"No."

I snag my nearly empty carton of Black Cats and stand to leave. I make it all the way to the doorway before his voice, deep and alluring, calls out to me.

"Is your plan to ignore me?"

I glance over my shoulder. He's got that vulnerable glint in his eyes again, like he's holding his breath. "Silas..."

"You need space?"

"Yes," I say plainly.

I'm desperate for space. From him. From these strange emotions running around my chest. They don't play nicely with my insecurities or my lingering heartbreak.

"Okay," he says.

It would be easy to fall into bed with him. He's eager. He'd listen. But he's seen too much of me, and I suspect he'd ask for more than what I can give. And I already know how that story ends.

"I'll prove I'm patient!" Silas yells as I walk away.

I can't stop the amused smile from tugging at my lips. I'm too tired to hide it.

Yeah, I would ruin him.

43

NORA

The meeting goes about the way I expect it to. I stay quiet during most of it, and that fact is not lost on Josie, Leo, or Wrath, given the confused looks they keep tossing me. And outside of some scolding for going rogue for nearly a month, they hold back their ire.

I'm unsure if I'm grateful for that or not. Would it not be easier for them to come in guns-a-blazing? To yell at me for endangering the Court? For running off with the Unseelie King to go murder my uncle—and the Seelie Queen too?

Our conversation ebbs and flows with details of the logistics, and soon, Silas is dragging Wrath out, a casual arm slung around the Sin's shoulder. Leo stands from his seat and approaches me, perching his ass on the table to my right. He crosses his strong arms over his chest.

"You know you had everyone worried, right?" Leo asks, and I imagine it's how a disappointed father would sound, gently reprimanding his daughter.

"You don't have to be concerned about me, Leo."

He clicks his tongue. "Shut down that idiotic fucking train

of thought right now, Nor. We can be pissed at you and still care about your safety."

Leo hops off the table, and his dress shoes smack the floor. I flinch when his hand lands on my shoulder and squeezes.

"We still love you, even if you're scary as shit sometimes," he says. He gives my shoulder another friendly pat, then walks off. "Don't be a stranger, okay?"

A puff of air escapes my nose as he saunters after the boys, leaving Josie and me behind.

There's a palpable tension between us; it's a new and strange thing to navigate.

"I'm glad you're okay—"

"I'm sorry about the way I left—"

We both huff short laughs at our overlapping awkwardness, but it does something to break down the weight bearing down on us. We are sisters—we've been through hell together.

And I missed her.

I jerk my head towards the door, giving her the only peace offering I've ever known.

"Tea?" I ask.

There's a vulnerability in the soft scrunching of her round nose as she replies, "I thought I took all the good stuff back with me."

I shake my head. "I hid a stash in my room."

A sliver of a white-toothed smirk flashes. "Of course you did."

I lick my lips nervously. "So, tea?"

"Yeah."

We don't talk as we trudge up to my room, grab the box I hid months ago, and take over the empty kitchen. The kettle whistles quicker than it ever has, as if the water can't help but sacrifice itself to the roiling boil. It must have a vested interest in getting us to whatever conversation is looming.

When my ass hits the bench next to Josie's, and my hands wrap around the hot ceramic, I decide to follow suit, throwing myself into the scalding depths of emotional intimacy.

"I'm sorry about how I left," I repeat. I want her to hear it without interruption. "I know that you can only say this kind of thing so many times before people stop believing you, but I'm going to try to be a better friend. You deserve better." I stare into the pink-tinged tea steaming in my cup, and recite the words I'd practiced all night as sleep evaded me. "I can't promise I won't be a bitch most of the time. Or that I won't piss you off. Or that I won't make mistakes. But I do promise to be more honest with you. And with myself."

I take a stuttering breath in, and let a lengthy sigh out. The heat of Josie's gaze warms my cheek.

"That's all we want, Nor," Josie says softly.

"I have a lot of shit to work through in here." I motion to my head, and then to my heart. "And here. And I realized the way I have been dealing with it is only going to cost me the things I care about most."

"Imogen?" Josie asks tentatively.

I shrug; I don't see a path in which Imogen and I pursue each other again romantically, as much as my heart still aches thinking about her. The more I ruminate on it, the more I realize I don't think I'm made for love. At least, not in the traditional sense.

We were a volatile pairing; propane and matches, fated to burn bright and then snuff out. Love like that isn't sustainable, in any sense of the word.

It would be unfair to pursue her again.

"It will cost me all of you," I clarify. "Also, I'm sorry for blindsiding you at the Sins' meeting. That wasn't the right way to pass on the title. But I stand by what I said. I believe you're what our House needs right now."

"Two apologies in one day might be a new record," Josie snarks, though her tone is laced with something somber. She takes a sip of her tea, slurping up the floral essence. "I accept them, by the way."

I snort and burn my tongue on my own sip of tea. "Good."

"A lot has happened since you left. Do you want to hear about it now?" Josie asks. I nod, and she launches into lengthy detail about our House. She recounts her struggles with the lingering sentiments from Wes's influence, a botched assassination attempt, and how she managed to end a workers' strike. All within no more than a month.

"That is a lot," I say, tongue poking my cheek. "It sounds like you had it handled, though."

"Thanks," she says. Josie's lips purse together, and her pointer finger scrapes along the ceramic lip of her mug. "There's something else, too."

"Okay," I say, slow. Dread creeps up my neck with every second she wastes pursing and parting her lips.

"Imogen and I—" Josie stops, sucking in a breath. "We kissed."

"Oh." I blink. That is not what I was expecting her to say.

I wait for the jealousy to rear its head, or the possessiveness I hold for Imogen to flare, or even for the ever-burning rage that lives in my gut to blaze. But the longer I stare into Josie's fretful brown eyes, the more confident I am that this doesn't upset me.

Not one bit.

Her throat bobs nervously. "Is that... okay?" she asks.

"Are you happy?" I ask slowly.

"Yeah," Josie says sheepishly. A light blush tints her cheeks.

"Is Imogen happy?" I ask, more importantly. Because if I couldn't make Imogen happy, then maybe my better half can.

"I think she's getting there," Josie answers honestly. "And I want to help her get there."

My soft smile quivers, and my eyes grow hazy; I blink away the swells of my heart. "Then, yeah, Joze, it's okay."

"It just feels weird—"

"Does it feel weird with her or is it because of me?" I ask.

"I don't want you to think that I—"

"I don't think anything," I reassure her with a shake of my head. Josie doesn't have to explain her worry to me. I know her better than that.

There's no malicious intent here.

And who am I to judge, anyway? I gave the Unseelie King a hand job in a fit of aroused mania after killing my uncle. There are worse things than a budding crush and a kiss.

"You don't think *anything*?" Josie repeats, lips suspiciously mashed together.

"Don't laugh at me—you know what I meant." I huff. "I'm trying to be supportive here. You know I'm not good at these things."

A beat passes between us before we break into nervous chuckles over our tea, sad little smiles dancing over our teeth.

"Thank you," Josie whispers.

"You don't need to thank me, Joze," I say. "Just keep her heart safe for me."

My head drops to her shoulder, and her head leans onto mine, a strange version of a hug. We've shared this moment many times over the years, but none have been so potent with change.

I know, with certainty, that once we leave this kitchen, our lives will look very different; but for now, we drink our tea. We sit still in the face of a shifting world, content in the quiet comfort of each other's company.

44
NORA

Chain smoking is the only thing getting me through this conversation. Bennie blabbers on about his childhood in some perversion of a eulogy for his father. It's as if this diner is the funeral home hosting the wake, and pastrami sandwiches with a side of pickle spears are the only refreshments being served.

I tuned out when he got to the part in his life's story where Patience tried to marry him off to a distant cousin. Bennie had gagged and then taken another disgustingly large bite of his sandwich.

In my pursuit of becoming a more amenable team player, I let my friends convince me I'd be able to handle this. I gave them, and myself, too much credit.

I imagine taking his fork, and stabbing it straight through the hand he's got splayed over a file folder. The folder supposedly includes a copy of his legal decree that will enact *The Kings' Deal* in Avalon. I had slid a copy of Silas's version over the booth's table thirty minutes ago, hoping that maybe it would quicken the exchange. It didn't, and now the daydreams of ruining his perfectly tanned hand with four equidistant holes continue.

But I can't stab the Seelie King with a fork. I can't stab him at all. Well, I *could*. But I *won't*. Josie better be fucking proud of me for my exercise in restraint.

"Why do you look like you want to stab me with that fork?"

"Hm?" I glance up from the utensil. "Because I do."

Bennie laughs, the sound full and deep. "You crack me up, Nora."

"That isn't my intention, but I'm glad I can be of entertainment," I mutter, sipping on the black coffee Bennie ordered for me. I opt to stab my dead cigarette butt into the ashtray instead, laying it to rest with its siblings.

"Am I boring you?" Bennie asks.

"Let's go with: I haven't been dying to know every detail about your childhood or its woes at the hand of your father..."

He hums thoughtfully. "Your candidness is hard to get used to, but I respect it."

I purse my lips, not knowing exactly what to say to that. *Thank you?*

"How about this," Bennie continues. He pops the last bite of his sandwich between his lips and pushes his crumb-laden plate to the side. "I can tell you're itching to leave, so answer a few questions for me and I will let you go."

"You sound just like Silas," I sigh, pulling another chuckle from Bennie. "Shoot."

"Tell me about your favorite parts of the Human Realm."

I pause at the question, one of my penciled-in brows ticking up with surprise. Questions about the Unseelie Court, my time as Pride, or—*gods forbid*—my trauma-filled childhood, were all in line with my expectations of the new Seelie King's interests.

But the humans? This city? That strikes a nerve deep in my chest.

I settle back in the booth and cross my arms, the patent leather seat squeaking.

"You really want to know?" I ask.

"Mhm. Don't you remember grilling me at Solstice about whether I'd actually been here? I was as fascinated then as I am now, but I haven't had time to explore. Give me the highlights."

I tongue my cheek, considering what to say; no one's ever asked me why I love this city beyond the obvious. It's not because I was born here, or because I spent the first six years of my life here. Nor is it because of the business House Pride runs here, although all of that is part of the equation.

"This realm overflows with potential," I say softly. "Humans, they have such short lives that it makes them daring in ways we're not. Maybe that's where I get my candidness from." My brows flick up teasingly. "It's busier than Faerie, more crowded, always something going on. Though back in Anwynn, that's changed in the past ten years. We get more like them every day."

Bennie nods, urging me along.

"And there's something comforting in the grit and grime," I say, staring out the window with longing. "The air is polluted, hazy. The water's murky. It reeks of hot garbage and piss one second and then of the most delicious street food the next. It's whiplash for your nose." I laugh, my smile growing. "This realm doesn't pull its punches. It forces you to accept it for what it is or move away."

"I get it now. It's a metaphor," Bennie says. And at my confused expression adds, "For yourself."

"Yeah, no," I say. "That's not what I was going for, *Your Majesty.*"

"You don't have to call me that, you know."

"What am I to call you, then?"

"Bennie," he says, as if I'm being stupid.

"You're the king now, not Benevolence," I say.

He clicks his tongue. "You know, I'm slightly offended that you don't know Bennie is short for Benjamin."

My brain freezes for a beat. "Pardon?"

"It worked out that it fits for both. *Benj*amin, *Bennie,* *Bene*volence."

I have to run my hand over my face to hide the silly little smile that forces its way on my lips. This is almost as funny a development as learning Wrath's real name is Robbie. Both are names of children who should be running around a playground, not running governments.

"Alright, *Bennie,*" I say, letting down my hand. I point at the folder. "Did I answer well enough to get that and go?"

"I guess," Bennie sighs dramatically, sliding it over. But when I try to pull it from his grip, he doesn't let go. "Remember: same time next month."

I roll my eyes. "A deal's a deal."

He lifts his hand.

I slide out of the booth, but then decide to leave him a parting gift. Call it an act of goodwill in response to him not poking at the hard parts of my past. I point at the dainty golden crown that sits atop Bennie's head.

"You gonna wear that thing everywhere you go?" I ask.

Bennie reaches for the metal circlet. "You don't like it?"

"Well, you do look ridiculous. We're not at a ball," I say. "But I only point it out because it's gonna draw attention from the wrong sort of people around here."

"What does that mean?"

I shake my head, chuckling softly.

"You're sitting in a diner in Moretti territory. You'll be fine if you've kept up your magic illusion or whatever cloaking shit you light-walkers do." I wave my hand over him, as if to mimic the bending of light by his magic. "Even so, I'm sure you'll find yourself bombarded by requests to meet with him soon enough. Now that you've been seen with me here twice."

"Who?" Bennie asks, confused.

"Moretti," I repeat. "Human Realm 101. Don't get involved with the mafia bosses if you can help it."

He eyes me warily. "I assume you learned this from experience?"

"Only twenty years of hearing about House dealings with them, ten seeing them for myself, and a few fighting in their rings," I say. "They'll eat you alive, chew you up, and spit you into the river. Fae or not."

"Good to know," Bennie says, holding back a grimace.

I salute him goodbye, muttering under my breath. "Or, knowing Moretti, he'll try to sell you his daughter in exchange for an endless supply of Seelie tributes for the Pits."

I snort a laugh, cracking myself up as I walk into the starry night.

45

IMOGEN

"**Y**ou can't wait until we're home?"

I kiss down Josie's smooth jaw as I press her against the cleaning closet's door.

"You're stressed. Let me make you less stressed," I hum against her warm skin.

"I'd be less stressed at *home*."

"But I'm all hopped up on bar pheromones," I whine, pulling back and giving Josie my best puppy-dog pout. "Just a little fun to take off the edge? Then you can take me home and fuck me in our bed."

I've learned that Josie tries to put up a big front, act all responsible and reserved in public. But if you push the right buttons, the heat ignites in those deep brown eyes. Like now, they're absolutely *glowing* with arousal as I dip my head and press kisses to all her favorite spots.

The edge of her collarbone, where her blouse flares open, two buttons undone.

The crook of her neck, where her flush blooms.

The hinge of her jaw, right near her ear, where I can whisper naughty things.

How fun it's been, learning someone like this again. And how nice it's been, knowing they're just as committed to learning me.

Josie chuckles, her chest rumbling against mine as she leans closer. Her fingers lace into my hair at the root, tugging my face to hers.

"You're so demanding," she says, smiling. Already, the crease between her brows is gone. "And yet I can never say no."

I lean into the subtle strength of her hands bracketing my skull. "I'm good at getting what I want."

"And what is it you want, exactly?" Josie rolls her bottom lip between her teeth.

"I told you already," I tease.

"Give me more."

Shivers roll straight down my spine.

"Hm, let me think." I trace my finger along the points of her shirt collar, then down the front seam, my nail catching on the buttons and tugging at them playfully.

"Imogen…" Josie warns. It's not a game, what we share, but the playful drawing out of the delicious tension between us.

"I want your kisses," I say.

Josie hums her satisfaction; I think she gets off on making me tell her what I want and then making me get it. It's healing, in a way.

"Where?" she asks.

"Here." I tap my lips.

"And?"

"Here." I drag my finger down my front, flicking my nail off the beaded fabric when I reach my core.

"Greedy. I thought this was meant to be stress relief for me?" she teases.

"Don't act as if it won't be," I tease back.

The blush I love to see blooming on her cheeks makes an appearance, a hint at the shyer side of the woman. Josie's hard when she needs to be, but soft when she wants to—a balance I admire.

"You're right," Josie says, leaning in until our lips graze. I feel her smile and soft snort of laughter more than I see it. "I can't believe we're doing this here. Again."

"It's fun being adventurous."

"I think it's more a slight form of exhibitionism on your part," she snarks.

"Stop talking and kiss me, please," I groan.

Her fingers tighten in my hair, and we're crashing together. There are no thoughts, just us. We're in synch, a symphony of strings, melding together in a drawn out harmony.

I squeak when Josie flips us around, one trouser-clad leg fitting between mine and pushing me against the door. My dress rides up with the action, my thighs prickling with goosebumps as they're exposed. I tug on her forearms, begging for her to release my hair. They listen, immediately running down my sides and gripping handfuls of my flesh over my dress.

I want more—need it. I'm already wound up from breathing in all my customers' heady arousal. My hips grind over her thigh in an attempt for more friction.

Josie breaks our kiss, both of us breathless. Her forehead falls to my shoulder as she burrows into my neck, running her nose along the taught tendons.

"I love how the world goes quiet when I kiss you," she whispers.

Awe in the form of warmth spreads from every place our skin touches. My heart clenches, along with my core, as she slides down to her knees. It's almost reverent, the way Josie pushes my dress up. She exposes my soaked underwear and hooks one of my knees over her shoulder.

I bite my lip, hard, as I watch her push my panties aside; I shudder at the first gentle graze of her fingers on me. Then her tongue is there, lapping at my heat and pushing me over the precipice of pleasure.

Time doesn't exist when we're touching each other.

Not here, fucking in the cleaning closet at the back of my bar. Not at our new apartment, snuggling in our bed. Not on the street, as we walk home every night with our fingers intertwined.

The spell is broken when someone knocks on the door—three firm raps that vibrate against my back.

Josie's head pops up from between my thighs, her cheeks even redder than before and her eyes bugging out. I slap a hand over my mouth to hold back my laughter.

"*Why are you laughing—*" Josie whisper-yells in a panic. She frantically rights my underwear and dress.

"Shh—" I smack my free hand on her head to force her to keep looking up at me. "If we're quiet, they'll go away."

"It's me. We're all heading out, and the others voted for me to say goodbye," Nora's awkward but businesslike voice calls through the door.

Now it's my turn to panic, all the color draining from my face.

Not because it's Nora. The three of us are fine, despite the few awkward moments we've had in the months since we broke up, this one included. But because I had completely forgotten that she, Wrath, and Hattie hadn't left yet.

Oops.

"I forgot they were still out there," I whisper, helping Josie up. I swipe at my hair in hopes of making it look less like I've been freshly ravaged. "Sneaky buggers always hide in the back with a bottle of wine where no one can see them."

Josie shoots me a glare that communicates her embarrassment—I'll say I'm sorry three different ways when we're home. Once with my voice, once with my fingers, and once with my tongue.

"It's *fine*," I reassure her before spinning around and pulling the door open.

Nora's leaning against the frame with one smug black brow cocked and those red lips of hers pursed. She leans to the side, glancing past me. "Doesn't it ever feel weird kissing her where I used to?"

I snort, my hand coming up to cover my amusement. Josie harrumphs at my back, before wrapping me in her arms.

"Honestly? No. I don't think about it at all," Josie says, and for good measure places a ridiculous kiss to my cheek.

Nora shakes her head, but the skin around her eyes crinkles.

"Oh, sorry, did you want us both thinking about you when we're making out?" Josie snarks. "I didn't realize you were into me like that, Nor."

Nora rolls her eyes; the green orbs cut to me when they finish their lap, darkening in that sad way they do lately. My magic reaches out to her on instinct, but she's still an iron vault.

Josie must sense there's a conversation to be had between us, so she places another peck on my cheek and says she'll be waiting by the bar. I shift nervously under Nora's soul-snaring attention.

"Are we still good?" I ask. It's something we've asked each other many times over the last couple of months.

"Always," Nora says. "Are you still happy?"

"Getting there, most days," I say, emotion surging to my

throat. My attention flicks down the hall where Josie's disappeared. "She helps."

"She's good for you."

I shrug sheepishly, but it's true. Josie is good for me.

"Better than me."

I go to open my mouth to say *not better, but different—*

"That wasn't a dig for compliments, Mo," Nora says. "Just being honest."

My jaw snaps shut. A beat full of tender affection passes between us.

I point down the hall. "I'm gonna get back out there, but I'll see you at the apartment this weekend, right? You're still coming?"

Josie and I are hosting a housewarming party to celebrate the new place we got together. We hadn't been using our old apartments much, and commuting to and from the cabin was getting tedious. Now, we're a fifteen-minute walk to all of our most frequented spots.

"You know that if she ever hurts you, I will kill her, chosen sister or not," Nora says.

I click my tongue. "That's not funny."

"It's not meant to be." She scratches her neck and looks away. Even after all this time, she hasn't shaken the shroud of melancholy she came back from Avalon with. Her jaw feathers, the cut of it almost painful before she whispers, "You'll always be mine to protect, Imogen, even if you're not *mine*."

There are many ways a heart can break, but hearing the yearning in her tone wasn't one I'd known about until now.

All I can do is offer her a sad smile and a comforting squeeze of her shoulder as I pass by. Nora needs to be needed. It's a small, easy thing for me to gift, as I whisper, "Okay."

46

NORA

I let myself into their apartment, the door left unlocked. I tsk, flipping the deadbolt after myself. This isn't the suburbs. They can't be leaving their place unlocked like that.

"Nora?" Leo shouts from the living room.

"Yeah, it's me!" I yell back. Thank fuck it was me, and not some vagrant.

Quick footsteps, bare feet slapping on the hardwood, rush around the corner.

"You're finally here." Imogen's beaming smile shines up at me.

"I'm here," I say, if a little awkwardly.

She pulls me into a quick hug and then waves me deeper into the apartment. "C'mon, everyone's already half drunk. You need to catch up."

"Good to know."

"You want me to make you something?" Imogen asks as we enter the large living room. Our friends fill the three couches that create a u-shape around the fireplace. "Everyone is serving as taste testers for a new recipe I'm trying. But you know I have the works."

"Do the sangria!" Hattie calls from her place snuggled up next to Wrath. The Sin's arm is wrapped protectively around her, and there's a dopey smile on his face as he stares down at my friend. Oh, how the mighty have fallen.

"That the consensus? Is it strong enough for me?" I scan over the rest of our friends. Leo, Earl, and Aisha take up one couch, all nodding their heads. Wrath and Hattie sit across from them. And then there's the white-haired bane of my existence, plopped in the middle of the last couch.

"Definitely strong enough," Silas says. He reaches back, holding out his empty glass. There's a mischievous glint in his dark eyes as they peek over his shoulder. "Be a doll and get me a refill?"

Someone snickers as I roll my eyes, but I snag the glass from his grip anyway. "I cannot promise it won't be poisoned when I come back."

"A risk I'll have to take. It's good sangria," Silas tuts.

I follow Imogen into the kitchen, where Josie is pulling out a tray of food from the oven.

"Nor!" Josie perks up, dropping the metal pan on top of the burners and tossing her mitts on the counter. "I'm glad you didn't ditch."

Imogen snorts as she takes Silas's glass from me and goes to fill our drinks.

"Almost did," I joke with a smile, though it doesn't reach my eyes. I'm happy for them, I am. But there's a tightness in my chest every time I see them take another step forward with their lives. Playing house isn't on my wish list, but I can't help but worry that I'm falling behind.

"You would have had hell to pay if you had," Imogen says,

handing me two glasses full of sparkling red wine with pieces of fruit bobbing in them. "Here. I'm going to help with the food. If you need to smoke, you can go up on the roof. We have direct access. Door's down the hall to the left, past the bathroom."

"Thanks," I say, and venture back to the living room. Hattie and Leo are in a heated debate over which games we're to play tonight. I tune them out, reaching over Silas's head to dangle his glass in his face. "Delivery for the Unseelie King."

He tilts his head back, exposing his long, pale neck. The front of his shirt is unbuttoned, showing off the curved line of that damn tattoo. The sight of it makes my back itch and my wings restless. Some days, they're quiet. Some days, they ache. And others, they scream.

Today is one of the aching days.

"I'm tempted to have you pour it into my mouth," Silas jokes. He opens his mouth wide, making a drawn out *ah* sound.

"Not happening!" Josie shouts, entering the room with two plates of snacks. "That is a brand-new sofa."

Silas winks up at me, then grabs the glass and rights himself. "I would never dare to ruin such fine upholstery, Josie."

"Uh-huh."

I round the couch, plopping down in the free spot next to Hattie and Wrath. Silas's head flicks my way, and a small frown adorns his lips at my choice.

Yeah, no way in hell am I sitting next to him again. The last thing I need is him whispering drunk jokes in my ear all night.

"Alright, everybody." Hattie claps her hands. "We need to get serious here and pick something to play before I lose my ever-loving mind!"

My cheeks are warm from the five glasses of sangria Imogen plied me with by the time I sneak to the roof to smoke. The party is roaring, though we moved on from games as more of Imogen's and Josie's friends arrived. We had a good little stint there, with the core group. But now, the apartment's packed, and there are too many bodies. The music is loud, and the drunk chatter even more deafening. It all dulls the second the metal door to the roof swings shut behind me.

Fresh night air hits my flushed skin, a cooling balm, even with the height of summer humidity.

I spy two loungers set in the center of the roof and take one. My ankles cross as I lie back, staring up at the sky. The city lights make it hard to see the stars, but up here, I can imagine them fine enough. Little dots of hope battling against a swath of obscurity, that's all stars are, anyway.

The creaking hinges of the rooftop door alert me to my visitor. I suck in a deep breath, already knowing who it will be before he walks into my line of sight.

The door slams shut, a loud clang ringing out into the night.

"Shit," Silas drunkenly murmurs.

"You're a clumsy drunk," I call out.

"And you're a mean drunk," he huffs, stomping over to the loungers. "Why are you out here?"

I dig into my pants pocket and pull out my smokes case and lighter. I waggle them at him. Silas squints, as if trying to focus on the items in the dark.

"Ah. I should have thought of that."

I click open the engraved tin. My nail taps over the three cigarettes I have left in here, but instead of pulling one of those out, I land on something stronger. Plucking the joint from its slot, I close and place the case on the table next to the lounger. The metal clinks on the glass top.

"Sit, if you want," I say to Silas.

Silas plops down on the lounger, eyeing me with suspicion while I light the joint. I take in one drag. Then another. It burns more than cigarettes, singeing my throat. In my periphery, Silas alternates between scrutinizing the stars and sneaking glances at me.

Smoke unfurls around us, blowing away in the southward wind.

"Are you going to share or..." Silas finally says, and I crack a smirk.

"Your funeral," I say, holding out the joint.

He's careful plucking it from my outstretched hand, avoiding my skin. Despite being a nosy thorn in my side and all his ridiculous attempts at flirting, Silas is always cautious about us touching. I've noticed, in the few times it's happened since Avalon, that it's always at my initiation. Never his.

I'm thankful for that.

He takes a drag and immediately devolves into a coughing fit.

"That is not giggle smoke," Silas chokes out. "That fucking burns—gods. What the hell is that?"

"Seelie drugs," I say. "Bennie hooked me up."

"Are you trying to kill yourself? You've already taken four hits. My head's already spinning."

"That's the alcohol, Silas. Drugs don't work that fast."

"No, I know the difference between drunk dizzy and drug dizzy." He hands the joint back to me.

"Yeah?" I lift it back to my lips.

The lounger creaks as he settles back on it, hands behind his head. "Mhm. I'm older than you. I've had more time to experiment."

I slowly exhale and flick ash onto the roof.

Life's been so heavy lately, in a way that's hard to explain. Because it doesn't make sense. Everything's fine. Bennie hasn't gone back on his word. I'm settling into a new routine, as are my friends. They're happy. I'm happy...*ish*. I simply can't escape this heaviness.

"Tell me more about these years of experimentation," I tease, allowing myself one guilt-free moment of levity. "You once told me you spent your teenage years with Wrath at boarding school. How much trouble did you two get into in the early days?"

"You remember that?" Silas asks.

"I remember everything," I say. I was trained to log information about others like it could mean life or death. Of course I remember he told me they went to school together.

"About me? I knew I was special to you," Silas croons.

"Not in the way you're thinking."

"She admits it!" Silas bolts up, ignoring me, arms lifted to the starry sky as he shouts.

"*Shut up, you're going to wake up their neighbors,*" I whisper yell. I quickly snub out the joint on the glass table.

"Do you hear that, Anwynn? She finally admits that she cares about someone! It's a miracle!"

"*Sit the fuck down, Silas.*"

Silas snickers, but listens. He lies down, facing me, and I can't help but laugh at his goofy smile.

The drugs finally hit, mixing pleasantly with the alcohol already in my bloodstream. It loosens that ever-present tightness in my chest enough that I can fully breathe. It settles my nerves, makes me float.

And it has my mind wandering dangerous places.

To his tattoos, peeking out from under his shirt. To his neck that begs to be marked. Fingerprints or love bites—either would do. To his lips. They're pouting at me. But they're pink, with a pointy cupid's bow crowning them. How would they taste compared to his essence?

It's been four months since I've touched anyone—since Avalon—and *gods*, am I fucking horny.

"You've been avoiding me," Silas says.

"What?" I say, blinking through the haze. Silas's frown has deepened, and his cheek squishes in a silly way against the lounger. I get the sudden urge to mirror him, curling onto my side. My hand fits between my cheek and the lounger cushion. "I've been avoiding everyone."

"Why do you do that?"

"Avoid you? Or everyone?"

"Both. Either." Silas copies me, one pale hand fitting underneath his cheek. "I thought you were feeling better."

I shrug with one shoulder. I was. And then I wasn't. It seesaws. "Define better."

"I'm too drunk for definitions," Silas groans. "You smile more, but it doesn't sparkle. Better means you're sparkling again."

"Hard to sparkle when there's so much night suffocating you," I say, my gaze flicking up to the sky.

"Is that why you're smoking Seelie drugs now?"

My face scrunches. He's close to the truth, but not at the heart of it. Things are changing, fast. I'm stuck, with the world whooshing by.

"I'm just trying to feel something again, Silas. That's all."

47
JOSIE

My first breath upon waking is brisk in my lungs, the temperature having dropped significantly overnight. However, under the covers, it's toasty warm.

Content.

The sensation wraps around me, a blanket layered between the sheet and the comforter.

I draw Imogen closer, closing the small distance that's formed between us as we've tossed and turned in the night. My hand indulgently runs over her hip and thigh, then bands around her belly. Nuzzling into the crook of her neck, I place sleepy kisses under her ear and suck in her rosy scent.

Peace. Quiet.

Imogen hums at my ministrations, lost in her dreams.

I'm glad it's a dream and not a nightmare. I can tell early on now; the difference lies in how fitful her sleep is, and tonight she's been all languid sighs and soft snuggles. After a particularly nasty panic attack on Wednesday evening, it's all I can ask for.

They aren't as common as they used to be. We've figured out some of what triggers the episodes, but they still pop up at random. And with us coming up on the one year of her shooting, and then one year from Casimir shortly after that, I imagine they'll rear their ugly heads often.

Wind whooshes against the fogged window. The sound draws my gaze, and my worries quickly flee when my eyes meet the falling specs of white beyond the glass pane.

"Mo, wake up," I whisper as I nuzzle against her cheek. She stirs, yawning. "It's the first snow of the season."

Imogen's rumpled blond head pops up from the pillow at the mention of the white fluff. "This early?"

I hum my laughter. "Seems so."

Imogen sits up fast, rubbing the sleep from her eyes. "Holy shit."

My laughter takes a louder form at her childlike awe. She may have turned thirty over the summer, but there are still moments where her inner youngling shines, drawing out everyone's innocent joy. I think it's a blessing to be able to embrace that part of herself so easily. It's one thing I've always struggled with, though the lack of a true childhood may be to blame.

My hand wraps around her waist and my fingers trace over the edge of her sleep shorts mindlessly. I've converted her to more practical sleepwear, at least for colder nights. Though she always finds excuses to parade around in various states of undress; I think she finds it amusing to tease and tempt me. And tempted I am; the pads of my fingers dip below the waistband and hook around her hip to pull her back down.

"Come here," I say.

"There's no time for that!" Imogen slaps my hand away

and scrambles out of the bed, bare feet slapping against the wood. She winces at the cold floor and hops over to the window, her arms banding around her waist to stave off the shivers. "We have to invite everyone over to the cabin!"

I groan, rolling out of bed and joining her at the window. Wrapping my arms over hers at her waist, I lean my chin on her shoulder.

"We'll have to wait until it's cleared enough to drive. Unless you're okay with being at the behest of the shadow-walkers' timelines..." My mutterings of logistics fade when the view outside the apartment registers in full.

The skyline is different.

Our building is the tallest in this part of the city—a newer build, standing above older structures—so we can see right to the city's edge. Usually it's all haze out there, over the river. You usually can't see the faint trace of a coastline across the water.

"Um, Josie, are you seeing what I'm seeing?"

"Yeah."

The shadow-veil that's encircled the Unseelie Court for half a century has fallen.

48

SILAS

The press conference took its toll on each of us in different ways. Me, most of all, because I'm the one who put the shadow-veil up. *Why would you let it fall?* The newsies asked repeatedly. *The people are scared. They don't know what it means.*

A million roundabout questions were thrown my way, to which I had to explain some bullshit politics about taking active steps in collaboration with the Seelie. It's not a lie, per se. We *are* taking active steps to foster a stronger relationship with those across the river. It's just that *this* particular event wasn't planned.

But they don't know that. And they don't know that I can't throw the shadow-veil back up if things go sideways with Bennie.

What they don't know won't kill them. Hopefully.

Relations have been positive between the Courts—one could even say they're thriving. We've established a small trade route through the Human Realm. Bennie's kept his word about scaling back their militia.

But I'm a paranoid bastard, and I haven't met with the Seelie King myself in months.

Nora assures me there are no whispers of war or betrayal, and it's only her confidence that has the vein in my forehead throbbing less.

Sometimes, it's stressful being king.

It's stressful being Silas, too.

I pluck the cigarette from where it hangs between Nora's lips, her hands otherwise occupied with the cards that Leo whipped out at the end of our friends' weekly night out. She's half a carton deep—where one ends, another begins. She hasn't even used her lighter, she lights the next with the dying end of the last one she's sucked down.

Nora shoots me a side-eyed glare over the cards she shuffles. I pop the cigarette between my lips, pressing over her lipstick lines in some pathetic version of an indirect kiss.

It's been seven months since the night we killed Patience and had our little... *moment.*

Seven months of giving her space.

Seven months of watching her slip away from all of us, despite the ways she's shown up for our Court. I don't think any of our friends have noticed the subtle way her fire's dimmed, or the way she leans on her vices in ways she didn't before. They all believe whatever bullshit she feeds them about *being better.*

Nora doesn't need to become a better version of herself for them, she needs to *accept* herself. That's the only way she's going to be able to move on like the others have. And I'm getting a bit frustrated with her for not giving me the whole truth when she *did* open up to me about this over the summer.

She lies to me. Even when she knows I know.

And then there's this unsatisfied craving, eating away at my chest. I feed it crumbs of her attention, small pieces I can steal during group outings or from lucky moments alone, smoking on a roof.

Smoke curls around my tongue and seeps into my lungs; I savor the scraps of her essence.

"You could've asked for your own," Nora grumbles.

"But then I wouldn't get to taste you on it."

She rolls her eyes, but I see the way her lips purse. I think she's more affected by my words than she will admit.

Nora's fingers curl around her neck, and she tries to subtly scratch at the exposed skin at the top of her back. My mood deflates with every red line she draws onto her pale skin.

Imogen and Josie say their goodbyes, walking off hand in hand to their apartment a few blocks away. Shortly after, Wrath and Hattie wink out like two shooting stars in the night.

Another round of cards and nightcaps later, Nora throws her hand down with a groan. Leo grins, rubbing his hands together, having swindled her again. I've been out for a while, content to watch them battle it out in the new game Leo brought to us.

"I never fucking learn," Nora says, dragging her hand over her face.

"No, you do not," Leo snickers. "I am the king of cards."

Nora shoves her chair back and throws on her jacket. "I'm out."

"Yeah, I guess it is time to head home." Leo yawns, his hands clapping on his thighs as he pushes to standing.

"I'll make sure you get home safe," I offer, standing with them.

"I don't need help getting home," Nora says dismissively.

Leo chokes on his laughter, breaking out into a cough—I shoot him a glare, and he gives me a thumbs up that says *nice try, bud.*

"Sure," I say. "But maybe I wasn't ready to go home and

thought a nice walk in the direction of the palace was a good idea. Not my fault your new place is on the way."

"*Gods above*," Nora grumbles, walking away. "Do whatever you want. Goodnight, Leo."

"See ya later, Nor!" Leo calls after her. He gives me a wink. "You got this."

With that thrilling vote of confidence, I use my shadows to catch up to Nora—she's a fast fucking walker and is already halfway down the block. We mostly stride in silence, and anyone we pass gives us a wide berth. Nora's reputation still leaves people hovering at a distance, despite Josie and I's efforts to shift the public's perception of her presence in the Court.

It's pleasant, though, the way our shoulders sometimes graze when one of us avoids a sewer grate or hops over a piece of trash. I only ever get to see her in meetings or in group settings, or in small moments like this, where I catch her on the tail end of outings. She's stuck to her promise of ignoring me. And I've stuck to mine with proving my patience.

All too soon, the walk to her newly purchased brownstone ends; we climb up the steps, and she glances at me as she jabs her key into the brass lock.

"Do you need to make sure I get inside and lock the door behind me?" she jokes in that deadpan way of hers.

"Is it Bennie?" I ask.

"Pardon?" she says, turning, leaving the key in the lock.

"Why you're scratching up your back again," I say, getting right to the meat of my worry. She wasn't doing that over the summer. "Is it Bennie?"

Her sharp eyes cut me with their clarity, shining under the single porch light that buzzes above us. She sighs. "Yes and no."

I wait for her to elaborate. I've learned that if you wait long enough, she'll fill the space with honesty. She's got this need to put up a fight before laying it all out, as if it's some kind of weakness to do otherwise.

"Seeing his... you know." Nora waves her hand in the air. She means his wings. "It makes it harder to ignore them."

"They still bother you that much?" I ask. "I thought after Patience it stopped."

Her head bobbles. "Sort of. It's not as bad without the tether. I imagine our magic being in constant contact made it worse."

"And now?"

"Manageable most days. There is the occasional bad one," she says. "Today's a bad one." Nora catches her rising hand before it can reach behind her back. It smacks against her trousers when she drops it; a grimace claws up her face at the action. "Distractions help. Cigarettes help. I try not to use the joints Bennie gets me too often. Got any other good ideas?"

"For distractions?" My teeth bite into my bottom lip. "I can think of a few."

"Get your mind out of the gutter."

"But I like it there—it's fun getting dirty."

A bark of laughter bursts from her, and the skin around her eyes crinkles. She reaches back, pushing down on the handle and letting the door creak open. One step and she's over the threshold, poised to shut the door in my face.

"Goodnight, Silas," she says.

"We never talk about that night," I mutter, leaning forward, putting one arm on the molding of the threshold. I trap her with my gaze; black and green, like her wings, crash together.

What I like about Nora is that she's tall. I don't have to look down when I bear my heart, or when she crushes it in her fist.

"What do you want to talk about? I gave you a hand job. That's it."

My tongue prods my cheek, searching for the right words. "Well, it's more me trying to figure out how to return the favor. Only seems fair."

"*Ah*," she says.

It's not a no.

Holy fuck, it's not an immediate no.

I hold my breath as I reach out, brushing her raven locks away from her neck. My fingertips ache to graze over the skin there, to soothe the raised edges of her scratches. Her head tilts, as if confused by my action. She studies me, brows knit.

I'm lightheaded by the time she speaks again.

"I guess using you wouldn't be the end of the world."

"What?" I say, sucking in a dizzy breath.

I barely blink before Nora's hand fists my shirt and pulls me to her. Her kiss is bruising, overwhelming; I'm drowning in it, the soft pillowy texture of her lips a contrast to the way they roughly slant across mine. Smoke, whiskey, and something rich bursts on my tongue. A groan rumbles in my chest, and my fists clench at my sides. I'm lost, and I don't know where to anchor my hands. Her fingers slip into my hair and yank me back, breaking our kiss. I burst out of the waves of *her*, sucking in lungfuls of air before the current pulls me under again.

"I lead. You listen. If you can't handle that, then leave." Her raspy breath washes over me.

"That's fine," I whisper into her lips—*perfectly fine*. "Can I touch you? Please?"

Her eyes flitter between mine. "Sometimes. I'll make it clear when I don't want it. In the same way, if you don't like something, you tell me. Understood?"

My head nods repeatedly, and she drags me into her brownstone.

The door slams shut. The deadbolt clicks.

I'm swept into the deep green ocean of her touch, brutal and demanding. I let go, surrender to it.

Which is how I end up suffocating on her bed, the juice from her approaching release dripping down my chin. It's a glorious death, one that I beg for by licking and sucking her sweet cunt. She braces one hand on the headboard for leverage, using it to grind herself harder onto my tongue. I tried to grip her hips and do that myself, but she slapped my hands away with a terse warning. Now they fist the bedsheets at my side and curl around my cock.

Nora leans back and the visual I peek is absolutely obscene as she arches.

A groan rips from my throat; she laughs, breathless and amused. The sound goes straight to my dick, triggering the first surge of my release. At the same time, I double down on the pressure around her clit. A single gasp falls from her lips as she comes, her hand dropping from the headboard and into my hair. Her fingers pull at the root, dig into my scalp, and I moan, flattening my tongue against her core. I lap up her sweet nectar as her orgasm fades.

A few blissful moments pass where our heaving breath fills the room.

"Please tell me we can do that again," I murmur against her core.

I stare up at her, and she stares down at me, slowly blinking away the haze of lust. Her tongue traces over her top lip, before she pulls it back, swallowing. And then she's climbing off me, scrambling off the bed.

"Nora—" I call out, panic spearing through me. She freezes at the pain and worry stitched between the syllables of her name.

Her hands run through her hair, gripping at her scalp. "Yeah?"

I roll off the bed, ignoring the ropes of cum dripping down my stomach; my attention is locked on the faded twin scars running down her spine. Above them are fresher red lines, made by her nails. I reach out, a brave act, and tenderly trace the lines. My gut twists something painful when she doesn't pull away, simply shivering at the small intimacy. Whether it be the post orgasm fog, or some kind of progress between us that keeps her still, I don't know, but I'm thankful for it.

"Why are you running away?"

"I'm not running away," she says. "I'm going to clean up."

"Can I help?"

"I don't need you to do that."

"But do you *want* me to?" My lips brush against her ear. "You already put my tongue to work, I'm good for other things too."

She still hasn't pulled away, and my thumb gets bold, running down the center of her scars. My mouth gets bold too.

"Can I see them?" I whisper.

"Really, Silas?" Nora says, almost exasperated, but more tired than anything. My thumb circles the lower edge of one scar, trailing back up the other. Nora sucks in a stuttering breath, and her body leans into my touch.

"Truly," I say. "Let me see them again. Please."

Another deep breath shakes her body. "Okay."

Magic tingles around my fingers, and Nora's wings unfurl before me. Inky splotches mirror each other on each wing, fanning out from where they emerge from her back. Green, a perfect match to her eyes, shines iridescent in the low light of her bedroom. My hand has a mind of its own, as I stand mesmerized by her beauty, and traces the edge of her upper wings. They're soft against my fingertips.

The action pulls a shocked squeak from her. Nora jolts, spinning around with wide-eyed horror.

"What are you doing?" she asks, the high-pitched tone unlike her.

"Admiring them?" I say. It's obvious.

"No one has touched them before."

"No one?" I ask.

Her head shakes.

"The only people who ever saw them before Casimir were Pride and Josie. And not even Josie wanted to." A beat passes before she whispers, "Can I put them away now?"

The question is so unlike her, so vulnerable; I immediately nod, and they quickly disappear.

I decide in that moment that these fragile parts of her need to be cherished.

I slowly reach out and cup her jaw. She lets me, and my thumb swipes over her cheek. I think this is the first time I've been able to do such a thing. It's surprisingly soft.

"I don't often make promises, Nora, but I promise you this. I will find a way to make the pain stop," I say.

"A tall task, even for a king."

I smile. "But I'm not a king with you, am I?"

Nora snorts, eyes cutting a glance at the bed. A hint of a smirk curls her lips. "No, I guess not."

49
IMOGEN

"Remember, we can turn around at any point. There's no shame in not wanting to come back here," Josie says.

"I know. But I want to do this."

Josie's hand squeezes mine, a burst of reassurance funneling between our magic from where our skin meets. "I'm proud of you."

I put on a brave smile, but it falters as soon as Casimir comes into view. The hulking white and pink castle looms before us, tucked in the center of the valley's lake. It's as I remember it—last December seems so long ago, and at the same time, like yesterday.

The only reason I agreed to come today was because I want to put this chapter of my life behind me. I'm viewing it as one final round of exposure therapy, a test to convince myself I can move past the trauma I gathered during those few weeks last year.

I still have bad days—sad days. Days I can't get out of bed.

Days I space out, unable to breathe while the world blurs around me.

But as Josie often reminds me, this journey isn't linear, yet I'm healing all the same.

"Alright, everyone ready?" Silas shouts, stopping us at the forest's edge.

All seven Sins, their dates, and an entire host of Wrath's guards watch on as Silas raises the land bridge between our Court and Casimir.

It's been two months since the shadow-veil fell, and we haven't heard a peep of trouble from the Seelie. Josie says the trust between the Courts has grown considerably since the new Seelie King was crowned—in large part due to Nora's arrangement with her cousin. But whispered worries of war have us all on edge.

And when Bennie extended the invite to *try again* at the yearly Solstice celebration, Silas agreed. It's not a multi-day trip this go around. To be on the safe side, we're attending the ball and then leaving.

I hope that the whispers are just that—rumors. Otherwise, we will all have a much bigger problem when we step into the haunted halls of Casimir.

I had forgotten how cute the sprites were.

One is particularly fond of me, zipping around my head as we make our way to the ballroom. My heart is pounding, but I'm safely tucked in a Josie-Leo sandwich; Nora's only a step ahead, and behind us are Hattie and Wrath. The pounding fades slightly at the reminder that I have the best family a girl could ask for.

Silas throws open the double doors, calling a stop to the Seelie revelry. It's a tense moment, one that resides between Silas's strides and the pause he takes to look Bennie up and down. The Seelie King's curled mustache quirks in the same way Silas's white brows do, and then they come together in that hand-shake hug that men love to do.

The smack of their hands on each other's backs punctuates a hushed exchange. A burst of laughter comes from the Seelie King—and all that mounting tension shatters.

It has an instant effect, the room whooshing with a collective release of held breath.

I lose my sense of self for a second, pushed to a seat at a cocktail table and handed both drink and food. I don't make much note of the decorations or the music, stuck in a loop of thought—about how the floor's *clean* when it was *red* last time. The air in my lungs becomes thin.

Someone drops a plate—and I flinch.

My gaze falls to my lap as I work on steadying my breath. A warm hand lands on my back, and I flinch again. But then a slow trickle of calming energy washes over me, and I know it's only Josie, doing what she does best.

Making me safe.

After a few minutes sitting with the unsteadiness, it passes. I'm able to sit up straighter, able to study the ballroom's details without seeing how it looked *back then*—able to breathe.

"Thank you. I'm feeling better now," I say.

"Yeah?" Josie asks.

I nod. "You should take me to the dance floor."

Josie tries to hide her smile but fails. "You want me to make a fool of myself out there for you?"

"I think you're a great dancer," I chide.

"Then you need glasses." Josie chuckles.

She takes me out anyway. We dance for an hour, on the Unseelie half of the dance floor. Bennie brought a much smaller host than last year, so there's plenty of room for us all to spread out.

Panting, with a thin sheen of sweat on our brows, we hobble away on tired feet. I point to the refreshments.

"If you want me to love you, get me water. And maybe a snack," I huff.

"You already love me," Josie teases in my ear, sickeningly sweet—but I crave it. "Be right back." She pecks my cheek and meets Leo and Nora at the table of hors d'oeuvres.

On my way to our seats, my attention catches on the Unseelie King, sitting alone. His elbow is perched precariously on the edge of his table, his chin resting on his palm. The dark stare Silas dons is the definition of yearning, half-lidded eyes gazing out into the crowd.

I approach him cautiously. Josie will be a while; she always ponders over the selection in great detail before making us a plate at these kinds of functions.

"Anyone sitting here?" I ask, expecting him to jolt at my intrusion, or at least peer my way. He does neither.

"No*pe*," Silas says, a distinct pop between his lips.

I've spent a lot of time with Silas over the last year, more than I ever thought I would. It's funny how close we are, given how rocky our relationship started. Blackmail and secrets somehow turned into weekly dinners and invitations out to the family cabin.

I know him much better now, enough to see something is clearly bothering him.

"Did Bennie say something that upset you?" I ask, curious.

"Hm?" His white brows crease, and he cuts me a quick side eye. "No. Nothing like that."

His dark stare moves across the room, landing in the direction of the refreshments table.

Ah.

There's only one person that could be make him fawn like a lovesick teenager, and that person isn't Leo or Josie.

They haven't exactly been forthright about whatever is going on between them, but it's obvious to everyone with eyes that can see. They're not subtle—at least, Silas isn't. Nora's still as locked up as a bank vault, though I do catch her glancing at him when she doesn't think anyone else will notice. It's always with a pinched and confused expression, as if she doesn't quite know how she feels about him.

A few bets have been exchanged within our friend group as to when her denial will end. To my chagrin, I'm the only one whose guess hasn't passed yet. Why they put down anything less than six months is beyond me. It's almost like they all forgot it took Nora *years* to kiss me in college, and longer still to admit to real feelings after we started fucking.

"Lover's quarrel?" I tease, though there's no bite to it.

Silas perks at that, a red tinge blooming on the pointed tips of his ears. His earring dangles and sways with the snapping of his head in my direction.

"Did she say something?" he asks.

"If she did, it wasn't to me," I say. "*Did* something happen?"

Silas sighs. "More like what *isn't* happening."

My expression softens, and I hum my understanding. I'm familiar with that wistful sigh—I've been the one huffing it far too many times. I'm about to make my exit, not wanting to pry too deeply into their business, when he asks me a question.

"Can I tell you a secret, Imogen?"

I shift on the edge of my chair. "Sure."

"I'm a soul-stealer."

My lips part, then close.

"Really?" I ask, unbelieving.

"Mhm."

I glance between him and Nora, memories flashing across my vision as it all *clicks*. "Is *that* why you were interested in her, in the beginning?"

He shrugs, but it confirms as much.

"Oh man..." I pat him on the back, two firm slaps from a kindred hopeless romantic, then I grip the base of his neck and shake him. "You are in for it."

A strange, shocked expression crosses his face, like he can't believe that I'd touch his skin after learning his secret. For a king who plots all these convoluted, cut-throat plans, he's acting very stupid.

"I've never been afraid of that magic, Silas. By all accounts I should be, but I'm not and never have been. Never thought the kind of magic you had should dictate your status as unlovable or not," I say. Then level with him, leaning close. "It took me ten years to crack open her heart. Good luck."

I give his back one more friendly pat before leaning back.

"I will need it, won't I?"

"Oh, that's a certainty."

"Even so, I'm okay to wait," he says.

Josie approaches, each hand holding a plate; confusion tilts her head, asking why I'm sitting with Silas.

"Even ten years?" I ask him.

"What's ten years in a life that will last hundreds? I know I already have what I want. I don't need her waxing poetic about how much she cares about me. But it'll be a fascinating day when it happens."

"So, your trouble isn't about love?" I ask, confused.

He waves his left hand in the air. "Something far more trivial."

"But you *do* love her?" I ask.

He shakes his head. "We have something different. Something that belongs to just us."

My heart keens with joy at his answer. He sounds so sure.

I'm glad he won't put the pressure of love on her.

"What's going on over here?" Josie asks as she reaches us, handing me a plate of delicious goodies.

"I was telling Silas he should go ask Nora to dance," I say.

"You were?" Silas asks.

"Yep."

"You think she'd say yes to a dance with me? *Here*?" Silas deadpans.

"She always said yes when I asked," I say, smug. Then jab a thumb at Josie. "So does she. They can't help but say yes when they know you want it that bad."

"She tells the truth." Josie nods her agreement.

"She'll say no," he says, but his black eyes have that determined glint.

"*Or*," I drawl, "maybe she won't."

50
NORA

The fae kings kept their word. I hope it lasts.

Funny, that feeling. *Hope.* I never considered myself a hopeful person. Determined, future-thinking, ambitious? Sure. But never hopeful.

As I glance out the ballroom window, watching the sky darken and splatter droplets all over Casimir's evergreen garden, I am reminded of my mother's whispered warning.

Storms are omens of change.

There was one the night I was born. Another the day my magic came to life under my skin. Rain and hail battered the windows the days I killed Pride and Patience, and a blizzard raged the night my heart broke over a blond beauty.

At the time, my mother's words were ominous, like the first page of a fable meant to scare children into behaving. But maybe it was simply her way of preparing me for the inevitable.

In a life as long-lived as we fae face, change will occur as often as it rains. There's no escaping the churning of nature's will. Although, it seems we've defied it, somehow, with the way we've managed to avoid a war between the Courts.

Fate is surely cursing us. But *hopefully*, she's laughing at our audacity instead.

"Nora, are you even listening?" Leo huffs, drawing me from my thoughts.

"No," I admit.

He groans, throwing his head back. "Then I'm going back to sit with the gang."

Leo—now Lust—trudges off to the cropping of tables where our friends sit. We're quite the intimidating group: three Sins, one former Sin, one unhinged shadow-walker, a king, and someone without a title or clear name for her magic.

How I—the *other someone*—managed to gain such an eccentric yet wonderful family is beyond me.

"Penny for your thoughts?" Bennie's joking lilt pulls my attention to my right. He leans back against the windows with me. "You seem pensive."

I shrug. "We're all dealing with what it means for us to be back here in different ways."

"Fair," Bennie says. He offers me a glass swishing with amber liquid. "Drink?"

"That the good stuff or the Seelie shit you folk manage to swallow down?"

"That is the good stuff?" he jokes. "Don't worry. I snagged this off some sprite's platter. Your precious taste buds are safe."

"Thank the gods," I mutter, grabbing the glass and taking a sip. A hum fills my throat—it's smooth, dangerously so.

"I assume that means it lives up to your expectations," Bennie says.

"You would assume right."

I've seen my cousin eight times since the night we killed his father, and each time I find myself getting more comfortable with him. It's not friendship, per se, but something that works for us right now. I don't need more friends; I need someone who understands, firsthand, the terror of the man that plagued me.

White hair flashes in my mind, with my fingers tangled in the strands.

"Thanks for bringing my brother back with all his fingers and toes," Bennie says casually, over the rim of his glass.

"He made it hard."

"I'm sure."

"The kid isn't *that* bad," I add. "He needs a wake-up call, though. Make him understand that this was it. He'll face worse than his grumpy older cousin and house arrest when he takes on his title."

"Somehow, I doubt that," Bennie says. "And don't think I'm going to gloss over the fact you haven't shied away from calling us family recently. I might be hiding it well, but I am positively giddy inside. Soon enough, you'll be joining us for—"

"Yeah, don't get ahead of yourself there."

Our conversation lulls, and we nurse our drinks, studying the tentative enjoyment of the Solstice festivities. It's not perfect, but it's something. I'm even somewhat proud of us for not letting this party start—or end—in a bloodbath.

"Remember how you told me to be careful about the humans?" Bennie asks, interrupting our peaceful coexistence.

"Yes..."

"I wasn't careful."

I shift, my hip and shoulder leaning onto the windowpane so I can scold him head on. "Bennie..."

"And now I'm in a bit of a bind," he winces.

I loose an exasperated sigh. "I can't solve your problems for you."

"*Okay, but* maybe you could lend some help to your dear older cousin?" Bennie asks. "Moretti, he wants me to—"

I hold up a hand, cutting him off. "You're a king. Help yourself. I've got too much on my plate as it is."

"Yeah, Bennie, go help yourself," Silas snarks from beside me, appearing out of thin air, though the telltale tickle of magic is nowhere to be found. "Nora's plate is full with official Unseelie Court business."

"Fine," Bennie groans. "I'll figure it out myself." He shoots us a heatless glare. "I'm going to get another drink."

He stomps off, but when he's firmly behind Silas's back, he winks at me.

I flip him off.

"You two have been getting along better," Silas says.

"He's awfully similar to someone else who likes to insert himself into my life without my permission," I mutter.

Silas leans forward, crowding me against the wall so he can whisper in my ear. "Oh, come on. I *absolutely* have permission every time I insert my tongue in your—"

My palm hits his face, and I shove him away; he stumbles back, a cheeky smile sparkling.

"That is not the same thing, and you know it."

Things between us have... devolved. I caved one vulnerable, horny night in October. And now, in the same way I'm at his beck and call for Court business, he's at mine for, well, other things.

Other things being fucking.

He's not terrible at it.

And there is an addictive quality to the way he *melts* for me —submits wholeheartedly to whatever I choose to give or take.

"*Nor-a,*" Silas sing-songs. "Where did you go just now?"

"None of your business," I bristle.

"Okay," Silas says. "I do have a question, though."

I cock a brow, knowing no matter my response, he'll still ask it.

"Will you dance with me?" he asks, almost shyly.

"You want me to dance… with you?"

"That is what I asked, yes." His void-like eyes twitch nervously to the side; the sudden switch of his energy puts me on edge.

"Okay," I say, brows knitting.

"I know it's probably not—wait, really?"

"Yeah."

His eyes narrow on me. "That was too easy."

I scoff. "Did you *want* me to make it hard?"

Silas darts forward, scooping up my hand in his, and drags me toward the slow-dancing fae. "Absolutely not. I will take easy any day of the week when it comes to you."

"I danced with Leo and Wrath earlier. It's not that big a deal," I mutter.

Silas stops in an open spot at the edge of dancers and pulls me to him. One arm snakes around my waist.

"*You* danced with Robbie?" he asks.

"Don't worry, it was one of those dances where you keep switching partners. I was hoping I'd get Hattie."

"Ah, I see." Silas nods, as if that makes it better.

We sway and twirl with the music, and he doesn't ask any more questions, for a time. It's surprisingly pleasant, save for the shocks he sends down my spine when his fingers toy with the fabric of my gown. The silk dips low at the back, bravely displaying more skin than I'm used to in public. Tonight felt like the right time to wear it, though.

Silas's hand presses me closer, and our chests brush. He dips his head to my neck, placing a quick peck on my pulse.

"*Silas*," I warn.

I may let him in my bed, but it's not something we advertise.

His head pulls back, mischief rampant in those black-holes he calls irises.

"Do you remember what I told you last Solstice?" Silas asks.

"You're going to have to be more specific," I say. I remember everything he said. But he could be referring to multiple rogue comments.

"When I told you that if you were a chess piece, you'd be a queen," he clarifies.

"*Yes...*" I say, tentatively curious as to where this is going. "Why?"

Silas leans forward again, cheek pressing against mine as he whispers, "Don't you want that freedom? That power? No rules. No consequences."

My hand tightens around his shoulder. "What are you getting at, Silas?"

"You're smart, you can figure it out," he says, smirking against my ear. His breath fans out over my neck, and his nose drags over my cheek. *Is he—*

"I have plenty of freedom. I don't need a *crown*." My whisper comes out harsh and rushed. "Are you *insane?*"

"A crown is never a need. It's a want," Silas says. "The idea of a promotion doesn't entice you? Not even a little bit? How many times have you said you wouldn't ever be my pawn? I can name a few from recent memory."

My heartbeat whooshes in my ear.

What would it be like, to have a clear place in the hierarchy of our Court again? Because that *is* what he's offering. To have a place no one could question. That potential future flashes in my mind for *one second* before I shut it down—but the thrill must reflect in my eyes, because Silas catches it, and I'm done for. He won't ever let this go now.

His hand leaves my waist for the exposed scars he loves to trace over; Silas does it every time I let him linger in my bed.

"*There*. There it is. The idea does tempt you."

"No."

"Liar."

"I considered it. There's a difference," I snap.

We spin to the music, and my attention wanders over Silas's shoulder. In the shadowy corner of the ballroom, Wrath and Hattie sneak a private moment. Leo holds court around the refreshments table; he's rising in the circle of Sins, having been deemed Sloth's new favorite. Josie and Imogen are beside him. Josie's arms are tightly wrapped around Imogen, and their laughter rings out like wind-chimes in summer.

I have yet to commit to change—to this new life—in the way they all have.

Maybe... no. It's too fast, especially for *this*.

The Unseelie King needs a reality check.

"We've been fucking. For *two months*. We are not even in a relationship," I say. "What made you think this was a good idea?"

"You have me wrapped around your finger, Nor. What else is a man to do but offer the one he's wrapped around the world?" He croons. "Plus, I made you a promise. I think this will help fulfill that."

I shake my head; I knew he was irrational, but I didn't think he was *senseless*.

"Too much, too soon, Silas," I say. I break his hold on me and take one step off the edge of the dance floor. But as much as I need some distance, I find that I don't want to completely break his heart. "Ask me again in fifty years. By then, you'll know if you regret your decision to pursue me as you have."

Silas grabs my hand, pulling me back to him. "I couldn't regret you."

My chest tightens. "That is a cheesy fucking line."

My stubbornness clashes with his fixation.

His pupils dilate.

My tongue swipes over my bottom lip.

"Did it work, though?" Silas asks, a soft, smug smile on his lips.

Thunder claps, pulling shocked yelps from the fae in the room, but not us.

Silas and I dance, unbothered by the sudden tempest. Seconds later, a deluge pounds against the ballroom windows, drowning out the band. Silas's black eyes are swirling storm clouds, and mirth glistens like raindrops at their center.

An omen.

I snort. His lips twitch. And soon, we're both bubbling with uncontrollable laughter.

"The answer is still no," I squeeze out.

Lightning strikes, flashing as we sway, and I cackle right along with the gods that hurled this storm at me.

They have a sick fucking sense of humor.

THE END.

WHAT'S NEXT?

To stay up to date with G.B. Bancroft's upcoming releases, bonus content, and events, join her newsletter: https://authorgbbancroft.beehiiv.com/subscribe

COMING SPRING 2026

THE BOY IN THE PAINTING

The first in the Meadowbrook Duet: an Alice in Wonderland inspired why-choose portal fantasy.

ACKNOWLEDGMENTS

Simply scrawling "thank you" onto the last pages of a book never feels sufficient in communicating my gratitude. But here we are, and these are all the amazing people who need to be screamed about, because they are pretty fucking awesome:

To my readers, who fill me with so much joy, and allow me to keep doing this thing I love. You champion my art, and for that I am eternally grateful.

To my editor, Maddi, for sharpening this story and helping me grow my craft.

To my cover designer, Maria, for nailing my vision for this duet.

To my proofreader and formatter, Kay, for polishing the manuscript when my eyes were burning from staring at it for so long.

To my betas, Nicole, Ann, Charity, Sarah, and Jenna, for refilling the fuel in my tank when I was running low, and for loving these characters as much as I do. And I'm happy to say that in the year since I wrote A Sin So Pure's acknowledgments, I've been able to read two of your books. Ladies, you are going to take the world by storm. I can't wait.

To the college lads, you know who you are. You also know how hard this year has been, and not once have you failed me when I needed you.

To Chelsea, you've kept me sane during this whole process.

Thanks for always being down for a bookstore run and a sweet treat. Proud of us for getting through 2025 mostly unscathed.

To my day one, Erin. What would I do without our three-hour phone calls discussing the *what ifs* for these characters? Seriously. I don't know. Probably lose my mind with choice paralysis.

To my family: you guys have always been my biggest cheer-leaders, and this year you've been my rock. Thank you.

To my writing buddy and fur-child: Miso, you give the best kitty snuggles.

And last, but not least, my soft love. When I finished line edits for this book, you so kindly wrote your own thank you via a WhatsApp text: *To my husband, who was gone the whole time I wrote this, thanks for nothing.* Love you babe, even if the ocean got to see you more than I did in 2025.

ABOUT THE AUTHOR

G.B. Bancroft, *aka Gabs*, is an event producer by day and author by night. She loves all things magical, gritty, and romantic, and is a voracious mood reader. Originally from New York, she's currently enjoying a few-year stint in sunny California with her husband and her grumpy orange tabby, Miso.

You can find her @authorgbbancroft on Instagram, Threads, and TikTok. You can also add her on Goodreads and Amazon.